I WANT YOU

"To be my mistress." Stephen said.

"I see." Actually Phoebe saw nothing at all but a man she thought handsome and charming enough to seduce a stable filled with women, a man who looked overly proud of himself with his chin lifted and a cocky grin plastered on his face. Goodness, he infuriated and intrigued her. However had he come to the conclusion she would be willing to agree to such a proposal? She tapped the toes on her left foot and twisted the reins into a tight knot about her fingers. "We hardly know one another. What makes you think such a relationship even possible?"

"Quite simply, I want you."

She knew he intended to kiss her. And no tree blocked her escape this time. Truth be told, wanton or not, she'd been waiting, even hoping, for this very moment. She watched his fingers, long and elegant, slide about her waist, and she trembled. His other hand gripped her chin. As his lips descended, she met him halfway.

Other *Leisure* books by Peggy Waide:
DUCHESS FOR A DAY

PEGGY WAIDE

POTENT CHARMS

LEISURE BOOKS   NEW YORK CITY

For Kevin, Dakota, Jordan and Alex.
I love you all.

A LEISURE BOOK®

March 2000

Published by

Dorchester Publishing Co., Inc.
276 Fifth Avenue
New York, NY 10001

ISBN 0-8439-4694-6

The name "Leisure Books" and the stylized "L" with design are trademarks of Dorchester Publishing Co., Inc.

Printed in the United States of America.

POTENT CHARMS

Prologue

Penrith, England, 1723

Lightning flashed across the sky. A clap of thunder shook the ground. The wind howled. The trees and shadows swayed as partners in an eerie dance to mother nature's music. Soon rain would pummel the ground. It was not a good night to be out. Yet, from beneath the canopy of his tent, Lord Badrick watched a shriveled old crone hover outside the circle of light cast by his fire.

"Duke," she called. "Dare you face me?"

She emerged from the mist, a creature of the night, one with the forest. Lord Badrick's two companions bounded to their feet, their hands gripping the hilts of their swords. One wave of the Duke's arm stalled their action. "What is the meaning of this?"

"I see you do not recognize me," she said. Three small steps brought her closer. Gold coin earrings glittered in the firelight. Her multi-colored skirt flared about her ankles as she walked.

"You are a gypsy."

"More than that, I am Juliana Romov, mother of Rosala."

The wind gusted, lifting the heavy wool of Lord Badrick's cloak. He shifted his weight from leg to leg, narrowing his eyes to reexamine the woman before him. "The name means little to me."

"Promising wealth and marriage, you seduced my Rosala. Without remorse, you discarded her to marry your noble lady. In shame, Rosala took her life. Now, she lies beneath the cold ground. You will pay."

"Wait a bloody minute—"

"*Ay, Romale, ay Chavale, sa lumiake Roma.*" The gypsy's voice rose in volume as she chanted the ancient curse. "*Ake vryama. Vi—*"

"For God's sake, speak English."

"God cannot help you now. Already, the crows gather, awaiting the deaths that shall follow."

"Cease this trickery. I will not give you a farthing."

"You think money can buy my forgiveness?" The gypsy spat on the ground before her. "Foolish man. Your title, your power and your threats mean nothing to me. Only tragedy will accompany your wealth." She pointed a tangled root at the duke while her left hand clutched a gold amulet around her neck. "For generations to come, the sons of your house will beget sons. Each son will marry noble ladies and each marriage will end in loneliness, misery and death as long as the Romany travel the pathways of this land."

An eerie cackling tumbled from the gypsy's mouth, taunting Badrick to step closer. She raised her gnarled fingers to the skies. "I call my curse from the heavens. May it canter hot on your heels to hell."

Potent Charms

A bolt of lightning split the tree beside the woman. When the smoke cleared, only a blue-black braid of hair laced with colored ribbons and gold coins atop a tattered scrap of red linen remained.

Chapter One

London, 1817

Couples twirled on the white marble floor, a stark back-drop for the rainbow of colored gowns that filled the long, narrow ballroom. Yet, regardless of the festive air, Phoebe Rafferty stood amidst three hundred people and felt more alone than she'd ever thought possible. After one week, she hated England and British formality. She despised the task of finding a husband even more.

The small orchestra played a country dance. Phoebe tapped her satin-colored toes to the rhythm of the music, fighting the urge to clap like she would have back in Georgia. Instead, she fisted her hand in the soft folds of her gown and cursed her fate.

The shrill whisper of her aunt's voice invaded Phoebe's dreary thoughts. "Yes, Auntie?" she asked.

Lady Hildegard Goodliffe shrugged her twiglike shoulders and shook her head. "Phoebe, do stop fidgeting. Everyone will wonder if fleas infest your wardrobe, such as it is, or if you simply lack the ability to sit still."

Charity, Phoebe's cousin, giggled behind her fan. The feathered wrens perched in her mud-colored hair bobbed dangerously from side to side until one toppled to the floor. Whyever anyone would purposely choose to wear a stuffed bird in her hair escaped Phoebe. Stifling the urge to ask just that, she gritted her teeth. In a small act of defiance, she straightened her spine and thrust her bosom out further than Aunt Hildegard preferred. She peeked at her new guardian and saw what she saw every day. Superiority and disapproval.

"Remember your purpose, girl. This quest bears substantial difficulties as it is."

Phoebe erased all expression from her face and fixed her eyes on the sputtering candles of one of the three massive chandeliers that hung from the domed ceiling. Lands alive, she had very little time. If she did not find a husband, her mother's fortune—by order of her will—would be forfeit.

"The fact that you offer a title and an estate as your dowry will appeal to any number of gentlemen, regardless of your shortcomings. However, I refuse to allow this task to become an embarrassment to me, or my daughter. I suffered enough when my sister eloped to the colonies with your father. He was a poor Irish nobleman with no future and even less common sense. You are most fortunate that my father left *you* Marsden Manor. Are you listening, young lady?" With her customary scowl plastered on her face, Hildegard swatted the inside of Phoebe's wrist with lethal accuracy. "Pay attention. We have visitors."

Phoebe glanced where directed, saw three men advancing and fought the overwhelming urge to turn tail and hide. In the lead was Sir Lemmer, a handsome enough man, though he tended to make strange noises with his teeth. Sir Milton, a pompous bore who resembled a green bean with a tuft of blond hair, strutted on Lemmer's heels. The Honorable Ellwood followed. He wore painfully tight chartreuse breeches, a white shirt with a ridiculously tied cravat and a green paisley jacket. Being prone to accidents, he nearly collided with a servant.

God's whiskers, not again. She'd already spent the better part of last evening playing whist with the three men. The cards had offered livelier conversation.

"Remember, girls, do not acknowledge their presence until I say. Show an appropriate amount of interest when I do. Smile."

Phoebe barely suppressed a groan. According to Aunt Hildegard, all three men possessed the qualities needed for viable suitors. They were second sons with no title, older than twenty but younger than sixty and virtually oozed aristocratic charm. She shuddered. To think, one of these men could possibly be her future husband. Phoebe wanted a love match. She'd have better luck pulling a hair from a bald man. With that thought, she did groan. Out loud.

"Phoebe," Hildegard snapped. "Stop making those hideous noises. People will believe you prone to stomach ailments. Charity, do try to maintain a normal conversation without any mishaps."

Looking as though she might swoon with anticipation, Charity nodded. The girl welcomed any and all suitors, Phoebe thought jealously. Since it was her first season, if Charity failed to make a match, she could wait another year.

Phoebe wanted to stomp her feet and scream. At ten and eight, she deserved the same opportunity. Unfortunately, she had only six weeks to complete the task.

Hildegard continued to lecture from the side of her mouth. "You may dance two country dances with each. I forbid you to waltz. And Phoebe, curb your tongue. Men

12

have little tolerance for women with bold notions, and
even less for those inclined to speaking their mind. Put
your past behind you. Remember, you now reside in England."

However could she possibly forget? Hildegard reminded
her daily. Phoebe opened her eyes to find Sir Lemmer at
her side, the oppressive scent of cedar emanating from his
clothes. Sir Ellwood, smiling with dimpled cheeks, circled
once, twice, then settled beside Charity, who wore the
same besotted expression as he did. Lord Milton satisfied
himself with the empty spot on Phoebe's other side.
Phoebe sighed.

The darkness fitted Stephen Lambert, Duke of Badrick's
mood. As a favor to his friends, he had promised to attend
this damnable anniversary ball hosted by Elizabeth's
uncle. And he regretted it. He'd seen the sidelong glances
and heard the whispers when he'd entered the ballroom. A
cursed title proved tempting fodder for the gossipmongers
of the Ton.

He calculated he had another hour of this fustian nonsense before he could bid Lord Wyman and Winston and
Elizabeth good night. Until then, this empty room, a snifter
of brandy and a cigar appeased him.

Sitting on a red velvet chaise, Stephen absently gazed
about Lord Wyman's private study. Four crystal wall lamps
beside the door and a candelabrum on a table shed enough
light to distinguish bits and pieces of his newfound sanctuary. Shelves of books lined the left wall near an alcove
concealed by a wooden screen. Erotic paintings hung on
the other two walls and a white marble statuary of women
in various stages of undress sat on pedestals hidden in the
shadows near the draped windows. Scanning Lord
Wyman's newest acquisition, an ebony nude astride a

dragon, Stephen wondered what the London matrons would say if they knew of Wyman's collection and the private parties held in this very room.

The brass doorknob to the study turned. Irked by what he considered an invasion of his privacy, Stephen stood and slid into the dark alcove. He felt no inclination for small talk. With any luck, the intruder would realize that this was not one of the party rooms and leave quickly. On the other hand, someone may have come to utilize the very chaise he'd just left. Dash it all, how bloody inconvenient.

Behind the screen, he peeked through the small heart-shaped hole near the top as the mahogany door swung open.

A fey-looking creature darted inside, slammed the door and collapsed against the solid barrier as if the dark room meant salvation. With a mass of copper curls framing delicate eyebrows against a background of ivory porcelain skin, the little beauty was a study in contrasts. A simple ribbon confined the curls to the top of her head, exposing a slender neck. A hint of peach color touched her lips and cheeks. She appeared fragile and delicate, but the thrust of her chin hinted at an inner determination. Her breasts were delightfully full, pushed up as they were in her gown. Their rising and falling with her breath was tantalizing.

Then she smiled. Stephen was accustomed to lust, but the response of his body, his powerful impulse to touch her, surprised him. But damn, this woman possessed a luscious little body that begged for a man's hand.

While he glanced to the study door, expecting her companion to follow—for surely she awaited one—she inspected her surroundings. She tiptoed to a painting and gasped at its risqué nature. Then another. And another. When she reached the fourth picture, she tilted her head almost upside down. "Well, I never."

Suddenly, he desperately wanted to know the color of

her eyes. Captivated by her indignation and unable to remain hidden another moment, Stephen seized the opportunity. "I certainly hope not. Unless, of course, sexual experiences in aberrant surroundings appeal to you."

The girl whipped about, her peach silk gown flaring like a midshipman's bell. She frantically searched the corners of the room. Then, irritation, of all things, flitted across her face. "How dare you not announce your presence, whoever you are."

"What do you think I just did?" Color rose on her cheeks, matching the flaming curls on her head. She was really quite lovely.

"Are you a thief?" she queried while edging toward the door.

"Hardly."

"I know for a fact you're not Lord Wyman. Why are you hiding in his house?"

Not the typical female, Stephen thought. Damn pawky, in fact. He could see now, that her eyes were blue or possibly green.

"Who says I'm hiding? You disturbed my privacy."

"A mishap easily corrected." She spun on her heels to leave.

"Wait. There's no need to hurry off." His voice sounded almost peevish, but he didn't want the girl to flee. At least not until he discovered her name or her purpose. Her companion had yet to appear and his mind whirled with the possibility that he could yet salvage something from this abominable evening after all. "Were you going somewhere in particular?"

She peered over her shoulder, her eyes narrow slits of speculation. "I was looking for the library. I figure I took a wrong turn." With a quick glimpse about the room, she added, "At least I hope I took a wrong turn."

"Are you meeting someone?"

"Whatever made you think that?"

"Feel free to take another look around. This is not the usual place for a lady to visit. Especially alone and without good reason."

That certainly garnered a reaction. She reversed her position and crossed her arms, which accented the fullness of her breasts. She thrust her lower lip out, a delightful lip, he thought, lush, full. Perfect for a man's kisses.

Obviously insulted, the girl marched forward several steps and tapped her left foot in agitation. Her eyes flashed with anger. They were beautiful, emerald green, like the Lincolnshire meadows in spring. A trifle amused yet more intrigued, Stephen wondered if she showed the same amount of passion in bed.

"Goodness gracious, as I said a moment ago, I got lost." She spoke with a distinct bite to each word, her irritation emphasizing the silky drawl of her voice that identified her as a foreigner.

The voice alone made him think irrational thoughts. She sounded like an outraged virgin, but Stephen knew better. No proper young lady—regardless of her heritage—wandered about, by herself, in the private quarters of a man's home. Suddenly, the evening appeared quite promising. He and his mistress had parted ways ages ago and he'd never replaced her. Perhaps the time had come.

"You don't believe me?" Phoebe asked, squinting at the alcove's mysterious occupant. "I find your insinuations insulting. I'm also tired of explaining myself to someone who skulks in dark corners."

"I don't skulk."

"Really? Besides bad manners, whatever do you call it when someone refuses to show himself?"

"A desire for privacy."

"Something altogether different comes to my mind, rude-

16

ness. It's suspicious, arrogant and secretive. I'm beginning to think you have something to hide after all."

"Impertinent, aren't you. All I hide is myself."

"How can I be sure?"

"I never lie."

"And just whom shall I ask for references? I have yet to hear a name or see a face. Come out of the corner and I just might believe you." Phoebe waited anxiously, wondering if the stranger would comply. She should leave. Now. To be alone with a man, any man, in a room such as this, if discovered, would surely be a social sin of the greatest magnitude. Then again, she'd learned long ago that running away accomplished nothing. Truth be told, she wanted to stay, to match the rich timbre of his voice to a face. For some reason, this man, this voice, intrigued her. "I'm waiting."

He stepped from behind the screen, and bowed slightly. "Stephen Roland Lambert, Duke of Badrick at your service. And you are?"

Allowing herself time to dislodge the breath of air trapped in her lungs, Phoebe executed a perfect curtsy. Oh la, she'd called a duke a thief. If he was a duke. Although she doubted he would lie about something so easily confirmed. She squared her shoulders and politely said, "Miss Phoebe Rafferty, formerly of Georgia."

"A pleasure, Miss Phoebe Rafferty."

While he crossed to the round oak table near a red chaise and lit three candles, Phoebe studied her mystery man for the first time. Glory, he was handsome and then some. He stood over six feet tall, was broad-shouldered and long-legged, and dressed in black all the way to the gleaming tips of his polished boots. A modestly tied white cravat was the only exception. His straight hair fell to his shoulders, matching the ebony mustache lining his upper lip, which curled slightly, and the brows that arched over the most astonishing cocoa-colored eyes she'd ever seen. He held a drink in one scarred hand. Everything about the man seemed dark, dangerous. Her heart seemed to dance when he moved closer.

"See," he said. "I'm quite alone. And I hold no priceless heirlooms in my possession."

She squelched the urge to voice the remark on the tip of her tongue. She'd practically called him a liar once already.

Splashing an amber liquid into his glass, he asked, "Would you care for a drink?"

"No, thank you." Unsure of what to do, she paced about the room. When she came eye to breast with a marble statue, her sense of reason returned, and then some. "I must go."

"And rob me of the one bit of pleasure I might find this evening? Come now. Need I worry about a jealous man barging in to challenge me to a duel for finding myself alone with you?"

"Goodness gracious, no. Need I worry about an irate female?"

"Nary a one. Therefore, neither of us need rush off. Besides, do you honestly wish to return to that mad crush, Phoebe?"

She knew she should reprimand him for using her name with such familiarity, but with his deep, refined voice, she liked the way her name sounded on his lips. When bay rum and heather filled her nostrils, she realized he stood directly behind her. Pivoting to face him, she exhaled and lifted her chin a notch. "I've overstayed myself as it is, Lord Badrick."

His rumbling laugh and full smile transformed his somber features to those of a charming rogue. Even his eyes twinkled with humor. "Don't go missish on me now, Phoebe. I'm not a lecherous fool. I promise to behave as the perfect host. We can be friends, simply two poor souls sharing a bit of solitude. I shall guard our secret with my life. What do you say?"

The thought of a friend appealed to her something awful. She doubted a man with his looks and charm lacked for company of any kind, but oddly enough, though never having met him before tonight, she felt a sort of kinship with him. Certainly the alternative of returning to Aunt Hildegard held no appeal. She crossed to the table. "A few more minutes then."

"Marvelous. Now tell me, how do you find London so far?"

"Do you prefer the appropriate social repartee or honesty?"

He chuckled, a warm rich sound. "Honesty, by all means."

"In that case, damp, soggy and insufferably gray."

"Are you referring to our weather or our conversation?"

She opened her mouth to say "both," but thought better of it. "The weather, of course."

"Of course," he drawled. "And why would a lovely young lady like yourself flee the festivities of a ball?"

"I was fresh out of things to say. Besides, I prefer smaller, less restrictive affairs. It's difficult to enjoy oneself when one must constantly remember what one can and cannot do. Even if you do behave as best you can, you still risk disapproval from the matrons, who seem to have nothing better to do than scrutinize everyone else's behavior."

The amber liquid in his glass swirled as he moved his hand in small circular motions. His eyes gleamed like those of a panther she'd once seen. "A woman after my own heart. Did you have such liberty in America?"

"Yes, indeed. My life was far simpler back home. There was very little I didn't do if it suited my fancy."

"You'll be hard pressed to find such freedom in England. Society is rather exacting about the way young ladies behave."

"I've already discovered that. I never heard so many rules in my life. It's quite tedious, if you ask me."

"Tell me then. What did you leave behind?"

The distant strings of the small orchestra filtered through the house and into the room. Swaying to the music, she considered all that she used to do. Goodness, life on a plantation was so different. Where did one begin? She paced a few steps until she stood in front of the painting that had drawn her full attention earlier, as stunned this time by what she saw as she was the last. A nearly naked man and woman sat on top of a black horse engaged in, well, a behavior that looked rather suspicious and equally impossible. At least, she thought it was impossible—and if not, likely improbable.

She whirled about and blurted the first thing that came to mind. "I rode Hercules every morning." Lord Badrick lifted a solitary brow. "My horse," she quickly added, knowing her cheeks flushed with color by the sudden flare of heat she felt. Silly chit. She silently scolded herself for her foolish reaction. The man had no idea what she was thinking. When she noticed the glimmer of amusement in his dark eyes, she quickly changed the topic.

"Sometimes we raced, but rarely did anyone beat me. Hercules was too fast. At night I sometimes played poker with Timothy and Teddy, our neighbors. They even taught me to cheat." Whyever had she said that? "Not that I ever did, or would, mind you. And on the hotter days, I fished with Tobias and the whole lot of us sometimes swam in the river behind our house."

Her mouth seemed to be running amok, traveling faster than Whiskey Creek after a heavy rain. She couldn't seem to stop herself from talking, or fussing with the lace on the sleeve of her dress. She paused, allowing him time to say or ask something. When he didn't, she decided he wanted to hear more. After all, he'd asked, hadn't he?

"My nanny drew the line at boxing, said it was no sport for a female, but not before I learned a few things which proved useful a time or two."

The duke opened his mouth as if he meant to speak, then snapped it shut. Glowering at his drink, he shook his head. "You're serious?"

She couldn't help but notice the disbelief in his voice. "Of course I am. Why would I make up something like that? I loved my home, my life."

"Then what brought you to England?"

He was clearly dismayed. Phoebe considered lying. But waiting only delayed the inevitable, a lesson she had learned at an early age. If Lord Badrick spent any time in society he would discover the truth himself. "I'm here to find a husband." The light disappeared from his eyes. Defensively, she said, "I see I've shocked you, although I don't know why. Everyone knows the season is designed to match young women with eligible men."

"Doing and telling are as different as chalk from cheese. Few women speak openly of such things."

"What do they do then? Lie?" He stared at her. Discomfited, she added, "My preferences matter little either way. I have no choice."

He swallowed the last of his brandy in one gulp and set the glass on the table beside her with a deliberate thump. "There are always choices, Miss Rafferty."

The stiffening of his spine, the rigid set of his broad shoulders, the way he used her proper name, all were sure signs of his withdrawal. Just like a man, she thought, to spook at the mention of marriage. "Perhaps for men. For women—"

Lord Badrick suddenly glanced to the door, grabbed her

arm and dragged her into the darkest corner of the alcove, behind the wooden screen. He held a finger to her lips. "Shhh."

"Let me go." Struggling against the duke's grip, Phoebe peeked around the side and saw the study door fly open. A man and a woman scampered across the threshold and fell against the wall in a tangle of arms before the door even closed. Phoebe needed no additional explanation.

With his expression more irritated than anything else, the duke whispered, "It appears someone intends to usurp our sanctuary. Follow me." He started to drop to his knees.

Phoebe held on to his elbow. "Excuse me, your grace. Whatever are you doing?"

"Avoiding unnecessary embarrassment for all involved and saving your precious reputation."

"Can't we cough or something? Perhaps they'll leave."

"I see you have a great deal to learn about the strictures of London society. Rather they'd demand we show ourselves. I'd hate to ruin your chances of making a suitable match. We shall crawl behind the curtains to the terrace."

"Surely they'll see us."

He peered over her shoulder. "Highly unlikely."

Curious, Phoebe followed his gaze. The woman, her back to the alcove, stood before the man, who now sat on the chaise. His head was nestled in her lap. "Whatever is he—"

Lord Badrick practically shoved her to her knees. "Not now."

Six feet of wooden floor loomed between her and the crimson velvet curtains. Her heart beat a frantic rhythm. She felt his warm breath on her ear, which oddly enough caused her heart to flutter even faster. "Excuse me, your grace. It seems we'd be better off if we stayed right here."

With an impatient motion of his head, he indicated that he found the suggestion preposterous. "As you wish. I, on the other hand, do not intend to remain here and witness an interlude deserving of privacy." He eased his way toward the terrace, and reaching the heavy drape, he slid beneath.

Phoebe sat on her heels long enough for his feet to disappear and decided she just might be better off with him. When she pushed herself under the curtain, Badrick grasped the brass doorknob. Wasting no time, he hauled her to her feet, opened the door and pushed her outside. Luckily, no one occupied the terrace.

Clutching her wrist, he stood and pulled her down the stone steps behind an evergreen hedgerow. In her haste, one slipper came off, but Lord Badrick retrieved it and then followed her into the garden below.

The scent of roses filled the cool night air. The sound of sprinkling water from a nearby fountain matched the fast, soulful warble of a nightingale. Small torches, which distorted their shadows as they fled Wyman's study, lit the maze of the garden's stone paths.

"I think that's far enough," the duke said as he searched their surroundings most thoroughly.

Phoebe lifted her hand from her mouth and giggled. "Oh, my goodness. I'm beholden to you, Lord Badrick. That's the most fun I've had in months."

Fisting his right hand on his hip, he dangled her slipper in his other fingers. Obviously bemused by her reaction, he asked, "You're not frightened?"

"Heavens, no." she answered. "I'm sorry. Should I be?"

He clamped his lips shut and led her farther away from the house. Once again she found herself in the shadows with this man. She stood near enough to feel the linen of his jacket against her hand, to hear his sudden intake of air. Her throat constricted and the urge to slide into his arms shocked her. When he cleared his throat, she practically jumped backwards.

Thrusting the lost shoe into her hands, he said, "I hope

tonight's escapade taught you an apparently well-needed lesson."

His words were clipped and impersonal. "Which lesson was that?" she asked nervously as she replaced her slipper.

"Do you not realize that if caught, your reputation would be ruined?"

Phoebe circled a white marble statue of Pegasus nestled in an alcove of a hedge, wishing the mythical creature could steal her troubles away. She loathed the idea of returning to the ball, to her aunt and the task ahead. Unfortunately, she had few choices left. Resigned to her fate, she sighed. "I'm not sure it matters a'tall," she answered quietly. "What of yours?"

"Mine would suffer little."

"Another rule created by men for the benefit of men."

"Hardly. For their own protection from men much like myself, ladies do not explore houses by themselves, especially those in search of suitors. Nor should they gad about gardens with strangers. Few women find humor in such circumstances, and I might add, these rules are usually for the ladies' own good."

"Or so men think," she muttered. "Well, I happen to be very good at thinking for myself—though I appreciate your concern."

He edged closer, pinning her between his body and the statue. The cold marble at her back and the heat of his body were a stirring combination. He gently cupped her chin and tilted it up, studying her intently with those amazing eyes. They were colored like Jamaican coffee, she now decided. Several breathless moments passed.

Finally, he broke the silence. "It's time to return."

She found herself oddly disappointed when he stepped back. Once the ability to move returned, Phoebe silently followed the duke, admiring the play of his leg muscles beneath his well-tailored pants, the grace with which he walked.

They halted beneath a large elm. Bright lights shone through the windows, casting shadows about the garden. The stone steps leading to the red brick mansion beckoned as if commanding her to return and do her duty.

Pulling a cigar from his coat pocket, Lord Badrick struck a match and lit the tip. He leaned insolently against the trunk of the tree. "If anyone asks, claim you came outside to enjoy a bit of air. All will be well."

"What about you?" she asked.

"I'll be along shortly. It's best for you not to be seen with me. Trust me on this. Go."

Her shoulders heaved and her mind whirled with possibilities. Lord Badrick claimed to be unattached. He was handsome and charming and aside from the mysterious comments about his character, he appealed to her as no other man had. Her breath exhaled in a rush. "I imagine you'll find this atrociously bold, but I ride in Hyde Park every morning about seven. In case you're ever out that early."

"I'll keep that in mind." He lifted her hand to his lips and placed a gentle kiss on the inside of her wrist. "Good-bye, Phoebe Rafferty. Good luck with the hunt."

It was a wonderful turn of phrase, and it gave Phoebe hope. She was the huntress like the mythical Diana, a female warrior who controlled her destiny with dignity and pride. Her small steps toward the house, although labored, were resolute. Another notion, though whimsical, gathered clarity in her mind.

Fantasy or fact, she needed to find a husband. And quickly. So far, during her first week in England, she had met a bushel of men, none of whom were even remotely attractive to her.

The idea swarming in her mind seemed unreasonable, irrational and foolish. Yet, as far as she was concerned, her predicament was all those things, too. Deciding she had nothing more to lose, she skipped back to the duke's side and grinned. "Perhaps, Lord Badrick, I'll hunt you."

Chapter Two

Dumbfounded, Stephen could have sworn the chit giggled as she fled. She skipped across the lawn, and up the steps to the top where she stopped, turned and dropped in a perfect curtsy.

He swore. How had he become a candidate for marriage? He wanted a mistress, not a blasted wife. After killing two wives, he had no intention of entering the state of matrimony ever again. The Badrick line—as well as its infamous curse—would die with him.

He flicked his cigar to the ground and crushed it with the heel of his boot. Deciding he had best discover more about Miss Phoebe Rafferty, he marched at a clipped pace toward the house in search of Winston. The man was a diplomat and Stephen's closest friend; he would have some information.

He found his friend leaning against a pillar in the corner, the man's broad shoulders nearly as wide as the marble. He wore a look of contained annoyance.

Circling from the back, Stephen leaned over Winston's shoulder and said, "You look ghastly. I warned you love and marriage led to misery."

The scowl on Winston's face deepened. "Humph. I'll be far happier once Wyman makes his toast to our continued happiness. Then I can drag Elizabeth home. Where the devil have you been?"

"Around and about." Like the matching half to a pair of bookends, Stephen mirrored Winston's stance and leaned against the opposite side of the pillar with one leg crossed at the ankle.

"In other words, you found someplace to hide. Can't say I blame you. The rumors that accompany your name constantly amaze me. I overheard Lady Tisdale tell Lord Peltham you post the skulls of dead animals about Badrick Manor to ward off gypsies. Did you know you also sleep with ropes of onion and dill about your neck? Thank goodness you no longer behead dark-skinned boys with black hair and eyes." Winston frowned, disapproval crossing his face. "My God, does Elizabeth intend to dance with that toad?"

Stephen followed his friend's gaze to see to whom he referred. Yes, Lord Hadlin definitely fell into the toad category. While listening absently to Winston ramble, Stephen scanned the rest of the crowded room for any sign of Miss Rafferty. She was nowhere to be seen.

"I apologize for asking you to come tonight," said Winston.

"Hmmm." Where the devil had the girl disappeared to?

Winston tapped Stephen on the shoulder, shifting his gaze between his friend and his wife. "This pillar carries on a better conversation than you. You're caught up to your elbows in something. What's going on?"

Not yet prepared to explain anything in detail, Stephen smoothed his mustache several times. "I heard you, Winston. You apologized. No harm done. Although I prefer my privacy, I grew accustomed to society's scrutiny long ago. It's never stopped me from doing what I wanted in the past and it certainly won't in the future."

"If you spent more time in London, the speculation would lessen. People love mystery."

"Perhaps. Do you happen to know a Phoebe Rafferty?" Stephen was eager to change the subject.

Winston's brows rose and his blue eyes gleamed with speculation. "The heiress?"

Now this was an unexpected surprise. "What do you mean *heiress*?" asked Stephen.

"You know, rich, wealthy, unusually attractive dowry. Why do you ask?"

"Then you've met her?"

"Not exactly. Elizabeth heard rumblings of a newcomer to town with an inheritance up for bid, so to speak. And you know Elizabeth. She talked with Charity Goodliffe tonight. Evidently, the American girl arrived last week. Hildegard Goodliffe is her aunt."

Unfortunately, Stephen knew Lady Goodliffe from previous business dealings with her now-deceased husband. The censure that curled his lips couldn't be stopped. "More's the pity."

"My thoughts exactly. Do you know this American?"

"What else did Elizabeth glean from her conversation with Charity?"

Pushing himself away from the pillar, Winston placed his hands on his hips. "I refuse to answer another question until you tell me what this is all about."

The last thing Stephen needed was interference, but he wanted answers. He pursed his lips and chose his words carefully. "I met Miss Rafferty tonight and I simply wish to know a bit more about the girl."

"Really?"

Knowing his friend's desire to see him remarried and noting the all-too-eager expression on Winston's face, Stephen gave him a scowl. "Don't go looking for something that's not there."

"Relax, my friend. I am not ready to summon the vicar." Winston waggled his eyebrows. "Yet. I've to meet the girl first. I haven't seen you talking to anyone, and you disappeared almost as quickly as you arrived. Where did you see her?"

"Wyman's private study."

"Surely you jest."

When Stephen shook his head, Winston's mouth fell slack. His friend's stunned reaction almost made Stephen laugh. Almost.

"Now, I must say, you've succeeded in piquing my curiosity. What the devil was she doing in Wyman's library? For that matter, what were *you* doing in Wyman's library? My goodness, I appreciate a naked woman as well as the next gent, but I find that room exceedingly . . ."

"Crude?" interjected Stephen.

"Precisely."

"It was the one room in which I believed I would find privacy until you made your announcement. Evidently she had the same intention, lost her way and found the study by accident."

"No wonder you want to know more about the girl." Winston rubbed his hands in delight. "We must talk with Elizabeth."

Stephen grabbed his friend's arm before the entire situation spiraled out of control. "Listen well. I met this girl. We had a simple conversation. Nothing else happened. She made a rather odd statement and I wish to ascertain her true circumstance. Nothing else. Do you understand?"

Winston's laughter matched his size and he chose to use it now. Stephen frowned again as a group of lords standing nearby turned toward them. He nodded a good evening to them while snapping at Winston. "By God, Winston, I'm warning you. Your last attempt at matchmaking nearly killed me. I know you think I need another wife and a son or two. I don't. The title dies with me."

"That curse is stuff and nonsense. You know that."

"Curse or no curse, with and without love, I've tried my hand at marriage twice already. I learn from my mistakes and I have no intention of repeating that one. Ever."

Winston vigorously massaged his chin, obviously contemplating whether to drop the subject.

"Winston, I am content," Stephen said. "Leave it be."

Scanning the ballroom with a resolute expression, Winston nodded. "All right. Let's rescue Elizabeth. She feels compelled to dance with every fellow who asks. That wretch, Lemmer, is waiting his turn."

When Winston mentioned his first wife's brother, Stephen suppressed a sneer. He had no use for the man. Though he appeared the perfect gentleman, he was a vainglorious little monster in search of a title, and, Lemmer's sexual appetites slanted toward what Stephen considered depraved. They had hated each other since Emily's death. Considering the rapid pace Winston set, his friend evidently felt the same.

It took only moments to cross the ballroom floor and reach Elizabeth's side. As a result of his prodigious size, most people quickly moved out of Winston's path.

Elizabeth, a petite woman with a heart the size of her husband, beamed as she watched Winston approach. His besotted expression matched hers. Good heavens, Stephen thought, love transformed people into idiots and fools. Still, no matter how loathsome Stephen found marriage, he wanted only happiness for his friends.

Winston wedged himself between Lemmer and Elizabeth, his display of ownership evident for even the simplest of minds. Stephen flanked Elizabeth's other side. Lemmer's eyes flashed for a moment and he appeared annoyed, but he merely nodded his head in greeting.

Winston faced Lemmer. "Were you leaving?"

With a sudden intake of air, Elizabeth glared at her husband. He merely shrugged his shoulders.

Extending his arm toward Elizabeth, Lemmer said, "As a matter of fact, your wife and I were about to dance."

"She looks a bit piqued to me," Winston apologized. "Do you not agree, Stephen?"

Swallowing a chuckle, Stephen cleared his throat. "For the lady's safety, she had best rest with Winston and myself." He could almost hear Lemmer's teeth grinding at the snub.

"Surprised to see *you* here, Badrick," Lemmer finally said. "I thought London too public for you. So much talk about gypsies, murder, dead wives and all."

"Many people with nothing to do spend endless hours exercising their tongues at the expense of others. I worry little about them. You of all people should know that."

"Ah, yes. The imperturbable Duke of Badrick. Are you here in search of another woman willing to take a chance on your dukedom?"

"Hardly."

With false sincerity, Lemmer placed his hand across his heart. "Pardon my indiscretion. I forgot. Finding a wife would be a trifle difficult, what with your reputation and two dead wives."

Refusing to give Lemmer any satisfaction, Stephen flicked at a small green leaf he found on his sleeve. "Reputations are funny things. They crumble quite easily when certain information, best kept between gentlemen, falls into the wrong hands—but I forget myself. This is not the place to discuss such things. Don't you agree?"

"For now," Lemmer said, his expression pinched and a

touch of red to his cheeks. He turned to Elizabeth. "Good night, Lady Payley."

Winston stared at Stephen. "What was that all about?"

"The man has despised my existence ever since I married Emily. Her death did not endear me. At least we're rid of his company." Grasping Elizabeth's hand in his, Stephen whispered, "As for you, my dear, we could still flee to the far ends of the earth and live happily forever."

Tipping her head slightly, her walnut-colored eyes sparkling, she glanced from one man to the other. " 'Tis something to consider."

Winston snatched her hand from Stephen's. "Best say no, darling. Else I would have to kill him."

"I had not thought of that." She stared at Stephen. "I'll simply have to find a wife for him as well."

As his eyes lit with mischief, Winston rubbed his chin. "As a matter of fact—"

Stephen cleared his throat. "Winston." He placed enough warning in that one word for an idiot to understand.

"What?" Elizabeth asked.

"Nothing," Stephen said.

"I've known you since I was four," Elizabeth said. "I recognize that tone."

Stephen wondered if he'd made a mistake in seeking information from Elizabeth. Winston needed no ally in his matchmaking schemes.

She squared her shoulders. "Five minutes alone with me and Winston will reveal everything."

Knowing there was no hope for it, Stephen gave in. "What do you know about Miss Rafferty?"

"The American?"

"Yes."

Leaning over her shoulder, Winston whispered, "He met her tonight. Nothing happened. He does not want her as his wife since he desires no wife at all. We are ordered not to interfere. The girl made an odd statement and he simply wishes to ascertain her true circumstance."

Stephen watched Winston adopt an innocent expression that Stephen imagined he used time and again when negotiating alliances.

"I'm merely repeating what you told me." Winston winked at Elizabeth.

Casting a speculative glance toward Stephen, Elizabeth said, "I see. I saw the girl from a distance. She's quite lovely."

Turning toward the twirling couples with practiced nonchalance, Stephen said, "I suppose."

Elizabeth tugged at her glove in defeat. "I can tell you are not prepared to reveal a thing." She paused. "Then I suppose I will. She is in need of funds, though she does have something to bring to the table. Whomever she marries will inherit the Marsden title."

Ah, no wonder the girl appeared unhappy about her fate, Stephen thought. Still, she seemed determined to do what was necessary. Unfortunately, Stephen had no intention of entering the marriage mart to save the girl from the poorhouse. Matrimony was, quite simply, not an option.

"Stephen," added Elizabeth.

"Yes?" he said absently.

"I believe Sir Lemmer intends to give suit."

Stephen felt his limbs stiffen. He stifled the urge to find Lemmer and physically redirect the man's interests. "Over my dead body."

Winston asked, "I take that to mean you intend to see Miss Rafferty again?"

The image of a smiling Phoebe, the charming dimple in her left cheek visible, filled his mind. The creamy flesh above her bodice, the sparkle in her eyes when she laughed completed the picture. Indeed, she was a rare treasure. He smiled at a curious Winston and Elizabeth. "I believe I will. One way or another."

Stephen squinted against the brilliant glare of the sun as it rose steadily over the treetops of Hyde Park, wondering once again if he had misplaced his good sense. Dawn was an unholy hour to make such a determination. For two days, with his normal calculated pragmatism, he had weighed all aspects of his plan, deciding his idea bore merit. He had no intention of allowing Phoebe to slip through his fingers and into the arms of another man, especially one like Lemmer.

Cavalier, his black stallion, loped down the sandy track of Rotten Row while Stephen watched for a carriage or buggy, any conveyance that might carry the little Colonial. All he saw were grooms or noblemen out for their morning rides. The thunder of hoofbeats garnered his attention moments before a large roan lumbered to an abrupt stop at his side and reared. The mare's front legs landed in a puddle, spattering mud everywhere. The rider laughed exuberantly, the sound as refreshing as the brisk morning air. Damn if Stephen didn't recognize that voice.

He turned in his saddle to assure himself that he was wrong. Much to his dismay, leaning over the mare, stroking the animal with the warmest of affection, was Phoebe Rafferty. The infernal female sat astride the huge red horse. Bareback. Not only that, she wore breeches. Men's breeches. A woolen cap slanted low over her forehead and covered the glorious wealth of red hair he had seen before. Her eyes, a deep green the color of lush clover, twinkled with mischief. At first glance, she resembled a young groom.

Stephen scanned the area for her chaperone. When he found none forthcoming, he felt the unusual urge, reminiscent of the night at Wyman's ball, to lecture Phoebe on good sense, or rather lack thereof. Then again, lecturing a woman moments before asking her to become his mistress seemed preposterous. He shook a glob of mud from his glove. "Typically, one approaches another rider with more caution."

Phoebe glanced at the numerous spots marring his trousers and boots, then hugged her horse around the neck. "Do forgive Flash. It's been days since we've ridden together."

"I was referring to you."

Phoebe threw back her head and laughed, sending her horse into a nervous shimmy from side to side. Displaying the skill of an accomplished rider, she controlled the horse with a simple squeeze of her thighs. Stephen wondered if she would react with such abandon when she rode him. He immediately regretted the impulsive thought; his arousal would likely not abate anytime soon. Forcing his undisciplined thoughts back to the present, he nudged Cavalier to a walk.

Flash followed at a sedate pace. Although anxious to pursue the business at hand, Stephen knew women expected all sorts of nonsensical chatter and frivolous conversation. He surveyed his surroundings, searching out a suitable topic for a woman's mind. Birds noisily chirped in the nearby evergreens. Dogs scrounged for breakfast or barked occasionally as a squirrel chattered from a nearby oak tree. A gentle breeze swirled the earthy scent of dirt and dew through the morning air. He said, " 'Tis a lovely morning for a ride, though I can't remember the last time I greeted the dawn in this manner. Flash is a fine-looking animal."

"Why, thank you, your grace." she said proudly. "I'm training him."

Remembering the horse's earlier display, he looked dubiously at her.

Phoebe laughed. "That's not fair. Hercules, my horse back home, would have let himself be ridden to ground if the need arose. Flash belonged to my uncle and has been ridden very little. Given time, I believe he'll come around."

"Then I compliment you on your ability. Such loyalty is hard-won with horses. Where is Hercules now?"

"He was considered part of my father's estate and sold." She averted her gaze to the horse's neck, but not before he glimpsed the sadness lingering there. She sighed, then said, "This is a pleasant surprise. I didn't really expect to see you quite so soon."

"It would appear we both made a miscalculation." She watched him and waited. He added, "When you said you ride in Hyde Park in the morning, I imagined something altogether different."

Her gaze followed his to her male-attired body. "I've ridden every morning since I was no taller than our front porch. I know it's a blatant disregard for another of your English rules, but I can't abide sidesaddles. The fripperies women chose to wear when riding are impractical. Do you find my behavior shocking?"

"Shocking is the wrong word. Unexpected, perhaps. Besides, I am the last person to cast stones. I do wonder why you respect the rules enough to dress as a stableboy?"

"Oh, sweet heavens. If discovered, my aunt would faint dead away and then some, only to wake long enough to administer a two-hour lecture on my impropriety. She considers me a classless hoyden as it is. Inferior. Until I'm free of her household, masking my behavior seems the easiest solution."

"Inferior? In what way?"

She stopped her horse and shook her head from side to side, waving her hands in the air. He presumed she was imitating her dear aunt's actions. The girl certainly had a flair for the dramatic.

"First, there is my father's Irish ancestry," she said, slowing her voice to a lazy drawl. "Therefore, my hair is too red, my eyes too bright. I am to move more slowly with less enthusiasm, an unlikely possibility because my legs are too long. But if I master the art of walking, it will benefit me since my oversized bosom would be less noticeable."

Halting beside Phoebe, Stephen allowed his gaze to wander over every physical flaw she named, difficult as it was given the clothing she wore. He remembered her dressed in silk, her red curls blazing in the candlelight and the powerful urge he'd felt to take her into his arms. She would make the perfect mistress. He clasped her chin, noting the softness of the alabaster flesh, and he lowered his voice almost reverently. "Your aunt is either jealous or in need of spectacles."

As though a hand gripped her neck, swallowing suddenly became difficult. She cleared her throat and licked her lips. "Did I mention my nasty little habit of speaking my mind?" Her voice seemed huskier, her accent more pronounced.

"I believe I remember something of that from the other night, but I feel tact is often overrated. Shall we walk?"

"If you like."

Right now his greatest wish was to glide every inch of her delectable little body against his, not the most prudent of ideas given the circumstances. "I'd help you down, but I think it might appear most peculiar if I helped my groom from his horse."

Veering off the path to a copse of elms and maples, Stephen tied Cavalier to a nearby branch. Spotting a clump of violets, he picked a handful and waited, watching Phoebe, her rear perched in the air as she slid from the saddle to the ground. She truly possessed a delightful derriere, a vision worthy of his appreciation when dressed in men's breeches. He'd always considered women's bodies one of life's greatest pleasures, partaken of excessively in his younger days. Older and wiser now, he'd learned to control his lust and usually limited his sexual encounters to mistresses or not at all. Nonetheless, the unbidden image of those soft mounds turned up trump on his bed, naked for his eyes only, flitted across his mind. His trousers suddenly fit tighter than he preferred.

When she stepped near, he held the flowers out to her. " 'Violets dim, yet sweeter than the lids of Juno's eyes or Cytherea's breath.' "

Accepting the gift, she grinned. "Shakespeare. *The Winter's Tale.*"

"You know our esteemed playwright?"

"You sound surprised. I'll have you know, sir, I've read all his works."

Passion and *stimulating conversation.* The time for idle chatter was over. He paced back and forth, slapping his leather gloves briskly against his leg while Phoebe stood silent for a moment, stroking Flash's neck. His proposition made perfect sense. He needed to explain his position clearly and thoroughly to allow for no misunderstanding. Why, then, did he feel like a misguided schoolboy on the verge of mischief?

"It seems something is clawing at your throat," Phoebe said. "I usually just blurt it out."

Stephen halted beside a large bayberry bush and watched a robin play tug-of-war with a worm. Phoebe was right. He gained nothing by waiting. As if delivering a speech in Parliament, he clasped his hands behind his back, braced his feet apart and spoke calmly and concisely. "I want you to become my mistress."

Phoebe's eyes rounded to the size of Dresden plates and her mouth fell open wide enough to swallow a small bird. Her mouth shut, then opened, then shut once again.

"It appears I've rendered you speechless."

"Lands alive. I don't know what to say."

"Then say nothing until I've explained. You will have a house of your own, an appropriate staff and a healthy monthly allowance. A carriage of your own choice will be given to you as well as a pair of horses for your riding pleasure. You will want for nothing."

Phoebe didn't look at him, but concentrated on the leather rein she twirled in her hands. "How very kind of you," she said, her voice now a shy whisper, void of its earlier enthusiasm.

This was going extremely well. The dear girl was overwhelmed with his generosity. She'd probably never received such a grand proposal before. Stephen couldn't wait for her to hear all that he offered. "At which time we choose to part, you keep the house, the staff and everything you have received during my care. I guarantee you your allotted income until you marry or find another protector."

"In return, you would expect me to . . . ?"

The red-silk-clad image of Phoebe, kneeling at the foot of his large feather bed, anticipating his arrival, forced a smile to his lips. He would kiss every inch of her, starting with the adorable little mole below her right ear. He lowered his voice to a seductive purr. "Be available to me whenever I wish."

"I see." Actually Phoebe saw nothing at all but a man she thought handsome and charming enough to seduce a stable filled with women, a man who looked overly proud of himself with his chin lifted and a cocky grin plastered on his face. Goodness, he both infuriated and intrigued her. However had he come to the conclusion that she would be willing to be his mistress? She tapped the toes on her left foot and twisted the reins into a tight knot about her fingers. "We hardly know one another. What makes you think such a relationship even possible?"

"Quite simply, I want you."

She wasn't quite sure how to respond to that declaration. He sounded as though that sole reason should be enough to convince her. The business of mistresses was not completely foreign to Phoebe. Although her father never had, many plantation owners took slaves as their lovers. Some went willingly, some didn't. When she was a child, she'd befriended some of the women on her own estate and heard them talk. The slaves foolish enough to care for the men waited like lost puppies, hoping for a scrap of time or a bauble to prove their worth. Phoebe shuddered to think of herself reduced to waiting on a man's whim. Good sense warned her to mount her steed and flee. Curiosity won. After all, she might never have the same opportunity to ask the questions she wanted to ask. "Shouldn't one's mistress require a certain expertise?"

"One can easily be tutored."

When his lips curled to one side he looked like a man confident in his skills. Her stomach fluttered strangely. No doubt he could tutor a woman on most anything. Pity, she thought. She needed a husband, not a protector. She looked him squarely in the eye, pasted her most congenial smile on her face and said, "Thank you very much for your generous offer, but I decline."

"I beg your pardon?"

"What you ask is quite impossible."

Suddenly he stood beside her, his hands fisted on his hips. "What game do you play, Phoebe?"

Straightening her spine, she tried to make herself appear taller next to his imposing height. "I play no game."

"Then why the deuce did you give me the impression you were interested in my proposal?"

"Is that what I did?"

"Yes," he snapped.

In order to satisfy her curiosity, she'd obviously hurt the

41

man's feelings. An apology was out of the question, but in goodwill—after all, she did like the man and hated to see him upset—she decided to explain. Skirting around the duke, she tied Flash next to Cavalier. "I found the information enlightening. No man ever asked me to be his mistress before."

His eyes narrowed to thin slits. "Come now, Phoebe. You hail from America, where you claim you had unlimited freedom to do whatever you wished. You fraternized with men on a daily basis, and your evenings, well, who the devil are Teddy and Timothy? You said your reputation mattered not. You clearly have no real desire to wed and you abhor and ridicule society's dictates, ignoring propriety at every turn. You invite, then meet me, unchaperoned, at this unholy hour of the morning. By God, you even proposed to me. What else am I to think?"

"That I have a will of my own," she shot back in irritation, regardless of the fact that he was possibly partly correct about her role in the misunderstanding. His glare grew fiercer and she sighed. Losing her temper right now certainly wouldn't help. "It's obvious you misinterpreted my boldness for something else altogether. I ran our plantation, for heaven's sake. Naturally I spent time with men, my father and our workers included. I grew rather accustomed to having my say. My neighbors, Teddy and Timothy, were only fourteen years old. As to my current dilemma, I must marry an English nobleman in less than six weeks. If I don't, I lose my only estate, Marsden Manor, as well as any other income. I'll be as poor as a church mouse."

"I know that much," he muttered, obviously still disgruntled.

"You do? How?" she asked, more confused than ever by his declaration.

"How what?"

"How do you happen to know so much about me when I know so little about you? That seems rather unfair."

"After you disappeared from Lord Wyman's the other night, I asked a few questions. Your plight is quite the talk of the town. I offer you an alternative. As my mistress, you'd be financially secure."

She wasn't sure which bothered her more: his arrogance, so typical of men who believed they needed to molly-coddle women, or the fact that her dilemma was no longer a secret. "Financially dependent is what I'd be. I'd be even more tied to you than if I married."

"That's ridiculous. Once married everything reverts to your husband."

"Not necessarily."

"Then, my dear, you would have managed to change the way of things since Adam was a lad."

He sounded so confident, so patronizing. Irritation warred with her determination to make him understand. "I aim to marry a man who agrees to *my* terms." He looked at her as if she'd grown a third ear. "If you understand my circumstance, then you know I bring a title to the altar. If I cannot find a man to love then I will find a man eager for that title and a stable income. Like you, I intend to be very generous. In exchange, I will ask for my freedom. He can go his way and I can go mine."

"Where do you expect to find these stellar candidates?"

"According to my aunt, there are any number of men who qualify. In fact, Lord Milton and Sir Lemmer seem interested."

Lord Badrick's limbs became rigid. Not a twitch or even a breath disturbed his body. Only his lips moved. "Stay away from Lemmer."

The hard edge to his voice was unmistakable. Although

she didn't particularly like Sir Lemmer herself, she refused to acknowledge that to Badrick. She shrugged her shoulders, wishing she was capable of standing as still as he. The man had incredible self-control. "I understand he seeks a title as well as money. I shall have both."

"The marriage will require a consummation. How do you intend to deal with that?"

"I haven't reasoned that through."

"I'll tell you this, Phoebe Rafferty. None of those men, especially Sir Lemmer, will keep you happy in that quarter."

This discussion was beginning to wear on her good mood. Probably because she knew he might be right, a possibility she found most disconcerting. "And you are such a great lover women flock to your door?"

For the first time in several minutes, obviously pleased with this particular topic, he relaxed. A sly, foxlike grin lit his face. He crossed toward Phoebe, slowly forcing her to retreat several steps until she backed herself against the trunk of the large elm. Flash stood on one side. Shrubs bordered the other, effectively blocking the couple from the road.

Stephen braced his arms on either side of her shoulders. "I assure you, Phoebe, the women who come to my bed do so eagerly and leave with no complaints."

"I did not question your—"

"Abilities? Oh, but Phoebe you did just that. Now I feel the need to exonerate myself."

She watched his brown eyes shift to black as he slowly brought his lips to hers, allowing her plenty of time to avoid his kiss. Her eyes fluttered closed the minute their lips touched. She had once kneed a neighbor in the groin and left him whimpering on the straw-covered barn floor after he had stolen a quick peck. If need be, she knew she could administer the same punishment to Stephen. Yet, she had no desire to do so. Timidly placing her hands on his shoulders, she leaned into the kiss. He smelled of heather and soap, and a masculine scent she recognized as his own.

She expected an assault, but received a tender persuasion with the soft blending of their lips. His tongue traced a light path across the crease of her mouth, teasing yet demanding entrance. When she opened her mouth ever so slightly, he deepened the kiss. The muscular length of his body pressed against her, her woolen jacket a sudden unwanted barrier to the heat she felt. His hands claimed her waist directly below her breasts, which ached in the most peculiar way.

He ended the kiss as gently as it had begun. "Now, my sweet, tell me my idea does not have merit."

With his withdrawal, she felt a moment's loss and licked her lips almost as if she might recapture his taste. Enough of this nonsense. She should have heeded her good sense sooner. Now she would regret what she must do. She pushed away from the tree and stepped away from Stephen. He continued to watch her, smug. When standing beside Flash, she grabbed a fistful of the horse's strawberry mane and swung onto its back. She faced Stephen and said, "I've always wanted love. By some demented twist of fate, I find I need a husband—with or without that luxury."

"Don't look in my direction, Phoebe. Love is for fools and dreamers. I'm neither."

"How can you say that?" Phoebe asked. To her, love heightened the senses, bound a man and woman together in devotion and comfort.

"Love is a perpetual wound. I have no need of it. I have no need of a wife. I will not marry you. Now or ever. I want a mistress."

It appeared that they disagreed on the very nature of

love, even its existence. "Well, then. It seems we have reached a stalemate, but thank you for a lesson I'm sure to find handy over the next few weeks."

Almost immediately, the lazy smile vanished. He became the predator again, his body tense and wary. "What do you mean?"

"If I cannot marry for love, I will control my own future and marry a man of my choosing. I had not fully considered the implications of the marriage bed until just now. I realize I shall have to test my candidates on that as well."

"You mean to bed them all before you decide?"

"Gracious, no. But a kiss or two will certainly help me make up my mind."

"*Phoebe.*"

She backed her horse from the copse of trees, away from the dangerous glint in his eyes. "And one more thing, Lord Badrick, regarding my outburst the other night."

He scrunched his eyebrows together as though trying to remember. She almost pitied the man. "About possibly choosing you as my husband. I must withdraw the suggestion. You simply will not do."

"Why not?"

"Why, sir, you'd never be a malleable husband."

Turning Flash to the track, eager to ride the wind, she spurred her horse to a gallop. Phoebe needed to calm the beating of her heart. She feared Badrick might follow. Her heart feared he wouldn't.

For the first time in her life she had met a man who made her feel the things the slave women back home talked about. What rotten, horrible luck! The man was all wrong for her.

Chapter Three

Phoebe crept up the servant's stairs of Aunt Hildegard's home, cautious of the creaking planks in the wooden steps. All the while, she searched for reasons to avoid Lord Badrick in the future.

He definitely disturbed her senses. No man had ever managed to make her stomach flutter or her heart pound the way he did. Even now, her pulse thrummed as she remembered his tongue stroking the inside of her mouth. Imagine, men and women kissing like that! She'd had no idea and hadn't minded the least little bit. She visibly shuddered at the thought of sharing a kiss the likes of that with either of Lord Milton or Sir Lemmer. Kissing Lord Badrick, she decided, was definitely a seductive argument of itself.

Nibbling her lower lip, she concentrated even harder. The man tended to jump to conclusions, and surely that was a deterrent. Twice now, he had incorrectly judged her actions. But she could hardly fault him for that, she realized. She was guilty of that from time to time as well. Hadn't she assumed he'd be the perfect husband?

Certainly the fact that he seemed accustomed to having his way was a reason to avoid the man. He wouldn't accept failure or defeat without a fight. She doubted that he'd marry her and leave her alone at Marsden Manor to live her life. Yet, was that a flaw or a virtue? She sat on a step, her elbow braced on her knee, her chin tucked in her hand. She further considered his confidence and high-handed behavior. It bordered on arrogance, but she admitted she liked strong men who knew their own mind. Unfortunately, what he wanted and what she wanted were at cross-purposes. The man even refused to acknowledge the need for love in a relationship. Well, there it was. The crux of the problem. Based on the censure in his voice, the rigidity of his body and his choice of words, his mind seemed made up. He wanted a mistress. She needed a husband. She wanted love. He wanted physical pleasure. Well drat, that was that. She mustn't see him again.

Determined to erase him from her mind, Phoebe stood, wondering how she could miss something so much when she never really had it in the first place.

Listening at the top of the stairway, and satisfied when she heard only silence, she tiptoed across the hall into her bedroom. Phoebe's servant, Nanny Dee, stood at the window, staring at the street below. Her ebony skin glistened in the sunlight. Both hands were clenched on her slender hips, and the red scarf that covered her head shook from side to side. She was clearly agitated about something.

Phoebe crossed the wood floor and glanced over her servant's shoulder to look outside as well. "Good morning, Nanny Dee. Is something wrong?"

Dee whirled and wagged her finger in Phoebe's face. "Don't you good-morning me, child. You're late, and that woman is already up and callin' for you."

"Aunt Hildegard? Oh, dear."

"Yes, indeed. She already come lookin' for you once this mornin'. You best be gettin' yourself out of those boys' clothes, into somethin' more presentable before she comes a lookin' for you again."

Quickly shucking her cap, jacket, trousers and shirt, Phoebe rushed to the room's white porcelain pitcher and grabbed a wash cloth. She bathed while Dee stuffed the worn riding garments into the bottom of a basket beneath the bed, clucking and mumbling the entire time, a habit Phoebe was long accustomed to.

"What did Aunt Hildegard want?"

"To ruin my day. She does that, you know. Ain't never seen no one with such a sour disposition. That woman is going to straighten my hair. And if she don't, then you surely will. Goin' off like this every day."

Dressed in a clean shift, Phoebe sat at the mahogany dressing table, grimacing when she saw her hair. She yanked out the pins.

"Good heavens, child. Leave a curl or two on your head. Give me that brush." Dee took over the task quickly and competently.

Phoebe smiled. Since the day she came into the world, she had relied on Dee for one thing or another. Phoebe didn't think she would have survived her daddy's death without Dee.

A free woman, Dee could have stayed with her husband, Tobias, but she had chosen to come to England. She'd watch over Phoebe before she left her charge in the hands of just anyone. That was that, she'd said, so here she was.

Dee weaved Phoebe's unruly curls into a tidy braid. "Why was you so late this mornin'?"

Phoebe's eyes locked with Dee's in the mirror. She remembered the excitement she'd felt when she first saw the duke in Hyde Park. Her smile broadened. Remembering their conversation, she frowned. "I saw Lord Badrick today."

"You mean that duke fellow you talked about the other night?"

Phoebe nodded, noting Nanny Dee's obvious censure. She held little regard for the positions men held. She constantly reminded Phoebe to measure a man's worth by his nature, not his name or some fancy title tucked on the end. Still, Phoebe had a feeling Nanny Dee would approve of Stephen Badrick, with or without the title. Well, up until she learned of his proposal.

"Umm-hmm," murmured Phoebe.

"What's the matter? You look like you did the day your daddy took away your first pony." Dee crossed to the armoire, an ornate concoction of wood, gold and glass. She pulled a peach muslin dress from the cabinet and a pair of matching stockings from the drawer. "Well, you going to tell me or you going to make me guess?"

Nibbling on her lower lip, Phoebe hesitated for the space of a heartbeat. Dee always provided guidance and direction without recrimination. Besides, Phoebe needed to talk to someone or go mad. "He asked me to be his mistress."

Dee tucked her tongue in her cheek, obviously chewing on that bit of information. "I pray to the sweet Lord that you told him no."

"Of course," said Phoebe, twirling her braid nervously.

"Come here, child. Get this dress on. You can tell me exactly what this duke fella said to upset you so."

Phoebe related everything except the kiss. All the while, she pulled and tugged on her fingers.

Dee listened as she fussed with the dress until every strap and bow fell into its proper place. With a swat to Phoebe's fanny, Nanny Dee said, "Sit down and put your stockings on. What ain't you telling me?"

Phoebe sighed. She never could fool this woman. "He kissed me."

"And what did you do?"

"I kissed him back. It wasn't at all like the time Jimmy Ray kissed me. I rather enjoyed myself." One stocking dangled from her hand when she asked, "Does that make me wanton?"

"That makes you a woman grown, who for the first time in her life knows what it feels like to have a real man take her in his arms. Now some men just plain know how to kiss a woman. And *sometimes*, it feels so nice because there's somethin' special goin' on."

"It's just odd. I mean, I only met the man two nights ago."

"You need a husband. You might as well enjoy his attentions."

Phoebe's laugh, devoid of humor, filled the chamber. "He made it quite clear, Nanny Dee. He wants a mistress, not a wife."

Clucking several times, Dee finally said, "Most men don't know their own minds. It's up to us women-folk to help them find the right direction. It don't take no big stick to move a mule. A man's no different. You got a choice to make. If'n he's the man you set your sights on, then I reckon you best make him realize it's you he wants—as a *wife*, not a mistress. Do I make myself clear about that? With that stubborn streak of yours, I figure the man don't have no chance a'tall."

"It's not as simple as that. He's arrogant and domineering. If I married him he would not be content to go his own way while I tend to my own matters. Besides, I don't think he needs money."

"I already told you that scheme of yours got holes bigger than Tobias's dreams."

"I am bound and determined to make the best of this situation. Surely if I can't find a man I love, I can find one who will marry me for my money and leave me be."

"Child, you best be taking a long, hard look at this plan of yours. You give up your dreams of a family and you'll be mighty lonely."

She remembered the feeling of contentment she'd felt within Badrick's arms. His frank rejection of her proposal and the reality of her situation resurfaced. She was penniless with no real home, relying on the charity of a mean-spirited relative, having to rush to choose a stranger for a husband, never knowing the love she wanted. Suddenly, the day seemed bleaker. "Oh, whyever couldn't he be the least bit interested in marriage?"

The tears threatened. She fought them back. Tears hadn't helped the day her daddy died, and they certainly wouldn't help now. She felt Dee's tender grip on her shoulders. Willingly, Phoebe rested her head against the woman's breasts.

"Go ahead and cry, sweet pea. You got enough right to. Sometimes it just helps to clear the soul."

Allowing herself the luxury, Phoebe let her emotions rule for a few minutes, wallowing in self-pity over the injustice of it all. Hiccuping, her shoulders shuddered as she gathered her wits. "Enough of this."

Dee gathered Phoebe's chin in her hand. "Listen, child, life's a funny thing. There's no guarantees, but you is a beautiful woman with a heart to match. I can't believe God would grant you a miserable life. It ain't His way. It may not be easy, but if you try hard enough, I think you'll find the happiness you deserve. You hold on to those dreams of yours with both hands. Once we lose sight of them we ain't got a whole lot left. Now blow your nose and get. I can almost hear that woman's voice screechin' for you."

Everything Dee said made perfect sense. Phoebe had been in London for one week and had met only a handful of men. There would be other opportunities. Lord Badrick would become a distant memory. Feeling better than before, Phoebe teased, "Want to come along?"

"Serve that woman right if'n I did. One look at me and she'd start wheezin' and coughin'."

Phoebe squared her shoulders as if she meant to offer a stern reprimand. "You have no one to blame but yourself. Telling her all those stories about the Caribbean and slaves and voodoo. You managed to convince her quite nicely that she best leave you alone."

Dee chuckled, her white teeth gleaming against her dark skin. "Yes, I did. Go on, now."

Reaching the foyer, Phoebe peeked around a plaster urn that reached her shoulders and into the dining room. Hildegard certainly liked extravagance, a bit too much if anyone asked Phoebe. Three walls boasted elaborate murals of gleaming chariots, mythical Gods, and lightning bolts. Gold plaster trimmed the red ceiling and a floral rug covered most of the marble floor. The chandelier glittered as morning sunlight filtered through one large window and reflected on the hundreds of crystal teardrops. The enormous mahogany table, inlaid with ebony and brass, seemed to consume the entire room.

Hildegard sat at one end, Charity at the other. Neither female conversed with the other—but then again, to do so they'd probably have to raise their voices, which according to Hildegard simply wasn't done.

With her brightest smile, Phoebe walked to the center of the table and sat. "Good morning."

Glancing up from her morning paper, Hildegard peered at the clock on the wall and pursed her lips. Charity merely nodded, returning her attention to her eggs and toast. Cook brought a silver platter filled with assorted meats and cheese and waited for Phoebe to make her choice. Selecting a bit of ham and a currant scone, Phoebe said, "I'm surprised to see you awake so early this morning, Aunt Hildegard."

"This entire sordid business is disrupting my routine. I actually found a post regarding you in the *Times* society section. I will have you know I do not like it."

Upon Hildegard's nod, a servant placed the folded newspaper beside Phoebe. She scanned the section and read aloud, "Who shall be the lucky man to win the prize offered by the lovely American, Miss P——— R———?" Lands alive. Had people nothing better to do with their time than report on the comings and goings of London society? Frowning, she said, "I fully understand, Aunt Hildegard. You've made your feelings quite clear. I'm as unhappy about the situation as you are. Still, I cannot stop the press from printing what they choose. As to the other, I have no choice. I could always find work and lodge elsewhere."

"Humph. And add more fat for the gossipmongers to chew? I think not. I cannot allow your sorry circumstance to ruin my daughter's chance for a prosperous match."

"Certainly not," agreed Phoebe, knowing Hildegard also anticipated generous compensation from Phoebe's estate. She turned toward her cousin. "Have you special plans for the day, Charity?"

Charity offered a shy smile accompanied by a soft twitter. "I thought I might go to the museum."

Hildegard glared beyond the large bouquet of daisies on the table to her daughter. "You need improve your feminine skills more than you need fill your head with frivolous poppycock. You shall stay home and practice your embroidery."

"Yes, Mother," murmured Charity as the joy faded from her face.

No wonder Charity wanted to marry as soon as possible.

Hildegard constantly ordered her about like a servant. Phoebe wanted the girl to stand up, toss her napkin to the table and demand to go to the museum.

"Phoebe," said Hildegard, her annoyance quite clear. "Correspondence and invitations have arrived all morning. I expect you to exercise proper etiquette in all your responses, unlike your mother who proved herself common and irresponsible, not worthy of a penny of my family's money."

Gritting her teeth, Phoebe squelched her rising temper. "Obviously, my grandfather thought differently. Otherwise, I would not have the opportunity to inherit Marsden Manor."

"True enough. A decision he made that I will never understand. He always held a tendre for your mother, even though she broke his heart."

"Hmmm." Phoebe stabbed a piece of meat with her fork. "I think it's going to be a lovely day."

"How would you know? You've barely been out of bed. Your father always preferred to lay about in the mornings as well, and see where that landed him. I knew from the beginning. The man showed absolutely no promise—"

"Aunt Hildegard," Phoebe said, her voice sharper than she intended.

"What is it?" snapped Hildegard, obviously disgruntled over the interruption.

Granted, her aunt had been kind enough to offer a roof over Phoebe's head, but enough was enough. Since her arrival, all she'd heard, day after day, was the ranting and raving of a jealous, splenetic woman. Today she was not in the mood to listen. Phoebe pushed the plate away, her appetite ruined. She folded her napkin once, twice, then flattened her palms over the piece of green linen.

"Aunt Hildegard," she began again, much calmer this

time, "I appreciate everything you have done for me. Truly I do. However, I think it best if we avoid any discussions about my mama and daddy."

"Are you telling me what I can and cannot speak of in my own home?"

"I wouldn't think of it. I loved my momma and daddy very much. I'm sorry you feel differently, but nothing you say will change my mind or my heart. I will not listen to their good names being trampled. I hope you consider my feelings in the matter. If not, I will have no choice but to find lodging elsewhere."

Hildegard squinted as her skin flushed with red blotches. Her forehead scrunched together to form a patchwork of wrinkles across her brow. Charity sat perfectly still, her eyes as wide as Hildegard's were narrow.

Considering the fact that dozens of things remained unsaid, Phoebe smiled, congratulating herself on her composure. "Now, was there another reason you wished to see me, Auntie?"

With stilted movements, Hildegard pressed herself from her chair and away from the table. Her chin angled such that Phoebe thought it just might snap like a cornstalk. She said, "You have correspondence. I recommend you give the invitation from Sir Lemmer some thought. We leave for the Halsten ball at eight. Come along, Charity."

Phoebe watched her relatives leave, Charity casting a backward glance as if to reassure herself that she had actually seen what had just transpired. At least her mouth was closed now. When they reached the door, the two nearly collided with the butler, Siggers, who held an enormous bouquet of flowers in a rainbow of colors out beyond his rounded belly. A small piece of paper dangled from the fingertips of his left hand. He announced, grinning proudly, "Flowers for Miss Rafferty."

Blatantly ignoring the fact that the envelope was

addressed to someone else, Hildegard grabbed the paper and tore it open. She gasped, then turned a vicious scowl toward Phoebe.

Before Hildegard uttered one word, Phoebe knew who had sent the flowers. The cook was in the kettle now. She stood beside her chair, masked her face with innocence and waited.

"I knew it all along," railed Hildegard. "You *are* exactly like your mother."

"Thank you."

"Humph." Hildegard's hand, the note now dangling from her fingertips, shook as she approached. "Explain this."

"May I read it first?" asked Phoebe, wondering what she would say, depending on what Lord Badrick had written.

Hildegard thrust the note into Phoebe's outstretched hand.

It was simple and to the point. "May the best man, *or woman*, win. Until tomorrow morning. Your greatest admirer." Needing nothing new to fuel Hildegard's foul temperament, Phoebe's mind raced for a rational explanation. Or a convincing lie. "My greatest admirer?" She tapped the note against her hand and affected an expression that had fooled her father a number of times. "How should I know who sent the flowers? He neglected to write his name."

"What of this morning rendezvous?"

"I'm as confused as you are. Perhaps the flowers were sent to the wrong household."

"Siggers," snapped Hildegard. "Who delivered these?"

He kept a bland expression on his face. "A street urchin, madam."

Hildegard glared from Phoebe to Siggers and back as if they had conspired with one another. She even threw Charity a passing glance of disgust before she declared, "Siggers, dispose of them."

"Aunt Hildegard," interrupted Phoebe, her voice calm but resolute. She intended to keep her gift. "Those were delivered to me. I believe I'm entitled to make the decision to keep or throw them away."

"A true gentleman does not send flowers without a proper introduction. And a *true lady* would never accept them."

"Who's to know, Auntie? I certainly won't tell." Phoebe rescued the flowers from the butler, knowing as long as he held them, he would feel bound to do his mistress's bidding. "If you don't wish to share their lovely scent, I will gladly take them to my room."

"Oh, mother," said Charity. "They are quite pretty."

"Go upstairs." Hildegard waved Charity away as easily as she might a chambermaid. With her daughter gone, she focused her full attention on Phoebe. "Let me make myself perfectly clear on this issue. I will allow you to keep those flowers because I wish it. If and when you discover the person responsible, you will tell me immediately."

The devil she would. "Of course," agreed Phoebe.

"And"—Hildegard leaned in—"do not think, for one moment, that you have me fooled."

Phoebe watched Hildegard storm across the marble floor, her shoulders squared, her chin held high. How exhausting. And how depressing. She still had five weeks left in this household.

Crossing to Siggers, who remained by the arched doorway, Phoebe placed her hand on his elbow. "Thank you for not divulging my little secret."

"I don't know to what you refer, miss," he said. He winked and departed.

Phoebe knew otherwise. In a very short time, with common courtesy and simple kindness, she had earned the servant's loyalty.

She buried her face in the colorful bouquet, absorbing

the texture and fragrance. Thinking of the scoundrel responsible, she frowned. Goodness gracious, the man was resourceful. She'd give him that. She'd left him not more than an hour ago, and already she had flowers. Dozens of them. Instead of honoring her wishes, he'd chosen to issue a challenge. Whether foolish or wise, she felt herself grin all the way to her toes.

Chapter Four

The females in the theater sighed collectively as the dark-haired soprano clung to a high note, her tale of misery captivating the audience. Aside from an occasional glimpse to the stage, Stephen barely paid heed to the production. He felt as he did often of late: irritated. And now he felt impatient, which, to his dismay, irritated him all the more.

Three days had passed since he'd met Phoebe in Hyde Park, since he'd submitted to the irrational impulse and sent her flowers along with a challenge. Perhaps not his most stellar of ideas, he decided. The illusive female hadn't bothered to take her early morning ride since. She obviously meant what she'd said about wanting a husband and not a protector.

Well, he meant what he had said as well. He had evaluated every detail of her situation forward and backward, circling around to do it all over again. Numerous times. He still believed that he, being a man, knew what was best for her. Men were supposed to take care of women. That was the way of things.

He shifted in the high-backed chair as he thought back to his rather hasty proposal. Clearly he had shocked the girl. Still, his idea was the logical solution. He sighed. She probably expected a jeweled trinket or two, soft words in the very least. He simply needed opportunity. Primed with anticipation like a hound on the hunt, he glanced across Covent Garden's horseshoe auditorium, trying to see his prey.

Opportunity had presented itself moments before *The Italian Girl in Algiers* began. Phoebe sat across the room in the company of her aunt and cousin. The opera's intermission couldn't come soon enough. As if by divine intervention, the audience erupted into exuberant applause, signaling the end of the first act.

Winston leaned over Stephen's shoulder. "A rousing first act. What do you suppose the chap will do to mend the fences he destroyed?"

Stephen wondered exactly what he had missed. "Who can say? How about you, Elizabeth?"

Flipping her fan open, she said, quite confidently, "Mustafa will plead momentary insanity and beg Elvira's forgiveness."

Winston snorted. "Darling, he cannot beg the woman to return. T'would be unseemly for a man in his position."

"Unless he is a man in love, who finally accepts that a woman will have her way no matter what," she stated emphatically. "Certainly, you would do the same for me." When Winston hesitated, she nudged him in the side with her elbow.

Winston laughed and wrapped Elizabeth in his arms. "Of course, my love. I would do anything to please you. I'd wrap you in silks and jewels. I'd swim the Thames—

although I'd probably perish shortly thereafter due to disease. I'd even sell my favorite stallion, all to prove my love and devotion." His comment earned him another swat to his ribs, only this time Elizabeth's laughter joined his.

Stephen watched the tender display with a hint of envy. As the image of Phoebe intruded on his thoughts along with a flash of longing, he immediately squelched the annoying sensation. Love was not for him. "I think I'll grab a bit of air."

"Splendid. We'll join you," announced Winston.

The three wended through the throng of people who milled about the upper balcony, some venturing to the upstairs verandah, others meeting friends in private boxes. Purposely, Stephen led Elizabeth and Winston to the other side of the theater toward his prey. A group of boisterous young dandies involved in a lively debate moved toward the entrance, leaving Phoebe in their wake. Stephen recognized her at once. Standing beside a painting of Henry VIII, her back to the mad crush, Phoebe wore a simple emerald gown. Her hair was swept on top of her head, which provided a lovely view of her neck and shoulders. A light dusting of freckles tinted her skin a touch of peach. Stephen anticipated the discovery of all the delightful places where freckles decorated her body.

Elizabeth prodded Stephen in the shoulder, breaking the spell. "Is that Miss Rafferty over there?"

He kept his voice as casual as possible. "I believe it is."

"Shall we?" Elizabeth never waited for his response, but charged ahead, wrenching the choice completely out of Stephen's hands.

Cheerfully, Winston said, "I suppose we had best follow. Otherwise we will never know her intentions."

Well, blast. Stephen wanted to talk to Phoebe, but certainly not with an audience. He lengthened his stride, overtaking his friends to reach Phoebe first. From behind, he whispered in her left ear. "You've missed your rides, Phoebe Rafferty, and I've missed you."

Whirling about to face him, her expression changed from surprise to annoyance. She drummed her fingertips together. "Lord Badrick, do you have any idea the trouble you almost caused me?" She lifted her chin in dismissal. "Go away before my aunt returns."

"Impossible." Not having a trinket anywhere on his person, he resolved to be sweet. "You look stunning this evening. I believe I prefer this choice of dress over breeches, darling."

"Do not call me that. And whyever can't you leave?"

Leaning closer, he noted the alluring scent of lilacs clinging to her skin, reminding him of their time alone in Wyman's garden. What he wouldn't give for a few moments of privacy. He whispered again, "Friends."

"Begging your pardon?"

"My friends wish to meet you." Glancing over his shoulder to guage the speed of Elizabeth's arrival, and realizing she was almost upon them, Stephen stepped back to a more appropriate distance. "Here they are now."

The transformation in Phoebe's face was remarkable. The panic and irritation vanished, replaced by an artful smile, one obviously polished from years of practice. Aside from the slight tint to her cheeks, she appeared calm, poised and confident. He'd wager last month's poker winnings her pulse was racing and her heart was pounding.

Winston, content to wait, hovered nearby. Elizabeth, on the other hand, moved very close, her eyes gleaming with excitement. Stephen could practically hear her mind hard at work with matchmaking possibilities. He almost moaned. Unfortunately, he couldn't very well ignore propriety, or his friends. Elizabeth would introduce herself anyway.

"Miss Rafferty, may I introduce my dear friends, the charming Lord and Lady Payley."

Elizabeth clasped Phoebe's hand in both of hers and squeezed. "I still consider Winston's mother Lady Payley. So please call me Elizabeth. I am delighted to meet you. I've heard so much about you."

Phoebe peeked at Stephen from the corner of her eyes.

Elizabeth chuckled. "Heavens, not from him, from your cousin, Charity. You and I are going to be fast friends. I can tell these things, you know. You must join us in our box. I wish to learn all about you and your home."

The emphasis on *you*, thought Stephen. Sending a warning, he straightened his lips and glared at Winston.

With wide-eyed innocence, his friend shrugged his shoulders, then gently pried Phoebe's hand from Elizabeth's. He bowed from the waist. "And call me Winston. Please excuse my wife. She barrels blissfully through life without a thought. Had she run the war, Napoleon would have surrendered within a matter of days. I married her to save her from herself. What say you, Stephen? Shall Miss Rafferty accompany us for the balance of this eve?"

Obviously intent on meeting Phoebe as well, Winston provided little assistance. Stephen practically growled this time. "A stellar idea."

"Thank you, but my aunt—"

"Not to worry," Stephen said, grasping Phoebe's hand and draping it securely across his forearm. "You and I shall move along. Elizabeth and Winston will gladly wait to explain your decision, spinning a reason so believable it will allow your aunt no choice but to submit."

Elizabeth, one hand on her hip, frowned. Winston plastered a silly grin on his face.

"All right, sir." Phoebe shot Stephen a look that clearly said, *I know what you're about*. "As long as you mind your manners."

Placing one hand across his chest, speaking most solemnly, Stephen said, "I will behave the perfect gentleman." He added mischievously, "Of course, everyone's expectations of a gentleman vary greatly. Come along." Stephen wanted Phoebe all to himself for a few minutes. He waved at Elizabeth and Winston. "Feel free to take as long as need be."

"Last I recall, you said I shouldn't be seen with you," Phoebe said as she walked beside Stephen.

"I've changed my mind."

"Why?" she asked absently.

"Perhaps I want everyone to know I'm an interested party," answered Stephen.

"This is not a game, your grace."

"Our relationship has exceeded formalities, Phoebe. Call me Stephen." He stopped beside an usher for a moment, exchanged a few words, then led her to another flight of stairs, hidden by a blue curtain. "Did you like the flowers?"

"They were lovely even though Aunt Hildegard now suspects the worse of me. Believe you me, I pled total ignorance. Wherever are we going? I thought we were meeting your friends."

"All in good time. First, I want a moment's privacy." Feeling pleased with his initiative, Stephen felt the scales tip in his favor for the first time in days.

"Don't misunderstand me," explained Phoebe, ignoring the warning in her temple, "but I have something better said in private as well." Determined to clarify her position, she moved ahead of Stephen, entering a small yet lavishly decorated room opposite the stage. A fancy table inlaid with jade and marble stood in the corner, a variety of liquor and crystal glasses set on top. A royal-blue settee was angled in the other corner. Four gold chairs faced the stage. A curtain of thin white netting covered the view to the stage, easily concealing the occupants from the people below. The room was obviously designed with privacy in mind. "Whose is this?"

"This, my dear, is the King's royal box. Of course, due to his illness, he is never seen here. From time to time, the Prince Regent ventures here, as does Queen Charlotte and other Royals. For a tidy sum, special patrons or couples who wish to remain anonymous and alone, may *borrow* it." Stephen closed the door and crossed to the table. "Do you wish for something to drink?"

Standing beside the table, dressed all in black, Lord Badrick exuded a maddening arrogance that aroused every fiber of Phoebe's very being. And she was alone with him. Her traitorous mind conjured the image of his lips on hers, their bodies melded together. She straightened her shoulders and strengthened her resolve. Alcohol might calm her nerves, but thankfully, good sense ruled. "No, thank you."

As if reading her mind, Stephen folded his arms across his chest. "Although the idea has merit, I have no intention of plying you with spirits and ravaging you in a theater filled with people."

Unable to stop the blush creeping from her toes to her face, she marched to the curtain and stared at the activity below. "Fine. A sherry, if you will." Lordy, due to the height of the room and the soft lighting, no one could possibly see inside, leaving her and the duke quite on their own. As long as they were quiet. She felt his warm breath on her bare shoulder and turned quickly enough to witness the lazy grin on his face, as though he'd read her private thoughts. She stiffened, swallowed her retort and squelched the trembling that threatened her limbs.

Extending the crystal glass toward her, he said, "When I make love to you, it will be somewhere and sometime when no one would dare interrupt us. I hold this fantasy of lingering over your body for hours."

Although unsure of what exactly one did when one made love for hours, her body seemed to like the suggestion. Or was it just the close proximity of Badrick? He did affect her in the most unusual manner. As dignified as possible, feigning an indifference she didn't feel, she said, "I'd say that is rather presumptuous and exactly why I came with you. You obviously did not hear a thing I said the other day."

"I heard. I simply chose to ignore it. One of the benefits of being a duke."

"That's a fine how-do-you-do. Well, sir, I don't have such a luxury. This is my life, not a day at the races or a game of chess with which you play."

"You make me sound like a spoiled lad who wants only his way. I believe I know what is best for you."

"How dare you presume such a thing. You don't even know me."

"Then tell me," he said, his voice warm and enticing. Using the soft pad of his thumb, he gently traced a path across her brow, her cheek and finally her lips. "Help me understand the secrets you keep, your desires, your dreams. Let me know what you require and I will endeavor to give it to you."

Whether bent on seduction or not, Stephen remained at the curtain. He waited patiently, giving her a chance to make the choice. He did seem sincere. Perhaps if she confided in him, he would see the necessity of what she did. She moved to the settee, perching on the very edge, both feet firmly planted on the floor. Her eyes focused on the claw foot of the chair in front of her while she contemplated how one explained one's dreams in a few short sentences. "Any choices or dreams I ever had vanished the day my father died. The day the banker knocked on my door to tell me my daddy owed everything I loved and held dear to the bank. Bless his heart, he left Ireland behind thinking

67

the colonies held the pot of gold at the end of the rainbow. Unfortunately, he was a good man with no talent for business. After my mama died, we moved several times. We finally settled at River's Bend. With age came a greater understanding of my father's foibles. I ran the plantation as best I could, trying my best to keep us financially secure. I was unaware of the debt he incurred with his final venture. When all was said and done, I had only an inheritance I knew nothing about until three months ago and enough money to purchase a ticket for England."

Inhaling a deep breath, she tilted her head to look Stephen squarely in the eyes. "You were right. I have no desire to wed. Not under these conditions. If I had my way, I'd find a man to love as my mama and daddy loved."

He waved his hand in the air. "A frivolous notion. As spoken through the ages in verse and rhyme, love marks every man and woman foolish enough to believe in the illusion. Most sensible young women wish simply for a suitable match. They are lucky to find even compatibility along the way."

Intent on matching his nonchalance with her determination, she crossed her arms beneath her breasts. "Sir, most women want *love*. Their *parents* hope for a suitable match."

"Perhaps. But more often than not, the pursuit of love robs a man's soul of reason."

In all her days, she'd never met anyone who didn't believe in love, who didn't dream of finding it in some way. Love was the greatest of treasures to be given and shared. It conquered all. Goodness, he made the emotion seen like a silly schoolgirl's dream and a rope around a man's neck. "What about your friends, Elizabeth and Winston?"

"Fine. I concede that some people, a minute few, are fortunate enough to find both love *and* compatibility, but let us revisit *your* situation. We established that you have no choice and little time. Suppose love is beyond your reach. Why tie yourself to a man you barely tolerate? I know you're attracted to me, Phoebe. I offer you an alternative."

She remembered Sarah Hastings, a sweet, innocent girl blinded by passion, who ran away with a gentleman from Atlanta, a man who used and then discarded her like an old coat. Sarah, unable to face alienation from her former friends and her own parents, had thrown herself off a balcony into the path of a passing carriage.

Phoebe didn't think herself so weak-willed, nor was she foolish enough to believe that Badrick had her best interests in mind. Consequences of some sort were always the result of one's actions. She pushed herself from the settee, circled to the other corner and placed her unfinished drink on the table. "Your so-called alternative leaves you in control of my future and me at your beck and call. It is an alternative that allows you to discard me whenever you weary of my company, one that eliminates any possibility of my claiming my only birthright."

"As a man saddled with such a destiny, I can honestly say you might be better off without the responsibilities you also inherit. But, if—and I say if—I tire of your company, you could return to America with a healthy income even without Marsden Manor."

"What about Aunt Hildegard? I owe her more than a scandal amongst her friends."

"Do you really care about your aunt's friends' morality? You don't even know them."

Armed with logic and calculation, he was obviously prepared to deal with every possible argument she might present. She briefly wondered if all his past mistresses had been hired so matter-of-factly. Likely so. His manner was the epitome of composure. She doubted many people, if any, ever saw him in a vulnerable position. Why in the name of Saint Mary did she like him so? "If you are so interested in me, why not ask for my hand?" Hesitantly, she asked, "Would marriage to me be so horrible?"

Since she stared at her slippers, she heard but never saw him approach. Standing only inches away, he did not touch her. "Not you, Phoebe. Never you, but marriage itself. Wedlock is not for me. I would not give you false hope."

Although his voice hinted at wry amusement, she sensed regret and even sadness. "You make marriage sound like a death sentence."

"For some, it is."

"Why? Certainly you must have a reason."

He pinched the bridge of his nose as though the thoughts crowding his mind required too much concentration. "Forgive my morosity. Suffice it to say, I am doing you a greater service by offering you the position as my mistress rather than that of my wife."

Scolding herself for the disappointment tugging at her heart, she added a false bravado to her words. "It doesn't matter anyway. I'm not quite ready to sell myself. I still have four weeks left."

"At a task you dread. Let me help. I wish to take care of you."

"Pardon me for saying so, but you've a wish to bed me."

"There is that, but something else draws me."

"Perhaps you want me simply because I injured your pride when I refused your proposition the first time."

"I am many things, but not a fool. I would never shackle myself to a female I disliked simply to soothe my wounded masculinity. I assure you, my reasons are far less noble. Shall I prove my point?"

She knew he intended to kiss her. And no tree blocked her escape this time. Truth be told, wanton or not, she'd been waiting, even hoping, for this very moment. She watched his fingers, long and elegant, slide about her waist, and she trembled. His other hand gripped her chin. As his lips descended, she met him halfway. The kiss, more sensual than she remembered, planted a seed of desire deep in her belly, one she sensed would grow and flourish with a few caresses. Even more compelling was the sense of rightness, the way her curves molded with his muscles. Lands alive, she had to admit she liked kissing this man, and when he used his tongue like that, she liked it even more. She pressed her body closer.

A soft, insistent tapping permeated the heady sensation. Startled, she jumped back. Her one hand nudged the table, which set the various glasses and tumblers rattling moments before Winston peeked around the door. Her other hand remained trapped within Badrick's, who refused to loosen his grip.

"Ahem," Winston said sheepishly. "Excuse the interruption, but Elizabeth requests, rather adamantly, that the two of you join us."

"Assure Elizabeth that Miss Rafferty remains well. We will be along in a trice." After Winston left, Stephen pulled Phoebe to his side once again, refusing to acknowledge the scowl she threw at him. "Do not be so quick to make a decision. Unfinished business lies between us, and I warn you, I intend to use all of my persuasive powers, which are considerable, to sway you to my way of thinking. You just might change your mind."

"And if I demand you leave me be?"

"Would you be so cruel? Besides, I attend a great many functions. As you hie yourself about London looking for your mate, we shall surely encounter one another frequently."

Pursing her lips into a doubtful frown, she boasted, "You are not the only one with persuasive abilities. Who's to say that I won't change your mind?"

"Shall you use your female wiles to force me to do your

71

bidding? Hmmm. Who holds the greater will within them? You or I?" He grinned at the obvious challenge. "It seems the next few weeks shall prove to be rather interesting. Come, before Elizabeth sends the royal guard in search of you." Without another word, they descended the stairs, Stephen's hand on Phoebe's elbow as he directed her to their destination. "Here we are."

The moment they entered their box, Elizabeth spun on her seat and glared at Stephen. "Shame on you. The second act is about to begin. How am I to acquaint myself with Miss Rafferty if you insist on monopolizing her time?"

"Elizabeth, my dear," Stephen said. "To my brewing consternation, I am most confident you shall find an opportunity to interrogate Phoebe to your heart's content."

"As a matter of fact," announced Elizabeth, her grin confirming Stephen's suspicions. "Saturday is the Doggett's Coat and Badge Race." She beamed then continued onward like a child in search of treasure, happy with her quest and not to be deterred. "Phoebe, you shall accompany us. It's an absolutely delightful diversion, as long as it doesn't rain. Simply everyone ventures to watch."

Caught up in Elizabeth's exuberance, Phoebe asked, "What is it?"

Obviously feeling left out, Stephen moved to Phoebe's side. "Apprentice seamen race from London Bridge to Chelsea. The winner earns the right to wear the grand scarlet coat with the silver Hanoverian badge. There shall be raucous crowds, heavy gambling, pickpockets and thieves, plus hawkers peddling their wares, not to mention a gathering of the scraggliest group of men who sail the seas."

Stephen's manner, somewhat like a preacher denouncing the sins of the local tavern, contrasted to Elizabeth's enthusiasm. Phoebe burst out laughing. "It sounds delightful."

"I told you she would accompany us. I shall send my

carriage for you about one. Besides, it might be one of the few times we can go about together. Stephen rarely shows his face in London and ventures into public even less. A bit of a recluse, he is."

"How interesting," Phoebe cooed, remembering his claim that they would meet frequently. The sneak.

"Elizabeth," Stephen drawled. "Do be quiet. The play is about to begin."

Waving one hand, Elizabeth patted the empty chair beside her with the other. "Phoebe, sit next to me. We shall whisper throughout the remainder of the opera, driving Stephen to distraction as he wonders what secrets I might reveal."

Phoebe sat as instructed, hoping that Elizabeth would become a trusted friend, one capable of easing her loneliness and offering council. As the theater quieted, Stephen reluctantly sat behind the two ladies, beside Winston. Throughout the remainder of the opera, Phoebe tried to focus on the actors and actresses on stage or on Elizabeth, who occasionally quizzed her. Try as she might to ignore Stephen, whenever Phoebe peered over her shoulder it was to discover his dark eyes fixed on her. As if drawn by his will, she found herself peeking more often. The corner of his mouth even curled upward as if he'd proved a point or gained some advantage. Once, the wretch even blew her a kiss. When the opera finished, she quickly bid good night to Elizabeth and Winston.

With Stephen at her side, Phoebe wove her way through the corridor, trying to return to the other side of the theater as quickly as possible. Likely Aunt Hildegard was frantic. As people crowded about, she found herself pressed against Stephen. Her body didn't seem to mind one little bit. Against her better judgment, which seemed to elude her whenever he was about, she purposely squeezed closer to him a time or two. From the corner of her eye, Phoebe studied the man. Glory be, he was a handsome devil. And charming, in a rather prideful way. His aversion to matrimony baffled her, though, and he refused to offer any insight. She considered Nanny Dee's suggestion that she change the man's mind about marriage, if in fact he was the man she wanted.

Before she decided one way or the other, or risked a broken heart, she intended to discover more about the Duke of Badrick than the fact that he turned her mind to mush and her insides to warm cider. If he truly meant what he said, then her time, which was short and precious, was best spent on other suitors. Elizabeth appeared to be the most likely person to help Phoebe find the answers she needed.

When they reached Hildegard's private box, her aunt paced back and forth, while Charity, sporting an enormous orange bow in her hair, sat, her eyes diverted to her lap.

"Good evening, Lady Goodliffe," Stephen said.

Hildegard, her back to the entrance, glanced over her shoulder and lifted her pointed chin a notch higher. "Lord Badrick."

He nodded, then asked, "Lady Charity, how goes your study in watercolors?"

Charity shifted in her chair and bumped her knee against the wooden rail with a resounding thud. "Sorry," she mumbled.

Sighing, Hildegard said, "Charity discovered she prefers a woman's duties to frivolous notions such as art," Hildegard explained, her words clipped and filled with reproach. Charity's face grew sullen as she sunk lower in her chair.

"A pity," said Stephen. "She seemed to be progressing nicely."

"Humph," snorted Hildegard. "How did you happen to meet my niece?"

Hostility swirled between Stephen and her aunt. Surely, Phoebe imagined it, but it appeared as though a battle were taking place between them as they both vied for supremacy. A flicker of apprehension knotted Phoebe's stomach as she tried to comprehend the reason. She started to explain how she met Stephen, noted the unpleasant twist of Hildegard's mouth and changed her mind. Instead, in hopes of lightening the mood, she pinned a bright smile on her face and said, "Actually Auntie, Lady Payley is responsible. While I waited for your return, she introduced herself, along with her husband and Lord Badrick."

"A happenstance for which I am quite grateful," Stephen added most eloquently.

"Really," said Hildegard, her mouth set in an even tighter line as she focused fully on Phoebe. "Sir Lemmer paid a call specifically to see you. He was gravely disappointed to discover your absence." She turned back to Stephen. "Thank you for your escort, but my niece's attentions are required elsewhere now."

Ignoring the apparent dismissal, he leaned against the wall and crossed his arms before him, his body as stiff as a stump. With his voice devoid of all warmth, he asked, "Where is Sir Lemmer?"

"Unfortunately, he received a message summoning him home."

"In that case, I shall take my leave. Until we meet again, Miss Rafferty."

Phoebe, already on edge, tensed as he lifted her hand to his lips, lingering long enough to fire speculation in Hildegard's already suspicious mind. Blast the buzzard. He fled while she had to stay and face the inquisition she was sure to get.

Hildegard didn't wait long. "You will not see Lord Badrick again."

"I assume you have a particular reason for that edict?"

"He is a cursed man who sold his very soul to the devil. His past is absolutely scandalous, which forces him to a life of isolation. Even then, distance cannot end the tales of his wickedness."

"Aunt Hildegard, whatever are you talking about?"

"Bad blood runs in his veins, noble or not. Immoral. He dallies where he should not. He collects young boys for God knows what. The Badrick line is cursed and evil, that young man as bad as his relatives before him. He murdered his first wife when she failed to bear a daughter. His second wife fled for her life only to be hunted like an animal and killed. Those are only two instances, mind you. There are many others, but I will not sully my daughter's ears by repeating them."

"Goodness gracious, you don't believe any of that nonsense, do you?"

"That man will ruin you, and my family as well." The rigid set of Hildegard's body meant she believed every slanderous word she spoke. "Stay away from him. Do I make myself clear?"

Land sakes. Phoebe wanted nothing more than to stand her ground, but how on earth could she argue in the man's favor when she knew so little herself? Imagine. Murder? Wickedness? Curses? Swallowing her arguments along with the urge to champion the man, Phoebe bowed her head. Tomorrow was soon enough to begin her exploration into the past of Stephen Lambert, Duke of Badrick.

Chapter Five

Sunbeams danced amid the leaves on the trees lining Park Lane as the carriage headed south toward the River Thames. Thankful to be outdoors and away from her aunt, Phoebe relaxed against the soft burgundy leather seat. For two days, she had suffered her aunt's relentless attacks on Lord Badrick's character and an onslaught of male visitors that rivaled the British siege of New Orleans. She deserved this little adventure. Besides, there were questions she planned to have answered before the day was through. But she knew the real cause of her excitement was the fact that she would see Stephen. She tipped her head to the sky, sighing audibly.

"You look as though you possess the world," said Elizabeth.

Lost in her haze of contentment, Phoebe said, "I declare, it is absolutely glorious to be free of *that woman* for the afternoon." She immediately realized she'd spoken her thoughts out loud. Her dislike for Hildegard was one thing, but to openly express her opinion of her family was terribly irresponsible, especially having just met Elizabeth. "Not Aunt Hildegard . . . I mean . . ." She sat up straighter, as if the action might make her words more believable. "She tries the patience of a saint, but . . ."

Elizabeth's gentle laughter filled the carriage. Her face, surrounded by a large pink bow attached to her straw hat, glowed with kindness. "Do not fret so. Your aunt is not the most accommodating woman."

"True, but she is family and she is providing a place for me to stay. I should feel grateful."

"As does an abused horse when fed." Elizabeth's white-gloved hand swiftly covered her mouth. She shrugged her shoulders, removed her hand and said, "There *I* go. Let us drop the topic of your aunt altogether."

More than willing to forget her aunt's unpleasantness and enjoy the afternoon, Phoebe nodded as their carriage turned toward St. James Park, joining a sea of extravagant curricles and ordinary wagons. Electricity filled the air as people waved and laughed. Some silly fools even attempted to race one another in the crowd. Phoebe felt a brewing exhilaration all the way down to her toes. "My goodness, is everyone going to the race?"

"To be sure, but we're perfectly safe. Stephen and Winston rode ahead to secure us a spot. We'll join them soon enough."

"It's absolutely thrilling. It reminds me of holidays back home, which were really quite wonderful. There were picnics, horse and boating races, and dances. One of my daddy's favorites was the watermelon-eating contest." Knowing she would never again share such a moment with her father, or possibly even return home, Phoebe's excitement ebbed, her mood changing to wistfulness.

Elizabeth placed a dainty hand on Phoebe's. "I know

how difficult this must be. When my father died, I missed him horribly. My mother told me I would always think of him, but one day the pain would leave, replaced by marvelous memories. It did. Then I met Winston. I trust you will find such happiness in England."

"I have hope."

"Splendid. Now, no more dreary thoughts. Tell me about your morning."

"It was downright tedious. Since word of my situation spread, I'm swamped with callers. Hildegard becomes more irritated, Charity crawls into herself like a poor baby bird afraid she'll trip or stumble or such, and my nanny sits in a corner, grumbling and grimacing. I simply find the mess exhausting. Lands alive, I never realized so many men lacked a title or funds."

Sunlight bounced off Elizabeth's pink parasol as it twirled in circles while she talked. "Please don't misunderstand me, but some men probably came out of curiosity. You are the current *denier cri*. The rage."

"What fiddle-faddle. Last night at the ball, I danced with a lord who wheezed the entire time while using his cane as a prop. After which he proposed. Only thing is, I wasn't sure if he was asking the marble statue he stood beside or me. Charity said he was fifty-two. Can you imagine? Why, just today I discussed the weather at least fourteen different times. My favorite card games and the flowers of my choice were also popular subjects. I made the grave mistake of mentioning Napoleon. You could have heard a mouse sneeze."

"Heaven forbid we should discuss such topics," Elizabeth confessed, "lest we embarrass ourselves."

"I fear I made an even worse mistake than that. I mentioned I read Dante's *Inferno*. Aunt Hildegard nearly fell from her chair. But I refuse to play an ignorant hen."

"Good for you. Thankfully, unlike many men, Winston enjoys intelligent conversation. Has anyone in particular garnered your attention?"

"Not the way I hoped. It's quite discouraging. Sir Lemmer hovers nearby at every opportunity, which pleases Aunt Hildegard to no end. Why just this morning, he intimidated poor Sir Ellwood, who really stopped by to visit Charity, into leaving after only five minutes. The poor fellow managed to exit without any accidents, but Sir Lemmer lingered a good hour." Remembering Lemmer's expression as he'd sat next to her, fuming like a jealous husband, she shivered. Real or imagined, the man's manner disturbed her in a most unpleasant way.

"Sir Lemmer has a rather unpleasant nature," said Elizabeth as she absently waved to a couple in a passing carriage. "I know for a fact that both Winston and Stephen dislike him, and Sir Lemmer despises Stephen. I recommend you look elsewhere for a spouse." Turning back to face Phoebe, Elizabeth said, "In fact, I am going to be a rude sneaky-beak and say I think you and Stephen might make a go of it. He needs a wife."

"I assure you, given my few encounters with the man, he'd disagree."

Elizabeth leaned forward, her parasol shading both women. "He has not been as preoccupied with a woman in years. He wants you but is afraid to take a chance. The stubborn fool is a dear friend of mine who seems doomed to isolation and loneliness. All of his own choosing. I, on the other hand, believe he deserves every ounce of happiness that comes his way."

Two deep notes resonated through the air as Big Ben signaled the new hour. Phoebe admired the distant gothic towers of Westminster Abbey, silently debating whether to pursue the topic of Stephen. She decided a better opportunity might not present itself, but she couldn't quite come out and ask if he had, in fact, murdered his first two wives. If he'd had two wives, she reminded herself. "How do you know Stephen so well?"

"Our estates bordered one another. Though he's ten years my elder, we spent a great deal of time together as children. When my father died, I moved to my mother's dower estate. I still saw Stephen from time to time. In fact, he introduced me to Winston, a debt I can never repay. Unless, perhaps, I can return the favor."

It was now or never. Remembering all of Hildegard's vile gossip, a part of Phoebe, perhaps her heart, wanted to discount everything she'd heard. At least Elizabeth, Stephen's friend, would tell the truth. "Has Stephen been married?"

"As a matter of fact, he was. Twice."

"What happened?"

Elizabeth concentrated on a flock of pigeons overhead, evidently considering Phoebe's request. She leaned against her seat and said, "I was only thirteen when Stephen married Emily. I think Stephen loved her for all the good and kindness she brought into his life. We moved away shortly thereafter. Emily died the next year. Two years later, he married Louisa. She died the following spring."

Nibbling her lower lip, Phoebe sucked in a deep breath, then forged ahead. "Did he murder them?"

Elizabeth's eyes rounded and her mouth snapped open, then shut.

"Oh, I'm sorry to just blurt that out, but I'm so confused and . . . well . . . my aunt said horrible things."

Recovering from her shock, Elizabeth gazed at the activity surrounding them, her lips pressed into a frown. "I imagine Hildegard filled your ears with a good deal of twaddle. Sometimes, my own peers irritate me so greatly I want to denounce them all. Unfortunately, when it comes to scintillating tidbits regarding the lives of other people, society has a long, if uninformed, memory. Stephen's desire for privacy fires speculation. Every time he comes to London, the gossip begins anew."

"Please. I need to know the truth."

"I'm not certain I can help. Stephen's rather taciturn about his past."

"The words mule-headed and shut-mouthed come to mind."

Elizabeth stared at Phoebe open-mouthed, then burst into laughter. "Dear Phoebe, I am so glad we met."

"I'm usually a tad more tactful, but I really do need to know. Did he murder them?"

"Of course not."

Thank goodness, thought Phoebe. She should have trusted her instincts all along. Stephen was not capable of murder. That meant there was a logical reason for all the rumors. "However did Emily die?"

"It was some sort of accident shortly after Emily birthed the Badrick heir. Stephen found her and the baby dead in the nursery. Or was it the bedroom?" She chewed on the tip of her finger.

"What of Louisa? Hildegard said she left Stephen—and died as a result."

"Actually, I believe she fell down a flight of stairs one night. I'm sorry I'm not much help. I was in the country at the time and Stephen refuses to speak of it."

"Hildegard also mentioned a curse."

"Lud. Stephen speaks even less of that than his two dead wives."

Phoebe recognized Elizabeth's reluctance, unsure if she truly knew so little or whether she protected Stephen. Thus far, most of the information made Phoebe wonder even more about Stephen's past. She pressed on. "Surely you have more accurate information than my aunt."

"It has something to do with his great-grandfather and a

gypsy woman, who cursed the Badrick men and their marriages."

"Does Stephen actually believe that malarkey?"

"When I was eight, Stephen showed me this lock of hair with ribbons in a trophy case. He said it was his heritage. I know his father believed it and became a bitter, nasty man. As for Stephen, if you live with unhappiness day after day, year after year, a part of you comes to believe anything—even if you are otherwise an intelligent man." Impatiently throwing up her hands, Elizabeth added, "Whether the curse exists or not, he believes both women would be alive if not for him."

"Phooey. Do *you* believe in the curse?"

"I do know that no family deserves so much unhappiness. Perhaps I disbelieve because I wish the best for Stephen." Elizabeth twirled the handle of the parasol between her palms. "Since we seem to be speaking so openly, will you tell me something?"

"If I can."

"Do you love him?"

Hiding her hands in the folds of her blue linen skirt, Phoebe once again considered the question she had asked herself the last few days. "Can you love someone you barely know?"

The way Elizabeth waved her hand led Phoebe to believe she found the question ridiculous. Her eyes became dreamlike and her smile turned languid. She looked every bit the woman in love. "The moment I saw Winston I wanted to meet him. After three dances, four glasses of punch and one game of whist, I was madly in love."

Phoebe tried to define her feelings. She remembered the immediate kinship she felt for Stephen when they met in Wyman's study, the warmth that settled in the pit of her stomach, caused by a simple flash of his dark eyes, the heart-stopping reaction to their first kiss, the disappointment when he said he would never marry. No man had ever made her pulse beat so erratically or invaded her dreams as he did. "I find the man wildly attractive and equally aggravating. He's arrogant and secretive, kind and intelligent. He creeps into my mind throughout the day and night. I love his eyes. Heavens, I even find myself thinking about the way he says my name." She clasped her hands in her lap. "Would I be a fool to try and win his heart?"

"I hope you will try and succeed, but I must be candid. Stephen will resist. No matter how hard you try and even if you succeed in making him love you, I cannot guarantee you marriage. He's bloody stubborn about that. If he does marry you, there is no guarantee he will allow himself to love you. Yet, if you're able to break the iron band about his heart, and he allows himself the luxury of happiness, he would give you the world." Grinning, Elizabeth relaxed against the seat. "In fact, I will help in whatever way I can. Winston is hosting a country party in two weeks. Of course, Stephen will be there. You can spend the entire weekend proving to the man that you would make the perfect—"

Before Elizabeth could finish her sentence, the two women slid forward in their seats as the carriage abruptly stopped. Traffic had come to a complete halt. In the middle of the road, tied to a wooden cart laden with trinkets and food, sat a haggard old mule. A young boy, no more than six or seven, tugged at a long rope, trying his best to coax the animal into moving. The gathering crowd, dismayed and delayed by the obstinate animal, hurled insults and solutions to the problem. A man with arms the size of platters kicked the animal while shouting obscenities at the boy. "Lands alive, doesn't that fool know that mule can't carry all that weight?"

"He probably thought to take advantage of all the people attending the race."

Phoebe watched with growing trepidation as the owner, a heavy leather whip in his hand, stomped toward the boy. Tears fell down the lad's cheeks as he boldly jumped between the mule and the man, accepting the blow intended for the animal. The image of Nelda, a young slave back home, taking an undeserved lash, crept into Phoebe's mind. The pain Phoebe felt when she herself stepped in the direct path of the next blow surfaced as well.

Fury gnawed at her stomach. Without another thought, she climbed from the carriage, racing to the boy's side before a second blow fell.

"Phoebe!" Elizabeth yelled from the carriage before hopping down to follow.

With one elbow balanced on the pommel of his saddle, Stephen slapped his leather gloves across his thigh. "Where the devil do you suppose they are? They should have arrived a good fifteen minutes ago."

Winston squinted against the glare of the sun reflecting on the water. "It pleases me to see you in a state of anticipation, something I have not witnessed for a very long time. It gives me hope."

Stephen crossed his arms, unwilling to slip into a debate on a subject his friend had attempted to broach for the last hour. "Stow it, Winston."

"Is this the manner in which you entice all those women to your bed?"

"What women?"

"Precisely," Winston grinned, obviously satisfied he'd found an opening. "Since you practically live the life of a hermit and a monk. Perhaps if you softened that acerbic exterior of yours, you might not scare people away so easily." Shifting his eyes to Stephen, Winston added, "Including Miss Rafferty."

Growing more restless, Stephen began to pace, stopping

now and again to survey the arriving curricles. "Let *me* worry about Phoebe."

"I intend to. I simply offer my assistance, my flair for diplomacy and negotiation should you desire it. How will you explain your illustrious ancestry? Phoebe's bound to hear a rumor or two or three."

"I imagine Elizabeth, whose machinations rival yours, disclosed all she knew—which thankfully is little—the moment she and Phoebe were alone. She'll be thrilled to have been a part of what she deems the greater plan. My future."

"True. She does like to meddle."

Stephen briefly glanced at Winston, ready to remind his friend of the proper roles between men and women. What was the point? His friend was hopelessly in love. Stephen scanned the road and field once again. Frowning, he fisted his reins in his hand and, with a natural ease, swung onto the back of his horse. "Stay here. I'm going to ride back and see if I can find the ladies. Perhaps Cosgell got himself into trouble."

Keeping a tight rein on the stallion, Stephen slowly threaded through the crowd. Thank heavens he sat a horse rather than a carriage. After half a mile or so, the narrow road became less congested. When he rounded the bend, he witnessed chaos at its pinnacle. Stalled carriages were everywhere. At the center of the commotion was a mule that looked as though he belonged at heaven's gate. Scattered fruit littered the ground. A cart on the verge of losing the balance of its wares tilted precariously on one wheel. Lord Albuld, a pompous philistine, made a ribald comment to someone near the mule, which elicited chuckles and additional comments from the spectators.

"Thank you, sir, but I do not recollect asking your opinion in the matter. Kindly mind your own business."

The voice—definitely female—set the hairs on the back

of Stephen's neck straight on end. He nudged Cavalier closer to the fray only to discover Phoebe, a leather whip in her hands, standing between a man twice her size and a small boy who had practically buried himself between her skirts and the mule. What the devil was the fool girl thinking? She could be trampled, or beaten, let alone disgraced in front of half the peers of London, who were occupying themselves by placing bets with one another from their carriages. And the brute of a man stood ready to attack.

Lord, she needed a keeper. Anger like a fever seeped into every fiber of his body. He closed his eyes for a moment, exhaled deeply, and tamped down the fear and his brewing temper. Slipping from his horse, he strode forward. Elizabeth, standing nearby, twisted her handkerchief in her hands. He should have known she would be close at hand. When she noticed his arrival, she had the audacity to wave. Unbelievable. Damn it to hell, both women needed keepers. Where the devil was the driver, Cosgell?

Suddenly the mule shifted his weight, jostling Phoebe and the boy. With the urchin tangled in her skirts, she stumbled to her knees. The peddler lunged forward, his muscled arm outstretched. A hush fell over the crowd. Stephen charged, ready to protect Phoebe at all cost.

With agility uncommon to most women and enviable by most men, Phoebe pressed to her feet, snapping the whip near the peddler's left ear at the same time. Stunned, Stephen stopped dead in his tracks. Surely his mouth hung open. The whoops and hollers from the audience jarred him into action.

Three long strides placed him behind Phoebe. He said, a distinct chill to his words, "I don't believe the lady wishes the boy, or the mule, to be whipped."

Phoebe whirled about, the anger lining her face diminished by her astonishment. "Lord Badrick."

He even detected a bit of relief. Not for long, he thought.

"Miss Rafferty." He nodded coolly yet said nothing else, knowing this was not the time to offer the lecture scalding the tip of his tongue. "Move to the carriage."

"I must see to the boy first." She bent to check the wounds on the lad's arm, clucking and cooing like a nursery nanny.

The peddler cleared his throat. His barrel chest puffed with indignation. "Hold on a minute. That lady owes me an apology and some blunt. She done ruined me animal and me wares."

If humanly possible, darts could have flown from Phoebe's eyes as she stood to face the man, her hands fisted at her waist, her right toe tapping at a rapid pace. "Why you good-for-nothing-bully. If I weren't a lady, I would—"

"Give 'em hell, miss," yelled a man from a nearby carriage.

"Five pounds says he plants a facer on the lady," cried another voice.

Another fellow held a note high in the air and announced, "Five pounds says Lord Badrick plants a facer on the chap, then plants a facer on the lady."

A flurry of renewed betting consumed the audience as Phoebe searched for the men who uttered the offensive suggestions. Stephen glowered at one of them, who had the good sense to close his mouth and sit down. Satisfied by that reaction, he leaned within an inch of Phoebe's face and whispered, "I suggest, most adamantly, that you hie yourself away from here and climb into that bloody carriage before I do something we both regret." He waited as she gasped, her eyes rounded, her face flushed.

Evidently feeling safe enough to step forward, Elizabeth tugged on Phoebe's arm. "Come along. I recognize that tone of voice. This is not the time to discuss anything. He's quite angry with us."

"Not just angry, Elizabeth," Stephen snapped. "I'm bloody furious."

"Well, I never," grumbled Phoebe. "What of the boy?"

"I will see to him."

She seemed to consider something of great import, then nodded. Proudly squaring her shoulders, wearing her dignity like a cloak, she mumbled and sputtered as she followed Elizabeth to the carriage. A portion of the assembled group groaned, disappointed the show had ended without additional violence. They'd likely lost their wagers. Others cheered as she passed. Every now and then, when someone spoke directly to her, she stopped, smiled cordially then moved on. Some bloody gent, pleased with the outcome of the fiasco, even kissed her hand. Money was quickly exchanged between those perverse enough to have placed bets on the incident, and men righted the cart, moving it from the center of the road, allowing traffic to disperse.

When Stephen deemed Phoebe to be a safe distance away, he turned his attention back to the peddler. "Are you of the habit of beating women and boys?"

"She interfered where she had no business."

Stephen's blood still boiled. He wanted nothing more than to pummel this churl for placing the blame on Phoebe. However, this particular play needed no additional scenes. Gritting his teeth, he turned to the lad. "What's your name?"

"Niles, sir."

Kneeling on one leg, Stephen softened his voice so as not to scare the young boy who shifted his weight nervously from leg to leg. "What happened, Niles?"

"Me and me mum helps Jakes from time to time when we needs the money. We need it real bad now. Me sister is sickly. Me mum cooks and Jakes peddles what she makes, but it's me mule. Angus got tired and Jakes beat 'im.

That lady stopped him from 'urting us. She's an angel, she is."

"Yes, she is. Now, listen well. Go to Number Twelve Park Lane. Ask for Davelman. Tell him Lord Badrick sent you. Send for your mother and sister. Stay there until I return. Do you understand?"

"Aye, sir," Niles said. "But what of me mule?"

Stephen ruffled the boy's hair as he stood. "I'd say you'd best take him with you."

"Yes, sir," cried the boy, beaming.

The peddler tapped Stephen on his shoulder. "Hey gov, you can't do that."

Stephen reacted instantly. He grabbed the man by the collar of his threadbare jacket, twisting the fabric tightly to effectively cut off the flow of oxygen. "It seems I just did. Now listen well, my misguided chap. I would like nothing better than to knock a tooth or two from your mouth. However, I shall refrain. In the future, I recommend you pick on someone your own size rather than women, young boys or neglected animals."

With that, Stephen discarded the peddler like a piece of rubbish and gathered his horse. Looking at the peddler, who lay on the ground gasping for air, Stephen wished the man had lashed out. He wanted desperately to punch someone. After tying his horse to the rear of Elizabeth and Phoebe's carriage, he climbed aboard, sitting opposite the two women. He leaned back in the seat and crossed his arms, silently demanding an explanation.

Phoebe matched his glare with one of her own. "What have you done with the boy?"

"I sent him to my home."

"Whatever for?"

He watched her eyes narrow suspiciously, her expression certainly more wary than a moment ago. What the devil was she thinking now? "The boy will send for his mother and sister, then I shall move them all to one of my estates to work. Satisfied?"

"Yes, actually. Now, am I to thank you for publicly humiliating me?"

Lord, he wanted to strangle the woman. One moment she endangered herself while making a public spectacle, next she blamed him for her behavior. "Of course not. You managed to do that all by yourself. I should be pleased. Your behavior today likely weighted my suit by at least a stone. I think an apology on your part might be appropriate."

"Fiddle-faddle, you arrogant—"

"Phoebe," cried a startled Elizabeth.

Stephen's voice remained aloof, distant. "It's quite all right, Elizabeth. I'm curious to hear what she has to say."

Leaning forward, her face a lovely rosy pink, Phoebe asked, "Would you have me sit and watch a boy be whipped?"

Stephen leaned forward as well, his nose a mere fraction from hers. "I would have you use that lovely head of yours for something other than sporting a hat. I would have you remain safe."

"Like all the other cowards who sat in their carriages and watched a man as big as a bale of cotton beat a young boy?"

"Truly, Stephen," Elizabeth added, her gloved hand softly nudging his arm. "No one seemed overly concerned with the boy's predicament other than the fact that he delayed their arrival at the race."

"Save your explanation for Winston. I'm sure he'll have an opinion or two on the matter."

Phoebe lifted her chin toward the sky. "Good heavens, leave Elizabeth out of this." She turned back toward Stephen, her eyes closed, obviously struggling to maintain a handle on her emotions. "I know the feeling of unjust punishment, being alone to face it. That boy did not deserve to be whipped. Neither did that poor animal. I've felt the sting of a lash, felt the pain. I know the brand it leaves."

That last bit of news spawned an unexpected wave of tenderness, dwarfing Stephen's anger. The desire to lecture vanished. Instead, he wanted to relieve her of her clothes, discover the heinous mark and kiss any lingering memories away. He rubbed his hand over his face. "I understand your reason for interfering. I even admire your fortitude. God knows few people are willing to stand up for what is right, but you must think before you plunge into something such as this. You could have been injured. And what do you propose to tell your aunt when word of this rumpus spreads? I assure you, gossip will fly from mouth to mouth faster than a plague on an infected ship."

Before she turned away to watch the activity surrounding them, a sigh heavy with acceptance slid from Phoebe's mouth. "I know."

Everyone fell silent. Stephen realized further argument would prove pointless. Phoebe understood the consequences but had acted anyway. She possessed a generous heart and a moral conscience, but damn it, unless coupled with a sizeable dollop of common sense, she would repeatedly find herself in unsuitable, potentially dangerous situations. Well, he would simply make it his personal responsibility to ensure that she exercised caution, which veered him back to his original thought. She needed a keeper. Him.

Chapter Six

"Here we are." Stephen jumped to the ground and helped Elizabeth from the carriage into a large open field. "I recommend we banish the last half-hour from our memory and enjoy our day. Of course you, Elizabeth, can decide to tell Winston now or later, for surely he shall hear of your antics."

Lifting Phoebe down, he slid the length of her body against his. He whispered in her ear. "Is all forgiven?"

"I'm not sure. And you, sir, are too bold."

Stephen's hands still gripped her arms. "Because I want you?"

With both feet firmly planted on the ground, she cocked her head to one side. "Wanting does not guarantee a thing, my lord."

He glanced over his shoulder to determine Elizabeth's whereabouts. She stood a good five feet away, her back turned in an attempt to offer him and Phoebe a moment's privacy that was blatant yet greatly appreciated. Grinning, he tilted Phoebe's face toward his. "Darling, I guarantee you pleasure and more, but do not keep me waiting too long."

"Keep you waiting? I haven't even decided to give you a chance."

Her mouth formed a delightful pout, the kind that made men like him appreciate all things female. Lord, he wished the woman would agree to his terms. And soon. He couldn't resist the temptation to stroke the delicate skin of her throat. To his male satisfaction, he watched her eyes flash, felt her tremble. He rubbed his thumb across her lower lip, slowly, finally caressing her chin. "I think you have. Otherwise you wouldn't be here."

Licking the lip his touch had abandoned, she swallowed and stepped to what she deemed a safe distance from him. "Elizabeth invited me. Remember? And I must say, we had a delightful and somewhat enlightening conversation."

Speculating on the subtle innuendo in Phoebe's voice, Stephen dropped his hand to his side. He'd never expected to keep his past concealed, but after years of censure and gossip, and unsure of Phoebe's reaction, he automatically felt the walls erect themselves around his pride. Why did Phoebe's opinion even matter? Placing his left hand in his coat pocket, his other on the wheel of the carriage, he assumed a casual stance. "Really."

"Yes, indeed. She willingly provided facts a *particular gentleman* I know deems unimportant. Minor little things like previous marriages, gypsy curses and all."

Just as he'd suspected. Elizabeth possessed a loose tongue when she felt her motives justified, and in her mind, finding a wife for him was a good reason to interfere. She knew little, but he could only guess what she had revealed. "Elizabeth needs to learn restraint," he muttered.

Tentatively, Phoebe placed her fingers on his hand. "You

94

can no more flee your past than I can. Nor can you predict your future."

"But I can control my actions."

"Precisely. And, I expect honesty."

"I have not been otherwise."

"No, simply closemouthed." He clenched his teeth moments before his expression turned flat, void of emotion. How she hated his ability to do that. Clearly, he disliked this topic. Well, that was just too bad. She had no intention of spending time with the man if dishonesty lay between them. "I am not accustomed to secrets and guessing games. If we're to have any relationship at all, I expect us to be honest with one another."

Like a summer storm on the river, his mood changed quickly and unexpectedly. His mouth softened and even twitched with amusement as a devilish sparkle lit his eyes. "By all means."

"Do you mind telling me what is so funny?"

"You just admitted we shall have a relationship. I see that as a direct step into my arms."

The infernal man had a way of dulling her wits and twisting everything she said all willy-nilly. "That is not what I meant."

"An individual is entitled to his or her interpretation." With that wicked grin on his face, the one that sent a ripple of excitement flowing through her, he draped her hand across his forearm and headed toward Elizabeth. "All right, you can turn around now. Winston seems trapped by the crowds. Let us go."

Phoebe stewed for all of a minute, finally admitting to herself that Stephen was right. Somewhere along the line, her heart and body had convinced her mind to take a chance on him, regardless of the unanswered questions about his past. It was no small wonder, considering all the men she had met over the last week, none of whom appealed to her in the slightest way. She nibbled her lower lip as she walked amongst carriages lining the dirt track where passengers stopped to watch the race. Peddlers hawked their wares at every opportunity while young boys dashed around the large field, which was covered with blankets and groups of revelers. She needed a plan. And a good one, if indeed she intended to marry him. She shook her head. Imagine, people believing a man like him capable of murder. And a curse? Poppycock. Pure nonsense. If the only thing standing between her and marriage to this man was a silly old curse, then she would simply have to convince him otherwise.

Winston stood beside a woolen blanket near the river's edge and waved. A bottle of red wine and four crystal glasses were neatly tucked in a large wicker basket, along with some fruit and a small wooden box of bread and cheese. Forcing her thoughts to the back of her mind, Phoebe sat opposite Elizabeth and asked, "When will the race begin?"

Sitting beside Phoebe, leaning on one elbow, Stephen stretched his long legs before him. He poured the wine and said, "Soon. We shall actually witness the end of the race. They start at London Bridge, roughly four and a half grueling miles of heavy rowing to win the opportunity to wear the symbol of the Hanoverians."

"Whoever are they?" asked Phoebe as she sipped from her glass.

Winston, his body practically a mirror to Stephen's, placed his hand across his heart in mock astonishment. "My Henry, girl, if you intend to marry a Brit, we'd best educate you. In 1715, the Hanover line succeeded to the throne. In honor of that miraculous event, Thomas Doggett, a common actor, started this race."

"Today, you shall witness a—historical event—as well as a very masculine tradition," Stephen added. "Grown men wagering wildly amongst themselves and sailors with their hearts and wills clearly shown in their muscles and backs."

"Then I'll try to give my full attention."

"Excuse me, Stephen," Elizabeth said, smiling sweetly. "Isn't that Lord Tewksbury and Lord Hathaway?"

"Yes."

"Phoebe, this is perfect." Elizabeth practically clapped her hands together, her eyes fixed on Stephen all the while. "I understand Tewksbury is looking for a wife. Although he's not a second son or such, he still has marvelous potential as a husband. Lord Hathaway is certainly eligible and a younger son with two older brothers, but I'd have to think on that. He's rumored to be a bit of a rake."

The group of men stood nearby. They cheered boisterously as two men shook each another's hands. "Which is which?" Phoebe asked, surprised at Elizabeth's sudden interest in her matrimonial candidates.

"The blond gentleman is Lord Hathaway. The fellow shaking his hand is Lord Ricland, Earl of Tewksbury. *A widower*. Stephen, you simply must wrest us an introduction."

"No, I must not."

Elizabeth frowned. Stephen, being his normal autocratic self, lifted a brow, silently challenging her to argue his decision. Fighting a grin, Phoebe turned to study the two men. Both were handsome, but unfortunately, unlike a mere smile from Stephen, neither made her body heat or her pulse race. Lord Hathaway, leaner than Tewksbury, appeared to be the same height. Lord Tewksbury wore a navy jacket and dark trousers that accented broad shoulders and long, muscular legs.

"Winston, wave to the man."

"Elizabeth," Stephen said, his irritation clear. "Leave Tewksbury alone."

"Whatever are they doing?" Phoebe asked.

Winston, silent up until now, answered, "I understand Tewksbury and Hathaway personally wagered one of their ships on the apprentices they sponsored. I imagine they're finalizing the negotiations."

Surely she'd heard incorrectly. What manner of man would make such an expensive wager? "I declare. A ship?"

Winston dug through the wicker basket, found an apple and polished it on the sleeve of his jacket. "Yes. Such behavior is common for Hathaway. I am surprised Tewksbury accepted the bet. He's normally rather prickly about propriety."

"How exciting," Phoebe said.

Stephen sat abruptly. He snatched the bread from the basket, waving it in the air as an extension of his arm. "I'd say its bloody stupid."

Why, if she didn't know better, Phoebe would swear Stephen was jealous. She pursed her lips. "Hmmm. His hair certainly is a fascinating color."

"I believe it's called *red*," said Stephen, his voice sounding more wonderfully annoyed by the minute.

"Lands alive, no," Phoebe said, pouring every bit of her Southern sweetness into her words. "More like sable with just a *touch* of cinnamon. I wonder what color his eyes are?"

"I believe they are blue," remarked Winston.

Stephen ripped a chunk of bread from the loaf. "Winston, must you foster this ridiculousness?"

Shrugging his shoulders, a mannerism Phoebe decided he used frequently, Winston proceeded to eat his apple. She crooned, "I just *love* blue eyes."

"Enough," snorted Stephen. "I did not come here today

to discuss the color of another man's eyes. Change the bloody topic."

Elizabeth waved her napkin toward Stephen before she turned to grin at Phoebe. "And he's quite rich. A benefactor for numerous charities, a—"

"I'm quite rich," added Stephen, trying with considerable difficulty not to lose his temper. My God, Elizabeth seemed prepared to nominate Tewksbury for sainthood. Phoebe's insipid fascination with the man, not that it mattered, wasn't helping.

A fanciful smile on her face, Elizabeth said, "But remember our task. We search for a husband for Phoebe."

Stephen's eyes narrowed to thin slits. Tugging none too lightly on the ribbons of her bonnet, he said, "You're toying with my good humor today, aren't you, Elizabeth? Matchmaking is for doddering matrons who chew with their back teeth and undisciplined young girls with nothing better to do. Leave Phoebe and myself to our own devices."

"Why would I do that?" Her blond brows arched and her mouth formed a pout honed by years of practice.

Stephen had fallen for Elizabeth's false innocence hundreds of times. Normally, he detected such transparent tactics. Today he'd fallen for her trap like an unwitting hare. He quickly excused his lapse to Phoebe's presence. Her behavior was rude, a shameless exhibition of bad manners. A lady simply did not stare at one man when another sat beside her as an escort. Stephen reminded himself to clarify for her that little lesson in propriety when Phoebe and he were alone. Stephen stood and pivoted toward the Thames. "Enough. We came to watch the race."

Feeling better, he concentrated on the fifteen boats moving closer. Three in particular raced head-to-head. The excitement grew to a deafening roar as the sailors rounded the bend, veering toward the finish line at the Chelsea Royal Hospital. He pulled Phoebe to her feet.

Elizabeth gleefully announced, "Here comes Tewksbury."

Stephen glanced over his shoulder to witness the earl's approach. Noting that Phoebe also watched the man, he remained indolently beside her, purposely closer than was proper. "Ignore him. The boats are coming."

Chuckling, Winston stood, as did Elizabeth. "Good afternoon, Tewksbury," he said.

"Good to see you, Payley." Tewksbury faced Stephen. "Badrick."

Stephen nodded in turn while Tewksbury assessed Phoebe with disturbing frankness. Blast, but this entire morning had been one annoyance after another. No matter how irrational he was being, he wished the man would turn about and leave. Now. Before introductions took place.

No such luck. Elizabeth cleared her throat.

"I believe you know my wife, Elizabeth." Winston said.

Tewksbury greeted Elizabeth with perfect comportment, then turned expectantly toward Phoebe. "And this must be the illustrious colonial."

Reluctantly, Stephen introduced Phoebe, who extended her hand far too eagerly to suit him. He stifled the impulse to grab her fingers and secure them in his lap. The thought of her hand within inches of his groin led to a tantalizing image that caused an uncomfortable physical reaction inappropriate to his current surroundings. He groaned. Today was not going as planned. In fact, none of his encounters with Phoebe Rafferty ever seemed to go as he intended. Right now she needed a reminder of his presence. He edged closer yet, going as far as to place a hand on her elbow. "Pardon us, Tewksbury, but we did come to watch the race." Stephen fixed his eyes on the river.

Attempting to pry her arm free of Stephen's grip, Phoebe twisted around Stephen and smiled. "I understand you placed a sizable wager. Is your sailor in the lead?"

"No, but fortunately Hathaway's apprentice is further back than mine. I shall gain a small compensation for that."

"Glory be. I'd hate to think of you losing a ship."

"You are exceedingly kind."

Prepared to relinquish her arm lest he appear like a buffoon, Stephen dropped his hand. Air puffed through his nostrils like an angry bull preparing to charge. He took three deep breaths before he finally muttered, "Impetuous, if you ask me."

"Mind your manners, Lord Badrick," Phoebe whispered. She exchanged glares with Stephen before whirling around to watch the race. Sunlight glistened off the Thames. The men used their entire bodies as they gripped wooden oars, their strokes hurling their boats forward. The excitement escalated as one young apprentice, Phoebe figured to be eighteen or so, exhibited a final burst of strength. His tiny scull flew the final few feet ahead of his competitor. The crowd cheered loudly. People continued to shout until the last of the racers crossed the line, at which time money exchanged hands and hawkers began to push their wares once again.

Stephen traded an almost adversarial look with Tewksbury, as though they shared some secret masculine conversation without the benefit of words. Phoebe thought she knew the topic. *Her.* Annoyed with Stephen, Phoebe said, "Lord Tewksbury, I must ask. Whyever did you call me the illustrious colonial?"

"I meant no insult, Miss Rafferty. Only that your prominence precedes you. It seems that after today's events, coupled with your unique situation, someone felt you aptly deserving of such a name. It's in the papers."

Clearly expecting an explanation, Winston said, "It seems I missed something of import. Would anyone care to enlighten me?"

"Nothing to worry yourself with, Winston," Phoebe

said. She knew every action had a consequence. Thinking ahead to the problem of Hildegard, she also knew this name business was utter nonsense and nothing but trouble. Phoebe peeked at Stephen to judge his reaction to this new information. Considering the scowl on his face, he seemed no less pleased than she was. "My, my, I declare, you British have a way of creating a rumor big enough to choke a cow."

Tewksbury laughed. "My dear Miss Rafferty, after making your acquaintance today, I wholly agree with my peers. You are a delight."

Stephen crossed his arms over his chest. "Thank you for your edification, Tewksbury. I believe Hathaway is looking for you. Good day."

Winston choked on his wine while Elizabeth clapped a hand over her mouth to stifle a giggle or a gasp—Phoebe wasn't sure which, nor did she care. She was so astounded by Stephen's rude behavior she could only stare.

After a seemingly inordinate length of time, Tewksbury bent slightly at the waist. He lifted Phoebe's hand to his lips. "Lord Badrick is correct. I am required elsewhere. First though, I've decided to hold a small, impromptu dinner party on Tuesday. I shall send invites today. I hope you shall attend. Until we meet again."

Drumming her fingers together, Phoebe faced Stephen, who had the audacity to smirk with self-satisfaction. Irritation bubbled below her calm surface. She waited for Tewksbury to venture a step or two away, then said, "That's a fine how-do-you-do. Your behavior was rude and then some."

"Mine? Hah! After listening to your recitation of the man's many attributes, I wearied of watching him ogle you before my very eyes. A man can only take so much."

"You hold no claim over me."

"Not yet, at least."

"Not ever, if this behavior is an example of—"

Winston cleared his throat and said, "Excuse me, children. Unless you wish to add a public argument to Phoebe's list of accomplishments, I suggest we change topics."

She wanted to stomp her feet or, at the very least, kick Stephen in the shins. He was infuriating. A bully. And judging by the twitching of the corner of his mouth, he was enjoying himself. Immensely. That realization checked her temper long enough for an idea, like a small seedling, to take shape in her mind. A plan. The very plan she needed. A way to spend more time with Stephen Lambert and pry information from his very own lips. A way to prove to the man that he was the only one she should marry.

Feigning exasperation, she threw her hands in the air. "Fine with me. Besides, I was wondering if I could ask a favor of Winston."

"By all means," Winston said.

"As you well know, I'm searching for a husband. I narrowed the list to several possibilities, but truthfully, I know very little about the men."

"A list of possibilities?" Stephen asked, his forehead creased with confusion. Surely he'd heard wrong. He'd left her to her own devices for three days and now she had a bloody list. "Since when?"

Elizabeth's gaze flipped from Stephen to Phoebe to Winston and back again to Stephen. Gleefully, she said, "It's certainly no surprise. Why Stephen, you should have seen the carriages lined up outside Hildegard's. As I told Phoebe, she's the rage. I can understand her need for counsel. Winston is a logical choice."

Stephen's confusion quickly shifted to irritation, Elizabeth the new target of his scowl. "Because?"

As though she schooled an unruly youth, Phoebe patted Stephen's arm in a patronizing manner. "Excuse me. I was trying to have a conversation with Winston." Dismissing Stephen once again, she said, "Anyway, what I was wondering is this. Would you be willing to tell me whether or not any of the gentlemen are suitable? I mean, I certainly don't trust Hildegard's opinion. She highly recommends the likes of Sir Lemmer, who already acts as though we're betrothed."

Abandoning any and all pretense of control, Stephen leaned forward. "Stay away from him."

She stiffened her spine. "I believe that's for me to decide. Anyway—"

"This little charade is not going to work."

"What charade?"

A calm settled over Stephen. Confident in his powers of deduction, he curled his lip in a familiar cocksure manner. He rocked back on his heels, his hands shoved in his trouser pockets. "This nonsense of analyzing your potential suitors, your attempt to make me jealous."

"Why on earth would I do that? You already told me you wouldn't marry me."

"He did?" Elizabeth asked. "When?"

"None of your business," Stephen answered, his eyes fixed on Phoebe. "You know my intentions."

"I certainly do. And you know mine." Phoebe's tone hinted of challenge. "If Winston can aid my cause, then so be it."

"What a splendid idea," Elizabeth added with an abundance of enthusiasm. "By the way, Winston, I invited Phoebe to our party. There will bachelors galore."

Phoebe was playing a game with him. Stephen was sure of it. Some form of manipulation that Elizabeth had seized with her front teeth. He had two choices. Stay out of the matter altogether or act as her go-between, which in turn would provide time and circumstance to persuade her to become his mistress. "Why Winston?"

Nestled beside Winston, Elizabeth squeezed her husband's arm. "He knows everyone."

"I know everyone," he rejoined.

Elizabeth *tsk*ed several times, wagging her head. "Stephen, you spend far too much time in the country."

"I do not."

Phoebe pursed her lips, deep in thought. She wrinkled her nose and drew an invisible pattern in the soil. "Why Stephen, if I didn't know better I'd say you were offering your services."

Folding one arm across his chest, he repeatedly stroked his mustache with his other hand while studying Phoebe, noting every nuance, every twitch, every blink of her eyes. The opportunity she provided was too tempting by far. He'd cling to Phoebe like a shadow, ever eager to reveal the peccadilloes of the overbearing lords of the Ton. By the time he finished, he'd be the prize worth winning. "I live to do your bidding. Remember. To the victor go the spoils. I shall plead my own case as well."

"Which case is that?" asked Elizabeth while kneeling beside Winston.

"None of your business," Stephen quickly remarked.

Elizabeth tossed a napkin into the basket. "What is the point of eavesdropping if no one intends to elaborate?"

Ignoring Elizabeth's frustration, he smiled at Phoebe. "When are my services required?"

"We can begin with Lord Tewksbury's party. With only four weeks left, time is of the essence. And I leave for Marsden Manor sometime soon. I hadn't planned on visiting before I married, but I received an odd note from the butler. Truth be told, I might enjoy a few days free of Hildegard's household."

"Where is your estate?" Elizabeth asked.

"Somewhere on the southeast coast, near a small town called St. Margaret's at Cliff. It's supposed to be quite lovely."

"Not far from Dover," added Stephen. "You can practically see France."

Elizabeth tapped her finger to her lower lip. "I have an idea. We'll make an outing of it. Winston and I shall gladly act as chaperones. We can wave to dear old Bonaparte."

"I doubt he'd wave back," muttered Stephen.

"As I was saying before I was so rudely interrupted," said Elizabeth, fixing Stephen with a baleful stare, "I haven't been to the coast in ages. And we can discuss eligible bachelors the entire trip. What do you say, Phoebe?"

"My companion is coming, but . . . are you sure you can spare the time? The trip will take several days. I don't even know what—"

While Elizabeth and Phoebe rambled on, Stephen considered an idea teasing his brain. To be alone with Phoebe away from London—without another suitable male in sight besides Winston, who was already married—was to tempting to ignore.

"I believe the idea has merit," Stephen announced.

"It does?" asked Phoebe, her surprise obvious.

"Undoubtedly. I am your new matchmaker, am I not? It will provide me with ample time to discern the type of man best suited as your husband."

"Splendid," Elizabeth crooned. "Why Phoebe, with all our help we shall have a list for you in no time. Add the weekend in the country, and you'll have a betrothal ring on your finger in short order."

Not if *he* had a thing to say about it, thought Stephen. He intended to use the five days with Phoebe to his advantage, wooing and seducing her into an agreement to become his. He clasped her hand and kissed her palm. "I look forward to our time together."

Chapter Seven

Phoebe tucked the invitation to Winston's country party in the panel of her morning dress. Thank goodness Siggers had remembered to give it to her and not to Hildegard. Ever since the escapade with the mule, which remained a secret for a paltry six hours, her aunt had been unbearable to live with, her sole purpose making Phoebe's life more miserable. Mercy, she was glad to be leaving for Marsden Manor in two days. She could still hear her aunt's blistering tirade over yet another savory tidbit in *The Times*, linking Phoebe's name with Lord Badrick. Someone had actually penned a cartoon with the American flag waving over Phoebe's head as she tugged at a mule. Stephen pulled from the other end, a British flag over his head. The caption read, "War? Again? Or is it soon to be nuptial bliss for Miss P———— R————, our illustrious colonial, and the D———— of B————" Wary of her aunt's constant scrutiny and changing moods, Phoebe had abandoned her early-morning rides in Hyde Park indefinitely.

And if that wasn't enough, the number of her suitors had doubled. Her newly found notoriety plagued her at every turn. She should have been pleased. After all, she needed a husband, and the more suitors, the greater selection to choose from. The problem was that Stephen wasn't amongst the group knocking at her door.

And she missed him with his do-as-I-say attitude and churlish remarks. The wretch. She hadn't seen him since the Doggett's race, yet every night he managed to invade her dreams, wicked fantasies complete with burning kisses and wanton caresses. She'd never had wicked thoughts before, at least not like these. She felt justified in blaming him for her restless condition. She needed to escape. Desperately. Trying to think of any plausible excuse to leave the house without her aunt's supervision, Phoebe stopped in the doorway from the breakfast room and stared.

Dee stood by herself in the foyer. She pulled a dead mouse from her red-flowered apron and stuck it on a three-legged table where Hildegard kept her dearest of possessions: her embroidery, her spectacles and *The Times*.

"Dee, whatever are you doing?"

Evidently quite pleased with herself, Dee chuckled. She covered the rodent with the social section of the newspaper. "I'm just wishing that woman never come back. She's been nastier than Widower Webster the day he lost his best piece of horseflesh to your father in that poker game."

Phoebe wrinkled her nose. "I'll admit, my aunt is not the kindest of women. Where is she?"

"She dragged that poor girl off to some singing lesson. Even the baker boy could tell that Charity don't have the voice for it. Downright painful it is. It's a wonder she don't just lock herself in her room and never come out." Dee grabbed Phoebe's chin and tipped her head up. "Why the long face?"

"I don't think I can endure one more afternoon of

callers. Winston's party is next week, and I've yet to think of a way to ask and convince Hildegard to let me go."

Grinning, Dee tweaked Phoebe's nose. "You'll think of something, Sweet Pea. You always do. You just need a little sunshine, not that you'll find any in this here city. Never saw a place as gloomy as this. But then again, at least it's not raining." Tucking her basket of mending, under one arm, Dee draped the other over Phoebe's shoulder. She turned toward the kitchen. "You know, child, I promised Siggers I'd go to the butcher for him, and my feet seem to be bothering me something fierce. I don't suppose you'd like to go for me?"

An escape! If only for a short time. If humanly possible, Phoebe felt as though her entire body grinned. "You know I would."

Within minutes, she had her cape, a straw bonnet decorated with bright white daisies, a list of purchases and the necessary coin. She waltzed out the front door. The sun barely penetrated the haze and moisture clung to the air, but Phoebe didn't care. She was free, at least for an hour. And it wasn't raining. She practically skipped down the lane toward Hyde Park, where people dawdled, enjoying the break in the weather. Nursemaids conscientiously watched their wards and ladies displayed themselves and their finery in their carriages while gentlemen displayed their horses. She found herself purposely slowing her pace, searching the dirt tracks for Stephen.

Instead, to her bad luck, she found Sir Lemmer, dressed in his typical peacockish fashion. Fine feathers certainly didn't make a fine bird, she thought, then caught herself before she burst into laughter at her own jest. He sat atop a black stallion whose sides heaved from exertion. The poor horse was lathered and carried marks consistent with the harsh use of spurs. Her dislike for the man increased with every encounter. She averted her eyes, hoping he'd pass her by.

"What have we here? A damsel, certainly in need of rescue."

"Good afternoon, sir." Nodding only slightly, she started back down the path.

He nudged his horse forward, directly in her path. The nervous animal danced in a tight circle several times before Lemmer uttered a harsh command and yanked hard on the reins, forcing the horse to stop.

"You might try a gentler hand, sir. I find an animal's loyalty is well worth the effort."

His gaze slowly slid down her body and up again, lingering on her breasts. Rubbing his finger across his chin, his lips parted slightly and he crooned, "I have an affinity for kindness when it suits me. Given the proper incentive, I would be more than willing to make all your dreams come true."

She felt naked under his stark appraisal. She almost grimaced. The odious man possessed the manners of a pig, and not just any pig, but one who acted as though he'd won a few too many blue ribbons at the local fair. She fought the urge to cross her arms in front of her. "That's a mite presumptuous."

He spoke softly, the slightest hint of warning in his voice. "Miss Rafferty, is that any way to speak to your future husband?"

She had never been purposely rude to the man, but neither had she given him any indication that she found his intentions the least bit flattering. Lifting her chin a notch, she said, "I don't recollect your asking me, nor my saying yes."

He pressed his horse forward. "It's only a matter of time. Lord Badrick won't marry you. He appears the perfect gentleman, but I know better. Count your blessings that you have me to protect you from him. Like my poor sister Emily, Badrick wives have a habit of dying mysteriously."

"Emily was your sister?"

"Didn't Badrick tell you? I'm not surprised. He talks little of his past. Don't blame the chap. Why would anyone disclose something so reprehensible as the seduction of an innocent young girl and murder? The curse has driven him quite mad. I recommend you stay far away from him. If you like, I shall see to it he doesn't bother you at all."

Phoebe digested the startling fact that Stephen was related to Sir Lemmer. However had she missed that scrap of information? She'd already heard the ridiculous accusations about murder, but the part about seduction certainly was a new window into Stephen's past. Still, she doubted that Sir Lemmer was the best source of information and she wasn't about to stand here and argue with the man. She stepped back, glancing from side to side. She realized he had effectively backed her into a small, secluded area surrounded by tall elderberry bushes. The discomforting sensation of being trapped skittered up her spine. She tapped her right toe and clenched her hands around her purse. "My patience is gone, sir. Let me pass."

One corner of his mouth curled upwards. Using the handle of his riding crop, he traced a line from her shoulder to the top of her breast. "And lose the first opportunity I've had to be alone with you?" He swung one leg over the saddle. "Not a chance."

Phoebe knew enough to know Lemmer was thinking something he shouldn't be. Considering the gleam in his eyes, if she continued to just stand there, he'd likely try to do exactly what he was thinking. She shuddered at the thought of his body next to hers, his hands touching her as he pleased. While he dangled with only one leg in the stirrups, she reached for the leather riding crop, tugging as hard as she could, effectively throwing him off balance. The horse finished what she began. He pitched to the left, throwing Lemmer to the ground on the right. Lemmer jumped to his feet, his face contorted with rage. He slapped the dirt from his breeches. "Why you little . . . I ought to—"

"Having trouble with your mount?"

Lemmer froze.

Phoebe skirted the horse and moved toward the familiar and welcome voice. Sir Lemmer's advances had definitely rattled her nerves, something not easily done. She practically kissed Stephen's boot right then and there. He sat perfectly still atop his horse, for all appearances calm. He didn't even seem to breathe, yet waves of anger emanated from him, charging the morning air with an uncomfortable silence. He locked a dark, savage glare on Lemmer, who had managed to straddle his horse once again. With nothing more than a whisper, Stephen said, "I shall attend to Miss Rafferty." His tone of voice, quiet but unyielding, left no room for argument.

With a false smile that never quite reached his eyes, Lemmer clenched his teeth so tightly his cheek twitched. With his hands knotted in his reins, he nudged his horse toward Phoebe. "Be assured, Miss Rafferty, we shall talk again."

Not if she had anything to say about it, which she wasn't sure she did. If only his horse would throw him to the ground once again and kindly trample him a time or two. Calling upon every ounce of arrogance she possessed, she tipped her chin in the haughtiest manner possible and remained silent as he spurred his horse into a canter. When Lemmer disappeared from sight, Phoebe finally spared a glance at Stephen. Surely he wanted to yell or offer a lecture of sorts. She pasted a cheerful smile on her face. "Why Lord Badrick, what a pleasant surprise."

He climbed down from his horse, his movements deliberate and rigid. "It seems I am to constantly rescue you from trouble."

"Now don't puff up about this. You just happened to arrive before I resolved things. It's your fault anyway. I was watching for you rather than paying attention to where I ought to have been."

"I assume that was your circuitous manner of avoiding a lecture." The tension slowly left his face and shoulders. He tucked a wayward curl behind her ear, allowing his hand to linger against her cheek. "You worry me, Phoebe Rafferty, plague, haunt and worry me."

Gone was the warrior, replaced by the man she feared was stealing her heart. One simple brush of his finger and she trembled like a school girl. On impulse, she leaned into the caress and placed her hand over his. His brown eyes darkened to black, not in anger, but with something just as dangerous. Lust, coupled with simple need. Both were more compelling than Phoebe thought possible. Just as quickly his hands fell to his sides. Whatever moment they had shared vanished like the flash of a lightning bug.

"Are you all right?" he asked.

"Truly, I'm fine, but I do thank you for your timely interruption. That man needs a lesson in manners."

"I have said this before. Stay away from Sir Lemmer."

"I intend to, although he seems to have other ideas. He sees himself as my champion."

He cocked his head to one side with a look of concentration she had seen several times as his mind dissected that bit of information. "Really?"

"Yes, indeed. He thinks to save me from a similar fate his sister, your wife, suffered. Would you care to elaborate?"

He shrugged matter-of-factly. "No."

"You can't avoid me forever."

"I have no intention of avoiding *you*, only the topic of my past."

Stomping her foot, she struggled to keep her temper in check. The man was worse than Tobias when he wanted to keep a secret. A person had better luck trying to change a dead man's mind. Just to let Stephen know what she thought of his behavior, she gave a satisfying squawk in the most unladylike manner possible and turned to leave.

He matched his steps with hers. "Where are you going?"

"The butcher and the milliner."

"A bit of a walk, isn't it?"

"My time these last weeks has been spent on teas, balls, dinner parties and the opera. I'm accustomed to more rigorous endeavors. Since you refuse to talk to me, the walk will be a welcome diversion."

"I didn't refuse to talk to you, but since you seem set on this course and since I see you have ventured off, again, without any sort of companion or chaperone, I will keep you company."

"How generous of you, sir." Didn't the man ever ask permission? She wanted to stay angry, she really did. But there was no hope for it. His company was exactly what she wanted. They walked leisurely, Cavalier trailing behind. "If I remember correctly, you were to give me counsel on my matrimonial candidates, yet you seem to have neglected your duties."

He tucked his tongue in the hollow of his cheek. "Did you miss me?"

"Like a case of measles."

When he laughed, she joined him. His good humor was contagious. She had missed him, but wasn't about to admit it. He was too sure of himself as it was. She pushed aside other questions about his absence, prepared to simply enjoy his company.

"You do realize your husband would forbid such behavior as walking about unaccompanied. He'd likely forbid your early-morning rides in the park and possibly limit your excursions altogether."

"I would likely test his patience daily."

"Then he might beat you and lock you in your room and be justified in the eyes of the House of Lords. Mistresses have so much more freedom afforded them these days. For your information, my dear, most husbands expect far more wifely obedience than you tend to exhibit. They dislike quibbling, whether the subject is a gift, a meal or a scrap of clothing. It upsets their constitution."

"That's a bag of moonshine, if ever I heard any. Don't you mean it challenges their need for superiority?"

"Only out of concern for their wives."

"Phooey! Out of concern for their pride."

"There is that. However, if they said the sky was green, they'd readily expect you to agree. If they preferred fish, they'd expect cod for supper. If they disliked velvet, you'd wear silk. If they abhorred Beethoven, you'd play Mozart. If they—"

She held up her hand to stay the flow of words on wifely obedience. "I understand, my lord. Is all this written in some book of rules or such? It might prove interesting reading."

"Goodness, no. A true gentleman acquires such attributes at birth, making a wife's life most boring. My point in all this is that few men enjoy a debate of any kind with a female. Unlike myself, of course."

"Of course." The rogue. He was thoroughly enjoying himself. She met his smile with one of her own. "You would allow me to wear breeches?"

"Daily, if you so chose."

"And ride in Hyde Park by myself, and discuss Plato and Socrates with you?"

" 'Twould be invigorating."

"You would eat gruel and black pudding, dance in the rain and allow me to cheat at poker?"

"Smiling at every turn."

Quietly pleased with herself, she flipped her bag over her shoulder and watched his expression. " 'Tis a good thing. I intend to find a man, one of the select few such as you, who has no need to exert his power over me."

Stephen admitted his defeat as he escorted her out of Hyde Park. He asked, "What was your aunt's reaction to Winston's invitation?"

"I haven't exactly asked her permission just yet."

He stopped and looked her squarely in the eye. "I hope you plan to ask her soon."

She lengthened her stride. "I've been biding my time. I plan to mention it before we leave for Marsden Manor. Hildegard has been absolutely horrific ever since that . . . well . . ." She kicked a pebble with her shoe. "I'm sure you know why. I hope the mention of us in the newspaper didn't cause you any problems. You'd think people had better things to do with their time than worry about the comings and goings of London society."

"Darling, it gives me no pleasure to be right about the incident with the mule if it caused you aggravation. Many people with too much idle time read the society section before any other part of the newspaper. Put the problem aside. I'll think of something."

As they walked, they discussed everything from King George to blackberry pie, which turned out to be Stephen's favorite. He even hired a street urchin to watch his horse so he could help her with her purchases. Determined to show her the benefits of being his mistress, he offered to buy her a pearl necklace, a new hat, a pair of shoes and a gold pin shaped like a seagull. She refused each and every gift, yet

117

bought the hat herself. She loved every minute of their time together.

As they neared Hildegard's house, she fidgeted with the small bag she carried, the thought of returning home now a worry. Her aunt had made her opinion quite clear. The Duke of Badrick was not a welcome suitor. Leaves danced about her feet as the wind blew. The skies turned a murky gray and the air grew heavy with moisture, a perfect reflection of her mood. Rain would soon fall.

Stopping at the corner of Hildegard's lane, intent on preventing any sort of a scene, she reached for the purchases he carried. "Thank you for your company. I had a delightful time."

He maintained a tight grip on his package and studied her face. "What's the matter, Phoebe?"

A fat drop of water fell on the tip of her nose, followed by another upon her forehead. She plastered a coy, flirtatious smile on her face. "Oh, silly me. I've just been gone longer than expected. I best hurry on. Good day."

His hand snared her wrist, effectively keeping her trapped before him. "You're a pitiful liar. The truth. Spit it out."

Rain began to fall in earnest and people with the tiniest bit of intelligence scampered to find shelter. The stubborn man would likely keep her in this foul weather until she caught pneumonia, but she couldn't very well tell him the truth. Soon, her cape clung to her body and water dripped from her hat, two of her spritely little daisies bowed over the brim in submission to the rain. Still, he refused to release her hand. Her shoulders heaved in resignation. "If you must know, my aunt doesn't like you very much."

"I thought it was something of importance." He started down the lane. "Do not concern yourself with such trivialities. Come along."

"She doesn't want me to see you. At all. She has no idea

118

you mean to accompany me to Marsden Manor either, and I'd appreciate that little bit of news be kept private."

"Trust me, I shall manage your aunt. Right now I am more concerned with finding dry space." He grabbed her hand, dragging her toward her aunt's home.

Chapter Eight

By the time they reached the front door, they were both drenched. Siggers appeared quickly and efficiently and, without so much as a blink of an eye, he directed them to the salon. He took their packages and withdrew from the room on a promise to return with suitable refreshments and towels.

Stephen shut the doors and moved close enough to tug on a lock of hair curling about her face. "You look quite lovely all soggy." Using the knuckle of his index finger, he traced a circle from her cheek to her chin to her other cheek. "Beautiful."

Yearning clawed at Phoebe's stomach. "Siggers? My aunt?"

"I know. We best not waste this opportunity." He nuzzled her right ear. "For the last few days, I've thought of nothing else." His grip tightened. Pulling her into his arms, his lips met hers.

Heat consumed her, every nerve ending alive with anticipation and fire. She forgot the rain, Hildegard's edict, even Siggers. Passion warred with her muddled senses. She couldn't continue to let him kiss her like this whenever he wanted. No matter the temptation. Didn't they need to stoke the fire or something, although heat was the last thing she required at the moment? Stephen warmed her better and faster than any old fire ever could. As his hand slid beneath her cape to rest on her rib cage, her breast swelled. Pressing closer still, she tried to blame the reaction on her damp garments. She knew better. Her body craved his touch. Stephen Lambert could kiss, and then some. As if he read her mind, his hand inched upwards. Slowly. Surely, she would die of anticipation. When his thumb grazed her nipple in a tender assault, she moaned. Her legs felt liquid and her body ached in places she never thought possible. Finally, his hand stilled and his lips left hers. A whimper, surprisingly her own, filled the void. She willed her eyes to open. "Oh."

Stephen dropped his forehead to hers. "You drive me to madness, woman."

Madness? Yes, she understood that feeling as well. Swallowing convulsively, she stepped to what she deemed a safe distance away, behind a large gothic library table with hideously ornate table legs shaped like dragons. She wrapped her arms about her waist. "You had best go. My aunt will return shortly."

"I detest repetition, and I told you once already, your aunt presents no threat." Stephen had no intention of leaving before he gained Hildegard's assurance that Phoebe would attend Winston's party. Moving before the stone fireplace, he removed the decorative screen and stirred the embers, warming the room.

"Easy for you to say," she muttered to herself as she removed the water-logged hat from her head and set it on the table. "Perhaps you don't realize the extent of her dislike for you. Hildegard said some rather horrible things for which I had no defense since you refuse to tell me anything about your past."

"I don't remember requesting a defense of any kind."

"Nevertheless I felt inclined to do so."

"Defending me is not a wise plan. My reputation is quite tattered. Few people will agree with you and, more importantly, you are likely to find yourself ostracized."

"All the more reason to tell me what I need to know."

"Give over, Phoebe. I have no need of a stubborn, single-minded female fighting my battles."

"Stubborn?" She planted her hands on her hips. "Hah. That's a tale tell coming from a man who chooses to play the martyr because of two dead wives and a fool gypsy curse."

"Tread carefully, Phoebe. You know not of what you speak."

"Then lands alive, tell me. Did you murder Emily?"

In exasperation, he threw his hands in the air. She was worse than a guard dog with a thief's britches in its mouth. He knew she would snarl and chomp until he offered information or escaped. Escape was not an option right now. At least her question was easily answered. "No, I did not. She fell from a balcony in our home. I arrived to find the body."

Phoebe stood rooted to her spot, tracing a large pink flower in the rug with her toe. She started to shiver. "Was that so difficult to share with me?"

He dropped his head to the palm of his hand which rested on his knee. So like a woman not to be satisfied. They wanted a man's soul. Well, his was not available. Prepared to tell her so, he shifted to the balls of his feet as a handsome Negro woman, obviously the companion Phoebe spoke of, sailed into the room carrying a silver tea tray. From the determined look on her face, he knew she had something on her mind.

"What are you thinkin', child?" Dee asked, placing the refreshments on a nearby table. "Getting yourself soaking wet."

Stephen stood, one hand balanced on the large Grecian urn beside him. "That would be my fault."

While Stephen and Dee silently took one another's measure, Phoebe made the introductions.

"Well, I can't say I admire your manner of caring for a lady. Most people have sense enough to come in from the rain. What's your excuse?"

"Dee." Phoebe glared at her maid in silent communication. Then she smiled at Stephen, one of those apologetic, my-servant-didn't-mean-it kind of smiles. "My companion worries overmuch for me sometimes."

"Understandable," agreed Stephen, undaunted by the woman's censure. Obviously Dee cared a great deal for her charge and took her responsibilities seriously. He couldn't blame her. He had similar feelings about Phoebe himself. "I plead guilty, Dee. Admittedly, Miss Rafferty bewitches me. My better judgment eludes me when I'm near her."

Dee stilled her hands. She tilted her head, raised her ebony brows to a formidable height and bestowed upon him a look that had surely felled lesser men. "You don't say?"

Charm from a distance seemed a good strategy right now. Stephen crossed to the tea service and filled two cups. He offered one to Phoebe, then moved to the window facing the street. "Quite so. Miss Phoebe is enchanting company, for which I'm sure you are partly responsible."

"You're right about that. I raised Miss Phoebe since she first saw daylight. I know exactly how enchantin' she can be. I also knows what men like you, Mr. Duke, like to do with enchantin' women, and I'm here to tell you, I didn't teach her to act a silly goose without a lick of sense. You just remember that."

The warning was perfectly clear. Dee protected Phoebe like Winston did Elizabeth—ferociously defending her anytime she felt her charge in any danger. Dee would make a formidable adversary, or a favorable ally. He would have to think on that. "Most assuredly."

Finally freeing herself from her sodden cape, Phoebe shrugged it from her shoulders, grabbed her hat, and placed the garments into Dee's waiting hands. "In case the two of you forgot, I'm still here in this very same room. If you—"

A screech, distinctly shrill and clearly female, sounded from the foyer. Phoebe snapped her mouth shut and rubbed her hand over her face, then glared at Dee, who grinned about something Stephen evidently knew nothing about. When someone, presumably Aunt Hildegard, squealed a second time, Phoebe glanced at Stephen and sighed, her breath fanning the damp curl on her forehead. From his secluded spot, he watched the doorway in anticipation.

Hildegard, her cheeks flushed and puffed with indignance, stomped into the room. One hand pressed against the lace neckline of her bright purple pelisse, the other fanned back and forth, her white handkerchief flowing from side to side like a flag of surrender.

Charity crept behind her mother, watching the scene with cautious yet avid fascination.

Hildegard stopped and glared at Dee. "You . . . you . . ."

"Somethin' wrong, madam?" asked Dee, her brows knitted in confusion. Stephen surmised the servant knew exactly to what Hildegard referred. This would be an interesting exchange.

"Don't you 'madam' me. What is the meaning of *this*?" Hildegard pointed to Siggers, who had moved to the doorway as well, a bland, almost serene expression pasted on his face. He held a dead mouse at arm's length from his body.

Dee's grin widened, revealing a row of white teeth. She flounced over to the butler and relieved him of his burden. "Goodness gracious. I best get rid of that. Wherever did you find it?"

"You know as well as I do," snapped Hildegard, her words flying fast from her mouth. "It's one of your tricks. You purposely placed it beside my embroidery."

"I did?" Dee scratched her head. "Goodness, I don't remember that a'tall."

"On no, not this time. I have had it," said Hildegard, stomping her foot. She pivoted toward Phoebe. "You, young lady, are responsible for this abomination. I imagine your father allowed such ghastly behavior in his servants as well. Not me. This is my home. I will—"

"Auntie," Phoebe interrupted.

"What?" Hildegard barked, her temper bound by a thread.

Nodding toward the corner, Phoebe directed her aunt's attention to where Stephen stood. "We have company."

Hildegard's head swiveled so quickly that had her feet not been firmly planted on the ground she would have toppled over into a heap of chartreuse and purple linen. He certainly admired Dee's backbone. The maid planted that ignorant smile on her face and latched on to him, which obviously irritated Hildegard all the more. He barely contained his grin. "Good afternoon, Lady Goodliffe."

Her expression shifted quickly from anger to disapproval to what some might call cordiality. Almost. She wasn't the least bit pleased to have him here. "Lord Badrick. You seem to have caught me unawares. As you have certainly ascertained, I've had a difficult day."

"Quite all right. Now and again, everyone, even myself, begins a day only to realize they'd have been better off to stay abed. Good afternoon, Charity. You look lovely."

Charity managed a curtsy.

"Charity, quit skulking in the hallway and sit down." Her mouth set with annoyance, Hildegard spared no glance for her daughter, but kept her eyes on Dee. "*You* may go. We will discuss this matter later."

"Absolutely, madam. Come on, Siggers, I can see we're going to need more tea for all these people."

Hildegard tucked her handkerchief into the sleeve of her dress and sat on the scarlet and rose floral chaise opposite Charity, who perched stiffly on a matching chair. "Pardon my trivial problems, your grace. To what do we owe this visit?"

"Hasn't Miss Rafferty told you?"

Hildegard glared at her niece. "Obviously I missed something of import."

Accusation radiated from her eyes. She truly was a most disagreeable woman. He pitied anyone forced to bear her company for any length of time, especially Phoebe, when Hildegard's dislike was so apparent. Phoebe busied herself with a cup of tea, then moved to the fireplace. Evidently, she wasn't about to offer an explanation when she had no idea what he was thinking. Smart girl. He crossed to Phoebe's side. "It is of minor importance, actually. I offered my services as counsel in her search for a husband."

"I see no need, your grace. I am fully capable of giving advice."

"Of course you are." He agreed readily while he studied the flamboyant two-handed silver vase decorated with an Egyptianesque motif sitting on the mantle. Conquests were all a matter of strategy and timing. "What an extraordinary piece."

"It happens to be one of my favorites. It was created by Paul Storr."

"I thought I recognized the work. Storr is quite talented,

but back to the subject at hand. Women are excellent judges of character, but men are often privy to some of one another's habits that women are not. Between the two of us, Miss Rafferty shall make a marvelous match. Which is, I'm sure, exactly what you seek."

"Indeed."

"After all, family ties bond us forever. I know it is your fondest wish to aid your only niece in every possible way."

"I do my best."

He swore he heard Hildegard's teeth grinding behind her pinched lips. Lady Goodliffe did not like this discussion, nor his interference. Phoebe, on the other hand, seemed content to remain a silent bystander. Stephen clapped his hands together. "Splendid. That being the case. I brought with me an invitation to Lord Payley's country affair next week. I believe a number of suitable lords shall be present."

Shifting in her chair, Hildegard squared her shoulders with revived confidence. "We have previous plans. Besides, it's far too late to accept. We should have received and responded to such an invitation weeks ago."

Like a conspirator, he lowered his voice to a whisper. "Who's to know, Lady Goodliffe? Did you not receive and accept Lord Tewksbury's invitation a mere two days ago?"

She managed to sputter, "That is different, your grace. It is a simple dinner party, not a weekend outing which requires a substantial amount of preparation."

"A slight inconvenience, nothing more, for a woman of your skill. Of course, Phoebe's companion may accompany her as well as yourself and Miss Charity, if she is so inclined." He spoke directly to Charity. "I believe Eustace Ellwood will be present as well. I heard through the rumor mill that his interests lie in your direction."

Bowing her head slightly, Charity squirmed in her seat,

gazing from Stephen to Phoebe to her mother and finally at the floor. The poor girl was more skittish than a young filly. Nervous or not, pleasure shined in her eyes.

"Forget Ellwood," said Hildegard. "I am considering a match with Lord Hadlin."

"But mother, he's been married four times already, and he's so old."

"He's also quite rich. Count your blessings that he wants a young, strong wife to breed an heir."

Stephen barely contained his disgust. He understood the business of making satisfactory matches. It was quite simply the way of things. His sudden interest in Charity's plight surprised him, but Hadlin was at least forty-eight with the personality of a stiff, unyielding bench and a propensity for virgins of any age. He might have money, but he seldom spent it on his wives. His mistresses, who were many, were far happier. But Hildegard cared nothing of those things, wanting only the prestige she'd receive for her daughter's match.

Smiling at Charity in an obvious attempt to offer support, Phoebe added, "Perhaps other lords we have yet to meet will attend."

"Undoubtedly, Miss Rafferty," added Stephen as he wearied of the game. It was time to exert the authority granted him simply by title. "I am certain your aunt realizes the merits of accepting such an invitation, the disadvantages if she doesn't. Don't you, Lady Goodliffe?" he asked, using his silky tone of voice as a blacksmith uses a hammer and anvil, bending Hildegard to his will.

Clasping and unclasping her hands, Hildegard cleared her throat several times. Her lips curved into the slightest of smiles. "Of course we accept. It would be foolish to do otherwise. I will inform Lord Payley of my decision to accompany Phoebe or not." She pushed herself from the chaise, her movements precise and rigid. "If you will excuse me. Siggers will see you out."

"By all means." Turning toward Phoebe, he whispered, "Close your mouth, darling, you're gaping. I told you your aunt was the least of your worries." He grasped Phoebe's hand and placed a kiss above her knuckles. "Until tonight, Miss Rafferty."

He nodded toward Charity, then proceeded to the doorway where Siggers appeared as suddenly as a puff of smoke. With a smirk and a wink, Stephen sailed from the room.

"Land sakes," muttered Phoebe, unsure whether to rejoice or run. Hildegard's foul mood would hover like a dark cloud for at least the rest of the day if not the balance of the week. Ready to skip around the room because she could flee to Marsden Manor, Phoebe remembered Charity. The poor thing. Charity's situation was no better than Phoebe's. In fact, it was worse. At least Phoebe had a say in the selection of her spouse. It now seemed that Hildegard planned to sell Charity to the highest bidder, and Phoebe doubted her cousin had the strength of will to disobey.

"Aren't you excited?" asked Phoebe.

"Mother will likely find a reason for us to stay home. Oh dear, whatever shall I do? Lord Hadlin is . . . a . . ."

"Your mother hasn't accepted his suit yet." She took the space Hildegard had recently vacated. "I'm truly sorry, Charity. Perhaps you'll see Sir Ellwood at Tewksbury's tonight. I'll do whatever I can to help."

Chapter Nine

Right now, this minute, an afternoon in the cotton fields back home held more appeal than the balance of Phoebe's evening. There, she wouldn't be worried about her manners, her dress, her every movement, about what she said or how she said it. This constant charade of proper deportment and her feigned excitement to find a husband was tedious not to mention depressing. Her future seemed dreary, and then some. And she had prepared for this evening with such anticipation.

Lord Tewksbury had been an attentive host until dinner, which was delicious, efficiently served, and dragged on forever. Now the men, Stephen included, had closeted themselves in the drawing room with their precious brandy and private conversation that was considered unsuitable for females. At the moment, waiting for the evening's entertainment, Phoebe suffered Hildegard's waspish countenance and a young debutante's inane attempt at conversation. Charity hovered nearby, seemingly as bored

as Phoebe. Likely her thoughts were with Eustace Ellwood, who conversed with the men as well. The young girl
beside Phoebe giggled yet again and she knew she had best
move elsewhere or go mad. Excusing herself, she fled
toward the conservatory. Perhaps if she hid behind a bush
or a potted plant, she'd find a moment's peace and quiet.

Rounding the cobblestone path lined with assorted
palms, Phoebe happened upon two older matrons, who sat
together on a stone bench tucked between the marble
sculpture of a large bird in flight and a rose bush. She
thought she might escape unnoticed until one woman
waved. Reluctantly, wanting only to flee outdoors, she
crossed to the bench, sat and awaited the introductions and
heaven knew what else.

Lady Ostlin, as she named herself, possessed bosoms
capable of sporting a small tea service. Nibbling on her
berry tart, she studied Phoebe. Finally, she nodded to her
sister, Lady Tipler, and placed her yellow-gloved hand
over Phoebe's bare one. "It is rumored, Miss Rafferty, that
you are in pursuit of a husband. Although Lady Goodliffe
is your aunt, I imagine she cares more for Charity's plight
than yours. My sister and I feel it our duty to aid your
cause, you being a foreigner and all."

"Yes, a foreigner," added Lady Tipler, a reed of a woman
with birdlike features and a high chirping voice to match.

"You are most fortunate," added Lady Ostlin. "You have
a veritable mélange to choose from tonight. All delightful
gentleman."

At that very moment, Sir Lemmer approached, carrying
a small plate. The men were evidently free from their after-
dinner caucus, one that Phoebe greatly resented at the
moment. He said, "Good evening, ladies. I must say, Lady
Ostlin, that you look exceedingly lovely tonight. And Lady
Tipler, your beauty puts the young girls to shame. I thought
you might enjoy a bit of refreshment." He offered them

crumb cakes, which the matrons accepted, beaming toothy grins of approval. They obviously enjoyed every bit of flattery Lemmer gushed. When he turned his attentions to her, Phoebe pasted a bland expression on her face.

"A pleasure to see you again, Miss Rafferty. Would you care to join me for a beverage before the concert?"

"I'm sorry, sir, but the ladies and I were engrossed in a rather interesting conversation. Thank you all the same."

With one hand behind his back, the other draped across his waist, and his head slightly cocked, he executed the perfect bow. "Until later, then."

Lady Ostlin waited all of two seconds before she tapped Phoebe's knee. "Mind that young man, my dear. Sir Lemmer is a prize, to be sure. And if my instincts are correct, which they usually are, he seems most determined."

Bobbing her head up and down, Lady Tipler agreed. "Most determined."

Phoebe didn't even bother to counter Lady Ostlin's opinion of Sir Lemmer. They evidently liked the man. Fine and dandy. Let *them* marry him. She alternated her attention between each woman. It seemed Lady Tipler was incapable of more than a word or two. All her thoughts belonged to her sister. What an odd pair, Phoebe thought, but she wanted information and they seemed willing to speak their minds. She directed her question to Lady Tipler, simply to see if the woman would answer. "Someone mentioned Lord Badrick might be here as well. I hear he's quite handsome."

Lady Ostlin tutted a dozen or so times, then pulled a white lace handkerchief heavily doused with violet water from her bosom and dabbed her brow. "He simply will not do. Avoid him, no matter what. Lord Badrick is dangerous."

Well, good heavens. There was no subtlety there. Phoebe fought the immediate impulse to roll her eyes and

132

offer the woman a piece of her mind. She smiled politely. "Surely one man cannot be as bad as all that."

"His grandfather killed a young girl and started the entire debacle. If memory serves me, at least six wives have died at the hands of the Badrick men. Shameful. As for the young duke, he killed his own wives with his bare hands. The beast stands naked before a full moon while he worships the creatures of the night."

"The beast," repeated Lady Tipler, nodding her head this time.

"And he collects young boys," Lady Ostlin continued. "Especially those with dark hair. Takes their toes and hangs them from the trees of his estate. It's to warn all gypsies, bothersome creatures that they are, from his lands when he could simply post a sign."

"A sign," Lady Tipler echoed.

Phoebe sat perfectly still, dumbfounded, by the accusations, which grew more absurd with every spoken word. These two women belonged in the company of Hildegard. Their misguided opinions meant more to them than the truth. Phoebe's racing pulse twitched behind her right ear, which began to itch. It spread down her arms until they grew rigid. Her hands clenched and released. If she sat here much longer, listening to these hateful and ludicrous lies, she feared what she might do. Yet she couldn't just walk away. She faced Lady Ostlin, who sat as straight as a porch pillar. "Have you witnessed any of these events or habits?"

"Of course not."

Phoebe swiveled toward Lady Tipler. "Then your husband saw these things and informed you of the circumstances?"

"Did he, sister?"

"Of course not, sister," answered Lady Ostlin.

She wanted to shake the women silly, loosen the prejudices collected in their minds tighter than bees in a honey jar. Forcing a deep breath through her lips, hoping it might calm her anger, Phoebe drummed her fingers together. "I understand. You're somehow related to Lord Badrick and read such factors in a family journal."

"Don't be absurd," Lady Ostlin cajoled. "His behavior is common knowledge."

"Common knowledge," agreed Lady Tipler, bobbing her head on her skinny little neck somewhat like a barnyard chicken.

That was it. Phoebe could not listen to one more vicious rumor. "Common is right, such as your behavior. How can you believe, let alone speak of, any of this? Why, you old withered busybodies, it's malicious gossip designed to wound, created by jealous men and women with nothing better to do with their time."

Her hefty bosom heaving with indignation, Lady Ostlin stood and extended her hand, which her sister grasped. "You ungrateful child," she huffed. "See if we offer *our* assistance ever again." They strutted from the corner, arm in arm, their pompous heads perched on their squared shoulders, their chins jutted forward.

Mercy, what had she done? Phoebe hoped she hadn't raised her voice. Glancing nervously over her shoulder to see if anyone had noticed her outburst, she crept through the nearest door into the night.

Darkness surrounded her like a shield. Noticing a light in the barn like a beacon, she sought comfort from the animals. She eased between the open doors and inhaled the familiar scent of horse and hay, a pleasant alternative to perfume. Closing her eyes, she could almost believe she stood in her barn back in Georgia, where she'd watched the birth of her very own horse; where Tobias had taught her to snap a whip and how to load a gun, both necessary means of defense for a woman running a plantation.

The image ebbed and shifted to more recent years. The stately plantation house of River Bend had finally gained a reputation for quality cotton, Phoebe's efforts finally paying the bills. She saw her tear-streaked face as she glimpsed Hercules one last time before the new owner hauled the horse away. She felt the stifling summer heat as she lay in the hayloft, crying over her father's death, his final betrayal.

She remembered the day she'd stood in a near-empty barn to say her good-byes to the people she had worked beside, laughed with and loved. The memories, good and bad, warred with one another as she sought to make sense of her current situation. One thing was certain, she never wanted to rely on the whims of a man or experience that feeling of helplessness again. The soft nicker of a horse followed by a small voice snapped her back to the present.

Stuff and nonsense. She wasn't alone after all. She pondered whether to stay or go when the tiny voice, a child's voice, spoke again. Phoebe crept forward until she reached the last stall. Inside, a little girl with wild blond curls hovered over a small black foal. The child wore a lovely red velvet robe that was now covered with straw.

Phoebe spoke softly. "She's quite lovely."

The young girl's gaze darted over Phoebe's shoulder and beyond.

Being a child that had tested her father's patience time and again, Phoebe recognized and understood the girl's wariness. She appeared to be about six or seven, likely Lord Tewksbury's daughter, and was probably supposed to be tucked in her room, asleep.

As though she shared a great secret, Phoebe whispered, "Please don't tell anyone you saw me. I simply had to leave the party for a bit of fresh air."

The child's blue eyes rounded, her worries now focused on Phoebe. "You don't like parties?"

135

Phoebe remembered her nasty exchange with Lady Ostlin and Lady Tipler. "Usually I do, but sometimes they give me a pain in the head. May I join you?"

The child nodded. "You talk funny. What's your name?"

"Phoebe Rafferty, and I'm from America so *that* is why I sound a bit different."

"My name is Meredith. You may call me Bliss. I live here. Do you like horses?"

"I *love* horses," Phoebe cooed, sitting beside Bliss without a care to her dress. "My father gave me my first pony when I was six."

"I'm seven," Bliss announced in a regal manner likely copied from her father. "This is my horse. Her mother died. I help take care of her."

"Your father must be very proud. Not all children are as responsible."

"That's what I tell my father. My mother died, so father thinks I need a new mother, too. That's why he's having this party. I heard him tell my grandmother. I told him if the new mother was for me, then I should be able to choose."

Phoebe wanted to laugh over Bliss's impertinence. "Did he also tell you that eavesdropping was poor manners?"

"No, but my nanny did. She grumbles over most everything I do."

This time Phoebe did laugh. What a wonderful child.

She imagined herself sitting like this, sharing secrets with a dark-haired, dark-eyed, child that resembled Stephen. She blinked the image away and straightened her shoulders.

Heavens! Now she was contemplating children, and not just any children, but hers and Stephen's children. Not a good thing, considering the man refused to marry her. It seemed a new rut lay in the path of her well-planned future. For all her protests that she wanted to marry and be left alone to run Marsden Manor, Phoebe knew it to be a false vow. Thunderation, she wanted it all: children of her own, a family *and* Marsden Manor. She wanted to keep Stephen as well.

"Good evening, ladies. I didn't realize the party had moved out of doors."

Startled from her woolgathering for a second time, Phoebe stood as Bliss hid behind her skirts. "Lord Badrick, may I introduce Lady Tewksbury."

When Bliss stepped forward, he kissed her hand and bowed. "Charmed, gentle lady."

Bliss giggled. Not a practiced artful twitter, but an honest-to-goodness giggle. Still grinning, she said, "Phoebe said the indoors sometimes made her head ache so she needed fresh air. Do you have a headache too?"

"No. I simply ache for the companionship of two lovely and intelligent women. Do you know where I might find any?"

A half-hour earlier, Phoebe had been ready to jump from a window and strangle two overbearing obnoxious women. A simple smile from Stephen and all seemed right with the world. She shared a conspiratorial look with Bliss. "I think we might be able to help you with that, kind sir."

"Splendid." He smiled.

Bliss nudged the straw with her right toe. "Actually I had best go. Nanny checks my bed. She turns grumpy when I'm not where I should be."

Phoebe said good-bye, then fidgeted with an iron loop on the door of the stall, waiting for Stephen to say something as he studied her intently.

"Phoebe, Phoebe, Phoebe." While shaking his head, he repeated her name like a chaperone preparing to discipline an unruly child. "Will you ever listen to what I say? Again you chose to wander off where you shouldn't. By yourself. After your adventure at Lord Wyman's and the park, I'd think you would have learned your lesson by now."

She couldn't believe her ears. The wretch had finally decided to talk with her and he had the audacity to offer a lecture. Mimicking his tone of voice, she said, "Stephen, Stephen, Stephen. Do you always ignore women in public, then seek them out in private? I mean, you've certainly managed to ignore me all evening without any difficulty."

Leaning against the frame of the stall door, he sighed. "We've been through this before. I am not your best choice of company when surrounded by my peers, especially considering our dual-appearance in *The Times*."

"I don't care about that silly old newspaper. How did you find me?"

"You left a wake equal to one left by a small ship. I started with Hildegard—who remains as disagreeable as ever—and ended with two very disgruntled matrons. You certainly set their bristles up. Whatever did you say to that pair of thatchgallows?"

She sailed past him, hoping to escape before he demanded to know all the sordid details. "You don't want to know."

He clasped her elbow, stopping her retreat. "Indeed I do, since according to them, you and I are suited to one another. It was not meant as a compliment."

"If you must know, I called them a couple of withered old busybodies. They said despicable things about you. I lost my temper. No wonder you avoid these people. And don't you dare get mad at me or I'll not speak to you again. Someone had to defend you."

With her words, the wall surrounding his emotions eased ever so slightly. She was so damned earnest. He warned himself to tread lightly, not to care overmuch. Nevertheless, her defense of him lanced his heart, a desire for

138

closeness he thought long-buried rising like the Phoenix from the fire. She was a treasure, to be sure, one he needed to protect himself against at all costs. He bent his head to kiss her forehead. "Likely a foolish thing to do. I'm not in need of your defense. I'm not even sure I'm deserving of such."

"Shame on you, Stephen Lambert, for even thinking such a thing. You're a kind, intelligent man."

"There's much you don't know about me, Phoebe."

"And whose fault is that?" She shifted her weight from leg to leg, waiting for any insight he might offer. He refused to say a word. She muttered, "I can see you have no intention of answering my questions. We had best return."

"I'd much rather kiss you." He moved forward. She stepped back. Stephen persisted until they lingered in the shadow of the tack room. "Why, Phoebe, m'dear? Are you afraid of me?"

"No. I just don't think this is a very good idea."

Slowly and seductively, he raked his gaze from one ivory shoulder to the other, over her breasts, down her torso, lower still and finally back up again. "I think you are afraid. Afraid of what might happen between us."

"Nonsense. I'd just rather go inside and discuss my matrimonial candidates. You are supposed to offer council and names."

His fingers toyed with the delicate gold necklace encircling her slender neck. "I'd rather make you mine."

Her nostrils flared and a gasp of air escaped her half-parted lips. "I'd rather you tell me about Lord Pennbright."

"The poor boy barely changes his trousers without his mother's approval. 'You marry him. You marry her.'" Stephen's hand drifted to the small cluster of pearls that rested between her breasts, his gaze focused on the shaded hollow. "Tell me, Phoebe, do you like my touch?"

139

Her shoulders rose and fell dramatically with each breath. "A true lady never enjoys a man's advances. What about Lord Hemsley?"

Stephen considered the St. Anne Orphanage near St. Giles, Hemsley's current philanthropic project. "He's a bloody bosky. Often drinks himself into oblivion and practically bleeds his money to make amends." Leaning forward, he traced the delicate curve of her ear with his tongue. "And you've been listening to Hildegard again. You didn't answer my question. Do you wonder what else lovers do?"

"I, um—" She cocked her head to the side, allowing him greater access. "Tell me about Lord Tewksbury."

Annoyance crept up Stephen's neck. There was little he could say against Tewksbury. In fact, he respected the man. Nibbling his way from her ear to her lips, he murmured, "He's as dull as ditch water. He'd never make you burn."

"What?"

Her skin flushed a lovely shade of pink and to his great pleasure her pulse pounded beneath his fingertips. "The hell with Tewksbury," he said as his mouth devoured hers. All conversation ceased as rational thought fled on the fluttering wings of sensation.

He'd set out to seduce her with words and had seduced himself. Touch was not simply desired but necessary to erase all other men from her mind. Passion ruled supreme.

When she molded herself to him, he whispered sounds of encouragement, nonsensible sighs that brushed her ear and teased his mind. He nibbled his way to her shoulder. His hand inched upward to cover her breast. Her nipple strained to greet his caress. With no consideration to time or place, hearing only her ragged breathing and whimpers of pleasure, he inched Phoebe's dress from her shoulders, feathering gentle, wispy kisses over her heated skin. Each alabaster inch he discovered aroused him more.

The silky fabric caught on the tips of her engorged breasts. When Stephen leaned back to witness the stunning vision, Phoebe opened her eyes and met his gaze with the same intensity that surely burned in his. She followed his eyes to the tops of her breasts and lifted her hand to cover herself. Stephen shook his head, his voice a mere thread and said, "Let me."

Phoebe wasn't sure if she spoke or not, wasn't sure if he asked or told. The sight of her breasts nearly bared for his perusal embarrassed yet inflamed her, weakening any and all of her defenses. She raised her hands to his shoulders as his hands slipped her dress to her waist. His fingers, slender and tanned, plucked her swollen nipple, shooting an arrow of heat to her very core. The caress of his hand sent a river of desire to Phoebe's belly and spiraled outward, skittering over her skin and down her limbs. She arched her back, not caring whether the action was wanton or not. Her body craved his touch.

Both his hands cupped her breasts. "You are so damned beautiful."

His praise, spoken in a husky whisper, thrilled her feminine pride. When his mouth covered one taut peak, she fell into a pit so deep, so powerful, she cried out. The sounds she made were foreign to her, but she couldn't stop them. Tension built and expanded. Restlessness tortured her body, all seemingly centered in the place between her thighs. She strained closer to Stephen, tugged his head upward. Wanton or not, driven by an unknown need, she had to kiss him, wanted his body pressed fully against hers.

His arousal strained against his trousers, and through the fabric of their clothes, he pressed against her very core, her soft cries of surprise melting to shock, then into a lusty groan. He continued the torturous rocking motion, driving them both to madness. He wanted her naked beneath him, every stitch of clothing piled on the floor. Such irrational thoughts

141

were not only dangerous, but impossible. That knowledge made his movements more desperate. He pressed his hardened length against her one last time, then ceased to move at all. Phoebe whimpered his name and clung to his shoulders, her head resting on his chest.

Seconds turned moments to minutes. The scent of passion filled the air. His body clamored for satisfaction. Likely Phoebe felt the same, although he doubted she understood the reasons why. The blasted female had no idea the extent of his restraint. He wasn't an untried youth incapable of controlling his baser urges, but surely this was the closest he'd ever come to taking a woman—a virgin, he reminded himself—in a barn at a social function of more than a hundred people. Damn his honor.

He wanted a bed and candles and satin sheets when he made love to her the first time. He wanted her full acquiescence. If he lived that long. An extended state of arousal couldn't be healthy for his well being or his throbbing cock. Lifting his head, he reluctantly pulled Phoebe's dress to its proper place. She kept her face hidden from his. Lord, his passion had probably scared her to death. Still he waited, prepared to explain the ways of men and women. Damned if he'd apologize though. Not when she'd moaned his name as she experienced the first stirrings of a woman's pleasure.

When she finally gained the courage to look at him, he nearly finished what he'd begun. Her eyes held no recrimination, no embarrassment or shame, only surprise and something akin to awe. Lord, how she humbled him.

She started to speak and he pressed his finger to her lips. If she spoke one word, uttered what he saw reflected in her eyes, he wouldn't be responsible for his actions. She needed the safety of people. A multitude of people. "Shhh, sweetheart. Say nothing." Allowing her no opportunity for rebuttal, he grasped her hand and led her from the barn in silence.

The stars shone brighter, the air smelled fresher, Phoebe's senses more alive than she'd ever thought possible. The breeze teased her skin, reminding her of Stephen's caresses and her uninhibited response stimulated by pure explosive pleasure.

She certainly had a better understanding of why some women did the things they did and she imagined there was more, so much more, to experience. Had Stephen not stopped, likely she would never have asked him to. The man, his touches, his kisses, obliterated reason.

When they reached the door to the conservatory and peered through it, she immediately sensed his withdrawal. She remembered her earlier conversation with those horrible women. No wonder he avoided his own kind, erecting walls around his emotions and private life. She knew enough to know one didn't change someone else's way of thinking overnight.

Like a small cotton bush, a seed had to be planted before new roots took hold.

Also, with a little nudge from her, maybe, just maybe, people might judge Stephen differently. Of course, a little cooperation on his part would be useful.

"You look like the barmaid trying to pull a pint from an empty keg," Stephen said. "What are you thinking?"

She knew he wouldn't discuss his status in society. She refused to discuss their little interlude in the barn, and she doubted he wanted to discuss her matrimonial choices. She lied. "I was thinking about Marsden Manor."

Kissing the knuckles of her fingers, he said, "If you wish, I can continue your lessons while we venture to the coast tomorrow."

She tilted her head to one side and pursed her lips. "I assume you refer to your offer to help me find a husband?"

He leaned close to her ear. "Think again, my dear."

A soft whisp of air teased the nape of her neck, making her tremble through her limbs to her fingertips. She cleared her throat, pretending not to be affected. She was thinking all right, but it certainly wasn't anything she cared to share at the moment. She had her owns plans for the trip to Marsden Manor.

Chapter Ten

Phoebe tugged the hood of her cape about her head in a futile attempt to keep the rain off her face, her eyes riveted on the massive stone structure looming before her. "My inheritance seems to be falling apart."

"Lord, child," Nanny Dee muttered as she stood beside the carriage. "You sure this is the place?"

"According to the vicar. This is Marsden Manor."

Gravel crunched beneath Stephen's feet as he joined the two women. He stood silent for a moment, then cleared his throat. "Phoebe, my dear, 'tis propitious this place is two days' ride from London. If a suitor managed to make it across those roads without losing his way, one look at this place and he would scuttle back to civilization with his betrothal ring tucked in his waistcoat pocket."

Regardless of the truth of the statement, Phoebe shot Stephen a quelling look. She certainly didn't need him to point out the shortcomings of her inheritance. They were as plain as day itself. Turning back to examine the build-

ing, she sighed. Marsden Manor was *not* what she had
expected.

Four ornate spires, one on each corner, rose to varied
heights above the three-storied mansion. Pointed arches set
with leaded glass lined the entire front of the manor along
with a score of gargoyles precariously balanced on crumbling stone ledges. Like battle-worn sentries who currently
spit water through their mouths, each seemed to be missing
an ear, a wing or some body part. She sighed again, this
time her shoulders falling with the deep breath. Marsden
Manor was an elaborate, poorly designed combination of a
French château and a house of horrors that was tumbling to
the ground, stone by gray stone. And it was all hers—or
soon would be. Once she married. Right now, at this very
moment, she wished her inheritance had been a small brick
cottage anyplace where dry weather prevailed.

Between Dee's constant scrutiny, Stephen's incessant
probing into the type of husband she wanted, Elizabeth's
sudden indigestion and Winston's worrying about Elizabeth, the two-day trip had been long and tedious. The poor
weather, the hour spent pulling their carriage from the
mud, coupled with the fact that they had gotten lost twice,
hadn't helped. They gained no comfort in the pitiful food
served at the inn last night either. Now, to arrive here and
discover this . . . well . . . a meal with Hildegard almost
became appealing. Hoping to hide her disappointment, she
said, "Perhaps the inside offers a different perspective."

Winston stopped beside Stephen with Elizabeth in his
arms. "Let us hope the roof repels water."

"Come on," Dee ordered. "We're all getting soaking
wet. We'd best go inside and see if'n it's any better."

Elizabeth struggled in Winston's arms. "For heaven's
sake, put me down. My stomach hurts, not my feet."

Stephen grasped Phoebe's elbow, following Winston
and Elizabeth up the steps as they pecked at one another

like two guinea hens. The massive double doors were patched with odd pieces of wood and the brass gargoyle knocker was missing its right hand. When no one responded to his pounding, Stephen turned the knob and crossed the threshold.

The sinking feeling in the pit of Phoebe's stomach plummeted all the way to her knees. The inside wasn't a sight better than the outside. Cracks in the plaster stretched across the bare walls like veins in an aging hand. A worn Aubusson rug covered the wooden floor while a rickety-looking bannister, missing a quarter of its rungs, led upstairs. The house needed a good cleaning, better lighting, new furnishings, and then some. All of which required money. Something she lacked.

Quicker than hell could scorch a feather, the formidable task of finding a suitable husband willing to keep her inheritance had become almost insurmountable. That is, if she couldn't convince Stephen to marry her.

Stephen rubbed a finger through the dust on a small table in the entryway. "You did say you sent word of your visit?"

"Yes." Her voice quivered slightly. "I wrote as soon as I received a note from my solicitor and gave our tentative date of arrival."

"Perhaps they never received the missive," Elizabeth interjected. She pressed her hand over her mouth. "Oh, dear, I think I'm going to be sick again."

Winston bolted toward the stairs, calling over his shoulder. "I'm going to try to find my wife a chamber pot and put her to bed."

"Well, this ain't how things are going to be while I'm here," Dee pronounced as she set down her bag. She drew her damp cape from her shoulders, tossing it over the arm of a wooden chair which, due to a missing leg, was balanced on a brick. "I'm going to find the kitchen and make us all a pot of tea and try to find somethin' to settle that poor girl's stomach." Dee turned to Stephen. "And don't you, Mr. Duke, be getting any ideas. I won't be far." She muttered this and that as she wandered toward the end of the long, dim hallway.

Phoebe watched Stephen scowl as he watched Dee disappear from sight. She ignored the desire to soothe his ducal sensibilities over her servant's brusque approach. She had enough to worry about. Freeing her head from her hood, she fought the urge to bury her face in her hands. Tears would accomplish nothing. "I don't understand any of this. However could this happen? Whoever would have allowed it to happen?"

"We'll solve that puzzle in short order." He moved close enough to tug on a lock of hair curling about her face. "Best to think of something else right now. You seem to be rather wet. Again." Using the knuckle of his finger, he tipped her chin. "All last night while I tried to sleep, I kept remembering a mere wall separated us."

The specks of gold in his dark eyes blazed with possibility. He obviously wasn't above coercion. She wanted nothing more than to curl into his arms and accept the solace and anything else he offered. Before temptation overwhelmed her good sense, she forced herself to step back and hang her cape on the lone peg of an oak coatrack, noting the trembling of her hand. "We had best find someplace other than this drafty hallway, else Dee will be wondering what we've being doing all this time."

"Dare we venture further? Dee might never find us." He waggled his eyebrows. "Then again, that idea has definite possibilities."

"Not likely. Nanny Dee is very resourceful."

"Trust me, darling. I do not underestimate your companion. It's evident she takes her job as chaperone quite seriously." His expression grew fierce, his forehead furrowed

148

with wrinkles and his chin lifted a notch. "She has no regard for my title or my preferences. Something to which I must say I'm not accustomed. What good is a dukedom if it earns you no respect? For two days, other than an occasional 'Mr. Duke,' she's done nothing but glare through me as though she's reading my very thoughts. Last night, before bed, she muttered strange words at my back. I thought I'd surely wake missing a toe or another essential part of my anatomy."

"That's absurd. She always mutters."

"Easy for you to say. She likes you."

The twinkle in his eyes caught her attention. The fox was teasing her. She finally laughed. "You're trying to distract me."

Grinning, the humor no longer concealed beneath an austere expression, he shrugged one shoulder. He crossed to the bannister, eyed it suspiciously, then placed his sodden garments on the post. "You had that wounded look in your eyes once again. It disturbs me. I promise, Phoebe, I will get to the bottom of this."

"Thank you. You know, Dee actually likes you."

"God forbid I should ever become her enemy. Come along." Grasping her hand, his thumb encircling her palm, he followed in Dee's path.

They passed an arched doorway and peered inside to find a dusty mahogany table large enough to accommodate at least thirty people. Only four chairs surrounded it. After three additional rooms, all noticeably devoid of furniture, they found what they considered a haven: the library. Books lined the shelves and the room boasted three chairs, a chaise and a game table. A small desk stood in the corner. A massive hearth with a marble mantel occupied most of the opposite wall. Within minutes, two lamps glowed, a fire crackled and Phoebe and Stephen sipped what Phoebe considered a rather nice brandy. Stephen fiddled with the fire while Phoebe browsed through the papers littering the desk. Nothing gave any indication to the why or wherefore of the estate's dismal condition.

Stephen brushed the dust from his knees and fingered the pages of a book left on the floor. "Do you expect your husband to be a literary man?"

Growing accustomed to his game of question and answer, which usually served his own purpose in some way, Phoebe answered without thought. She was also learning a great deal about Stephen. "It would please me if he read, yes."

"Hmmm. Many men prefer dim-witted, uneducated women, wives whose sole aim in life is to please their husbands, in *all* ways, Phoebe—ways that have nothing to do with reading, embroidery or the running of a household. Would you like to know some of the manners in which a man expects to be indulged?"

His voice had dropped to a provocative whisper, purposely slow and silky, laced with the promise of unspoken things she had yet to experience, she was sure. "I believe, sir, this topic is not at all appropriate."

"But a woman such as yourself might benefit from knowing her husband's expectations," said Stephen. He knew Phoebe's passion firsthand. He hoped she was curious as well. She needed to realize the fire that lay between them, not yet fully explored, was missing in most relationships.

Her mind needed to know what her body already recognized. She wanted him. He felt it in her response every time he took her into his arms, the manner in which her eyes turned a darker shade of green when she sensed his arousal, every time she pressed herself closer to absorb his heat. Damn if he'd share that with another man. He fixed his eyes on the book, which rested on his leg as he knelt by the fireplace.

"Based on some silly notion that a true lady dislikes passion, some men prefer a quick tumble while practically fully clothed in the dark, their only purpose to gain an heir. Likely they have a mistress to satisfy their other needs." He paused for effect. "But some men believe pleasure essential to lovemaking, whether married or with a mistress."

"Like yourself, I imagine."

"Absolutely. I believe immensely in giving pleasure as well as receiving. I like a room shadowed but not dark—so touch can be seen as well as felt and sighs can be observed as well as heard." He noted the rosy color creeping up her neck and the tension in her hands as she gripped the stem of her glass. Her eyes flashed with an awakened awareness he knew he had taught her. His hands slid over the soft leather of the book, stroking the binding from end to end, and damn if his little game wasn't affecting him as well.

However uncomfortable, he was compelled to continue. Crossing to her side, he turned her palm upside down and lightly traced the length of each of her fingers. "Did you know there are books that describe, in great detail, the methods for men and women to pleasure one another? Where to touch? How to touch?" Lifting her hand to his lips, he scraped his teeth across the soft pad of flesh near her thumb.

"Really?" Phoebe's voice came out as a squeak, no small wonder considering the provocative images that leaped into her mind. They were a vivid combination of her own imagination, her newly awakened desire, her precious encounters with Stephen, and they were not at all appropriate. But she could not stop them. Judging from the jaunty tilt of his mustache, he knew exactly how this conversation was affecting her. The scamp.

Well, she wasn't above such manipulations herself. Two could play at this game. She pulled her hand from his, balling it into a tight fist to stop the disturbing sensations.

"May a wife demand pleasure? I mean, it seems only fair. If her husband neglects his duty to her then she should be free to tell him what she needs, *where* she likes to be touched, *how* she wants to be touched."

"Such women are rare indeed," Stephen said, his voice heavy and a touch ragged.

"Then she would be all the more appreciated by her husband."

When she referred to a husband once again, he dragged his fingers across his mustache. "Or her protector."

Before he could utter his next thought, a short, round man as old as dirt, dressed in brown woolen breeches and a long, dark coat, wobbled into the room. A large oilskin hat covered his head, water dripping from its brim. He'd obviously been outdoors. A black patch covered one eye.

He gazed nervously from Phoebe to Stephen to the corners of the room, as if searching for someone or something. Wheezing, he said, "Pardon me, but might you be the American?"

Before she nodded, Phoebe looked over her shoulder, half-expecting someone to be there. "Yes. I'm Miss Rafferty. You must be Mr. Hampson."

"Wibolt, miss." He wheezed again then glanced nervously toward Stephen. "We wasn't expecting you today, nor did we expect company with you."

"Let me introduce my acquaintance, the Duke of Badrick."

Stephen stood, his ducal air sliding on like a second skin. "Remove your hat, for heaven's sake. Miss Rafferty also brought a companion and two friends. Is that a problem?"

Wibolt's face turned a deeper shade of red. He removed his hat to reveal grey bushy eyebrows and a wild cap of matching curls. With his grip tight about his hat, he shuffled his feet from side to side. In between puffs of air, he said, "No, sir. I'll have the other rooms prepared."

"While you're at it, see to bathwater and rouse a cook." Stephen leaned forward, his hand outstretched. "Are you all right?"

In between a hacking cough and another raspy bit of breathing, Wibolt managed to say, "I was running, you see. 'Twill be fine shortly, your grace, but I thank you for asking."

Stephen didn't look convinced. In fact, Phoebe thought he was preparing himself to catch Wibolt should he collapse. Beneath Stephen's contrary facade lay a kind man. She said, "My chaperone is in the kitchen as we speak. I think we shall eat here since this seems to be the one room with suitable furnishings."

"That'll be fine, miss. I can have Mary Potter come over to help, but . . ." He swayed to the side. "Well," he wheezed, a hollow hissing sound. "It's only . . ."

Stephen clasped the man by his elbow and lowered him into the nearby chair. "Spit it out, man."

"Hampson will be needing funds for pay and likely Mrs. Potter won't stay the night due . . ." Wibolt glanced between the doorway and Phoebe several times.

"Due to?" she prompted, hoping he'd manage to finish his sentence before he fainted.

"Due to the ghost," he whispered.

Phoebe gasped, the brandy stinging her throat, which ignited a fit of coughing. She managed to sputter, "Ghost?"

"Aye, milady." The poor man glanced to the doorway one last time, then to the tops of his sodden boots. He appeared as though he might tie his hat in knots while trying to decide something of great importance. He squeezed a deep breath of air into his lungs, looked up and blurted out, "Lord Marsden, your grandfather. We can't keep decent help. Augustus scares them all away."

"Oh, for the love of Mary," Stephen snapped. "You don't expect us to believe that pile of rubbish, do you?"

"Sir, it's the truth. If you stay here long enough, you'll see what I mean."

"Enough. We'll discuss Miss Rafferty's ancestor another time."

Phoebe finally managed to find her voice. "Are you telling me there is *no* money in the estate account?"

"Well, miss—" Wibolt cleared his throat, then muttered, "Thank heavens."

Phoebe followed Wibolt's gaze to the doorway, afraid of what she'd see, and then she couldn't believe her eyes. If Wibolt seemed as old as dirt, then the man who'd just arrived was older still. Above the starched collar, wrinkles climbed up his neck to the top of his bald head. Although his shoulders stooped a bit, his upright posture exhibited years of service. His eyes seemed kind, alert and intelligent, assessing the situation quickly and thoroughly. He sent a searching look to Wibolt, who shook his head. This had to be Hampson.

"In truth, your Lordship, Marsden Manor is extremely low on funds at the moment," the newcomer announced.

Leaning his hip on the edge of the desk, Stephen surveyed the newcomer. "Hampson, I presume?"

"At your service, sir." He nodded to Phoebe. "Welcome to Marsden Manor, Miss Rafferty."

Speechless once again, she only nodded.

Wibolt pulled a handkerchief from his pocket and dabbed at his brow. He inhaled deeply while his left eye twitched. The man looked about to faint.

Stephen held up his hand. "Do not start wheezing again, Wibolt. In fact, you can see to our rooms. Lady Payley is a bit under the weather. She and her husband are upstairs somewhere. Please see them settled. Hampson, go to the kitchen and bring Miss Rafferty's companion here. We shall decide the sleeping arrangements for the night."

"Aye, yer lordship." Hampson pivoted to leave. Wibolt, looking thoroughly relieved, quickly hobbled behind.

Phoebe rose from her chair and moved to the front of the desk, taking a spot beside Stephen. Curiosity was gnawing away at her patience. "Wait a moment. Hampson, whatever happened here?"

"I'll handle this." Stephen moved toward the servant. "We will explore the deplorable affairs of this estate in great detail and decide what has to be done, but tomorrow will be soon enough."

"Excuse me," Phoebe interjected.

"Hold a moment, Phoebe. Miss Rafferty will want to review all the ledgers first. I'd say you have a great deal to explain. For now, hire whatever help you need. I personally guarantee any wages."

With his dismissal, Hampson looked one last time at Phoebe with such hope, such trust, that she wondered if she'd imagined it. Massaging the drumming in her head, she turned on Stephen and advanced like a rabid dog. She tapped his shirtfront with her finger. "If you've a mind to take my life over, you might ask first. I happened to be standing right here in this same little old room, or were you so busy running my affairs you simply forgot I existed? What right do you have to hire more staff? And what about Wibolt and Hampson? Aren't you a tad bit curious about my servants? And what if there *is* a ghost—not that I believe my grandfather's eavesdropping or such, but obviously something peculiar is going on. I might have had a question or two."

Pressing on the bridge of his nose, he paced before the fire, then stopped and placed one hand in his pocket, the other on the mantle. "Is there any particular order in which you wish me to address your questions?"

"It's late. I'm tired, wet, just a little bit disappointed and fresh out of patience. If you didn't happen to notice, Marsden Manor is my very own personal setting for a Shakespearean comedy of errors. I already have my ghost. All I need are three witches and a fairy or two."

"Calm down. You're becoming hysterical."

"Hysterical?" She finally allowed herself the laughter that had threatened for the last half-hour. "Perhaps I am, and if I am, it's my choice, and given the circumstances, I feel mighty justified. I don't appreciate your high-handedness right now."

"Pardon me. I have no designs on managing your life for you, although I'd likely do a damn good job. I thought you might like a bit of time to think things through. Your house is tumbling down about your ears. You seem to be broke. Your staff is horrifically old, possibly incompetent, complete dolts or liars and thieves. I haven't decided which."

She drummed her fingers on the desk. "I realize something is amiss."

"Amiss? Hah! As to the wanderings of your dear departed relative, we'll deal with that issue if and when he arises. As to the staff, I desire a decent meal and a decent bed. I do not mind paying for them."

"I don't have extra funds to be hiring people right now. I can cook, as can Nanny Dee, and I've certainly made my share of beds."

Bracing his feet apart, he placed his hands on his hips. "You won't act as my servant. Do you understand?"

"And I won't have you paying my bills."

"Consider it a gift."

"Making me indebted to you. Hah. Mistresses accept gifts."

"Phoebe, you're beginning to upset me."

156

She crossed her arms over her chest. "And I imagine—"

Nanny Dee sailed into the room, effectively bringing an end to the dispute. A tantalizing aroma filled the library as she set a tray laden with warm tea and bread on the lone table. "There is something mighty strange going on in this household. I met this man too old to be breathing who told me I could leave the kitchen right this minute. I gave him a piece of my mind and I reckon he won't be bothering me no more. I thought he might fall over then and there. He was as nervous as a long-tailed cat in a room full of rockin' chairs. I don't trust that man. Not one little bit." She propelled onward, allowing no one a word. "Now, Miss Phoebe and I are going to see about our sleeping quarters. I hear they have a nice room in the west wing suitable for yer lordship. We'll be takin' a suite in the east side."

"That is, if you think we mere women can find our way there?" Phoebe sarcastically added.

Stephen practically growled. He plastered a bland look on his face. "Be my guest. Since you *women*," he emphasized the word, "seem to have things under control, I shall take my feeble man's mind in search of Winston and Elizabeth."

Chapter Eleven

Stephen silently maneuvered down the back servant's stairs leading in the general direction of the kitchen. The single tallow candle, which produced a faint sheeplike odor, tormented his nostrils. After what some might call dinner served in the library, he had lain awake thinking about Phoebe and her inheritance, staff included, when he heard the soft fall of footsteps outside his door. He swore he'd smelled pipe tobacco as well. He knew Winston was tucked in bed with Elizabeth, so he had immediately followed.

Reaching the lower floor, he peered around the doorway, looking in both directions. Nothing stirred. As he listened for any noise, he thought again of Phoebe and her newest predicament. Marsden Manor was a disaster, the amount of money required to restore the place astronomical, not to mention the odd collection of servants.

Regardless of his need for a title, a man would have to be a supremely self-sacrificing fool to invest funds in this mausoleum. With no additional financial support and a coastline of cliffs unsuitable for use by most sailors, Marsden Manor had little future, which made Phoebe's task to find a husband near impossible. His proposal made even greater sense now than it did before.

Odd, but he found no joy in her current state of affairs. He knew, as surely as he knew himself, that regardless of all his warnings, she still hoped he would marry her. Not a chance. He'd already killed two wives. He refused to add Phoebe to the list.

The image of his first wife came to mind. Emily had been so damn trusting, so easy to please. She had wanted a balcony added to the original structure of Badrick Manor, joining her room to his. She'd asked for so little, he'd gladly seen to the arrangements. The balcony had become her favorite place to sit, to read and enjoy the morning sun. If only he had known.

Both Emily and his child had died while he sat in the comfort of his study, sipping a brandy and reading the bloody newspaper. They'd fallen to their deaths while he'd pondered the coming races at Ascot. His first marriage and its abrupt conclusion seemed a lifetime ago, yet to this day, the pain struck like a dagger to his heart. He clenched his fist around the candle. Lord, why couldn't his past stay buried?

A door creaked and a dim light glowed down the hall near what he'd learned from earlier explorations was the old music room. The flame of his candle flickered. A cold rush of air brushed his body. He barely contained his excitement. The culprit sneaking about would soon be caught dead to rights. He crept forward using every bit of stealth he could muster and peered inside. Hard to believe, but the room was empty.

"Damn," Stephen muttered. Cursing a second time because it improved his mood, he froze when he heard the light fall of footsteps. Didn't anyone in this bloody household sleep? He sneaked over to the arched doorway.

An apparition, cloaked in white and suspiciously familiar, tiptoed toward him. Much to Stephen's surprise, when the ghostly figure whacked her toe on a loose floorboard, she swore like a sailor on shore leave.

Within two long strides, he gripped her wrist and whirled her about. Before she could scream, waking everyone else, he covered her mouth with his hand. "Are you out of your mind? What the devil do you think you're doing?"

Phoebe twisted her head to the side and whispered furiously, "Me? You scared the very wits out of me."

"Answer my question."

"I couldn't sleep and then I heard someone downstairs."

"So you decided to investigate?" When she nodded, he dragged his hand through his hair, ordering himself not to yell. He certainly didn't need anyone else lurking in the hallways. The woman was like a willful child, always going where she wanted, when she wanted, with little thought to the consequences. "That was bloody stupid."

"What about you?"

"I'm a man. I'm supposed to seek out adversaries, protect the woman, the home and all that."

"Nonsense." When all the muscles on his face tensed, she planted her hands on her hips. "Well, o great defender of hearth, whatever did you find?"

"The person sneaking around waltzed into the music room and disappeared. Hardly normal comings and goings."

Her eyes rounded and she looked from side to side like someone trapped in a cemetery long after dark. "No need to fret, Phoebe. I do not believe your ancestor dropped by for a nightcap. Ghosts tend to walk through obstacles. Our intruder used a door. He must have slipped by me."

"However did you let that happen?"

He started to answer, then decided to keep his churlish remark to himself. Given his current mood, he'd likely end with a blistering lecture on common sense, which she'd likely resent. Turning on his heels, her hand in his, he headed back down the hall. "Where is Dee? And don't tell me she allowed you to sneak down here unaccompanied."

"She never heard me. Once she's asleep, a barnyard full of roosters couldn't wake her before sunrise."

That little tidbit certainly garnered the full attention of both his mind and body. Stopping dead in his tracks, he allowed his eyes to travel down Phoebe's silk-clad body and back up again. Tiny pearl buttons ran the length of the robe all the way to her neck, where she'd forgotten to fasten the uppermost three. A touch of delicate pink lace peeked above the collar. Her hair fell in auburn waves down her back. He lowered his voice to a purr. "That's not exactly the wisest thing to tell a man bent on seduction."

She swallowed quickly, yanked the robe tight about her neck and thrust her pert little nose high in the air. "I assure you, Lord Badrick, I'll be seduced if and when I decide I want to be seduced. In all likelihood, that won't happen *until* my wedding night."

Stephen merely grunted. He tightened his grip about her hand, pulling her with him, unwilling to enter into a discussion on matrimony at this hour of the night.

"Wherever are we going?"

"The music room. There has to be something I missed."

"Like Grandfather Augustus."

"Doubtful."

A damp chill had settled over the house like a shroud as the rain continued to pour. Whispers of cold air from the cracks in the windowpanes danced about hall, reminding Stephen he wore only a thin shirt hastily tucked into his breeches. Phoebe wasn't wearing much more than he did. Here they were, alone, without the benefit of a chaperone, barely dressed, in the middle of night, and he was leading her down a dark drafty hallway. He was going mad. "Did that cook say anything of use?"

"No," she answered regretfully.

"No worries. You'll have time tomorrow to ask Hampson your questions. Here we are."

The music room occupied the back corner of the first floor. The light from Stephen's candle brought shadows to life on walls in dire need of painting. A harp occupied one corner, and a small decanter and several glasses sat on a table, one lone chair nestled beside it.

Phoebe plucked her hand from Stephen's, stood on her tiptoes, and peered around his shoulder into the darkness. "Shouldn't we wait until morning? Lots of sunlight and all."

He felt her breasts against his back through the fabric of his shirt. Blast it all, he wasn't a bloody saint. How was a man supposed to uphold the best of his intentions with her body parts pressing against him? Delightful body parts. He pivoted about, prepared to offer her fair warning. Placing one hand behind her neck, he held her captive. "I'm fairly awake now. I probably couldn't sleep if I tried. If you wish, we could revisit our discussion from earlier today. I'd even be willing to demonstrate a technique or two. Shall we return to the safety of the library and—"

He sensed the fires within her begin to heat. Her eyes rounded and her nostrils flared. "Ah, hell," he muttered, then dropped his lips to hers, speaking more eloquently than with words. Her breath hitched and her pulse raced beneath his fingers. That was all the invitation he needed. Without further thought, he molded his body to hers, his hands plumping the soft globes of her buttocks. Thigh to thigh with his chest glued to her breasts, he slid his tongue into her mouth. This was not a timid kiss, but one of fire and heat, expectation and promise. He removed his mouth from hers to nibble on the mole behind her left ear that drove him to distraction every time she wore her tidy braid.

She managed to speak between her reedy gasps of delight. "I don't think this is a very good idea. I mean, we might not be alone." Circling to the front of him, she pressed her backside against his front and said, "The least you could have done was bring a bigger light."

He managed a groan before, out of self-preservation, he wandered to the nearby wall. She followed him like the sweet scent of perfume. Occasional warm wisps of air fanned the sensitive spot behind his left ear. Ignoring the impulse to drag her into his arms, which would surely lead to other improper impulses, ones he was trying very hard to resist, he traced the space above the wooden molding.

"Whatever are we looking for?" she asked.

"I'm not sure. If someone came into this room, they had to have left by another exit."

"Like a hidden passage? How exciting."

Slowly circling the room, he thoroughly inspected each wall panel, periodically tapping the wood. From time to time, Phoebe imitated his actions, but mostly she hovered at his heels, leaving little space between them, chattering at a rapid pace.

"Did you know Wibolt's been at Marsden Manor for three years?" she said. "Hampson has been here forever. Anyway, Wibolt claims to know nothing about the finances, only that money was scarce. He mentioned other people and some nasty woman who used to come and go. I never quite understood that part. He began to fret something awful when I asked questions about Hampson or Grandfather, whom he claims he actually saw."

"Phoebe," Stephen said on a sigh. "You're talking about an old man you just met who might be responsible for this very mess. You're also rambling."

"It helps me think of something other than what I am

currently doing, which right now is somewhat unappealing. I'm not in the habit of seeking ghosts in the middle of the night." She paused. "Anyway, one evening, on his way to the kitchen, on the lower floor of the south wing, Wibolt saw Augustus carrying a box while he smoked a pipe and whistled. He disappeared directly into the wall of family portraits in the west wing. Do you think that passages connect various parts of the manor?"

"Possibly." He tapped a panel one last time. Nothing seemed out of the ordinary, but bother, *someone* had come into this room. And he didn't believe in ghosts. At least not the kind that rose from the dead. He rubbed his fingers back and forth across his mustache. "Well, raise a bloody breeze."

Phoebe crossed to the window seat, balanced on her knees and peered into the night. "Whyever would someone be up and about on a night like this, anyway?"

"Hmmm." Stephen pondered the same question. He lit another candle, found a single crystal decanter on a small table, removed the brass stopper, then sniffed and smiled delightedly. " 'Tis something we shall discover sooner or later."

Lightning ripped across the sky. The sight of Phoebe's nightclothes pulled taut over her derriere brightened Stephen's mood faster than the anticipated brandy. After filling two glasses, he joined her on the window cushion. Another white light flashed outside, causing Phoebe's skin to practically glow.

The cream silk nightgown and robe clung to her body, accentuating the curves Stephen had already imagined and memorized. Her red hair fell in waves down her back. She was temptation in its purest form. It was easy to imagine her naked beneath him, the rain pounding on the windows as he offered her his body heat. He would remove her clothes bit by bit, starting with the tiny pearl buttons, then ease his way to the shoulder nearest him. Using his mouth, he'd work his way toward her breast. He watched her tongue lick a drop of brandy from the corner of her mouth. Lord, he wanted to devour her.

Her eyes, softened by the alcohol and the late hour, gleamed with something akin to adoration. It was the kind of look that assaulted a man's heart, willing him to believe all things were possible. Even escaping gypsy curses and tortured pasts. Damn and blast, he thought, shaking his head, what was he thinking? She was beginning to plant impossible dreams in his head, and it frightened him to his very core. He shifted to the edge of his seat and crossed his arms and legs. "Don't look at me like that."

"I beg your pardon?" Phoebe asked. She was startled by the brusque tone of Stephen's voice.

"You heard me. Wielding that come-hither expression that incites men to ponder impossible things, turning them into blithering idiots. Only my frustration, which is your fault, makes me susceptible. If you were any other woman, you would be flat on your back right now, regardless of the consequences."

Phoebe watched Stephen move across the room with the animal grace she had come to appreciate. His movements were more agitated than normal, stemming from an inner restlessness she didn't comprehend. "It seems I arrived at the play after intermission."

He uttered a terse response from the doorway, his face concealed by shadow. "Do you intend to carry on with your preposterous plan?"

Trying to determine the reason for his mood shift, she answered slowly, cautiously. "I have no choice."

"Give over. The task you now face is impossible."

Phoebe recognized the truth. She'd thought of nothing less since she arrived here, since she'd finished a meager meal of potatoes and what she thought was ham cooked by

Mrs. Potter, who flinched whenever a noise echoed elsewhere in the house; a meal served on chipped earthenware plates by Wibolt, who had worn a tattered livery. Marsden Manor was a hangman's noose about her neck. She kept her voice cheerful, almost flirtatious. "To which task do you refer, sir? It seems I have many these days."

"You have three weeks left to find a husband. Add this monstrosity of a home and your chances of making a match that won't make your life a living hell are slim."

"Granted, my task is more difficult."

"Humph," he snorted sarcastically. "Exactly what manner of man do you think to marry? Will you lie to him?"

All pretenses evaporated. She leapt from the window seat, her night robe whipping behind her as she advanced on Stephen. "How dare you? I intend to be frankly honest. If he wants his title, he'll have it. If he wishes to never set one foot here, fine and dandy. Don't you think I understand my circumstance? Do you think me a feather-headed pea brain with no scruples? I assure you, I am made of sterner stuff. I've worked before and I'll do so again if I have to, but I'm bound and determined to keep Marsden Manor even if I use one room at a time. Lands alive, it's not as if I need forty-eight rooms."

She shoved her hands into her pockets before she could do something stupid. Violence would accomplish nothing. She stomped from the music room, took four steps and exhaled, trying to purge her mounting frustration and anger. She whirled about. "I told myself I would not have another outburst like the one earlier today. Can't you even see the possibilities here?"

Joining her in the hallway, he said, "To be perfectly frank, no."

"That's because you're a man. You dream with logic and your pocketbook. Women dream with their hearts."

"It's a damn good thing we do, else the world would be

in financial ruin. At least tell me why? You never saw this place before today."

If she convinced him of the importance of this place, he might at least understand her determination. She walked a bit, knowing he followed her. Three beautifully carved panels lined the hallway. She stopped beside one, allowing her fingers to drift along the dusty curves of the lifelike fruits and flowers draped with flowing ribbons. "Lordy, I know there's a lot to be done, but my mother was born and raised here. She loved the sea, the hills. She kept a miniature painting on the dresser in her bedroom. When I was young, I'd sneak into her room and imagine myself living here. It seemed like a fairy castle, a safe haven, the perfect place for a princess to live and wait for her prince to come."

"Don't expect a prince to come unless he has two thousand pounds and a hearty appetite for discomfort, disorganization and bad food. Besides, I hardly expect you'll find a prince amongst the candidates sniffing after you and your title like mangy curs."

"Oh, *you* . . ." she bit back a scream. "It must be a blessed thing to be a man and rule the world. To have so much money you can do whatever suits your fancy and never worry if you'll have enough to pay your bills, whether or not you'll arrive home to find your property sold from underneath you. Believe you me, Marsden Manor will be mine. No one will take it from me except myself. *My* actions will determine the consequences."

An unearthly shriek pierced the darkness. Any thoughts regarding Stephen's stubborn behavior evaporated with the eerie silence that followed. Phoebe slapped her hand to her chest. "Dear heavens. What was that?"

"Stay behind me," Stephen ordered. "No matter what.

He didn't need to ask twice. He whisked her behind him, locking her hand in his as they ran down the hall. Stopping beside the wood bannister, they froze, listening, their rapid breathing the only sound. Another shrill cry echoed off the bare walls.

"The cook," Stephen cried. Evidently, the earlier activities were only the prelude to tonight's events. Splendid. He might never sleep. By the time they reached the cook's quarters, an eerie silence lingered. Stephen frowned. The door, slightly ajar, opened easily. Mrs. Potter lay in a crumpled heap at the foot of her bed, her face ash-gray. A broom lay at her feet.

Phoebe's nails pinched his hand as her grip tightened. "Do you think she's dead?"

Moving quickly, Stephen pried his hand loose and placed two fingers beneath Mrs. Potter's nose. "She's fainted."

"Whatever happened?"

"We shall have to wait for her to wake," he said as he lifted the cook to the bed. "See if you can find another candle. I don't suppose you have smelling salts, do you?"

Giving him an expression that clearly said she found the question insulting, Phoebe found a rag and a small bowl of water on the nightstand.

"Sweet Delilah, what was that?" Dee cried as she sailed into the room, Hampson right behind.

"The cook screamed," answered Stephen.

Dashing into the room hand-in-hand next were Elizabeth and Winston. They might have served tea for all the blasted commotion. "For the love of Mary, who was murdered?" Winston asked.

"No one. Cook fainted," added Phoebe. "Like you, we heard the scream all the way in the library, came running and found Mrs. Potter in a dead faint."

"Oh, dear," murmured Hampson, his face rigid.

"Here, give me that," said Dee, grabbing the rag from

Phoebe and crossing to the felled cook. While dabbing the woman's brow, she shot Stephen a questioning glare. "You wanna tell me exactly why you two was up and about in the middle of the night?"

Stephen decided this was the perfect time to exert ducal authority. "Not particularly."

"Do you want to tell me?" Elizabeth asked as she studied Stephen and Phoebe's faces for any signs of mischief.

"No," Stephen snapped.

Evidently realizing there was no immediate threat to the household, Winston leaned against the bedpost, a grin tugging at his lips. "Would you like to tell—"

"Oh, good grief," Phoebe mumbled, right after she stepped on Stephen's toe with the heel of her foot before he could say something rude. "We heard noises and were investigating. That's all."

"It seems Wibolt is the only one missing from this little party," Winston said, knowing Stephen likely wondered the same thing. "Where do you suppose he might be?"

"I believe he is still abed," answered Hampson, standing a good inch taller while shoving his hands deep into the pockets of his flannel robe.

Mrs. Potter sputtered, gasped twice and snapped awake. Obviously still panic-stricken and dazed, she reached for the handle of the broom. "Is . . . he . . . gone?"

Stephen patted her hand, reassuring her all the while. "Who?"

"His lordship." She raised a finger toward the corner. "Standing there at the foot of me bed, big as life. Scared me near to death, he did. I'll never be able to cook a decent meal again."

Stephen refrained from mentioning that Mrs. Potter didn't seem to know how to cook as it was, but felt that now was probably not the best time to criticize her culinary abilities. She was still shaking like a banner in the breeze. "I assure you, Lord Marsden made no appearance tonight. You had a dreadful dream, that's all."

"Hah. I told Mr. Hampson I'd cook, but I won't be spending me nights here no longer."

"Shhh," Stephen cooed. "Certainly an intelligent woman like yourself knows better than to believe in ghosts. In either case, you can share Miss Rafferty's room for the rest of the night." He looked to Phoebe, who nodded. Shifting to the foot of the bed, Stephen addressed the group. "It's settled. Elizabeth, please help Mrs. Potter gather her belongings while Winston and I check a few things. Go along, Phoebe. We'll muddle through this mess tomorrow."

Judging from the looks Dee exchanged with Stephen, Phoebe wished she'd left the room five minutes earlier. She needed no lecture, no warning, no interrogation. Not from anyone. Not tonight. Stephen had provided enough for her to think on.

"Come on, child. Back to bed," said Dee.

Without an ounce of energy to argue, Phoebe simply turned on her heel, heading for the stairs. Phoebe swore she could hear Dee's mind silently spinning with questions. "Speak your peace. Otherwise, you'll toss and turn all night, which will only keep me awake." Phoebe glanced over her shoulder. "But before you do, I'll tell you this. Nothing happened. At least not what you suspect."

Dee matched Phoebe's steps, taking the stairs briskly. She clasped Phoebe's hand and squeezed. "I know that, Sweet Pea. I'm just testing the man's mettle."

Phoebe chuckled over that revelation, which didn't surprise her one little bit. Yawning, she removed her robe, climbed onto the lumpy straw mattress, pounded a spot here and there, finally gave up and lay down.

Humming, Dee pulled the cover all the way to Phoebe's chin. "Why so glum?"

"Dee, I'm trying, truly I am, but it's difficult to even find the rainbow this time, let alone the pot of gold. However will I find a decent man to marry me with this place as my inheritance?"

Dee stroked Phoebe's curls from her forehead as she had done so many times before. "Don't count yourself out, Miss Phoebe. Miracles, big and small, happen everyday. Go to sleep, child. Things will look brighter in the light of day."

Chapter Twelve

When Phoebe awoke the next morning, all the light of day showed was more dirt, more cracks and the overall dilapidation of Marsden Manor, which was considerable. Hampson and Wibolt were still too old to do serious work and a pot of gold had not magically appeared from the end of a rainbow. Stephen's words—the truth, but annoying all the same—replayed again and again in her mind. What was she going to do? How would she ever find a man to marry her with Marsden Manor as the lure?

Restless and seeking answers, she skipped breakfast to wander the halls of the manor, every torn curtain, each bare room a greater source of confusion. Finally she faced her ancestors, their paintings a contradictory mix of either forbidding, imposing people or affable souls that she knew so little of. The portraits depicting her mother's easy laughter and her grandfather's kind eyes only increased her melancholy.

"Your mother was a lovely young woman."

Spinning about, Phoebe spied Hampson standing at the end of the hallway, a somber expression on his face. His livery, cleaned and perfectly pressed, was worn at the elbows and the knees. She simply couldn't imagine him masterminding a plan to rob her of her inheritance. She glanced at the painting again. Her mother sat on a stone balcony, the deep blue ocean and endless horizon her only backdrop. "How old was she?"

"Eighteen. The portrait was commissioned only two months before she sailed with your father. She was so happy. Your grandfather stored the picture in the attic for years. When she died, he returned it to its rightful place as a constant reminder of his foolish pride. He often stood here as you are and stared at the painting. He never forgave himself."

"She died when I was only six. I remember certain things she told me, but I wish I knew more about her life, her childhood. Daddy never spoke of it. He said it hurt too much."

"If you will allow me, miss, I think I can help."

Curious, she followed Hampson as he proceeded down the long hallway. Stopping now and again, he generously offered her a window into her heritage, something she'd never truly had before. She learned that her great-grandfather, a gentleman pirate for part of his life, commissioned Marsden Manor because of his love for the sea. He'd actually kidnapped her great-grandmother, which created a scandal only marriage could quell. They had loved one another desperately. Her Great-uncle Herbert, whose nose was enormous, loved hunting. Great-aunt Rosalund commissioned the building of an orphanage in London against her husband's wishes, and Phoebe's grandmother had been an expert horsewoman.

Feeling better than she thought possible, clinging to her newfound family, she stopped beside Hampson who waited near a pair of French doors. When he pushed them open, she stepped outside onto a long balcony a hundred feet above a sapphire sea and witnessed the most breathtaking sight she had ever seen.

Waves pounded the cliffs, crashing and echoing for what seemed miles, calling to her in a hypnotic rhythm. Gulls cried as they soared high above the cliffs, celebrating their freedom for all to hear. The wind blew, crisp and fresh, the feel of salt heavy against her skin. The setting was vast and desolate, just as Stephen had described, and she loved it.

Hampson braced his feet near the stone wall. "Your mother possessed a most delightful imagination. She sat here for hours, watching for a mermaid to wash ashore or a helpless boat to flounder so she could dash down the cliffs and rescue each and every soul."

"She used to tell me wonderful stories of pirates and their vessels filled with gold."

"No doubt inspired by your great-grandfather the pirate," Hampson elaborated, his voice growing more animated as he spoke. "Your grandfather joined her every afternoon for tea. They sat here, their heads tucked together, plotting their travels around the world. When they grew tired of that game, they entertained one another with the most unbelievable tales."

A small iron table and two chairs in need of painting were nestled in a small alcove on the balcony. It was easy to imagine the scene Hampson portrayed. Attempting to reclaim a tiny portion of her mother's life, Phoebe sat in the nearest chair, placed her elbows on the table and stared out to sea as her mother must have done. "You must have known her very well."

"I practically caught her from the womb."

"And you loved her." She smiled at him as he bristled

ever so slightly. "So did I. Thank you. Today you have given me the greatest of gifts."

Blushing over the thanks she offered, Hampson crossed to a stone seat that faced the ocean, suddenly uncomfortable meeting her gaze. He stared off in the distance. The pained expression on his face started to worry Phoebe, but she waited. After a time, with the uttermost care, he pulled a brown linen package from beneath his arm. Removing a bundle from the fabric, he revealed a lovely wax doll. He placed it on the table. "I saved this for you."

She pressed the small figure to her breasts. Tears gathered in the back of her eyes. "I'm surprised my grandfather allowed you to keep anything of hers."

"Truly, Miss Phoebe, he loved her more than life itself. The joy in his heart vanished when your mother died." If possible, as though a great burden weighted his soul, his eyes grew wearier, his body more fragile. He pulled a white scrap of paper, which looked like a letter of sorts, from his pocket. When he handed it to her, he murmured, "I deeply regret my inability to do a better job of caring for this place. When you and Lord Badrick are ready, I will answer all your questions." He left without another word.

Afraid of what she might find based on Hampson's sudden change of mood, she twirled the envelope in her fingers as if a clue to its contents might appear. When she had finally managed to gather the necessary courage, she opened the note and absorbed the scripted words. Then, she read the note. Twice.

The news was the same, still as shocking and just as depressing as the first time. Suddenly exhausted, she wrapped her mother's doll to her chest, lay her head on the table and closed her eyes.

While searching for Phoebe, Stephen slipped through the doors Hampson had described. The sight was undoubtedly breathtaking. The person responsible for the location of Marsden Manor had selected well. It was unfortunate the other relatives had neglected to care for the old mansion.

He saw Phoebe with her head nestled in her arms on the table and decided the poor girl was exhausted. No small wonder. Last night had proved to be rather tiring for everyone. While he considered allowing her the rest she seemed to need, he noticed her hand fisted about a scrap of paper. He crossed to stand beside her, and unable to resist the urge, he nibbled on the exposed ear that her bent position afforded. "Good morning."

Lifting her head, she balanced her elbows on the table and rested her chin in her hands. "Good morning to you."

He sat in the chair and saw her face for the first time. More than mere exhaustion haunted her this morning. Her skin seemed translucent and her eyes lacked their normal vibrancy. Although her lips curled slightly, her smile showed no real pleasure. In fact, she looked downright dreary, defeated. Tipping her face toward his, he asked, "What happened? Judging from the pallor of your skin, you look as though someone handed you a death sentence."

She averted her face and handed him the scrap of paper. It was crumpled and damn if he didn't notice a spot he swore was a tearstain. He read the note and understood her mood. Not only was Marsden Manor broke, but back taxes, likely a considerable sum, were being called for immediate payment. While muttering a curse under his breath, he crumpled the foolscap into an even tighter ball. "Other than I'm sorry, I don't know what else to say."

"I feel like a marionette controlled by someone who insists on jerking the strings every time I find myself close to a solution. Nanny Dee always says that dealing with problems develops character. Well, I feel like I have enough character to last me a lifetime. At least now I understand the odd message my solicitor sent. Does *that* seem a fair amount?" She indicated the note.

"It depends upon the last payment your solicitor made and the size of the estate. It's rather complicated. Besides a dozen sundry things, we pay taxes for manservants and the land. There are the tithes due the Church of England, and your parish requires money for roads and the local poor. The estate ledgers, if maintained, should reveal a detailed accounting. What shall you do?"

"The cliff has a decent height, but with my luck I'd land on the only soft spot on the entire beach." His shocked expression must have left her feeling a bit guilty, for she quickly added, "I'm teasing. I feel despondent and then some, but I promise the mood won't last long. I've never been one to sulk. Besides being unproductive, it's tedious. Hampson is ready to explain things in detail if you like. After that, I'll decide what has to be done."

Most distressing was the hopelessness in her voice. The urgent desire to shelter and protect Phoebe surged over him like the waves crashing on the rocks below. It had been years since he'd felt any need to rescue a woman. His wife Louisa had never stirred such self-sacrificial thoughts or tugged on his heartstrings or conscience as Phoebe did.

He ordered the nagging thoughts from his mind. He wasn't prepared to offer what she truly wanted. Besides, if he offered any advice right now, she'd likely pitch *him* over the cliff. What she needed was a diversion! Something to take her mind off the debt, her troubles and the condition of the estate. An adventure. Besides, he'd waited all morning to substantiate his findings from the night before. Wibolt was on his way to the village. Winston and his wife were indisposed—the local doctor had come to see to Elizabeth's condition. Mrs. Potter, Dee and Hampson were upstairs setting the servant's rooms to rights. If Stephen's suspicions paid off, they would have more to confront Hampson with than the condition of the estate.

Pulling her chair out, he clasped her hand in his. "Right now, I suggest you think about something else. Come along."

"Where exactly?"

"To the cook's room."

"Whatever for?"

"I'd wager my best mare that our nocturnal visitor is quite human and someone in your employment." They wound their way to the north side of the manor, carefully avoiding everyone. To guard against any unwanted interruptions, Stephen closed the door and began a systematic search of the cook's room in the same fashion he'd investigated the music room the night before.

"Do you still believe the house has secret passages?" Phoebe asked. She studied the sparse furnishings, glad for the distraction Stephen offered.

"It's a distinct possibility. Few servants' quarters have shelves such as this. It struck me as odd." With his ear pressed to the wall, his fingers probed the wooden edge framing the recessed shelves. A quiet but definite click came from somewhere inside. "Here we go." He pushed against the wood with his shoulder and the entire shelf opened to reveal a set of stairs that descended to a lower level. Grabbing a nearby candle, which he quickly lit, he slid into the tunnel. "Let's see where it goes."

Phoebe watched him duck his head and hunch his back. Goodness, his shoulders practically touched the sides of the old stone walls. "Now?" she asked. "Down there? By ourselves?"

"I wish to know as much as possible before we talk with Hampson," Stephen said, his excitement barely contained. "His response should prove interesting."

She stepped to the top stair and stared down into shadow. Dank and musty air wafted through the opening. She hated dark, enclosed areas. Aware of the sweat forming on her palms, she swiped her hands against her dress and steadied her voice.

"That must mean you think Hampson's the ghost, although I can't fathom why he chose to scare us. Surely he can't expect to gain anything if I up and leave. Perhaps it was Wibolt. He failed to make an appearance last night. But he seems so sweet. If you do think they're guilty of something, wouldn't this be dangerous to go down here, alone? Perhaps we should get Winston."

She felt Stephen's hand on her chin. His eyes, filled with concern, met hers. Ever so softly, he said, "I doubt either man is capable of any true violence, but now that you mention it, perhaps it would be best if you remained here to make sure no one disturbs me."

Bless the man, he didn't laugh or scold or taunt. He simply accepted her fear and offered a way to maintain her dignity. The thought of sneaking down a spooky tunnel that led to who knew where with only a puny candle was uninviting to say the least. Facing her fear, she admitted that likely a mouse or two was the greatest danger they'd encounter. Prompted by the belief that Stephen would take care of her, she squared her shoulders and pasted what she hoped was a valiant smile on her face. "You'll keep me safe?"

"With my life."

On his vow, she followed, gripping his arm like a vise. When he took a step, she matched his with one of hers. The small tunnel barely seemed large enough for a child, yet she knew grown men must have utilized this passage time and again. At the bottom, the stairway opened to a larger chamber that split in two different, very dark, menacing directions. Her stomach churned with anxiety. By the time she'd managed to calm herself down a bit, several rats skittered into the blackness, their tiny feet scraping the walls and floor in their haste to escape. One stray rodent scampered across her slippered foot. Phoebe practically vaulted onto Stephen's back, swallowing her scream at the same time.

Stephen pulled her to his side, extended the candle high in the air, and peered down both passages. Pulling a small piece of charcoal from a handkerchief, he marked the left wall with an arrow. "If I'm right, this should lead us toward the music room."

"You were quite prepared, weren't you?" The thick walls absorbed most of the squeak in her voice.

Winking, thoroughly enjoying this little adventure, he slowly led the way, occasionally testing the stability of their path with his foot or arm. He never left her side. They passed two more forks, each as uninviting as the first. Every time Stephen checked the new tunnel for signs of use. So far all the passages seemed to be undisturbed or too dangerous to risk entry. He marked the wall again. After countless minutes, they reached a small room, eight feet or so across. A collection of candles sat on a wooden box and a white robe hung on a wooden peg with a tin can of powder beside it. Nearby, several blankets lay on a straw pallet. Four wooden stairs led to a raised section in the ceiling above.

Stephen stared and mumbled, "Amazing."

"What? Tell me," Phoebe nervously asked. "Are we below the music room?"

"I believe so." He climbed the stairs and tapped on the wood. "And this would be the window seat you sat upon last night. I never thought to check there. Very clever." After searching a few more moments for a latch, he shoved against the barrier with all his strength. "Blast. It seems to be jammed or locked from the other side. But look." He swiped at a handprint the size of a man's on the bannister and held his finger in the air to reveal white powder. "I think this proves your ghost to be quite human."

"I just don't understand why Hampson or Wibolt would do this."

"I'm not sure either. Let's go find out."

She sensed that he would have stayed longer and investigated further on his own, but she jumped at the chance to leave without a second thought. Together they threaded their way back to the beginning, approaching the stairway to the cook's room. Phoebe didn't remember it being quite so dark. When they reached the stairs, she understood why. The panel at the top was closed. Stephen poked, pushed and shoved, all to no avail. They were thoroughly trapped in the bowels of the mansion.

A wave of apprehension flowed through her. She sucked in a deep breath and tried to relax. No matter how unreasonable, how unwarranted, she couldn't vanquish the child's memory of being trapped. Stephen's presence didn't help.

"What to you propose to do now?" she asked, pounding on the wood. Stephen continued to calmly probe the wall, with no success. "Do something," she ordered.

He grabbed her hands and pulled them to his chest. "Phoebe. We closed the door to the bedroom. Mrs. Potter won't be spending her nights here. There is no reason for anyone to enter this room."

"Well that's a fine how-do-you-do. What do we do now?" she asked, her voice an octave higher.

"We have several choices. We can sit here on the steps or we can venture back to where we were. The odds are greatest that someone shall hear us there. We'll have more candles and a place to sit. I left Winston a note. He'll know to look for us."

"What about the other passages?"

"I'd rather not risk it. Most of them appear unused and possibly unstable, and I'm not sure where they might lead."

Her nerves calmed somewhat. After all, what he said made perfect sense. "I'll say one thing. When you offer a lady a diversion, you certainly keep your word."

He clasped her head to his chest and stroked the back of her head, his touch soothing and provocative at the same time. "Trust me, darling. Winston will find us. Besides, when both of us fail to appear for lunch or tea, Dee will initiate a search that would rival any led by an army of Bow Street runners. The staff shall have no reprieve till they find us. I promise to keep you safe until then."

The warmth of his embrace and the gentle stroking eased the tightness in her chest. The man had an uncanny effect on her. She did trust him. She lifted her head to tell him just that and noted the gleam in his eyes. A flicker of excitement skittered across her skin. Who would keep her safe from him?

Beneath the music room for a second time, with the full understanding that they were possibly stuck for hours, she studied their meager supplies and said, "I'm hungry and cold."

Lordy, she sounded like a petulant schoolgirl, and it seemed so silly to be thinking about food and all, but she was hungry. She hadn't bothered with breakfast, and last night's supper barely qualified as a meal. The chill clinging to the walls seeped into her bones.

Stephen lit several candles. The light didn't dispel the cold, but improved her mood nonetheless. He spread the robe they found and the woolen blanket on the straw mat, sat down and extended his arms. As her teeth began to chatter, she willingly slid into his arms, eager to absorb some of his heat. He briskly rubbed his hands up and down her arms. As she relaxed, the tension faded from her body and she yawned.

"Why don't you try to sleep. It might be hours before they even search for us. If I hear anyone, I will pound on the floor and raise such a noise they shan't miss us."

Lying there as the flickering flames undulated on the walls like a dozen fiery dancers, she considered his suggestion ridiculous. Yawning again, she didn't even intend to close her eyes. Still, the warmth of Stephen's body, combined with his calming touch, lulled her toward drowsiness. Within moments, lack of rest from the previous night pushed her over the edge to sleep.

Chapter Thirteen

Stephen watched Phoebe as she slept and contemplated the last time he had simply held a woman. Other than his very first wedding night, not one other circumstance came to mind. Usually after lovemaking, either he dressed and tended to other business or moved to his own bed.

Emily's blind faith had fed his youthful arrogance and made him feel powerful. Their lovemaking had been pleasant but had lacked real passion. His second wife had possessed the passion but lacked the kindness. Their relationship had relied solely on lust and greed. He didn't think he'd ever spent one complete night in Louisa's bed. Phoebe was kind and passionate; she had a zest for life rivaled by few women. If they were together, he doubted he would ever let her sleep elsewhere but in his arms.

This train of thought was not the wisest. The fact that they were quite alone clouded his better judgment. All attempts to wrest Phoebe's presence, her delectable body pressed against his, from his mind were pointless. He dipped his head and, pulling in a deep breath, he savored the scent of lavender clinging to her hair. As she burrowed closer to his chest, the growing awareness of their situation rose solidly and uncomfortably in his lap. He brushed his hand across her forehead, each eyebrow, his gaze riveted on her face. He traced the contours of her mouth with his finger. She stirred, rubbing against him like a kitten seeking a caress. The moist heat of her breath fanned his cheek. Her stomach grumbled.

Lost in the haze between dreams and reality, she opened her eyes and graced Stephen with a lazy grin. "I'm hungry."

"So am I, darling. So am I." He hadn't intended to kiss her, knew the folly of such action, but with her heavy-lidded eyes filled with the dewy gleam of sleep, he couldn't overcome the impulse.

Phoebe mewled, a soft sigh of satisfaction, as she reveled in Stephen's mouth on hers, the abrading of his mustache against her skin. *What a lovely way to wake from a nap.* She touched her tongue to his, and taking the initiative, deepened the kiss. Her mind whirled and her pulse quickened. Her skin heated and like a glowing cinder; warmth swamped her entire body. Stephen's kisses seemed endless, arousing, often gentle, sometimes playful, all demanding her response.

His fingers grazed her cheeks, her neck, and the high-laced collar she wore suddenly seemed too restrictive. As though he read her mind, she felt his hand on her gown's buttons, which proved to be minor obstacle's for his clever fingers. The cool damp air rushed over her nipples, but she felt only heat as his hands hovered in the valley between her breasts. She arched her back as if to say "Yes, touch me." His mouth replaced his touch, trailing a path of heat from one turgid peak to the other, caressing her inflamed flesh, stoking her body's need, her mind's curiosity. An unexpected and disturbing yearning, palpable in its intensity, spread from her breast to the juncture between her thighs, the secret place long dormant until she had met this man. She crushed her legs together in an effort to ease the discomfort, the insistent throbbing she didn't quite understand.

Thank goodness Stephen understood. While cooing sweet words of encouragement into her ear and kissing her time and again with magical thrusts of his tongue and persuasive lips, he slowly edged the hem of her dress higher, his hand following in its wake to finally tease the tiny nubbin she never knew existed. She thought she just might faint then and there. Forgotten were the dank walls surrounding them, the chill hanging in the air. She felt flushed, feverish. Then he moved his fingers in the most delightful, unexpected way. Brilliant colors of violet and orange danced in her mind. Nothing else mattered except the incessant burning deep within her body. Instinctively, in a rhythm as old as time, her body demanded she lift her hips to greet and welcome his caresses. Her explosive reaction left her breathless, humbled and awed, and truth be told, unsure of what to do next.

Stephen smoothed the wisps of hair from her brow, and he burrowed his forehead in the curve of her neck as he commanded his own desperate body to forget its baser urges. Sweet mercy, remembering this passionate moment, her uninhibited response, he wouldn't sleep for a week. He should never have allowed this interlude to go this far. Thankfully he had kept Phoebe more or less dressed. Otherwise he doubted he would have possessed the strength to refuse the warmth, the solace, he would find buried deep within her body.

She shifted, pressing her hardened nipples against his arm. Damn, if he didn't move, he would loose very ounce of willpower. Lifting his head, he pulled the edges of her jacket together, covering the lush bounty of her breasts before he lost his good intentions. He tucked her chin back to his chest. "My dear darling Phoebe, what am I to do with you?"

Marry me. It was the first, unbidden and fanciful thought to leap into her mind. Thankfully she held her tongue. She shivered with the aftershocks of pleasure and waited for the shame. None came. Wanton or not, she treasured the touches, the pleasure that Stephen had wrought upon her body. The yearning to understand him, the need to understand his past, overwhelmed all else. Wrapped in the comforting warmth of his embrace, she quietly asked, "Will you tell me about the curse?"

His body tensed, but his arms remained tight about her. Fighting the impulse to prod and push, she waited and accepted his need to consider her request. He wasn't accustomed to sharing parts of himself with many people, of that she was sure.

"Knowing the details won't change the outcome," he said. "The only reason I tell you this is so you know why I will not marry again."

"I would like to understand."

With a deep, cleansing breath, he relaxed his shoulders. "My great-grandfather was betrothed to a prominent noblewoman. Nonetheless, two months before his wedding he seduced a young gypsy girl. Pregnant and shamed when she discovered he had no intentions of marriage, the poor thing killed herself. The girl's mother, a Juliana Romov, cursed my great-grandfather. No daughter would be born to our line and every male heir would know only death and sorrow in his marriages. No daughter has been born since. Five women married into the Badrick line. All died within two years of their wedding night, my own two wives included. I refuse to add a sixth to the family cemetery."

"How did they die?"

"You want the gory details?" Disentangling himself from her arms, he stood and marched three steps to the corner of the tiny room. His face fell into shadow, hiding any expression that might have revealed his feelings. "My great-grandmother died in a carriage accident as she fled her husband's temper. Another fell from her horse during some idiotic race. The last drowned in her very own bathtub. I already told you about Emily and our two-week-old daughter. Louisa fell down a flight of stairs, a bottle of brandy in one hand and a diamond necklace in the other." His voice sounded horribly cold and ever so empty. She felt his withdrawal with each word he uttered.

"Accidents happen, Stephen. More likely, those women suffered from a combination of poor judgment and bad luck."

Moving to her side, he towered above her, his head only an inch or two from the ceiling. He snorted, more from disbelief than laughter. "Unlucky because they chose to marry my ancestors or myself. Emily was the perfect lady, the perfect female to quell the gossip of the Ton. I believed I could protect her from all the evil in the world, including myself. I seduced her into marriage as surely as I breathed. Death was her reward.

"Louisa wanted my money, nothing more, nothing less. She had it for as long as she lived. For years, I railed against the fact that my ancestors were right, that the Badrick line was indeed cursed. But young women have died. Sweet mercy, if even one had lived a normal life, I would maybe hope, believe otherwise, but . . ."

He dragged both his hands through his hair. "You once asked if I believed in love. Perhaps I did at one time, but love can bring me no joy. I never asked to be cursed, Phoebe. I won't allow myself to care so deeply again. I won't be responsible for the death, inadvertent or otherwise, of another woman. I won't bring another child into this world to suffer the pain of such a legacy. The Badrick line dies with me."

The fervor with which he spoke revealed the extent of his belief, the anguish revealed his despair. And now, Phoebe thought, Stephen refused himself a future. He refused to allow himself to care. The odds of changing his mind seemed astronomically small. How did someone combat such conviction, one based on the most honorable of reasons? Given his current state of mind, now was not the time to try. "It seems, my lord, that we are forever at this crossroads." His eyes met hers, challenged them, his body held in check as though he anticipated an argument. A bit sheepishly she asked, "You didn't happen to find anything to eat while I was sleeping, did you?"

He relaxed. "And here I'd thought you suitably satisfied."

Hot color raced up her neck to her cheeks. "I was talking about food. The sustenance needed for man's very existence."

Crossing to her side, a twinkle popping into his eyes, he said, "So was I."

It was foolish to allow him to kiss her again. He'd clearly stated that he would not marry her. She was better off forgetting the man's persuasive lips and clever hands. Still, her body refused to accept what it considered nonsense. But, the moment she leaned forward, the floorboards above them creaked and groaned, wiping away her thoughts of kisses or anything else. It sounded like a small army tromping around in the room upstairs. Just about the time that relief flooded her mind, the barrier at the top of the stairs opened and five familiar heads peered into the darkness below. Squinting against the sudden infusion of light, Phoebe recognized Dee first. Judging from her stony expression, appearing to see more than was humanly possible, Dee looked none too happy. Elizabeth seemed shocked, Winston appeared nonplussed. Wibolt and Hampson looked like two men who'd just met their maker.

"You intend to stay down there?" Dee asked, a hint of challenge in her voice.

Dee's words mobilized everyone into action and suddenly six pairs of lips were flapping at the same time, sounding something like a squabbling flock of seagulls. Phoebe climbed the stairs while Stephen shook his head and extinguished the candles. By the time she set her feet on the floor of the music room, Phoebe had discovered that Elizabeth was not ill, but pregnant; and that Mrs. Potter had fainted yet again. At least two dozen questions had been asked and she was trying her darnedest to answer them.

Stephen, now beside her, cleared his throat. The chatter continued. He tried again to no avail. Evidently deciding it was time to assume control, he clapped his hands together. "Enough. Let us move to the library and sit down. We will answer everyone's questions, but one at a time for mercy's sake."

Phoebe sat behind the desk, trying to maintain the cool facade she felt necessary to compensate for her appearance. A few strands of hair loosened from her braid, which curled about her face, and dirt smudged her dress. Her appearance could be fixed later. Right now her future needed tending. Quickly and efficiently, trying her best not to remember those charmed moments in Stephen's arms—for surely her face confessed to every memorable touch, every delicious moment—she retold the events of the afternoon. Stephen sat in a chair across the room, one leg crossed over the other as a silent observer. His face revealed nothing.

Dee left for the kitchen to fix tea and prepare a bath. She

mumbled the entire time as she made that long, deliberate walk to the doorway, then imparted a final warning glare to Stephen. Winston, who stood behind the chair Elizabeth occupied, kept a restraining hand on his wife's shoulder as they received congratulations on Elizabeth's pregnancy. They both looked as if they might burst with happiness.

Wibolt sat on the now-closed window seat, his eyes fixed on the battered hat in his hands. Hampson, who knew the attention was now focused on him, stood perfectly still, his old bones as rigid as a marble pillar. If the poor man continued to stand so stiffly, Phoebe thought he might just snap in two. She softened her voice. "Hampson, I'm not going to order your execution. I simply want answers."

His thin shoulders relaxed a fraction, but his expression remained sullen. "I don't deserve your kindness. Interrogate me as you wish, my lady."

Assurances wouldn't ease his worries. "I have no intention of treating you like a petty thief. Simply explain why and how Marsden Manor is in its current state."

Nodding, he clasped his hands behind his back. "After your mother died, your grandfather wrote the king for a special dispensation, transferring the property to you."

"The king must have been feeling magnanimous that day to grant such a request," Stephen said.

"Indeed, sir," agreed Hampson. "His lordship notified your father in the Americas. Your father never responded; nonetheless your grandfather kept the will intact. Over the years, as your grandfather became ill, he paid less and less attention to such details as the repair and upkeep of this place. When he died, your aunt came."

"Lady Goodliffe?" Phoebe asked, surprised.

Wibolt slapped his hat against his leg. "She came to take things, she did. To take them and sell them."

Hampson faced Phoebe once again. "I reminded Lady

Goodliffe that the furnishings belonged to you, Miss. She'd hear nothing of it. After her second visit, we devised a plan to keep her away."

"Let me guess," Winston interjected. "The ghost of Grandfather Augustus."

Hampson turned his head slightly. "Yes, sir. We used the old tunnels, the ones in decent repair and if I may say so, the plan worked grandly. Lady Goodliffe never came back."

The image of her nasty aunt being roused from a deep sleep by her very own, very dead father lifted Phoebe's spirits slightly. "Why did the ghost make an appearance last night?"

Wibolt twisted his hands back and forth, his battered hat the innocent victim. "I didn't mean no harm. I just thought . . . well . . . maybe you'd be angry with us and if we scared you, you'd leave us be." He wheezed a few times before he continued. "Hampson didn't know. He told me it was foolish. I apologize if'n I scared any of you."

"Truth be told," whispered Elizabeth, "I thought it was rather exciting."

"Might we continue?" interrupted Stephen.

"Go on, Hampson," prodded Phoebe. "Why is the estate in such shambles?"

"Your grandfather neglected to consider the financial ramifications of his will. Without other properties to subsidize this place, it quickly fell into disrepair after his death. That's when Wibolt came. He was an old retainer of your granddad's. Together we used our pensions for as long as possible, even sold a piece of furniture or two, for which I have an accurate accounting. We simply ran out of money."

"Didn't you think to contact my aunt?"

"I did, miss. The first time was a year ago. That's when I wrote you. The last was a few months ago. She basically told me to go to the devil."

"She never said a word to me," murmured Phoebe, not really surprised by her aunt's unwillingness to help, but rather at the extent of Hildegard's bitterness. She massaged a spot at the back of her neck that had begun throbbing with the barrage of questions and was now hammering with the discovery of the woman's duplicity.

"I apologize, miss. I failed your father and I failed you."

"*We* failed you," Wibolt added dramatically.

Silence stretched uncomfortably throughout the room. Phoebe stood and crossed to Hampson. "You did what you could and more. Thank you. I'll think of something. Now go along and help Dee."

Stephen waited until the two servants had shuffled from the room, single-file, like a line of prisoners on the way to the gallows. Poor devils. He turned to Phoebe, noted the weariness in her body, the ashy pallor of her skin, the near defeat haunting her eyes. It pained him all the way to his heart. The greater agony came from the fact that he knew he would not offer to ease her worries in the manner she desired.

He escaped to the window to stare at the distant horizon, his hands laced behind his back lest he succumb to the urge to take Phoebe into his arms and promise her the moon. "What will you do now?"

"We must return to London tomorrow. Somehow I will set the matter to rights."

Stephen faced Elizabeth and Winston. "May I have a word with Phoebe?" Elizabeth remained in her seat, an expectant expression on her face. "Alone," Stephen added.

Winston, a wise and compassionate friend, eagerly pulled his sputtering wife from her chair and escorted her from the room.

Stephen straightened his spine. He tipped his chin. He spread his feet to the exact width of his shoulders. "Please

193

know that I gain no satisfaction by this turn of events, but I do have a suggestion."

"Stephen Lambert," Phoebe said, wagging her finger toward his face. "If you ask me to be your mistress right now, I declare, I am liable to throw something."

"You are the most stubborn female I have ever encountered. I was going to suggest you sell the mansion today and be done with the entire affair."

"I cannot believe you would suggest such a thing."

"Certainly not because I enjoy being right, simply because I see the practicality of the situation."

As though prepared for battle, she crossed her arms over her breasts. "I intend to keep my home. Hampson has lived here since he was eighteen. He served my grandfather well and although misguidedly, he did his best to protect my inheritance. Wibolt has nowhere to go—and in his condition it would be impossible to find work elsewhere. My heavens, they spent their pensions trying to save this place."

"Fine. I have another suggestion. Secure a loan."

"Whomever from? A banker would only laugh in my face."

"Me."

"You?"

"Yes."

"You're serious?" She continued to stare. She slowly rose from the chair, her movements sluggish. Crossing to the window to stare at the gray skies outside, she considered all she'd learned in the last half-hour. There was no discernable reason for her aunt's secrecy.

Hildegard had never mentioned her visits, the ghost, nothing. Phoebe shook her head.

What could she do? She grudgingly admitted she needed Stephen's help, no matter the embarrassment it caused her. He seemed willing enough to help, and only a fool would turn away such an offer. She felt Stephen's breath on her neck and fought the impulse to turn and rest her head on his shoulder. "Fate seems to have placed another hurdle in my path, one I cannot leap without your help."

"If I give you—"

"*Loan* me the money," she interrupted as she turned to face him. "I shall be the collateral."

He paused and looked at her with intelligent eyes that flashed with speculation. A moment passed before he said, "I doubt any future husband would appreciate the fact that I hold such a promissory note."

"That is a chance I am willing to take."

"Why not simply agree to my terms now and end this charade?"

"Why not agree to marry me and end my worries?"

He only scowled, the thought obviously so unsettling that he avoided the subject altogether. "I shall draft a note giving you two thousand pounds at your immediate disposal to do with as you wish. No tricks, no ties, no rules. Take as long as need be to repay me."

"That's too generous."

"You'll need every pence."

With her hands behind her back, she leaned her head against the cold windowpane. "Knowing I must marry and knowing you seem decided against such a fate, may I ask why the generosity?"

He leaned forward, his body flush with hers, and he placed his hands on each side of her face, trapping her within the prison of his arms. "Believe me, I haven't given up hope of changing your mind, but, if you come to my bed, if you allow me to make love with you, it will be because you so choose—not because you feel indebted to me, not because you owe me money."

The heavy beating of her heart and the dampness

between her legs was the immediate answer to his touch. How easy it would be to climb the stairs and tumble into his arms, to take what he offered. He took her lips, then, and she returned his kiss with abandon; using her tongue as he had taught her, she tried to show him without the benefit of words the passion, the emotion he stirred within her soul.

She knew she teetered on the edge of love, feared she might have already fallen. When she withdrew from his embrace, she saw the fire burning in his eyes, the desire and lust. She wanted more. She wanted what he kept locked away. Like a soft breeze, an idea had teased the edges of her mind ever since the morning. Standing here with this man, she knew what she would try to do. She would end this nonsense once and for all.

If a gypsy had placed a curse on Stephen, couldn't a gypsy remove it?

Chapter Fourteen

"Are you sure this is the right way?" Phoebe studied the narrow serpentine track shadowed by a dense wall of trees on either side.

"Yes," Elizabeth confidently answered. "At least I believe so," she added. "In fact, it shouldn't be much further." She consulted the scribbled map in her hands then pointed to a wooded slope to the left of the carriage. "There is the stone cross set into the rocks. According to that farmer, we have only a mile or so left."

"We had best continue then." Phoebe kept her voice cheerful. Her idea to seek a band of gypsies had seemed far better when they had been sitting in Elizabeth's salon back in London. Oh, well, too late now. As Phoebe fought to avoid a gaping hole directly in their path, the carriage lurched to the right. Her efforts were rewarded with a jarring thud and a resounding thwack, which left the carriage tilted precariously to the left. "Goodness gracious," she muttered as she peered over the side. "It seems we've cracked a wheel."

Both ladies stared down the dirt road that suddenly appeared far more uninviting than a moment ago. Determined to follow her course and help Stephen, Phoebe scrambled down to survey the damage. The carriage wasn't going any further. "If we're traveling in the right direction, it shouldn't take us long to find the camp. We'll simply hire one of the men to fix our wheel. Can you walk?"

"I'm pregnant, not crippled." Elizabeth's shoulders slumped as soon as she spoke. "I'm sorry. That was unbearably rude. It's simply so bothersome, not to mention embarrassing, to be ill in the mornings. And with his questions and constant worry, Winston is driving me to distraction." Climbing down to solid ground as well, she asked, "What of the horse?"

"He'll be needed to bring the carriage to the camp." Phoebe unhitched Flash from the buggy and led him to the side of the road. She tethered him to a large elm that was already in blossom. To bolster her confidence, she fingered the small pistol tucked in her purse. After all, she had learned how to use a gun at an early age and wasn't above doing so if the need arose.

Together, shoulder to shoulder, hand in hand, the two women picked their way down the path, doing their best to avoid the holes, ruts and pockets of mud. When they crossed an old gray bridge, Elizabeth tripped over a loose stone, twisting her ankle.

Guilt pricked Phoebe's conscience. If not for her, Elizabeth wouldn't be here. Once Phoebe had revealed her plan, Elizabeth refused to be left out. Together, they had inquired into the whereabouts of a gypsy camp, informed Elizabeth's maid of their true destination, and then told Dee, Stephen and Winston that they'd be gone shopping for the remainder of the day. Now they were stranded.

Well, there was nothing for it.

After resting for a time or two, they reached the crest of another small hill. To their relief, nestled in the valley below was a circle of lavishly decorated wagons with odd rounded tops. Several men tended to horses while three women prepared a meal over a central fire. Two boys and a dog chased a young girl, who squealed in delight as she darted in and out of the wagons, cleverly avoiding her pursuers.

Elizabeth stared at the scene, her hands tightly wrapped about the parasol she had insisted on bringing. "Are you sure about this, Phoebe? What if they truly hate the English?"

"Nonsense. Besides, what choice do we have? Even if someone can't fix the carriage, you certainly can't walk back to the village. We must secure a ride." Her chin tipped with determination, Phoebe marched down the hill. Elizabeth limped awkwardly behind. Like the setting for a still-life tableau, a hush fell over the camp and all activity ceased.

"Good afternoon," Phoebe called cheerfully. No one uttered a sound. Not even the dog.

"What if they don't speak English?" Elizabeth whispered.

Lands alive, Phoebe hadn't considered that. "Of course they do. However could they trade horses?" Beaming her friendliest smile, she turned the gypsies. "Our carriage broke a wheel a ways back and we were wondering if someone would be able to retrieve the carriage and, well, fix it. We'd be happy to pay for the services." She was greeted with blank stares and muted conversations spoken in a language she didn't understand. "Excuse me, does anyone here speak English?"

Silence.

Elizabeth lowered herself onto a rock. "What now?"

The hems of their dresses were covered with leaves and mud, their shoes were completely ruined and Elizabeth's ankle had begun to swell. A precious hour or more had already been wasted. "You can barely walk," Phoebe said. "Even if I thought it best, I refuse to trudge through that muck back to the carriage, then back to the village for help. I came here for answers and I intend to find them."

A shaggy dog the size of a small pony growled. A burly man with thick eyebrows and a faceful of hair crossed his arms and grunted. The dog scuttled under a nearby wagon and laid his head on his paws. Everyone else just continued to stare. Phoebe thought the dog just might have the right idea. Retreat seemed the better choice, but she'd come all this way for a reason. One grumbling male, an oversized mutt and a little hostility wasn't going to scare her away.

A rumbling of conversation began as everyone gazed past Phoebe. She spun about and spied a gorgeous woman with midnight hair, who wore a brightly colored skirt and a white blouse that fell sensuously off her left shoulder. The gypsy ambled toward them, her expression a mixture of arrogance and what Phoebe thought might be contempt. Smiling her brightest smile yet, Phoebe said, "Good afternoon."

The gypsy girl sauntered right past Phoebe and Elizabeth without a backward glance, Flash in tow.

"Pardon me, but what exactly are doing with my horse?"

Shrugging her shoulder, the gypsy girl said, "I found him wandering free. He is mine now."

Phoebe was unsure of what shocked her more: the fact that the girl claimed Flash as her own or that she spoke heavily accented, but otherwise intelligible, English. "I think not. I left my horse tied to a tree beside my carriage."

"You dare call Ariana a thief?" The girl's eyes heated with anger.

Given the sudden turn of events, Phoebe decided to give

the girl the benefit of the doubt and continued as diplomatically as possible. "Never mind, Ariana. May I call you that? Anyway, if Flash was found loose, then someone else obviously freed him. Thank you for finding him for me."

Ariana's dark eyes flashed before she simply walked away. She bandied comments back and forth with people in the camp, rousing a few chuckles, as she crossed the clearing. Then she tied Flash beside a magnificent white horse.

"Goodness gracious," Phoebe muttered.

"Now what?" Elizabeth whispered.

"I'm certainly not going to allow that woman to keep my horse." Phoebe marched to Ariana's side and tapped her on the shoulder. "Excuse me. You obviously didn't hear what I said. That horse is *mine*. If you'll just answer a few questions for me, I'll take Flash and be on my way."

"Enough, gadjo. I weary of your company. You go now."

They had been dismissed as regally as Phoebe assumed one might be if dealing with the King of England. Ready, willing, even eager to teach the black-haired witch a well-needed lesson in manners, Phoebe stepped forward.

Suddenly the ground shook. Both Elizabeth and Phoebe whirled about to witness a man gallop into camp seated atop a stallion very similar to the one beside Ariana. He rode directly toward them and swung from his horse with the ease of a man long accustomed to riding, his movements lithe and fluid. He glanced beyond Phoebe and Elizabeth to Ariana, then to the assembled group that watched the scene with avid fascination. Grinning in a manner that had likely turned the heads of young girls aplenty, he bowed. "Good afternoon. My name is Rhys. I did not know visitors were coming today. Why are you here?"

Phoebe was quite weary of explaining herself. However, this man spoke perfect English with only the slightest accent and his bearing clearly demanded she answer.

Maybe he could help them. She explained that Ariana had her horse, casting an accusatory glance toward the girl, who merely turned up her nose and continued to groom Flash. Though her cheeks were beginning to tire, she plastered a smile on her face and added, "So, if you'd be kind enough to answer a few questions and convince that woman to give me back my horse, we'll be on our way."

Crossing his arms, Rhys studied Phoebe intently. He fingered a loose curl lying over her forehead. "I like your courage, little one."

"You . . . I . . . Of all the . . ." She sputtered like a dried up fountain. "You may call me Miss Rafferty, and this is Lady Payley." She emphasized the lady part. "How *dare* you take such liberties."

"I dare, because you, a beautiful woman who obviously belongs in one of the finer salons of London, has landed in my camp without the benefit of a chaperone or a man. Since you are here, I will tell you I am accustomed to taking what I desire."

And she'd thought Stephen was arrogant. His behavior paled by comparison to this libertine. "Well, you can just undesire me. Our companions are overdue. That's all."

He snorted.

His voice softened to a caress. "If you were my woman, I would never allow you from my sight."

"Good thing, that. I'd surely die from boredom, and quick-like."

He was still chuckling when Ariana flounced—for there was no other way to describe the way she walked—to Rhys's side. Under Phoebe's watchful eye, the two spoke heatedly to one another until Ariana tossed her hair over her shoulder and advanced on Phoebe.

Before Phoebe could question Ariana's motives or her intentions, she found herself tumbling to the ground in a heap of green linen to land with an unladylike plop in a puddle of mud. Her screech and Elizabeth's startled cry filled the glen.

Rhys yanked Ariana to one side and spat a string of not-so-subtle threats. She merely crossed her arms beneath her breasts and matched his stare with her own. He took a menacing step forward. "Your jealousy is unfounded and your actions could very well have undesired consequences."

"Jealous? Hah. I take what is mine. Nothing more, nothing less."

Shaking his head, he said to Phoebe, "I am most sorry. Ariana's temper often causes poor judgment. Come. We shall find you new clothes."

"No."

"Blessed saints"—he threw his arms into the air—"spare me from stubborn women. Do not argue with me." He extended his hand. "Come."

Pushing away his hand, Phoebe pressed herself to her feet. She shook the mud from her hands. Enough was enough. She didn't want new clothes. She wanted her questions answered, her horse released and she wanted to leave. In that order. It was apparent that the situation required an entirely different strategy. She reached into her purse and withdrew her pistol, which she leveled at Rhys's head. By God, if anyone made a single solitary move, she'd plant a bullet between his eyes.

Stunned silence was her reward. Both Rhys and Ariana appeared suitably shocked and thoroughly subdued. At least that was what she thought until Rhys's stark appraisal gave way to a mischievous grin, and finally deep rumbling laughter.

"I swear I know how to use this, and don't think I won't. Now give me my horse."

Wiping tears of mirth from his eyes, he said, "I cannot do that, little one." Within the space of a blink and a sigh, he lunged, trapped her arms at her sides and wrested the gun from her hand. As Phoebe struggled against his embrace, he loosened his hold and stepped back. "You are full of surprises, gadjo. Unfortunately, Ariana believes the horse to be hers. I cannot intervene. We shall have to find another way to settle this matter."

Elizabeth planted herself beside Phoebe. "We won't leave without our horse. You may torture us or starve us, lead us into the forest to be lost forever, but I warn you, my husband will hunt you down and tear out your heart with his bare hands."

Phoebe had never believed her friend to be so dramatic. But their options *had* dwindled from zero to none. Gripping Elizabeth's hand in hers, she faced the chortling, rude barbarian, whose behavior in Phoebe's mind now equaled Ariana's. "What exactly did you have in mind?"

"Phoebe," cried Elizabeth, "you can't think to—"

"I want nothing more than to ask my questions and leave this place. We are quite on our own. We have no choice but to bargain."

"The horse is mine," Ariana spouted, her hands on her hips, reasserting her claim as boldly as possible. "I am the one to strike a bargain."

"Hah!" Phoebe snorted. "You're a thief. I certainly have no intention of giving you coin for *my* horse."

"Be quiet, Ariana," Rhys ordered.

"Why? Because she is a lady with fine clothes?"

"This jealousy of yours is unreasonable. I'm warning you. Behave. Miss Rafferty, come with me."

"If you think for one little minute that Lady Payley or myself intend to go anywhere with you, think again. I want my horse. I want it now. You said there were ways to settle disputes such as this. What are they?"

He steepled his fingers together and studied all three women, looking as though he might just strangle them. "Gypsies take their treasures very seriously. They also possess great honor and pride. There are games of chance, fights or races, which can be extremely dangerous. I am sure they hold little appeal for a lady like yourself."

If he thought to frighten her, he had another think coming. Phoebe barely contained her excitement. By gosh and by golly, she'd win Flash back. "What sort of races?"

"We ride the horses, you foolish English," spat Ariana, a victorious smirk on her face.

"Oh," whispered Phoebe, thanking the heavens for assumptions that ladies were incompetent once removed from the drawing room. "How difficult could that be?"

"They have lost their collective minds. I swear I will—" In his fury, Stephen couldn't complete the sentence. Locating the abandoned carriage with the broken wheel had done little to appease his worries or his brewing temper.

"My sentiments are the same as yours, my friend," agreed Winston as he nudged the shattered wood with his boot. "Elizabeth and Phoebe are indeed a pair to be reckoned with. The one saving grace is we know that Rhys will keep them safe. He allows the gypsies no nonsense when they camp on his estate."

"True, but what of Rhys himself? He has the devil's own reputation. My God, I've witnessed the man in action. All he needs do is utter a sentence or two in Romany and women practically swoon into his bed."

Winston's eyes lit with amusement. "Now I understand. I never thought to see you so possessive toward a woman again."

"Possessive, hell. I'm furious to be inconvenienced, that's all. Besides, I loaned her money. I'm protecting my investment."

"Really?"

"Of course. Hildegard could truly care less about her well being. Someone has to watch out for her."

"Rhys might be happy to accept that responsibility. I heard he decided to finally claim his title. Odds are he means to claim a wife as well."

"Bloody hell," Stephen muttered again. He had known Rhys since they were fourteen years old. He was a good man and one of the few Stephen called a friend. Rhys would make any woman a fine husband, but blast it all, let him find his own female. This irrational wave of jealously irritated Stephen all the more, which he quickly excused to prolonged lust. Noting none too happily the laughter in his friend's voice, he nudged Cavalier into a gallop, leaving Winston in the dust.

They crested the hill and without stopping cantered into the camp, which seemed to be a whirlwind of activity. Scanning the wagons for any sign of Phoebe and Elizabeth, he finally spied Rhys, who stood with his feet braced apart and his arms crossed over his chest like a sultan. Stephen swung from his saddle and shouted, "Where the devil are they?"

Rhys merely grinned. "Is that any way to greet an old friend?" He enveloped Stephen in a powerful embrace. "I assume from your question that you come for the redhead. Pity. She is an intriguing mix of womanhood, packaged in quite a delightful body."

Winston joined the two men and exchanged a warm embrace with Rhys. "Tread lightly. Stephen sees himself as the girl's protector."

Rhys lifted one brow. "You will marry again?"

"Hell, no. You of all people know my circumstance. It's simply . . . never mind."

"I understand. She is a handful. I also recognized your wife, Winston. It has been an interesting afternoon, my friends. I thought to teach the ladies a lesson. I believe six-year-olds would be better students."

"Where is Phoebe?"

"At this moment, she prepares for her race."

"She what?"

Shaking his head, Winston said, "You'd best impart the whole of it."

When Stephen heard the entire tale he didn't know whether to offer Phoebe a medal for her bravery or a lecture for her foolishness. Likely she was deserving of both. He knew one thing for certain: He wanted to see her. This instant. "Phoebe Rafferty," he thundered. His voice boomed across the glen.

Dogs scuttled under the wagons and children tucked their heads in their mother's skirts. Rhys and Winston stared in amused silence. Phoebe peeked from behind a nearby wagon and hid once again. But not before Stephen saw her. "Phoebe Rafferty, no point in hiding."

"The same goes for you, my dear," yelled Winston.

"Oh, spit," Phoebe muttered. Granted she was glad to see Stephen, thrilled in fact, but the murderous expression plastered on his face meant a lecture or maybe something worse.

"What now?" asked Elizabeth.

"We take the offensive." Phoebe stomped over to Stephen's side, matching his glare with one of her own. "I've had a miserable day, Stephen Lambert, and as far as I can tell the fault lies at your feet, so don't you dare yell at me."

Elizabeth hobbled behind, trying her best to look dignified, no small feat with an ankle that was surely the size of her thigh. "The same goes for you, Winston."

A snort, suspiciously like laughter, escaped Rhys's lips. He slapped both men on their backs and walked away shaking his head.

Phoebe felt like throwing a rock at Rhys's head. In fact,

at the moment, she felt like drubbing all males in general.

"Elizabeth, do you realize that you could have been seriously injured?"

Winston's tone of voice, one Phoebe had never heard him use before, indicated his mood. Thunderation, *he* was angry too. "It's not her fault," Phoebe said. "I forced her to accompany me."

"Humph," Winston grumbled. "Like you, she possesses a decent amount of intelligence and common sense when she elects to utilize them. Today, you both seem to have lost all reason."

Elizabeth's eyes started to tear. "I injured my ankle." On a sigh, Winston opened his arms. She curled into his chest and winked at Phoebe.

For all of two seconds, Phoebe contemplated such a ploy. One look at Stephen's scowl and she knew it was a waste of time. "If you intend to lecture me," Phoebe said, "you can just mount your horse and ride back to London."

"I should, you know. I should ride away and abandon you to your own devices. I don't know why I bother."

Because you care, she thought to herself, knowing he'd laugh himself silly if she offered that suggestion. "This is all your fault anyway."

"You dare blame me for your lack of judgment? Sweet Mary, I've been in residence all day. What the devil did *I* do?"

"You exist," Phoebe snapped. His eyes rounded and his jaw clenched. She sighed, knowing she'd have to explain all of it. Even if she didn't, Elizabeth would likely tell Winston, who would then tell Stephen. "I came here for your benefit. I figured if a gypsy could curse you, then a gypsy could uncurse you."

"I . . ." He snapped his mouth shut. His stride devoured

the distance between him and Phoebe when suddenly he veered toward a nearby tree stump. Back and forth, back and forth, he paced, stomping about like an angry troll.

Suddenly, he marched to Phoebe's side, gripped her chin in his hand and claimed her parted lips. He released her just as quickly.

"Do not think for one minute that we are finished with this. Be careful," he commanded before he stomped, once again, to the edge of the clearing beside Rhys to watch the race.

Gratified to see Phoebe rendered immobile and speechless, Stephen crossed his arms over his chest. When she realized she was standing there watching him like a frightened hare, she frowned and ran to her horse. She likely thought him insane, yelling one minute, kissing her the next. Truth be told, he felt as though he were teetering on the edge of insanity, and had been for days.

Whenever unwelcome and impossible ideas of marital bliss invaded his mind, he remembered Emily's crumpled body, her limbs askew and broken. Any thought of Phoebe, limp and mangled in such a manner, was unthinkable. Thus far his resolution to have her as his mistress or not at all had held firm. Silently, he renewed his vow.

With a mix of trepidation and pride, Stephen watched Phoebe mount Flash. When she hiked her skirts above her knees and tucked the fabric between her legs, he fought the impulse to stomp across the clearing to tug the fabric back down to her ankles. Instead, he studied the horses and the course.

After circling the glen, the riders would ascend a hill to the north, then travel back down again to dash for the finish line, where Stephen stood along with most of the observers. Three obstacles blocked their path: a small creek, a downed tree and the wooden hitch from a wagon.

The white mare Ariana rode was magnificent, athletic and agile with a strong, short-coupled body. Colored ribbons decorated the horse's wavy mane. As if she knew she had an audience, the horse swished her tail with the same arrogance with which Ariana tossed her unbound curls.

Flash, on the other hand, was all grace and elegance with powerful hindquarters and a deep girth for maximum lung expansion. The thoroughbred excelled in sports demanding great strength of will, stamina and speed. Stephen nodded toward Ariana's horse and spoke to Rhys. "One of your Spanish breeds, I assume?"

With his arms crossed over his chest, Rhys grinned like a proud father. "The mare is spectacular. Like her brother, she will breed a fine line of steeds. How well does Miss Rafferty sit a horse?"

"I have little knowledge firsthand, but she claims to be quite proficient. Either way, I'm sure she'll do her best to try my patience during the race."

Chuckling, Rhys added, "You know, men and women are like horses. With the right pairing, a fine family line can be established."

Stephen eyed Rhys. "Do not start."

"Do not scowl so. Miss Rafferty is a package worthy of worry, my friend. That is all." With that, Rhys signaled Torio, Ariana's father, who stood between the two women, a blue scarf in his outstretched arm. Both riders watched it drift downward. The moment one corner touched the ground, Phoebe spurred Flash into a gallop, her head low over the horse's neck. His hooves hurled dirt into the air, his powerful muscles pumping as he fought to give her his all. Ariana kept pace with Phoebe, her face determined. Stephen couldn't help but admire the skill of both women. A horse gave its heart only to a rider who knew how to ask for it.

The crowd cheered wildly as both riders cleared the creek together. The hill lay ahead. The animals dug their hindquarters into the soft ground, disappearing into the trees and, much to his dismay, out of Stephen's sight.

Chapter Fifteen

Birds scattered and a small rabbit scampered to safety. A squirrel chattered noisily, protesting the invasion of its shaded sanctuary. Phoebe ducked even lower to avoid a branch on her right, the sound of Flash's labored breathing music to her ears. Mercy, the horse could run. She had sensed his power before, but today, he was running with his heart. For her. She cooed words of encouragement into his ear. His hooves crashed through the bracken and leaves, climbing higher and higher. She felt as if she were soaring, floating through the air like a bird's song.

The top of the hill came suddenly. She burst through the trees, whirled the horse about and started down. Ariana was right beside her. Phoebe admired the skill of the woman and the power of the mare. Sharing a bond, the love of the race, the thrill of freedom, both women smiled. With a shrill cry, Ariana spurred her horse, leaping forward. Phoebe did the same, thundering down the hill and laughing all the while. Despite the steep decline, Phoebe centered her body, her weight in the stirrups to combat the slope of the descent. Miracle of miracles, at the bottom she gained a slight lead.

Stephen's hand clenched about the limb of a tree as the horses sprung from the shrubbery at neck-breaking speed, Phoebe a hairsbreadth ahead. Flash jumped the downed log with ease. Only the open meadow and the wagon hitch remained. Soaring over the final obstacle, Flash's hind legs bobbled as his feet touched the rocky ground, forfeiting Phoebe's slight lead. Stephen's heart plummeted.

Seeing his tension, Rhys said, "Relax, my friend. Watch her. She knows what she is doing."

"Damn reckless female," Stephen complained. "I told her to be careful." He watched as she righted herself, gripping the reins low to the horse's neck. Her hair, loosened by the wind, flew like a scarlet banner behind her. He saw her lips move, knew she coaxed Flash to victory with soft words and praise. Neck and neck, the lathered mounts raced toward the finish. Twenty feet lay between her and the spot where Torio stood, the scarf held high once again. With a burst of strength and sheer will, Flash surged into the lead. Phoebe plucked the scarf from Torio's hand and raised her arm over her head, her face aglow with unabashed pleasure. Her eyes sparkled with vitality and her cheeks were flushed pink. Stephen didn't think he'd ever seen her look more beautiful.

Emotion filled him. First came pride, followed by an unbearable longing that made breathing difficult. He recognized the stirring of something other than lust, and it terrified him. Like a window to her heart, Phoebe's open gaze met his. She beckoned to him.

It was an offer to share her victory, but more, it was a promise to ease his loneliness. She offered the key to unlock the emotions he'd successfully buried for all these years.

Rhys clamped a hand on Stephen's shoulder. "What will you do?"

"What can I do?"

"That is a question only you can answer, my friend. But look at her, the way she watches you. A man would be a fool not to listen to eyes that speak from the heart the way hers do."

Ignoring his friend, Stephen fought to recall the image of Emily's twisted limbs amid a pool of blood, her last gasp of life. Maybe he did choose the coward's way. He didn't care, he couldn't afford to. Desperate to escape, knowing that if he went to Phoebe now he might not have the power to refuse what she silently asked of him, he stomped into the shelter of the forest.

Her disappointment keen, Phoebe watched Stephen separate himself from Rhys and disappear into the woods. What did he expect from her? She'd seen his eyes as she dashed across the finish line, witnessed the pride and much more. Stuff and nonsense. Maybe she saw only what she hoped for.

Rhys sauntered to Phoebe's side and lifted her from the saddle. "Now we celebrate."

Rhys led her to a small wagon and pushed her inside. A mound of blankets and pillows topped a bed that stretched from end to end near the back. Two chests sat beneath the bed. Boxes and baskets were stacked on top of one another along the sides. Brightly covered shawls, silky scarves and pots and pans hung from a wooden bar. A gypsy named Anna moved about the cramped space with an ease born from years of experience that one learned when all one's worldly possessions fit in a wooden box on wheels. Anna placed a bucket of water and a rag on top of a three-legged stool and gestured for Phoebe to wash.

Stripping down to her shift, Phoebe asked, "Why is everyone being so nice? I won."

"True, but nothing was lost. The horse was yours to begin with." The gypsy laughed at Phoebe's wide-eyed expression. "Do not be shocked. Ariana found the horse. Had you not appeared she would own a fine animal. When you did come, it became a matter of pride. Also, she saw Rhys look at you. She forgets he is noble and can never be hers."

"Rhys is a . . . he's not a . . ."

"Rhys is a bastard. Half gypsy, half English. This is his land. Does that shock you?"

Phoebe had wondered about the bond the three men apparently shared, but she would never have guessed that bit of information. She answered, scrubbing her face vigorously. "I know better than to make assumptions. I'm just surprised. Rarely are things as they appear."

"Very true and very wise. Today you rode like a gypsy." Anna pulled a woven skirt and a flowing white shirt from one chest. "Tonight you dress like one. Your man will be pleased."

"He's not exactly my man. I mean, I'd like him to be, but he has other ideas."

"Fire burns in his eyes. Tonight it will be difficult for him to refuse you. Rhys said you had questions. This gadjo nobleman, he is why you came here?"

"I had hoped to gather some information," Phoebe said, as she fingered the skirt, a luscious blend of purples that seemed to shimmer with life. Casting aside any modesty, she slipped her shift to the floor and slid her arms into the shirt. It fell from one shoulder and draped suggestively across her breasts. The skirt came next, flowing to her ankles. She twirled in the cramped confines of the wagon, relishing the freedom of movement in the outfit, the soft swish of the fabric.

Anna tossed the water from the wagon and pointed to the small stool. "Sit. Ask."

Phoebe explained the curse, providing what details she knew. Anna asked several questions as she loosened the remnants of Phoebe's braid and silently combed her hair. Finally Anna asked, "Does your man believe in the power of such a curse?"

"I believe so. Certainly, he credits himself responsible for the death of two women and refuses us a chance to be together as man and wife. I hoped to find a way to change his mind."

"Cursed or not, who can say for sure. A curse or a charm of any kind usually works with a man's beliefs, his guilt, his fear or his greed. Like a child, if told enough times that he is ugly, he will come to accept it as truth. Your man's heart holds the answers he needs, but he must find them himself. Let me see your palm."

Phoebe extended her hand. Anna gently flattened her fingers over Phoebe's and began to trace and study the lines. She rubbed back and forth several times. "I see a long life for you, my child, with many children."

Long life was good, thought Phoebe. And children. She wanted children, but whoever was the father?

Anna continued, "You will fall in love with one man, but the man you marry will be different."

Phoebe didn't like the way that sounded. "You mean I won't marry Stephen."

"The palm does not tell me a name. It shows me a life with different paths. You will marry and you can be happy if you allow it."

Phoebe was more confused than ever—and she'd hidden from Stephen long enough. By the time she emerged from the wagon, the shadows of night had overtaken the day. Flames shot skyward from a roaring fire. Laughter, music and the tantalizing aroma of food drifted about the glen.

As she crossed the encampment, searching for a familiar face, she realized why Ariana walked as she did. The skirt danced about her ankles, the soft muslin shirt slid sensuously over her unbound breasts. Her hair fell uninhibited down her back and swung back and forth across her hips. Tonight, away from the scornful eye of her aunt, the constant scrutiny of the Ton, Phoebe felt free for the first time in weeks. This time was only a brief respite, a false image of reality, but she would enjoy every single moment nonetheless.

Elizabeth and Winston talked with Anna on one side of the fire while Rhys and Stephen sat on a blanket, their backs pressed against a log. When Phoebe approached, unsure of what Stephen might do, she stood perfectly still. The minute he noticed her, he edged over and extended his hand. Evidently he'd forgotten his earlier private tantrum.

A woman brought a plate heaped with food. Phoebe's stomach growled in response. No small wonder. She hadn't eaten since early that morning. Tearing away a piece of roasted meat, she asked, "Where are Winston and Elizabeth going?"

"It's likely Elizabeth's attempt to leave you and I alone together."

"So you can murder me without witnesses," she grumbled.

"It's doubtful that witnesses would factor into the equation. I'd plead my case and the House of Lords would likely find in my favor."

Beside them, Rhys chuckled.

She momentarily considered arguing the point, but instead chose to ignore the rude men and their silly opinions. She would let nothing dispel the magic of the night. She was with Stephen, far from London, amongst people who led a life unlike any she had ever known. Possibilities abounded. "Then I guess I'd best enjoy myself for as long as I have to live."

"What are you contemplating now?" Stephen said.

"Whatever do you mean?" Phoebe asked, wondering how he knew her mind as well as he did.

"I recognize that gleam in your eye, the manner in which you nibble your thumb when you've thought something through and reached a conclusion of sorts. Given our past encounters, it makes me wary."

She jerked her thumb from her mouth and placed another bite of food in its place. "Has anyone ever told you that you are a suspicious man? What trouble could I possibly find here?"

He crossed his arms over his chest. "Given sufficient time, I'm sure you could propel England into a major war."

"Surely you jest, my friend," Rhys said, as he reached for a pitcher of ale. "She is but a mere woman."

"Mere woman? I'll have you know women are not mere anything. We are capable of great things. It's the men who bind us to our embroidery, menus and balls."

"I see what you mean," Rhys agreed. "She is a handful. The kind that a man would possess and never want to lose sight of." Grinning, he left Phoebe and Stephen alone to join a burly man who held a strange-looking violinlike instrument.

She asked, "What did he mean?"

"Nothing." *Everything*. Rhys had been very direct in his observations. He considered Stephen a blind-eyed lobcock, tied to his past.

"How do you know Rhys?"

"I imagine our friendship took you quite by surprise. The Ton would likely find some nefarious reason for our relationship."

"Are you going to tell me or just make cryptic, self-deprecating comments all night?"

"Pardon me, I forgot your decision to act as my champion." He draped one arm over his bent knee and stared into the flames, recalling a time long ago. "By the time I was fourteen, my heritage was well and goodly ensconced in my mind. After all, I'd heard the stories of my ancestors since the day I was born, and society's harsh critics had reminded me often enough in case my father had neglected his duties. We'd been discussing the infamous three witches from *Macbeth* when a schoolmate made the mistake of taunting my illustrious background. Something snapped. I beat him to a bloody pulp." He noted her shock. "No need to worry, Phoebe. That was before I learned to control my anger."

"He deserved whatever he got."

A smile tugged at his lips. Her unconditional loyalty always surprised him. Clearing his throat, he said, "Bloodthirsty wench, aren't you? Anyway, I was suspended from school for two weeks and sent home, where I suffered a long lecture from my father all about accepting my miserable fate. A band of gypsies happened to be traveling nearby, and feeling justified—for surely they were the cause of all my troubles—I sought someone, anyone, to punish. Rhys was the unfortunate recipient of my ire.

"He was sitting by a lake tossing rocks into the water. Little did I know that he was dealing with his own demons. It's not easy being the bastard son of a nobleman who refuses to claim you. Needless to say, when we came together we were like two quarreling hounds set on destruction. We near killed one another. Bruised and bloodied, realizing there would be no victor, we both collapsed to the ground in exhaustion. One thing led to another and we struck a mutual friendship. Over the years, both of us have learned to accept our lots in life."

That blind acceptance was what she fought, the passive resignation when she wanted Stephen to rebel. Tracing a deep purple thread in the skirt with her finger, she said, "I feel rather silly now for thinking I could come here in your defense. I'm sure you've asked questions aplenty about the curse."

"Until I realized I'd never truly have the answers I sought. All I discovered were riddles, none of which altered the fact that five women married into the Badrick line and died. There are some things in life that simply can't be explained." He entwined his fingers with hers. "Or changed."

His message was clear, and it was no different than the one he'd given her since they first met. But foolish or not, she refused to listen. She turned from the chocolate eyes that pleaded with her to accept, to submit, and allowed the hypnotic rhythm of the gypsy music to flow through her. Soon her feet were tapping. She clapped to the pulsing beat.

Ariana stood and with nimble feet began to move. She circled the fire and stood before Phoebe, her hands boldly fisted on her hips. "Today you rode like a gypsy. Tonight let us see if you can dance like one."

Phoebe stared open-mouthed for a moment, unsure whether to accept the challenge, for surely that was what it was. Like the pounding of drums, musical notes bombarded her body, gathering power. She watched Ariana sway to the rhythm. With her arms high above her head, her hands extensions of her arms, she opened and closed her fingers one at a time like the circular motion of a fan. Phoebe rose from the ground with grace and determination and matched Ariana's movements.

Her feet began to shift, a mix of tapping and stomping movements. Phoebe allowed her mind to drift, her body caressed by the cool night air, the heat of the fire and the burning appreciation she witnessed in Stephen's eyes. Several women joined them, and Phoebe thought it the most exquisite, most decadent thing she had ever done.

Stephen had seen gypsy women dance before, had

enjoyed their lithe movements, their open sensuality, but nothing compared with watching Phoebe. She circled the fire with her face deep in concentration and her eyes half-closed. Her hair, a cascade of flaming curls, shone like a sunset over the Caribbean. God, he wanted her. Right now. More so than the first time he'd lain with the servant girl who'd first seduced him, more than Emily and Louisa, and more than every mistress since. Phoebe vanquished all women with the gentle swirl of her hips.

His fingers ached to touch the bare alabaster flesh of her shoulders, to kiss the slightly parted lips, to suckle the breasts that teased him with every dip and rise of her arms. He wanted, no, needed, to bury himself deep within her heat and claim her as his. The music grew bolder, more urgent. Ariana grasped Phoebe's hands and, with their arms extended before them and crossed at the wrist, they spun in a tight circle, their faces tipped to the heavens, their hair flying like black and auburn pennons behind them. With a wild thrum of strings, the music came to its end. The pulse drumming in Stephen's head, throughout his body, continued to pound.

Without a thought to the consequences, he leapt up, marched to Phoebe and grabbed her hand. The submission in her eyes humbled him. As though they both realized tonight was indeed special, a time to forget, a time to pretend, she followed him away from the fire.

The music had begun again but this time the men took to the forest floor in a more robust, virile display. When Stephen snared a blanket from the step of a wagon, Phoebe gave the dancers no more thought. Without a word, she allowed him to lead her away, the rhythm of the music still a wild echo in her body. She had never felt so alive before. This was foolishness, insanity. But she trusted Stephen to take care of her.

They found a small clearing near a brook. Somewhat

221

like her emotions, the water rushed over the stones toward an unknown destination. Stephen spread the blanket, knelt, and for a second time that night she accepted his invitation.

She hadn't intended to come with him, couldn't believe she'd agreed so readily, yet here she was, alone with him. When she'd ceased dancing and met his eyes, she couldn't refuse him. Knee to knee, chest to breast, they studied one another, silently acknowledging what might happen. His lips descended to her lips. She reveled in the texture of his mustache abrading her skin, and she whimpered in a soft sigh of longing.

Without thinking beyond the moment, trapped in the sensual haze created by the magic of the night and the soul of the music, she touched her tongue to his. Like a star bursting in the heavens, the kiss exploded.

Passion was no longer new to Phoebe. She understood the dampness between her legs, her body's answer to Stephen's touch. She understood the hunger that seemed unquenchable, the thirst for more, the endless pit of desire that only Stephen's caresses could quell. The rhythm of the earlier dance hummed through her body, singing praises to each caress, every kiss.

Lifting his mouth from hers, he loosened the ties on the front of her shirt with trembling fingers. His reaction amazed her and inflamed her already fired senses. His hands drifted downward, sliding the soft fabric from her shoulders to expose her breasts, the nipples taut with anticipation.

"Do you realize how drawn I am to you?" he asked as he brushed the back of one hand across the peak of her breast.

She dared not breathe, let alone speak. She shook her head.

"More than the bee to honey." Both hands caressed the tender mounds of her breasts, squeezing ever so gently. "More than the waves to the shore." His tongue lapped one breast, then the other. "More than the song to the nightingale." He suckled on her left breast.

The tugging of his mouth and the swirling of his tongue upon her breast shot a sea of flame to her core. She threw back her head and clasped her hands to Stephen's shoulders for fear she'd collapse to the ground. Then his lips were devouring hers again, thrusting deep into her mouth as though he meant to capture her soul.

He drew her hand from his shoulder, guided it downward and placed it across the proof of his desire. Except for their reedy gasps of air, neither moved. Slowly, cautiously, and ever so clumsily, she traced the length of him.

"Sweet mercy," he gasped. He thrust himself into her innocent embrace, marveling that trained courtesans had never elicited from him such hunger. The threads of ecstasy lay somewhere between pain and pleasure, he was sure. Somewhere from the depths of passion, the hazy plateau between sensation and reality, Stephen heard the rustling of leaves. His one fleeting hope was that a fox, a rabbit, any creature of the night, invaded his sanctuary. Not one of the humans that he knew were just through those trees.

"Stephen," sounded Elizabeth's ever-familiar voice, soft yet determined. "Where the devil are you?"

When he felt Phoebe tense, he lifted his lips from hers and stared at his hand still wrapped around her breast, seemingly powerless to remove it. Her hand hovered a hairbreadth above his groin. Perhaps if they said nothing, if they remained perfectly still, the female interloper set on ruining his life would take her leave.

"Stephen, stop whatever you're doing this instant and show yourself. Do you hear me? Phoebe? Are you all right?"

A loud thwack preceded several ripe curses from an agitated Winston. "Sweet Mary Jane! Be careful with those bloody branches. Give Stephen a moment and have a care with your ankle. A mother-to-be should not be traipsing through the forest at night. Elizabeth, are you listening to me? It would serve you right if I left you here."

Stephen judged Winston to be twenty or so feet to the right, arguing none too quietly with his wife. The image of his friend tromping through the forest, acting the watch-dog, was too much to overcome. Stephen lay his chin on the top of Phoebe's head. A rumble of laughter started deep in his chest until it boomed across the clearing. "Cease your worries, Elizabeth," he finally managed to sputter. "I'm not ravishing Phoebe." *At least not any longer,* he thought.

Phoebe fumbled with the lacing of the shirt. "I don't know what came over me," she whispered.

Stephen understood her embarrassment. He gently removed her hands and assumed the task of repairing her appearance. "Don't. Please. You are a passionate woman. The music, the mood, the night, fed that passion and I took advantage."

She slapped his hands away. "Goodness, it's not your fault. I could have stayed right where I was."

"Could you have? Truly?"

She never answered, but stood and brushed the nonexist-ent wrinkles from her skirt. Grasping the blanket, he took her hand, kissed her knuckles and headed toward the grum-bling voices of Elizabeth and Winston.

"Either you want them together or you don't," Winston said. "Make up your mind."

"I don't understand," Stephen said as he pushed through a hackberry bush to face his friends. "Would you care to enlighten me?"

"Spare me your droll sense of humor, Stephen. I'm not in the mood," Elizabeth said.

"If I remember correctly, you and Winston have disappeared into the forest a time or two."

Smiling like the tiger with the mouse between his teeth, Elizabeth limped to Phoebe's side. She clasped the girl's hand and headed toward camp, managing the most elegant of hobbles Steven had ever seen. Over her shoulder, she said, "*We* were engaged. Let me know when you intend the same."

"Don't ask me why, but I love her to distraction," Winston said. He slapped Stephen's back. "Let's go home. You'll have the entire weekend at Payley Park to impress Phoebe with your skills and drive Elizabeth half-crazy with worry."

Stephen grinned. His life was no longer recognizable. The fact that he was smiling over the debacle of the last half-hour only solidified his conclusion. This American bit of fluff had careered into his arms and blasted him like a fourteen-gun frigate.

He'd been content on his estates, traveling to London now and again to visit his mistress or tend to business. Aside from a select group of friends, he'd avoided society.

Phoebe had freed him from his protective cocoon. His mouth curved downward. Sweet heavens, he feared he might never be able to return.

Chapter Sixteen

Payley Park occupied the good portion of a hill overlooking a lush valley of budding trees and shrubs, its beige stone walls forming a three-story rectangular shape that in its simplicity spoke of elegance. A long circle drive lay in the middle of a manicured lawn Phoebe thought any Southerner would envy. It suited Elizabeth and Winston, and it evoked the longings for a life she'd likely never see again. The estate was magnificent, and a welcome sight.

Aunt Hildegard, her mood as waspish as ever, had issued rules and commands the entire three-hour journey. Lands alive, that woman was contrary. She had been more so ever since Phoebe had returned from Marsden Manor and bombarded her with questions. Of course, Hildegard had pleaded forgetfulness and acted contrite. It was clear that Phoebe would get nothing from her aunt, the wretched woman. However, if listening to Hildegard grumble and complain meant spending more time with Stephen, Phoebe would tolerate the lecture. Surely once they arrived, she'd have time to herself.

Elizabeth must have read her mind, for she quickly deposited Charity and Hildegard in one room. Against Hildegard's not-so-subtle objections, Elizabeth placed Phoebe two doors down. A large four-poster bed occupied the corner near the window and a door opened onto a small balcony.

Promptly at seven, dressed in a simple rose-colored silk gown, Phoebe ventured into the drawing room. At least thirty people milled about the room. When Elizabeth saw Phoebe, she separated herself from a group of women and crossed to her side. "Did you find everything to your satisfaction?"

"It's glorious." Phoebe nibbled her lower lip and cast a quick glance over her shoulder to watch Sir Lemmer as he conversed sociably with a small group of people. "I must confess, I didn't expect to see *him* here."

"Neither did I. Although I don't find the man overly charming, he does have access to the better parlors of London. Since he arrived in the company of my step-uncle we couldn't very well ask him to leave. If he becomes bothersome, simply pretend he doesn't exist."

"Easier for you than me. You're married. I'm the bait waiting mercilessly for the fish—and I think Hildegard would gladly hold the line for him as well."

Elizabeth patted Phoebe's arm. "Oh Lud. Winston and I shall monopolize your time. If you find yourself trapped, garner my attention and I shall save you."

One question remained unanswered, actually the most important in Phoebe's mind. Scanning the room once more to make sure the scoundrel wasn't lurking in a dark corner somewhere, she said, "I don't see Stephen."

"There is no need to feign indifference with me, Phoebe

Rafferty, but not to worry. Stephen will be here. In fact, his room is next to yours."

Wicked images popped into Phoebe's head, suddenly and vividly, thoughts that heated her skin and parched her throat. She really needed to gain control of these unwanted impulses. Afraid her face revealed her thoughts, she shuffled her feet while she stared at her soft pink slippers. "Elizabeth, you're shameful."

Clasping Phoebe's hand in hers, Elizabeth said, "No. Hopeful. My role as matchmaker began weeks ago. I'd like nothing more for Stephen to marry you—however, I have no intention of allowing the man full liberties." She whispered behind her fan. "Being married, I know about these things." She cleared her throat. "Having said all that, I am not above manipulation, enticement and pure, unadulterated temptation. I leave the rest in your capable hands. Imagine you and Stephen so near each other for three days. It will drive him insane. Lord Tewksbury will be here part of the time as well. I can't wait to witness Stephen's reaction to *that* surprise. Until then, let me introduce you to my friends."

True to her promise, Elizabeth entertained Phoebe while easily performing her duties as hostess. Before and during dinner, Phoebe never had a free moment; neither Sir Lemmer nor Hildegard had a chance to speak to her.

The evening progressed fairly well until she found herself cornered by Lord Milsip, who warned her to mind herself this weekend. After all, her name had been linked with Lord Badrick in *The Times*. Shortly after that, Lord Renoke trapped her in a game of cards during which he, too, expressed his odious thoughts about Stephen.

She tried to remain silent, she truly did; however, honesty won out. Neither man appreciated her opinion. Finally free of both men, she glanced over her shoulder and saw Hildegard and Sir Lemmer together once again, their heads bowed together in a most disconcerting manner. Stephen had yet to appear and unfortunately, it was far too early to escape to her room. Phoebe dropped her forehead into her hands and massaged her temples.

"As bad as all that?"

Phoebe smiled at Winston, who stood before her with a glass in his hands. She eagerly accepted the drink. "I fear I have insulted Lord Renoke and Lord Milsip."

He chuckled. "Do not fret. They thrive on controversy and gossip. Few people whose opinions truly matter pay them any mind. Needing their support for a bill in parliament, I tolerate their company. It's all quite bothersome sometimes and must seem rather shallow, but alas, it's the way of things. Who was their target tonight?"

"Who else? Stephen." Her temper resurfaced in full. She wanted to stomp her feet and shout. "The things they said were atrocious. If I didn't think they believed what they said, I'd laugh myself silly."

Tucking his tongue in his cheek, he appeared to fight the urge to laugh. "So you became Stephen's champion?"

"It seems he needed one."

"He might not appreciate your intervention. I, on the other hand, applaud you. He deserves a woman with your strength and kindness. As his friend of many years, I ask you not to abandon him just yet."

"To tell you the truth, I'm not sure I could even if I wanted too." She paused, sorrowful. "In my heart, I know he's capable of love and wants to be happy."

"A habit of self-preservation, I fear. Trust me when I say some of his actions are justified—others are caused by years of expectation. One day, hopefully soon, he will recognize his good fortune and accept what you so generously wish to offer. I pray you shall give Stephen a good deal to think about over these last few weeks." He grasped her elbow and led her toward a group of people seated in chairs beside the fireplace. "Come join us for charades, after which you can play cards, billiards, or, if you like, retire early."

She settled beside Winston as Lord Renoke stood before the group, executing a ghastly impression of what Phoebe thought might be the Prince Regent riding a horse. Winston whispered a suggestion in her ear, eliciting a burst of laughter. The gathered players blurted their assumptions, one lucky soul guessing Napoleon at some battle or other. Several people took a turn, Phoebe included, while others simply watched. As Lady Ashby assumed the floor, prepared to take a turn, Winston moved to stand beside Elizabeth. Lemmer quickly snatched the empty seat, prompting Phoebe to inch further to the edge of the settee.

Leaning close enough so that his breath, which smelled of onion and a touch of mint, fanned her cheek, Lemmer said, "You have neglected your duties this eve, Miss Rafferty, and ignored me, yet you bat your lovely lashes at others. You are quite naughty."

"I can do whatever I like."

"Once my ring sits on your finger, you will behave quite differently."

Phoebe jerked to one side, checked her reaction and simply straightened her spine. Maybe if she ignored the man he'd simply leave her be. She focused on Lady Ashby, who slid back and forth across the floor with her head tilted majestically.

Lemmer applauded Lady Ashby's efforts, as did several other people. He chuckled with some sort of perverse satisfaction and whispered for Phoebe's ears only. "A silly game, charades. Grown men and women behaving like utter fools. What is becoming of our society?"

She hated his conceit, his high-and-mighty attitude. "The game is harmless and fun."

"I admit, you did quite well with *Pride and Prejudice*."

She tried to concentrate on Lady Ashby, who now pretended to kneel on the floor, her head cocked oddly. Unfortunately, Lemmer's presence proved an unnerving distraction. Phoebe's mind was a blank.

"As a matter of fact, I believe pride is something of which you have an abundance. I look forward to eradicating that flaw."

She was full up with his possessive remarks. This man would not ruin her evening. "No matter what you think, you shall never have such an opportunity." Hesitant to stand too abruptly and cause any sort of scene, she rejoiced when someone shouted the correct answer to Ashby's pantomime. Applause and laughter erupted. Thankfully, the game was over.

Winston stood, clapping his hands together. Slowly, the room quieted. "My friends, a light repast shall be served shortly in the salon. Best remember we have a fox to hunt tomorrow bright and early. Until then, there are cards or billiards, and if some of you wish to retire, Lady Payley and myself bid you good night."

Phoebe stood. Lemmer stepped boldly in her path. He nodded politely toward a passing couple as they left the room, then spoke sweetly to Phoebe. "Retiring so quickly?"

"Actually, Lord Eaton invited me to play cards."

"You cannot avoid me forever, my dear."

A small group, which included Elizabeth and Winston, circled toward the door. Winston halted beside Phoebe. "Is there a problem?"

"Not at all," cooed Lemmer, backing a more discreet distance from Phoebe, his smile one of false humor. "I was simply telling Miss Rafferty I intend to show her my appreciation by bringing her the fox tail tomorrow."

A few gentlemen chuckled at the bold statement, adding their opinions on the matter. Soon the conversation gathered the attention of others in the room and much to Phoebe's annoyance, wagers were placed with her affection as the prize. She looked desperately to Elizabeth for help.

Clearing her throat, Elizabeth said, "Excuse me, but I believe Miss Rafferty should have a say in all this."

Hildegard, wearing her ever-familiar pinched expression, chose that particular moment to interject. "I find the idea satisfactory enough. After all, my niece is looking for a husband. This is somewhat like a jousting tournament. Men have always found a means to display their esteem for a particular young lady. This is no different."

No different? Phoebe had no desire to be anyone's prize, leastways not Sir Lemmer's—and certainly not at the expense of some poor fox. She found herself wondering if this was a scheme Lemmer and Hildegard had orchestrated with their heads tucked together earlier in the evening. If so, to what end?

Well, try as they may, they'd see how difficult it was to manipulate her. "Begging your all's pardon. But there are other lovely ladies in attendance as well. Shouldn't they be included?"

Elizabeth placed her hand on Winston's arm as if to remind the audience that she possessed his full support in whatever she chose to say. "A splendid idea. I do suggest caution. Society often has large ears and long memories." She fixed a pointed look on Lemmer. "I'd hate to think a harmless wager might endanger someone's reputation."

Lemmer shook his head in agreement. "Of course not."

"In that case," Elizabeth explained, "the gentleman who reaches the fox first shall have the opportunity to select the young lady of his choice as a dinner companion, with a maximum of two dances at the ball."

"And what if a lady happens to win?" asked an older matron.

Elizabeth exchanged a glance with Phoebe, then grinned. "Then I suppose she would have her choice of companions."

Laughter accompanied by a few ribald comments were volleyed back and forth across the room. One man promised to choose his wife, which sparked another bout of jokes. One older wife announced that if she won, she intended to choose a younger, more vigorous dancing partner. The men howled. The women giggled. The overall idea obviously appealed to everyone. Everyone except Phoebe.

Winston nodded in approval as others in the room expressed theirs. "It seems our hunt tomorrow has a purpose. May the fox be fleet of feet, but not too much so. Coming, Phoebe?"

"In a moment. I wish to have a word with Sir Lemmer first." She had every intention of wiping the smug expression from his face. She waited for the crowd to disperse, then lifted a brow, taunting him just the way Dee had taught her. "I don't understand your game, but don't underestimate my ability to play as well. I'll rejoice at your loss tomorrow."

"But I intend to win, after which you will find it impossible to ignore me—and Lord Badrick shall not be able to interfere. Heed my words, Miss Rafferty. I said this before and repetition is ever so boring, but Lord Badrick will not have you."

"I would never presume to speak for Lord Badrick. Only he knows his mind. I, however, know I shall never marry a pompous, self-indulgent little rodent like yourself. Good night."

"Of all the miserable, low-down marsh rats." Phoebe yanked the pins from her hair and massaged her scalp.

"He'll rue the day. Yes, indeed." She hurled one shoe toward the balcony door.

"For the love of Mary, watch out," muttered Stephen as he limped from the shadow, rubbing his shin. "Had I known the extent of your temper, I would have made my appearance downstairs."

"Stephen? Are you all right?" She stopped in her tracks, narrowing her eyes and placing her hands on her hips. "What are you doing in my room?"

Sweet mercy, she looked magnificent in her fury. He briefly wondered about the apparent anger, but found his thoughts quickly drawn to the creamy skin of her bosom. Having loosened her curls, Phoebe's hair cascaded about her face in a fiery waterfall. Having purposely avoided her for the past several days, he had arrived later than planned with no desire to dally with his peers. He'd come directly to his room. Shortly thereafter, he'd found himself in hers. Waiting.

Considering the lustful thoughts swarming in his mind, he decided he would have been wiser to wait until morning. He tossed the balance of his brandy down his throat. "I came to see how you fared and to say good night."

"Good night."

"I'm truly sorry to be so late."

"Lands alive. I'm not the least bit concerned that you chose to arrive eight hours after the party began, although you might have saved me from antagonizing a couple of rude old men. And maybe, just maybe, I could have escaped a game of cards with Lord Eaton, who happens to find my accent a trifle annoying, though he is willing to overlook it for my sake and marry me all the same. And, had you been here, Sir Lemmer might not have goaded me into riding that infernal fox hunt tomorrow."

"Lemmer is here?"

"He came with Lord Wyman. And he remains as conceited as always. That man plays a game of sorts and I have the uncomfortable sensation he makes his own rules. I don't know what he plans, but I refuse to be tested."

Heaven help him, but he needed to hold her, to taste her. His hands itched to touch her. If he hoped to sleep at all tonight, touching her was definitely out of the question. He moved to her side. Pulling her against his chest, he felt her relax instantly, invoking a surge of pure male satisfaction. It felt wonderful to hold her in his arms, enough so that he almost forgot his good intentions and that Lemmer was at Payley Park. "Tell me exactly what happened."

She remained within the cocoon of his arms and explained the wager in great and animated detail. When all was said and done, Lemmer's game and its final outcome remained a mystery. Whatever he planned, it certainly wasn't above board. "All will be well. Wait and see." He bent his head to press a tender kiss to her forehead. "I've missed you."

She pushed away and crossed to the wardrobe. "Tell me about a foxhunt."

Dumbfounded, he balanced the emotions that warred with his body. By George, he'd been experiencing a tender moment and she concerned herself with foxhunts? "Excuse me?"

"Tell me about a foxhunt."

He recognized the fire in her green eyes, the way she pursed her lips and nibbled her thumb as she methodically considered something he knew she shouldn't, something that would likely keep him awake all night. Her devious mind was hard at work. "What are you planning?"

"Nothing." She practically skipped to a chair and sat like a pupil waiting her next lesson. "I wish to know what to expect tomorrow."

Balderdash. He would have to watch her closely. He

occupied the chair opposite her. "Very early this morning, the game boy shall find the foxholes and cover them to prevent the animal from returning to his den. Hence the fox shall be forced to seek cover above ground. After breakfast, the field will assemble and—"

"The field?"

"The riders, all of us grand and noble folk, along with a dozen or so yapping hounds and Winston's huntsman, the man in charge of the animals. We shall all depart from the stable yard at what's deemed an appropriate hour and give chase until the dogs roust a fox in a thicket or bramble bush. Then off we go, riding like lunatics over hill and dale. Everyone tries their best to remain seated in their saddle until the hounds trap the fox and subsequently kill him. The first man to arrive is awarded with the tail or paw as a trophy."

Judging from the frown on her face, Phoebe possessed no appreciation for the longtime tradition. A shudder racked her shoulders. "That poor animal. The sport sounds barbaric and not the least bit fair."

"Nevertheless, it is a time-honored tradition. Normally we avoid hunts in the spring, but the local farmers have been losing chickens."

"What if the fox escapes?"

"T'would be highly unlikely, but everyone would return, sip their tea and discuss all the reasons they turned up trump."

"And no one wins the wager." Beaming, she marched to the door that led to the balcony. "Thank you, Stephen. You had best go now. Tomorrow's events sound quite exhausting."

The blasted female had dismissed him, actually requested he leave—and he had waited for her until midnight. By golly, he'd have the last word before he left her to her own devices. With very deliberate footsteps, Stephen cornered her and, using his entire body, pressed her against the cloth-covered wall. Her eyes locked with his. She swallowed, then cleared her throat.

His every nerve ending trembled with a heightened awareness, yet he made no move to kiss her. When he felt her pulses pound like a drum throughout her entire body, then and only then did he let his mouth descend. He captured her lower lip between his teeth and suckled gently. Swallowing her gasp and then her sigh, he possessed her mouth completely, endlessly.

A gentle knocking at the door snapped him back to reality. Lifting his lips from hers, he kept his hand on her chin, studying the dazed look in her eyes and feeling a deep masculine pride. " 'Tis likely the maid. I will go now, but I shan't sleep a wink for fear of what you contemplate. I'm warning you. No nonsense tomorrow. Let Winston and me worry about Lemmer."

Other than his uncomfortable state of arousal, he felt quite pleased with himself. If she trembled like this after a simple kiss, imagine how she would react after he introduced her to lovemaking.

Chapter Seventeen

"Once the fox is spotted, stay to the back of the field. The ride turns wild rather quickly. I shall keep my eye on Lemmer. Remember what I said last night. No nonsense."

Yawning behind her hand, Phoebe spared Stephen a glance. Goodness, he was agitated this morning. She hadn't slept all that well either, but she didn't blame him for her lack of rest, even though if she had, she would have felt justified. His kiss had left her yearning for his company long into the morning hours. Admittedly, her preoccupation with the hunt had also prompted her to wake earlier than normal. She intended to show Lemmer that she was not easily intimidated. Or manipulated. She yawned a second time. "I heard you the first time, sir."

He slapped his gloves against his hand, likely aggravated over her lack of argument, before he stomped away to gather his own horse. She turned her attention to the stable yard. It certainly took a lot of people to orchestrate a fox hunt.

Stableboys and groomsmen saddled the horses. The hounds howled and yapped and tugged on the tethers that as yet, bound them to a large pole. As the fog melted away, a gentle breeze teased her face, carrying the fresh scent of spring and sunshine. Fraught with purpose, she seemed unable to enjoy the activity.

Winston occupied himself with the huntsman. Elizabeth stood at Winston's side, one hand on his sleeve. Their affection for one another was so obvious that Phoebe sighed. That sort of tenderness and devotion was all she wanted. Was it too much to hope for?

A horn sounded, prompting the forty or so lords and ladies to mount, herself included. Enthusiastic chatter carried through the morning air, sounding somewhat like the spirited audience of a cotton auction back home. Imagine, thought Phoebe as she climbed atop her horse, a tiny little fox was the cause of all this excitement.

The huntsman, dressed in a lovely red coat, rode to the front of the group and raised one arm. On his signal the stableboys released the dogs. They obviously knew what they were about, for they made a mad dash across the clearing in the direction of the nearest cover. The riders followed at a steady lope, maintaining a comfortable distance from the hounds. No one seemed overly concerned about where he or she rode or how quickly.

Stephen rode beside Winston and Elizabeth. Periodically, he switched his gaze to Phoebe, a firm warning in his eyes. Lemmer, also riding near the front, primped while his horse pranced. Every now and then he slid her a backward glance, his expression more like a leer. It took every bit of restraint not to stick out her tongue at him. All in good time, she reminded herself. If the hunt went as she planned, the overgrown braggart would be eating crow by dinner time.

She trotted near the end biding her time, listening to

Lord Kendall, her self-appointed companion, babble end-lessly about the skill required to tie a proper cravat. An occasional bird squawked, no doubt annoyed by the cacophony of baying hounds that tore through the wooded glades. She kept her eyes open, alert and watchful, looking for the path the young stableboy had mentioned.

After a half-hour, the riders passed a rotted oak that resembled a hunchbacked witch. This was the moment she had awaited. She placed her hand to her forehead and swayed in her saddle. "Oh, dear, I feel a bit lightheaded. If you don't mind, sir, I believe I shall rest."

Lord Kendall immediately stopped his horse. "Of course. Let us retire to the shade of those elms."

"And ruin your chance to win a dance with me? Please, go. I shall either catch up or return to the stables."

His eyes shone when she mentioned the little wager. After he glanced a time or two between the parting group and Phoebe, Kendall nodded abruptly and galloped away. She waited for him to disappear behind a large bramble bush, then yanked her horse around and cantered in the opposite direction. She stopped and pulled from her bodice the tiny map the game boy had given her. In the distance, she heard a peculiar bray, followed by a loud yell and a horn. The fox had been sighted. She didn't have much time.

Cavalier jumped the three-foot hedge with the ease Stephen expected. Eager to witness Phoebe's skill as a rider, he veered off the leaf-covered path and waited. When Lord Kendall flew over the obstacle, alone, Stephen knew his earlier assumptions to be true. That caper-witted female had concocted some sort of idiotic plan and had traipsed off to parts unknown. By herself.

Wasting no time, he urged his horse to a gallop. Finding

the spot he had last seen Phoebe, he stopped, trying to decide where she might have gone. A small flock of magpies screeched and fled high above the trees. He smiled. She wasn't far.

Maintaining a lengthy distance, he spied Phoebe as she circled the woods toward some destination only she seemed to know. After five minutes, he was rewarded with her plan. Somehow or another the clever girl had managed to learn the location of the foxholes. She had every intention of uncovering them, allowing the fox to go to ground. Although annoyed with her decision to exclude him from her plan, he grinned. There would be no winner today. Lemmer would be suitably vexed. Quickly and quietly, Stephen tied Cavalier to a nearby maple, advancing on foot until he startled a small rabbit that dashed across the clearing. Stephen ducked behind a large bush.

Spying the frightened animal, Phoebe froze. Her gaze darted from tree to tree. At least the girl had the good sense to be nervous. She hesitated another moment, obviously decided she was alone, then resumed the task of pushing a large rock from the hole. Suddenly jerking her finger to her mouth and sucking on it, she uttered a rather earthy expletive.

Stephen stepped into the open. "Phoebe Rafferty, you have the mouth of a sailor! Was the hunt boring you?"

Jumping to her feet, she brushed the dirt and leaves from her knees, her head tilted to the ground. "You know exactly what I'm doing."

"True. And I should be angry. I leave you to your own devices and off you go to kick up a lark." He shook his head from side to side, wishing she would lift her face. He couldn't determine her mood. "What am I to do with you? Not that I disapprove of the concept, only the consequences if you're caught. What do you suppose the others will think when both you and I suddenly turn up missing? What if someone else saw you and decided to follow? Not everyone is a gentleman like myself."

She thrust up her chin with determination and fisted her hands on her hips. She was dressed in a delightful blue outfit, and her breasts thrust forward to tease him mercilessly. She had even loosened the top two buttons, exposing the creamy flesh of her slender neck. "Is that so? If you are the gentleman you claim to be, then come over here and move this infernal rock."

Blast, the woman was a tempting armful, but now was not the time to act on his baser impulses. He intended to find privacy first. Shaking his head once again, Stephen pushed her aside and easily lifted the rock away. "Most men take their hunts very seriously. I wonder if you realize the extent of your interference."

"Will Winston be angry?"

"Knowing him as I do, I imagine he will consider Lemmer's proposal, place your absence with mine, and come to a reasonable conclusion on his own. Of course, he will investigate to ascertain if his assumption is true. This little scheme of yours could cause the stable lads a fair bit of trouble. How did you discover the location of the foxholes, anyway?"

Tugging on the ends of her gloves, she shuffled her toe through the grass. "I sort of, well, I, more or less bribed the game boy. He shouldn't be punished, though."

With deliberately casual movements, he brushed his hands together and said, "If you willingly spend the afternoon with me, I shall explain the situation to Winston and swear him to leniency."

"Exactly what do you desire, Lord Badrick?"

You. In my arms. Beneath me. Joined with me. If he hoped to gain her company for the afternoon, he dared not share the images wreaking havoc on his body. He lifted her hand to his lips and pressed a gentle kiss to the inside of her wrist. "A ride. Conversation. The rest remains to be seen and is totally in your hands, Phoebe, but we'd best hurry lest the hounds find our scent and you and I become the targets of great speculation and ruination."

"Goodness gracious. We'd best be off, then." When she folded her hand in his, she felt safe and content, anticipating the afternoon with renewed interest.

They located the second foxhole and together dispensed with the barrier. The hounds brayed in the near distance and they knew time had run out. With luck, the fox would return to his burrow.

Mounting their horses quickly, they cantered across a wide field alive with yellow primrose and purple violets. Along the edge, budding cherry trees burst with color. But Stephen was the most magnificent sight of all. An expert horseman, he moved as one with the animal. His toffee-colored breeches molded to his thighs as he rode. The wind teased his raven curls, exposing the strength of his jaw. He smiled contentedly, evidently as pleased with the prospects of the afternoon as she.

Following a path beside a rocky stream lined with ferns, they slowly climbed a small hilltop. "Wherever are you taking me?" she asked.

"Chanctonbury Ring, a place of magic and mystery. An ancient Roman temple once sat on top of this hill. Winston and I came here as lads and imagined ourselves embroiled in all sorts of adventures."

Trees grew everywhere, towering to the sky, flowering ash and young budding sycamores, majestic oak and grand old elms. They formed a dense, eerie ceiling, effectively blocking much of the sun. Not a bit of wind stirred and the heavy scent of dirt and new foliage filled the air. In the center was a circle of crumbling stone monoliths. Patches of wildflowers and grass grew amongst the rubble. Although the hounds sounded in the distance, she felt as though she and Stephen were the only two people in England. She whispered, "It's quite wonderful."

"They say that if you run seven times around this circle of trees, backwards, at midnight on Midsummer's Eve, the devil himself will offer you a bowl of porridge."

"Did you and Winston ever try?"

"Once. We made it to the sixth turnabout and decided we'd best find a very large stick—after which our stomachs began to grumble in a most disconcerting manner. We elected to return to the manor in dire need of something to eat lest we'd have too little strength to face our adversary."

His dark eyes gleamed with an intriguing mix of mischief and pleasure. His spirited mood and sudden willingness to talk about his childhood drew her to his side. Laughing, she said, "You were cowards."

"Never. We were ten and we feared the story might not be true. Legends are great fun, but unfortunately, they vanish like the shadows on the moor in the light of reason."

"Tell me more."

He climbed from his horse and lifted her down from hers, brushing their bodies together ever so slightly. The simple contact shot shivers up and down her spine, electrifying the tips of her fingers and breasts. Surely he felt her tremble. When she blushed his lips curled to one side; he had the expectant look of a man ready to savor a cigar and warmed brandy.

Taking her reins from her, he tied their two horses to a nearby branch, clasped her hand in his and led her to a grassy spot centered within the ruins. "A white-haired man, perhaps a druid, centuries old and searching for treasure, also inhabits this hill—as does a ghostly army. Every now and again, if you listen carefully, you can hear the hooves of invisible horses."

"Have you seen the old man?"

"Now that is another tale in itself." He shed his jacket, exposing a white muslin shirt molded to his chest. After placing the jacket on the ground to serve as a blanket, he knelt and extended his arm in invitation. Willingly, and unable to stop herself, she sat beside him.

"We made our first visit here," Stephen said, "shortly after Winston's father shared the story of the old man. Tell a young boy of treasure and there's no stopping him. Like two cross-eyed lobcocks, we spent nearly a week traipsing through the woods, digging at every plausible hiding place. One night we stayed later than we should have. A horrific storm came up. The wind blew relentlessly, wailing in an eerie song throughout the trees—like a choir of the dead. Or at least it seemed so in our wild imaginations. Suddenly a figure in white with fierce, burning eyes and hideous, wheezing laughter appeared from over there." He pointed to a gnarled tree near the edge of the ruins.

"Winston, the poor lad, stood dumbstruck. As the ghostly intruder edged toward us, I, of course, collected my wits, grabbed my friend's quaking hand and dragged him to safety."

Leaning insolently on one elbow, his face seemed dangerously close to her breasts. She perched her folded hands on her bent knees. "Why Lord Badrick, if I didn't know you better, I'd say you were trying to frighten me."

He placed his hand across his heart, his expression one of shock. " 'Tis the honest truth I tell. Winston will gladly corroborate, although he will do his best to portray himself as the hero. Anyway, we abandoned our shovels and darted for home, our legs pumping as fast as possible. We dashed into Winston's father's study wild with excitement—partly out of fear but mostly joy of our adventure. Come to find out, it had been Winston's father in disguise. When all was said and done we had quite the laugh over our folly."

"How wonderfully exciting." Intoxicated by the rich

timbre of his voice and his mere presence, she knew that remaining with him, alone, on top of this secluded hill was likely not the best of ideas. Their problems forgotten, she couldn't resist the attraction they shared.

"I knew you to be an adventurer at heart, Miss Rafferty."

She wasn't feeling much like an adventurer right now. This was dangerous ground she tread upon. His fingers toyed with a curl loosened from her braid near the nape of her neck, and she felt herself shiver with delight.

His eyes blazed with an intensity that beckoned to every nerve in her body. Swallowing convulsively, she feared she would sound like a shy little church mouse. "Most definitely. When I was eight or so, a slave told me a tale of a casket of coins left behind by a French pirate. I even discovered a map. I was determined to make the treasure mine. I found the cave with the help of Tobias, Dee's husband. I was frightened and thrilled at the same time. We found a skeleton and a weathered box. Then we looked closer. In his one hand he clasped a golden locket. Inside was the picture of a beautiful woman. In the other hand lay a crumpled scrap of paper. The nearby box contained a ring engraved with two entwined hearts, and a packet of letters, obviously the ones she wrote. I believe he died thinking of the woman he loved. It was quite sad yet terribly romantic."

"What did you do?"

"We left everything. We concealed the cave as best we could and I destroyed the map. I know that's silly because someone probably discovered it again sooner or later, but it seemed somehow sacreligious to disturb him."

Stephen's hand entwined with hers. He studied her fingers as he traced the delicate lines of her knuckles. "You have the heart of a romantic."

She was lost. Right now, at this moment, as they shared bits of their past, she fell over the edge and into love's abyss. She had expected such for days, ever since their time together at Marsden Manor. Now she was sure. She would grant him anything. With the realization came a sense of despair, which saddened her all the more. The discovery of love was a moment to be celebrated, not feared. "And you, Lord Badrick? Have *you* a heart to give?"

"Most definitely. And if I'm not dreadfully vigilant, I'll likely lose it."

"If ever given, I would cherish your heart as the greatest of treasures."

A flicker of longing flared deep in his eyes, but it was buried just as quickly beneath a haunted look. "Foolish girl."

She wanted to weep for him, for all that forced him to lock his emotions away. Unable to stop herself, hoping to erase the agony in his voice, she reached for him and cradled his cheek in her hand. "I'm afraid I have little choice. The deed is done."

"You can't—"

She placed her fingers across his lips. "Stephen, my heart, the way I feel, is a gift freely given."

Freely? Stephen wanted to shout. Nothing in life came without a cost, a consequence. He knew he had best leave her now. Her declaration hurled his mind into a maelstrom of needs and demands. To consume. To possess. To take what she offered.

Shifting his position, he pressed her to the ground, his gaze riveted on her face, studying the features that invaded his sleep at night. Light brown eyebrows that arched over green eyes the color of a spring meadow. Skin soft and dewy. Lips, full, parted and ready for his possession.

"Phoebe." Her name was a plea. He hated the weakness he felt, but seemed unable to control the need. It clawed to be free like a beast from its cage. His lips brushed hers lightly, reverently, knowing that kissing her was the last thing he should do. A wise man would run for his horse, ride away fast and hard as if demons followed. He admitted demons did chase him, his own private demons, ones that refused to allow him a life, a future. He would not deny himself this brief respite. Stephen crushed his greedy mouth to Phoebe's willing one.

Stephen had shared kisses with other women as a prelude to lovemaking, a task necessary to prepare a woman for the physical act to come. Kissing Phoebe was a banquet in itself. With the dueling of tongues and reckless melding of lips, they feasted upon one another. Like a madman unable to discern right from wrong, driven only by need, his tongue explored the fullness of her lips, the recesses of her mouth. He savored her gasps, her breathy sighs of assent.

His hands caressed the bounty of her breasts. Her desire was evident and his fingertips tingled, down through his hands to the very part of him that demanded satisfaction. One by one, he loosened the buttons of her jacket and slid the garment from her shoulders. She offered no objection.

Shifting himself to his knees, he loosened the tie on her skirt and slipped the fabric from her body. He froze.

With an unwavering stare, he raked his gaze from her boot-clad ankles up her long legs, over the shadow beneath her shift at the juncture of her thighs to the soft, supple mounds of her breasts, the peach-tinted nipples already swollen and hard. He slowed his breathing, a difficult task when all he thought to do was bury himself deep within her warmth. Damn, she'd told him she loved him. She was *his*. He had all the time in the world to make love to her in all the ways he'd imagined.

He lifted first one of her feet, then the other, removing her boots and stockings. Using his knuckles, he massaged her tender soles until her toes curled in response. Next came her calves, his stroke slow and steady, kneading the muscles of her legs. As he inched his way to her thighs, the fabric of her shift moved slowly upward. He straddled her body and as his hands hovered at the top of her legs, he waited until she looked at him, forcing her to acknowledge what they meant to share.

She opened her eyes, burning him with a look of such love and trust that he paused. Lord, what was he thinking? But he knew. His hands scrunched the fabric into a tight ball. He was thinking to make love to the woman who'd just told him she loved him. She wanted him. What more did he need to know? This was right.

"Lift yourself a bit." When she did, he edged the shift to her narrow waist, beyond her shoulders, and up over her head. He needed to see her in all her naked glory. The garment fell to the ground unnoticed.

Using the backs of his fingers, he brushed a featherlike caress from her collar bone, over the rise of her breasts. He circled her nipples, running his hand down her stomach through the thatch of curls, over her legs to her feet, only to repeat the torture until they both were panting.

Phoebe lifted her head. "Am I to be the only one without clothes?"

He sat on his heels and shed his shirt, then lowered himself on top of Phoebe, pressing chest to breast, male to female. His tongue thrust deep into her mouth. Her calm, the last shreds of her control, shattered with the hunger of his touches and kisses. The need to feed that passion overwhelmed all else. She could deny him nothing. The feel of his naked body pressed against hers was unlike anything she had ever imagined.

His hands slowly crawled in a slow, torturous path to her very core, where he toyed endlessly until she writhed against his seeking fingers. She stilled for a moment when he placed a finger within her body, the shock of such action foreign to her but enticing all the same. Two fingers, then, and the steady rhythm he set enveloped her body with a marvelous tension, a suspense and need, a wanting of the unknown.

Then and only then did Stephen lean away to discard his trousers. When he lay atop her once again, she felt the proof of his desire pressed at the juncture of her thighs. She spread her legs further to adapt and accept the nourishment he offered, the only sustenance that would end the gnawing hunger of her loins.

Probing gently, he pressed into her allowing her to accept the part of him so different from her. She felt a slight burning, horrifically awkward, for she knew not what to do to ease the tightness. Then he thrust forward, joining them in the manner a man and woman were meant to be joined. Unable to control her reaction, she gave a rather mouselike squeak. Stephen lay perfectly still, his head burrowed in her hair, his gasps of air teasing the strands at her temples.

She waited, the clawing need she'd momentarily lost building once again. Still, Stephen lay perfectly still. "Is that all?" she managed to ask. She felt the rocking of his shoulders as he chuckled.

He raised his head to meet her gaze. "No, my sweet. We're far from finished. I was giving you time to adjust."

Fighting the embarrassment of actually talking while joined as such, she nibbled her lower lip. She really wanted to continue. "I believed I've adjusted enough."

He laughed again, this time deeper and fuller. She felt him deep inside her, his slight movement causing the most intriguing sensations. "Oh, my," she sighed. He pulled away ever so slightly, only to plunge into her depths again and again, his movements gaining power. He kissed her fiercely, his body's rhythm matching the thrusts of his tongue. Her body rose to match his movements. Stephen groaned and, she discovered the benefit of moving, participating in this act of love. Tentatively, she matched his rhythm, pumping and heaving toward a destination she knew existed, a plane of completion like none she'd ever experienced. The pounding of her heart matched the throbbing in her loins until a pleasure ignited so great that she could do no more than shudder beneath its fiery release.

A moment later, Stephen gave a final thrust, emitted a lusty groan and bent his head to her shoulder. They collapsed, sated. With a sigh, Stephen slid from her body, rolled to his side and leaned on his elbow, his head tucked in the cradle of his hand.

Reaching her arm high above her head, languishing in the warmth of the afternoon sun, she felt like a cat, too content to do more than stretch. Love was a remarkable thing. Her lips curved slightly as the racing of her heart began to slow. She raised her eyelids to find Stephen staring at her, his gaze no less intense than it was earlier. In fact, if possible, his eyes burned brighter, his expression fiercer, almost triumphant.

Smoothing the wisps of hair from her brow, he said, "Darling, as soon as we return to London, we shall find you a place to live."

She still felt like purring. "A house?"

"You can chose whatever you like, I care not. Cost is not a factor. I simply want you in my bed as soon as possible."

The brusque matter-of-fact tone of Stephen's voice penetrated the sensual fog that had wrapped about her body. She'd declared her love, and truth be told, she hadn't known what to expect from him—but certainly not this. He'd obviously misunderstood. She sat up, distancing herself from the man. "What do you think I agreed to?"

For the first time his expression wavered slightly. "To be my mistress, of course."

"Of course." Reaching for her shift, she dragged the garment over her head. She pushed her arms through the sleeves of her blouse, stalling for more time looking for the words to explain. Her skirt came next, the dampness from their lovemaking evident. Which only increased her discomfort as she realized what she had done.

No, she thought. She had willingly given him her virginity and would never regret her actions.

She had surrendered her love, yet she wasn't prepared to surrender her future. Two weeks remained before her inheritance became Hildegard's. Ample time yet to sway the stubborn man's mind, to prove he couldn't live without her. "I admitted my love, but I did not mean, in any way, to give you the impression that I—"

"Spit it out, darling. What's the matter?"

"I am not going to become your mistress."

"The devil you say." He jumped to his feet, entirely naked. He seemed not to care. "No other man will touch you. You just gave me your virginity."

"Believe you me, I'm well aware of what just happened."

His eyes narrowed suspiciously as he yanked his trousers over his hips, fastening the flaps with abrupt movements. He threw his arms into his shirt. He marched about, towering above her like the wall of trees surrounding them. "What game is this? Do you think to force me to marry you?"

"You idiot." She stuffed her feet into her boots without her stockings, which she tucked into the pocket of her jacket. "Why must everything be a game, a ploy, a trap? Can't I give you something without your suspicions taking over? Listen to me, you stubborn man. I chose to make love with you and that's that. I'm not ready to give up hope for a future I've dreamed of all my life."

Stephen continued to prowl the wooded area, his movements, normally graceful and fluid, were agitated and stiff. The muscles she had caressed and felt their sinewy strength now bunched with tension. Stopping to stare at a squirrel that chattered from a nearby tree, his terse response came from beneath a large oak, his face cloaked in shadow. "You just experienced a woman's pleasure. Tended to by me."

"I realize that," she said hesitantly, unsure of the direction of his thoughts.

"Such pleasure is not often shared between a man and a woman."

"Why do you suppose that is, Stephen?"

"I have no bloody idea."

Love, she wanted to shout. Love made the difference. Damn his soul.

"Do you think to find another man who can make you respond so readily?"

"Probably not."

"Then abandon this ridiculous search of yours!"

"I have no choice."

"There are always choices."

She focused on the loosened buttons of her jacket. "So you keep saying and I keep wishing."

He ripped a scrap of bark from the trunk of a tree and tossed it to the ground. "I do not understand your willingness to go to a man you hardly know, one you might dislike, simply due to a piece of property. We shared more than a kiss or two, Phoebe Rafferty, and don't even think to forget it. I guarantee my caresses will haunt you no matter the man you take as husband."

The truth of his statement was paralyzing. No man made her feel as he had. She hated the fact that he knew it. She stood and brushed the crushed leaves from her clothes, which only fueled her discomfort. His blind refusal to acknowledge what they had shared, what she had freely given, hurt and shattered what little patience she had left. Her body throbbed with rekindled passion. Anger. For the first time in weeks, she questioned her ability to change his mind. "Since we seem to be speaking so openly, I venture to say that you, Stephen Lambert, will remember the response I freely gave and will spend the rest of your days despising the thought of another man touching me as you did. Think on that."

Like the ancient trees that surrounded them, he stood rooted to the ground. Then without another word, he stomped toward their horses.

Phoebe considered his silence a good sign; her comments had hit their mark. She still had a slight chance of convincing him to marry her. With a conviction born of years of hardship, she resolved to give the man one last chance. Of course, she was a dreamer at heart.

Chapter Eighteen

Phoebe tore her gaze from Stephen, who stood on the other side of the ballroom refusing to give her the time of day. She stared at her aunt's pinched expression—the knitted brow, her normally pale coloring flushed with anger—and sighed. Hildegard was in the mood to lecture.

"Your willful behavior, Phoebe Rafferty, casts doubt on your character, which in turn affects me and my own. I have heard the whispers about your disappearance this morning. The fact that Lord Badrick vanished near the same time stimulates gossip amongst my peers. I shall not have my name linked with his."

Hildegard's words rolled off her tongue with little care as to who might hear while her arms flapped in every direction. A bit of the devil prompted Phoebe to widen her eyes with false innocence and, knowing she would be better off saying nothing, she spoke nonetheless, her voice a whisper laced with shock. "Why, Auntie, do people think you were with Lord Badrick?"

Hildegard sputtered twice, then snapped her mouth shut. She frowned at Phoebe, then cast a glance to her daughter, who had giggled quietly. "Charity, what do you find amusing? And quit your slouch. Your dress hangs like a worn grain sack when you do."

Charity jerked her shoulders backward and thrust her chest forward. However Charity managed to tolerate her mother's constant attacks was beyond Phoebe's imagination. But then again, so was Hildegard's cruelty.

"And *what*, pray tell, did you say to Lord Renoke and Lord Milsip?" Her aunt continued. "They seemed absolutely horrified when someone mentioned your name. Not that I care overmuch for their opinion. When I consider your mother's sins, I am not surprised at your behavior. She traipsed off to the colonies without a care to what happened to me, leaving me to accept what meager proposals came my way. People talked then as well."

Gritting her teeth, wishing she were anywhere but where she was, Phoebe purposefully smacked her lips. "Auntie, if I may say so, I think that too many people spend far too much time hashing over other people's lives as it is. As to my disappearance this morning, I felt faint and went for a walk. Remember?"

"At the same time as Badrick!" The disdain carried over into Hildegard's words. "Even Sir Lemmer commented on the so-called coincidence."

"Sir Lemmer's opinion means nothing to me."

Hildegard's lips twisted into a sneer. "You say that now, but circumstance often changes quickly and unexpectedly."

Ignoring the warning that clamored in her mind, Phoebe tried to think of a way to escape her aunt's company, though she hated to abandon Charity. She grinned when she saw Sir Ellwood and Lord Kendall heading in their

256

direction. A dance with either man was better than a lecture.

"Here come Sir Ellwood and Lord Kendall," Hildegard muttered. "Remove that wobegone expression from your face, Charity. As I reminded you earlier this eve, do not waste your time with Ellwood."

"But Mother, surely one dance wouldn't hurt."

"Humph. And for heaven's sake, try to think of something to say other than 'yes sir' and 'no sir.' "

"I am not a simpleton, Mother."

Clutching Charity's hand in hers, Phoebe squeezed. She could offer no words, only support. Waiting until Charity had secured a dance with Sir Ellwood, Phoebe herself spun away with Lord Kendall.

Her aunt scowled, but Phoebe only laughed.

The unbidden image of Phoebe, her lips parted with surprise and passion, flashed repeatedly across Stephen's mind. Tantalizing, unwelcome memories had taunted Stephen throughout the day, making him more irritable than anyone ought to be. With his thoughts scattered and distracted he'd actually played one of the worst hands of whist he'd ever encountered. He glared across the ballroom to the woman responsible for his foul mood.

Lord Eaton stood beside Stephen and sipped a glass of sherry. "What do you suppose happened to the fox, anyway?"

" 'Tis a puzzle, indeed," Winston said, looking purposefully at his friend. "What do *you* think, Stephen?"

"One can only speculate, my friend."

"Bloody shame if you ask me," muttered Eaton for the third or fourth time—not that Stephen was counting, but the bore refused to change the blasted topic. Eaton tugged his red waistcoat lower over his extensive belly. "I rather fancied the business of impressing the women. Oh, bother. I shall have to rely on my wit and skill as a dancer. If you gentlemen will excuse me, I for one intend to make the most of the evening."

With a ridiculous flourish of his wrist, Eaton abandoned the discussion, circling the dance floor, seeking the lady of his choice. Already guessing the prey Eaton sought, Stephen grimaced. His scowl deepened as Phoebe gave Eaton a winsome smile and a giggle. The damned woman had flaunted her charms all evening, dancing with gent after gent, talking and laughing as if she actually enjoyed their company.

It was an abomination. Why just this afternoon, she had bestowed upon him one of the greatest gifts given a man. Now she was allowing every man-jack to touch her. At least Lemmer had the good sense to stay away. Stephen doubted he could have remained on this side of the ball-room, as he had all evening, if Lemmer had so much as breathed in Phoebe's direction.

Clearing his throat, Winston grabbed two glasses of champagne from a passing servant. He handed one to Stephen. "By the way, my friend, how is that headache of yours?"

"Fine."

"Truly?" Winston pursed his lips and studied Stephen's face. "It appears as though you suffer for need of a physic this very moment lest you expire at my feet. Unless, of course, there is another reason for a scowl worthy of all scowls to be plastered on your face?" Winston waited patiently for a response, any response, from Stephen.

When none was forthcoming, he continued. "Eaton does have an interesting point. I myself wondered what happened to the fox today. Sir Lemmer seemed quite upset over the debacle. Much to my chagrin, Lemmer came to his senses before he insulted my gamekeeper's skill. I rather liked the thought of planting a facer on him. Imagine my surprise when my men investigated and discovered not one, but two of the foxholes uncovered. Very odd."

In the arms of another man, Phoebe circled past Stephen. Her laughter, like the effervescence of a fine champagne, floated above the music and set his teeth to clenching. His fingers curled around the stem of his glass, wishing it were Eaton's miserable neck instead. "Hmmm."

"Sweet mercy, Stephen. What the devil happened?"

Stephen pivoted away from the dancing couples to face Winston. Perhaps if he ignored the girl his mood would improve. Rubbish. "You are more persistent than a harrier with a rabbit between his teeth. I have a fair idea you already know what happened and torment me for your own enjoyment. Phoebe decided—on her own I might add—to save the fox from his fate and remove any chances that she be saddled with Lemmer for the eve. When I discovered her little plan, I naturally gave assistance—as any gentleman would."

Winston lifted a solitary brow, a silent request to elaborate. He waved his hand impatiently. "And?"

"After which, we rode to Chanctonbury Ring where I foolishly subjected myself to her manipulations and an afternoon of frustration and torture."

Clearing his throat, likely hiding a chuckle, Winston said, "My dear friend. Go ask the female to dance. You might be more fit company for her than Eaton"

Not bloody likely, thought Stephen. He'd strangle the woman or drag her from the room, peel her clothes from her body and kiss her into submission—or he'd admit that he loved her. Bloody hell. Where had *that* thought come from?

Guilt, he quickly decided. He'd not asked for her full agreement before they made love; he'd assumed her declaration meant that she'd accepted his conditions. He hadn't bothered to clarify what she meant, but rather taken her virginity, and now he felt guilty. Thinking to ease his guilt, some twisted piece of logic was convincing him he loved her.

But that was impossible. He'd locked the door to those emotions and buried the key with his two dead wives. He slapped his hands behind his back. "Considering the speculation caused by our absence this morning, that is the last thing I should do."

"As long as no one knows the truth, no harm shall be done. Let everyone wonder. Other than Renoke's and Milsip's misguided opinions, it certainly has not affected her allure. Even Tewksbury asked about her earlier this eve. At this rate, she'll make a match in short order."

"Like hell she will."

Shaking his head, Winston placed a brotherly hand on Stephen's shoulder and squeezed. "The girl is perfect for you. The curse is nonsense. Marry her and be done with it, else I fear you shall be the most inhospitable company for all time."

"I can't."

"You won't."

He viciously cursed. "Am I always to be plagued by those who worry over my matrimonial state as if it were their own?" Not bothering to wait for an answer, Stephen stomped off in the general direction of the card room. He wearied of watching every man and boy ogle the woman he considered his.

He had warned Phoebe about her feelings. Lord, *he* seemed to be the one unable to control himself. Infernal woman. When would she realize she belonged to him?

Phoebe watched Stephen storm from the room. Stubborn oaf. Let him brood. He had ignored her all evening, which suited her just fine. Unless he had something different to say or was prepared to apologize, she intended to keep her distance. She pasted a false smile on her face and turned back to Charity. The poor girl stared at Sir Ellwood as though the man held the moon in his hands. Phoebe knew the feeling. She sighed and watched the lords who circled them like vultures after a kill. How she wished for a few moments alone.

Hildegard's nagging voice cut through her thoughts. "Phoebe, I see you need something to divert your attention. I seem to have left my fan in the portrait hall. Go fetch it."

Before Hildegard had an opportunity to blink, let alone ask a second time, Phoebe jumped to her feet. "Gladly, Aunt Hildegard. I welcome the exercise to waken me after dinner."

The oddest look, one almost like anticipation, flashed in Hildegard's eyes, then vanished. A feeling of unease jolted Phoebe's body, which she quickly dismissed. After all, what harm could come from fetching her aunt's fan?

In no hurry to return to the dancing, she slowly found her way to the room near the back of the house where they had earlier viewed Winston's newest acquisition: a lovely painting of the Thames by some artist named Joseph Turner.

Other than an occasional chair set about the long rectangular hall, the gallery contained little furniture. Paintings dotted the walls and statues occupied spaces on the floor. Although the subject matter varied greatly from that in Lord Wyman's private study, the room reminded her of her first encounter with Stephen. After today's events, Wyman's paintings held new meaning. Disgusted by her preoccupation with Stephen, she crossed to the table Hildegard had described but found nothing. Knowing Hildegard, she'd spitefully sent Phoebe on a fool's errand just so she could lecture Charity.

A light breeze drifted across her shoulders. She whirled

about to find Sir Lemmer leaning insolently against the now-open door to the terrace.

"You look displeased, my darling dearest. Were you expecting someone else? Lord Badrick perhaps? 'Tis a pity he's engrossed in a card game at the moment."

Phoebe noticed the disapproval in Lemmer's voice and knew he'd clearly chosen words to incite fear. A flicker of apprehension skittered down her spine. She squared her shoulders and leveled at him a look of disdain. "Excuse me. I was just leaving."

Strutting forward like a barnyard rooster, he stepped directly in her path. Cedar, the scent she recognized as his, assaulted her nose. His hand shot out to snare her wrist. "Do you know what happens when a young lady is discovered alone with a bachelor in a, shall we say, compromising situation?"

She felt trapped, very much like the afternoon in Hyde Park. His eyes blazed with unleashed passion. She certainly didn't expect Stephen to come to her rescue this evening. Her wits would be her only protection. "It matters not to me. I certainly have no intention of compromising myself in your company and I doubt anyone will rush in here anytime soon to discover us."

"Society is extremely fickle. Ruination requires little. Even the young toads interested in your title or your funds will be hard-pressed to ignore propriety. 'Tis a sacrifice, but alas, in the grandest of gestures I shall wait and kindly relieve your aunt of her responsibilities to you."

"Precisely, sir. You *shall wait*. Forever, if that is your objective. Now get out of my way." She tried to wrench herself free from his powerful grip. When she failed to loosen his hold, she lifted her knee toward his groin, almost losing her balance in the process. She cursed the confining fabric of her dress.

He grabbed her about the waist, yanking her hard

against him. "You have such fire, Phoebe. I have not forgotten that incident in the park, and I assure you at another time, another place, I will remind you of it in great detail. As to our being interrupted, your dear aunt and I have a bargain. In the company of a lord or two, she shall seek her errant niece and her missing fan—only to discover us."

No wonder Hildegard had looked as though she'd won a chess match. Phoebe had known her aunt disliked her, but had never anticipated such a vile act of betrayal. Unfortunately, there was little she could do about her aunt right now. Lemmer required her full attention. "Personally, I don't give a damn if the entire party enters. No one will believe I willingly came here with you."

"Shall we see?" He crushed his lips to hers. Her stomach roiled. No matter how hard she fought the embrace, the scoundrel's arms held her captive. As she struggled in earnest, Lemmer chuckled into her mouth, seemingly enjoying her efforts. When his hand grabbed her breast, she bit his lower lip; to her satisfaction, she tasted blood.

Lemmer lifted his head and clutched her chin in his hand. Like a snake poised to strike, he hissed. "That was very foolish."

Her jaw throbbed from the pressure of his hold. Before his lips descended again, she was free, tumbling backwards into a marble statue. She barely recognized Stephen. His face was contorted with rage, his eyes clouded with fury.

Air whooshed from Lemmer's mouth as Stephen slammed a fist into Lemmer's stomach. He continued to hold Lemmer by his no-longer-perfect cravat and pound the man's body. Mercy, if she didn't do something, surely Stephen would kill the man, not that she cared. But Stephen's reputation was an altogether different matter. Society needed no additional tinder to fuel their tales and rumors. She grabbed his arm before it connected again.

"Stephen, you've done enough. We need to leave before Hildegard arrives."

His iron gaze bored into Lemmer, who remained standing only because Stephen gripped his shirt. "I care not whether your aunt comes or not. This scoundrel dared touch you!"

"Look at me. I'm fine. Come."

Stephen hurled Lemmer against the nearby wall, where the man crumpled like a sack of grain. Stephen turned toward Phoebe. Accusation blazed in his stony glare. Good heavens, not only was he furious with Lemmer, he was furious with her as well.

Pressing himself to a sitting position, Lemmer swiped his hand across his bloodied lip. "You bastard. Must you ruin Phoebe as well, add another woman to the Badrick cemetery? Was it not enough to seduce and murder my sister?"

"You sanctimonious hypocrite," Stephen spat, every bit of wrath wrapped in those three words. "I know all about your brotherly devotion to Emily. My God, she was your sister! You can't forgive the fact that she chose me over living in a house in which you presided, your insidious behavior growing bolder with every day. My actions pale in comparison to yours."

Lemmer's face flushed red. Spittle flew from his mouth. "That's a lie."

"Emily spared me no detail. I know all your ugly little secrets—and if you think I'd allow you near Phoebe for one moment, think again. I'll kill you first."

Lemmer pushed himself to his feet, leaning against the wall. "Phoebe, let me help you."

"I don't need or want your help."

A mask of anger contorted the features of Lemmer's face. Beyond reason, his words flowed like a river of hot lava, set to obliterate everything in its path. "Fine. Go with him, but do not forget I warned you. You will regret this. I swear on my sister's grave." His voice shook with fury. "You waste your time with this bastard. He's not good enough to kiss your boots. He'll seduce you just like he did my sister, and if he marries you, which I doubt he's man enough to do, he'll kill you just the same."

"You disgusting leech," Stephen warned. "You're lucky I don't call you out at dawn. Unfortunately, Phoebe's reputation is at stake." He thrust his hand through his hair. "Emily's dead. Nothing you or I do will ever bring her back. Let it end. Here. Tonight."

Chapter Nineteen

Stephen barely spared Lemmer another passing glance. He collected Phoebe and tromped from the room, weaving his way throughout the house. Silence reigned between them, the air too charged for speech. She knew she should return to the ballroom and appear as though nothing had happened, but she couldn't leave Stephen in his current frame of mind. He'd likely go back and beat Lemmer another time or two.

Stephen stopped outside a door she didn't recognize and thrust her inside. The room was dimly lit, but she recognized the objects of war. Swords and shields of every shape and size adorned the walls. A wooden case housed daggers big and small, each sharpened to deadly points. When Stephen slammed the door behind him, she realized his anger had not yet cooled. She was about to become the recipient of a blistering lecture. She positioned herself beside a full suit of armor on the far side of the room, hop-

266

ing the stuffed mannequin might somehow offer support. She feared she would need it.

"Are you so desperate for a husband you now lure your prey into dark corners? To test my patience? To allow other men to touch you then make comparisons?"

"Allow me to explain."

"I have warned you repeatedly about that man."

"My aunt is responsible. She was supposed to enter, discover Lemmer and I together and somehow or another make me appear the wanton, forcing Lemmer and I to marry."

"Any number of men could have followed you after you paraded yourself before them all night long. Your behavior was irresponsible. This would not have happened in the first place if you had bothered to think."

He circled the room, pacing, very much like he had earlier at Chanctonbury Ring. His voice was brittle. He dared to accuse her? After he had ignored her all evening? After her uninhibited response to his touch just this afternoon? Her temper, fueled by his unwillingness to listen and heightened by Lemmer's attack, exploded. "Don't you dare lay this at my feet, you arrogant, egotistical prig. You're blinded by jealousy and have already set your mind to my fault and refuse to see my side."

"Hah. No man will sit back and deny himself when something is flaunted so openly. I think we proved that most effectively earlier today." Stopping beside a round oak table, he planted his hands on either side of an ornate helmet with a ghastly spike on the top. "If he does, he is a fool."

"And you are anything but a fool?"

"Exactly."

She marched across the room, no longer content to stand idly by and defend herself. She had a point to make as well. "Yet you deny me because you fear a woman you never met, a ridiculous curse." She tossed her head toward the ceiling and snorted. "And you dare call me foolish! You act the injured party simply because I choose to grasp my fate with both hands."

He leaned forward. "You grasp a cold piece of earth and stone. You've chosen wealth rather than the pleasure I know you find with me. You cling to dreams of love like a naïve child. I hate to remind you, but love is an illusion glorified by idealistic poets and grasping, melancholy mothers. Love does *not* conquer all. Love does *not* guarantee happiness."

She mirrored his position and boldly met his gaze, her nose mere inches from his. "I'd rather believe in something good and pure than cling to my cynicism and fear like a coward. Marsden Manor is more than a place to live. If I can't have my freedom, then allow me to choose a life I can tolerate." She stared at him with fire in her eyes. "Yes, I dream and wish and pray for love, for a husband who greets me with affection and respect. He will listen to me, talk with me, and grow old with me. And what of children? Little ones to tuck into bed at night, to carry on the legacy I leave them. If I become your mistress, I lose all hope for all those things. You would win the battle, but in the end, we both would lose the war."

Dear God, how her words burned deep within his heart. He wanted all those things. With her. Only he was terrified. If he married her, he sentenced her to death. Even if the curse were an illusion, a reflection of his own actions, how could he take the risk? He already cared more than he dared.

"Fine. Hold fast to your childish dreams, the illusion, and dare to find the man to give them to you. I cannot marry you. I *will not* marry you. Take your remaining days.

Try to make yourself a match. I shall be waiting." He whirled on his heels and fled the room.

A solitary tear rolled down Phoebe's cheek. Her heart felt tattered, ripped in two. The fool man. He cared. She knew he did. He fled his own demons, and she could not overcome them. Phoebe felt her mood tip precariously toward despair.

In the looming silence, metal clanged against metal like a parish bell. She froze as her mind wildly considered the unfortunate possibility that someone else occupied the room and had witnessed her scene with Stephen. She almost laughed. With her luck, the Prince Regent, his entourage and forty or so other people hid in a corner. How dare someone eavesdrop? She fisted her hands on her hips and reeled about, her stance one of belligerence. Her gaze searched the room. "Who's there?" She waited, tapping her toe in agitation as she often did. Finally a shadow parted from the wall near the far corner of the room. As the apparition moved closer, Phoebe recognized his bold features. She groaned. "Lord Tewksbury."

He bowed slightly. "Good evening."

The time for pretenses had come and gone. "Well, kick a rock. It seems my life is to be invaded by men whether I like it or not. How long were you present, sir?"

Avoiding her probing stare, he absently studied a pair of crossed swords above the doorway and cleared his throat several times. At least he had the good grace to be embarrassed. He'd apparently heard every miserable word she and Stephen had shared. "Never mind," she muttered. "My luck continues to go from bad to worse. Why were you hiding?"

"I came here to ease the pain in my head. You and Lord Badrick entered on my heels. I never truly saw an opportune time to make my presence known. If I may say, Lord Badrick is making a mistake."

"On that we agree."

"What shall you do?"

"My task remains the same."

Tewksbury walked forward, stopping a respectable two feet from her. His blue eyes held compassion and understanding. No recrimination lingered in their depths. He offered her a quiet smile. "In that case, there happens to be a small country fair tomorrow. I would be honored if you would accompany me."

Oh la, what to do? His request added to her already present confusion. She couldn't very well hide for the balance of the weekend, and Stephen had more or less abandoned her. She needed time alone to collect her thoughts and the opportunity to reason with Stephen one last time. Then she would decide what she would do.

She almost laughed. What could she do? Her choices were few. "You've caught me quite by surprise. May I give you my answer in the morning?"

"Of course." He draped her hand across his forearm. "Now, I suggest we find our way back to the ballroom before trouble finds you yet again tonight."

When she remembered Lemmer's words, revealing Hildegard's role in his little scheme, her temper flared anew. "Likely too late. I have something to say to my aunt."

Phoebe easily spotted her aunt, who, thankfully, stood in an alcove tucked away in the corner of the ballroom. Good. Privacy suited the conversation to come. As she approached, Phoebe realized Hildegard doted on an older gentleman who hovered over Charity, who was busy feasting her eyes on Sir Ellwood.

Was this the infamous Lord Hadlin? A few stray hairs

adorned the top of his bald pate, and thick, bushy eyebrows lined his forehead like a furry caterpillar. He laid his hands on top of his protruding belly and leered at Charity as though she were a stick of peppermint. If this was Lord Hadlin, it was no small wonder Charity found the thought of marriage so unappealing.

Suddenly Hildegard's crimes grew even more horrified. The woman cared for no one but herself; her obsessive need for power and esteem had become the driving force behind her actions. Phoebe almost felt sorry for the woman. Almost.

She marched directly to Hildegard's side. "Pardon me, but I need a word with you. Alone."

Phoebe's demand elicited varied reactions. Lord Hadlin's eyes narrowed with disapproval, his caterpillar brows burrowing even closer together. He said nothing as he stomped away. Charity blinked several times, obviously astonished by Phoebe's actions.

Hildegard squared her shoulders, wearing her dignity like a shield. She opened her fan and furiously waved it before her face. "You rude, ungrateful child."

Even though Phoebe wanted nothing more than to wring her aunt's deceitful neck, she kept her voice calm. "My, my, my. I see you found your fan."

"Actually, *I* did," announced Charity. "The fan was beneath mother's dress all the time. She tried to find you and tell you."

"That will be enough, Charity," snapped Hildegard, her face beginning to flush.

"And who accompanied her?" asked Phoebe, all innocence and sweetness.

"Lord Renoke and Lord Milsip," Charity eagerly said.

"Imagine your surprise when you discovered the gallery empty, neither Sir Lemmer nor myself anywhere to be found."

After a moment's hesitation, Hildegard scanned the crowded ballroom, the behavior the only confirmation of the woman's sins that Phoebe needed. "You won't find him," she said. "He fled to his room to nurse his bruises."

"Why would I care about Sir Lemmer's whereabouts?"

"That is a question I have asked myself repeatedly. He mentioned a bargain of sorts. It had to be something of great importance for him to sink to such disgraceful conduct."

Hildegard simply stared straight ahead, her face drawn in a smug look.

Shifting her gaze from one woman to the other, Charity finally stared at her mother. Sadness and understanding filled her eyes. "What have you done now?"

"Mind your own business, you foolish girl."

"I don't think so, mother. Not this time."

Hildegard's lips twitched several times before she managed to find any words. Then she found a mouthful, her fury directed at Phoebe. "Do you see what you've done? This is your fault. Now my daughter displays insolence! I won't have it."

"I'm pleased to witness the strides Charity has made. As for me, I shall remove myself from your household shortly and take up residence at Marsden Manor. If Charity chooses, rather than marry an old fool you force on her, she can live with me."

"Marsden Manor will never be yours, you ungrateful, impertinent hellion! Had Lord Badrick not interfered, I would already have everything I deserved."

Animosity rolled from Hildegard's body in waves. Anger had certainly loosened her tongue. Determined to discover all her aunt's secrets tonight, Phoebe assumed the role of the accuser. "You lied to me about Marsden Manor, didn't you? You knew about the debt all along. Did you hope to pay the taxes yourself and make a claim?"

"It should have been mine all along. You might have escaped tonight, but I shall persevere. Wait and see."

"Which brings us back to Sir Lemmer and your plan. Unfortunately for you, Sir Lemmer has had a change of heart."

"Impossible. The man wants a title and he shall have yours."

"Is that what you promised him?" asked Phoebe.

Charity sighed. "Mother, you didn't." Shaking her head, she said, "Phoebe, I'm so very sorry. I had no idea."

Hildegard snapped the closed fan across her daughter's palm. "If I wish your interference, I will ask for it."

Color swamped Charity's cheeks and her eyes clouded with tears. "I am not a child any longer, and I am sick to death of your bitterness. It's obvious you failed in whatever it is you tried to do. Let Phoebe find a bit of happiness. Mercy knows, there are so few people who ever do."

"Never. When no one comes sniffing with an offer, she will gladly accept Lemmer's suit or be cast to the streets. He will have his title and I will occupy Marsden Manor."

Any compassion Phoebe might have had vanished. "I never realized how much you hated my mother and obviously me. She was kind and generous with qualities you'll never understand. Grandfather loved her and you never forgave him."

"He never gave me a chance," Hildegard spat.

"I wonder. I think you've been angry for so long, you no longer recognize the truth." Suddenly exhausted by the emotional upheaval of the night, Phoebe clasped her hands in front of her. "I have ten days left to find a match, after which you will never have to claim me as relative again. Until then, leave me alone. I will not marry Sir Lemmer or any man you push in my direction." She turned to Charity. "Are you coming?"

Nodding, Charity joined Phoebe. They left Hildegard

273

sputtering in the corner, wrapped in her own disbelief, rage and frustration. Neither cared any longer.

"Which do you prefer?"

Phoebe smiled as Lord Tewksbury extended a garland of pink and white wildflowers and a halo of bluebells toward her. They were shopping at the fair. She gave both equal consideration, then tipped her head to the side and studied his face. "I think either would match your complexion, although the bluebells accent your eyes quite nicely."

He laughed easily, a warm rumbling sound from deep in his chest. It was a nice change, thought Phoebe, since Stephen seemed more inclined to grumble most of the time. She remembered Stephen's devilish grin, the twinkle in his eye as he told the stories of his childhood, and she knew she lied to herself. Those dark, brooding eyes, probing questions and penetrating gazes haunted her still.

"I meant for you, Miss Rafferty, and well you know it."

"In that case, I think the bluebells."

He balanced the wreath of flowers on her head. "Lovely."

"Thank you." Uncomfortable with the praise she knew he sincerely meant, she crossed to the next cart and toyed with a lace scarf. She sensed his gaze as he studied her from behind and fought the urge to straighten her spine. She had no reason to question the man's behavior. He had been nothing less than a perfect gentleman all morning. In fact, if she stopped worrying about Stephen, she might even enjoy herself. Determined to enjoy the sunshine, the laughter and the excitement of the festivities surrounding her, even the company of her companion, she smiled brightly and whirled about. "We've talked about me all morning, Lord Tewksbury. I insist you tell me about yourself."

"What do you wish to know?"

"Whatever you wish to tell me."

"I imagine you know I've been married before." Walking beside Phoebe, he locked his hands behind his back, his eyes focused on the ground. "Miriam died three years ago. I also have a daughter, Meredith. Her nickname is Bliss. She is seven, and she bowls through life without a care, heedless of danger. I love her to distraction, yet fear I shall age beyond my time much sooner than my due."

"I confess we met the night of your party. She's delightful."

He looked thoughtful. "Yes, I suspected you would appreciate her disposition."

"In a world run predominately by men for men, I believe a young girl had best reach and grasp whatever she can while she can." When Tewksbury abruptly stopped, she glanced to the brightly woven shawls folded over a wooden rack, then back to his face. She searched his eyes for any sign of anger or reproach and found none. "That must sound horribly insensible and single-minded."

"Does malice control the whim?"

"No. Only the desire that women should have a say in their own lives."

Grasping her hand, he draped it across his forearm, and they continued to stroll through the merchants hawking their wares. "Considering what I know about your circumstance, I certainly understand why you might feel that way."

Passing a silversmith, Tewksbury bought a silver rose pendant for his daughter. They circled a juggler tossing four colored balls in the air as he whistled a jolly tune.

She stopped them for a moment to buy a purple length of ribbon for Charity, who remained a captive of Hildegard's at Payley Park. All the while, they shared stories and bits and pieces of their lives with each other. In fact, it surprised Phoebe just how easy it was to talk with Lord

Tewksbury. Eventually they moved to the shade of a large elm, where they sat to share a berry pie and wine they purchased from a shopkeeper.

Phoebe sat with her legs tucked beneath her dress on the blanket Lord Tewksbury retrieved from the carriage. He leaned against the rock a good foot from her with one leg bent, his arm casually draped across his knee. She nibbled on the pie and waited. It seemed Lord Tewksbury had something on his mind.

"Miss Rafferty, I know no subtle way to say this. You need a husband. I want a wife. I realize we hardly know one another, but time is of the essence. I would like to take this next week to determine our possible suitability."

She watched him through lowered lashes. He was certainly a handsome man. Likeable, jovial, although a tad reserved. However, she felt no tingling in her limbs, no rapid beating of her heart, no ache in the pit of her stomach. But neither was she repulsed or annoyed by his company. They seemed to share a comfortable ease and he did offer her the solution she needed.

She waited for a surge of joy or even relief. Instead, she felt frightened and confused. She wanted Stephen, dreamed of hearing those same words from him.

"I imagine any number of British ladies would vie for your attentions. Why me?"

Deftly twirling a thin reed in his slender fingers, he kept his gaze locked on the stem as if the answers to her question lay therein. "For one, I find you attractive. A plus, I think, for a husband and wife. I believe you to be honest, forthright and kind. You seem to be intelligent, therefore our time spent together would not be lost to vapid conversations. In truth, I like you."

"That's all well and good, but unless you have to . . . I mean . . . why would you be willing to marry me without knowing whether or not we"—she finally blurted out the

276

question foremost on her mind—"I don't love you and you don't love me. Why would you marry under such circumstances?"

"I deeply loved Miriam. When she died, I struggled for a goodly time. I miss her still."

"Again, I ask. Why marry?"

"To be truthful, I prefer not to lose my heart again. I do not want the soul-searing love I experienced with my first wife. I need an heir and Bliss needs a mother. I think you would suit perfectly. I ask you, does that sound insensible and single-minded?"

"No. Merely honest." Her fingers toyed with a loose string on the cuff of her jacket. "Since you witnessed that little scene with Stephen last night, you surely must realize where my heart lies. And yet you are willing to court me?"

"Stephen must chose his own path. I will not ask you to dismiss him at this point, only that you give my offer consideration and when the time comes to make a decision you tell me the truth."

The money owed Stephen for repairs to Marsden Manor stuck in her throat like a chicken bone. Tewksbury needed to know the entire situation before any decision was made. "There is one last thing. My estate was in need of funds. I borrowed two thousand pounds from Lord Badrick."

His gaze followed the activity of a juggler entertaining a group of children. "Miss Rafferty," he said, his manner offhand. "Money is of little importance. If you and I come to some sort of agreement, I shall settle the matter with Badrick."

His offer was too generous by far. Knowing she might not ever receive such a proposal from Stephen, she would be foolish to refuse Lord Tewksbury's request. "Then, I guess, kind sir, my answer would have to be yes."

Chapter Twenty

"You going to prune that bush or hack it to pieces?" Nanny Dee asked as she wiped her forehead with the back of her hand.

Witnessing the carnage at her feet, Phoebe winced. Leaves and stems lay strewn about her feet, wilted petals witness to the massacre. A red rose, the lone survivor of the attack, swayed in the gentle breeze as if in surrender. Hildegard's favorite bush now resembled a one-armed scarecrow.

It was no small wonder, thought Phoebe. She was a jumble of nerves. She had been since her return from Payley Park, when Lord Tewksbury had begun to court her. Stephen remained conspicuously absent. "I don't know why I'm behaving like such a ninny."

Dee arched one black brow. Her hands kept busy weeding a small patch of violets.

"All right, I do know," Phoebe said. "But it's so silly. I

should be overcome with joy. Lord Tewksbury is everything I sought in a husband when I came to England. He's gentle and kind and seems devoted to me." She started to snip at a nearby bush, realized her intent and quickly lay the pruning shears on the stone bench beside her. The plants deserved no further abuse. She stood and paced back and forth on the pebbled path. "He's intelligent, appreciates the fact I can cipher and read, and he wants children as I do. I'll never want for anything."

"Who you trying to convince, child?"

Unable to ignore Dee's directness, or the feelings in her own heart, Phoebe dropped to the bench. With her shoulders slumped, she rested her elbow on her knee, her hand tucked beneath her chin. "If I accept Stephen's offer I'd have his protection, but for how long? I've lived with uncertainty all my life. However can I knowingly enter the same situation again? Is it so wrong to want a home and children?"

"You already know the answer to that, child."

"I called Stephen a coward. I'm a coward as well. Even if I could get beyond the uncertainty of my future with him, I don't think my pride could abide the whispering behind my back, the stares or the pity. I experienced enough of that back home." Thinking of Stephen, she ripped a small daisy from a nearby patch and shredded it in her hands. "Why on earth did I have to meet the likes of Stephen Badrick, anyway?"

Dee sat back on her heels and sighed. "Some men are like a stone wall. It takes a whole lot of rocks to build. Some of those rocks might be stacked year after year. Once it's done, it takes a heap of strength to move or destroy that wall. Some men can, some men can't."

"I'm not sure I understand."

"Your past is what you are today. It takes more strength

to change a lifetime of action than most people think. It's more comfortable to do what we know. And changing— even if we're unhappy—is mighty hard."

Nanny Dee held up her hand and continued. "If'n you decide to choose to be Lord Badrick's mistress, that pride of yours will see you through, but you make darn sure you can live with yourself. There won't be any going back, and there's no guarantee of how long he'll stay or how long you'll love. Life ain't like that. You just gotta make your choice and believe that you're in God's pocket."

Pulling the worn pair of gloves from her hands, Dee pushed herself to her feet. She lifted a callused palm to Phoebe's cheek and smiled with tenderness. "I loved you and raised you since the day you was born, teaching you as best I could. I know it's hard to think clearly right now, but look beyond today and tomorrow. I think you'll find your answers. I'll be inside if'n you need me. Don't dally too long, you got that museum party later."

In that moment, sitting there alone, Phoebe understood what Dee meant. Because of his past, Stephen feared his future. She was no different. The instability of her childhood influenced her own decisions. More importantly, she knew her wants had shifted without her even knowing it.

Her original plan had seemed so clear to her when she arrived in England. But Stephen had awakened all sorts of unexpected stirrings. Suddenly, she wanted someone to love and return her love.

But, if that wasn't possible, she'd accept the next best thing, a ring, a wedding, a husband, a son or daughter and a home.

"By Queen Mary's crown," Elizabeth muttered impatiently. "You stare at her when she's not staring at you and she stares at you when you're not staring at her. You are behaving like dunderheaded fool. Tell me what happened."

Although he wasn't truly concentrating on the artifacts before him, Stephen kept his eyes fixed on the marble frieze lest Elizabeth think he was actually listening to what she had to say. Once he uttered one word, a single syllable, Elizabeth would probe and wheedle like the worst of busybodies until the entire story unfolded.

Having accompanied her and Winston to this special exhibition of the Greek marble from the Parthenon, he wished he had lingered at home in his self-induced isolation. He never would have come had he thought for a moment that Phoebe might be here. And she wasn't alone. Lord Tewksbury served as her escort. Foolish or not, refusing to allow Phoebe Rafferty one whit of satisfaction by revealing the extent of his annoyance, he swore to ignore the woman. In fact, he'd ignore both women.

"Stephen," said Elizabeth, using that patronizing I'm-not-finished tone of voice. "Since Winston's party, when you so rudely and unexpectedly departed a day early without so much as a by-your-leave, you have hidden yourself away. Now you and Phoebe seem to barely abide one another's company. And what did you do to Sir Lemmer? The doctor said he'd broken a rib and his nose. Something happened and I want to know what."

Since Winston seemed content to let his wife badger him, Stephen remained stoically silent. He would gawk at this highly prized collection of Lord Elgin's, offer an opinion or two of his own, then leave at the first possible opportunity. He watched Tewksbury place a guiding hand on Phoebe's elbow; the man spoke far too closely to her ear to be at all proper. Her carefree laugh carried above the din of conversation in the already ridiculously crowded museum gallery.

Not just carefree, thought Stephen, her laughter was downright cheerful. A red haze flashed before his eyes. Knots the size of small cannonballs formed in his stomach.

He clenched his hands at his sides. What right did she have to be so bloody feckless while he stewed in a foul temper—as he had for the four days since he'd lain with her?

Good heavens, the thought of doing so again and again seemed to consume every moment of his day, sleeping or waking. And she had declared her affection for him, yet she appeared here with another man. No wonder he was irritable.

Elizabeth stepped directly in front of Winston, who concentrated on the marble slab nearby. It was decorated with maidens carrying sacrificial vessels. "Don't just stand there. Do something."

"What precisely do you suggest, darling? That I whisk Stephen and Phoebe away from here, confine them in a room at our home and summon the vicar?"

"Is someone to marry?" Rhys asked as he joined the small group. "If it is one of my friends, I hope I receive an invitation."

Stephen grabbed the opportunity to change topics like a lifeline in a stormy sea. "Rhys. What the devil are you doing here?"

"My life as a wanderer is officially over."

"It's about bloody time you claimed your title."

"I had little choice. I could not allow my scoundrel cousin to inherit. Didn't Winston tell you?"

Grumbling a moment or two, Stephen admitted, "I've been unavailable lately."

"You've been hiding," Elizabeth added.

"I've been forced to hide from interfering females who refuse to allow a man a moment's peace."

Rhys crossed his arms. "It seems there is a story here, if someone would like to tell me. I have a peculiar feeling it involves the redhead I saw on the arm of Tewksbury."

"Perhaps you," Elizabeth explained, "can convince this befogged imbecile that he is making a horrendous error in judgment; that the best thing we could do since he seems determined to ruin his one chance at happiness is hire a vicar and force him to marry Phoebe. She is a perfect match even if he is too stubborn to realize it. If we rely on him, he'll ruin everything. And what of an heir? He needs children of his own."

"Unlike you, darling," Winston interjected, "not everyone is thrilled with the thought of tiny creatures underfoot. It is his life and he is a man full grown, capable of making his own decisions, foolish or not. Whether he wishes to marry or not, continue the line or not, it is his choice. Not yours. Not mine."

"Besides," Rhys added. "The man's as stubborn as a tick on a hound's ear. I doubt you could force him to do anything he chose not to. I failed once myself."

If one more person called him a fool or such, he might have to hit them. They had taken to discussing him as if he weren't there. Feeling like a stallion on the auction block at Tattersall's, Stephen cleared his throat. He cast a baleful glare at Elizabeth. "Would you like to examine my feet, or perhaps my hindquarters?" He curled his lips. "How about my teeth?"

"He speaks," Elizabeth said, slapping her hand against her cheek and widening her eyes in mock surprise.

"I was waiting for a notable topic. None seem to be forthcoming. Until then I shall ply my attentions elsewhere. Understood?"

Elizabeth showed no sign of retreat. She was becoming as single-minded as Phoebe. Showing her his shoulder once again, Stephen asked Winston, "What do you think of Lord Elgin's coup? I wonder if Napoleon ever regretted not purchasing them for France?"

"Probably not," Winston eagerly said, obviously content to change topics. "What do you think, Rhys?"

"Granted, they are rather old, but I certainly do not see

them as a great investment. Someone said the government paid Elgin less cash than he extended for the retrieval of the marbles from the bottom of the ocean."

"Perhaps 'tis why some people have called them Elgin's folly," added Stephen. "But alas, Elgin shall have his name immortalized along with the stones."

Elizabeth once again marched in front of all three men. "Enough. This idle chatter will not alter my course. I want to know what you intend to do about Phoebe."

None of them acknowledged her demand. Suddenly her expression shifted. Self-declared victory shone in her eyes. If Stephen hadn't known better, he would have sworn she knew something he didn't.

"Why Stephen, look who's here. Miss Rafferty and Lord Tewksbury." She shifted to the side of the little group, extended her arms in greeting, and kissed Phoebe on the cheek as all three heads swiveled about. "We were just talking about you."

Elizabeth was practically crowing. She would dangle by her slipper strings before the end of the day if Stephen had any say about her interference. Winston wasn't helping matters, either. The least he could do was offer a reprimand or two, but no, he participated in the innocuous greetings. Rhys simply grinned like a court jester. He was pleased to see Phoebe again after their last encounter, and he was eagerly telling her so. Stephen pasted a bored expression on his face and nodded, valiantly trying yet unable to ignore the scent of lilacs clinging to Phoebe's skin, the rosy blush that adorned her cheeks, the fullness of the same lips that had welcomed his kisses. He also noted the wariness in her vibrant green eyes.

She had reason to wonder what he might do. He'd sent her flowers. She'd returned them. He'd sent her a pearl necklace. She'd returned it. She'd never bothered with the simple courtesy of a note. Now he knew why. She was too busy fawning over Tewksbury to respond. Fine!

She had five days left before she needed a wedding band on her finger. Stephen would not relent, *could* not relent. She'd said she loved him. Didn't that mean she belonged to him? Perhaps she needed a reminder. "It appears, Miss Rafferty, that you have a fondness for antiquities. I remember your appreciation of old Roman fortresses. Our *discussion* was illuminating. In fact, quite stimulating."

"Hmmm." Phoebe sighed as she watched the predatory gleam flare in his eyes. She had hoped to avoid Stephen tonight. Elizabeth had other ideas. And now the wretch wanted to play word games. Phoebe's wariness quickly shifted to discomfort as she remembered that particular *discussion*, one that had shown her the stars.

During the past week, she'd thought of little else but his gentle caresses and magical kisses, the way her body had sung at his touch. Shaking her head as though confused, she said, "I do recollect that event, sir, and regard the moment with fondness . . . and *regret*."

"Regret?" snapped Stephen, his expression fierce, his brows knitted together.

Yes, she wanted to shout. She regretted that private moment and all the others they had shared, for now his touch haunted her. "Indeed. It's a pity your opinion on the subject and mine differ so greatly. If you'll excuse us now, Lord Tewksbury and I are playing whist with friends this afternoon."

"Really? Then I offer my congratulations. I'd thought you inclined to games. Now I know it's the truth. It appears you have learned to *play* and continue to *play* exceedingly well, if Lord Tewksbury intends to join the game. I imagine the stakes are quite high."

"As Nanny Dee always says, necessity forces one to

learn what one must." Unsure of how far she could go, yet unwilling to allow Stephen the last word, Phoebe asked, "Given a high-stakes game, what would *you* do, Lord Badrick? Play? Or avoid the match for fear of the consequences? I wager you would chose the latter."

"Do you bait me intentionally, Miss Rafferty? Or do you strike out like a spoiled child deprived her toy?"

Elizabeth squeaked and Phoebe thought she heard Winston groan. Rhys actually chuckled. Tewksbury, evidently curious enough to let the two combatants have at their verbal swordplay, stood silently watching. If Stephen's voice chilled any further, icicles would soon hang from the noses of the small group.

The pain that swelled in Phoebe's heart was beyond release through tears. She tried to ignore the misery she felt. What right did he have to be angry? He was the one who ill-accused her, had callously disregarding her declaration of love. Then the scoundrel had plied her with gifts in a futile attempt to buy her consent; that hurt all the more.

She had spent the week waiting, hoping that each time she returned his gifts without so much as a simple note, he would realize his stupidity, change his mind and come to her. As each day dawned and set, the possibility of a future with Stephen faded, her hopes replaced by disillusionment and resignation.

Choosing between her needs and her love for this man, she felt torn in half. "Me? Childish? Someone I know recently accused me of the very same thing. I, of course, consider the accusation pure nonsense. I believe *that person* cares only for himself."

Stephen's mouth curled into an insolent expression. "As you said a moment ago, necessity forces one to learn what one must."

Tewksbury, who had watched the debate with great

interest, slipped closer to Phoebe's side. "As intriguing as this discussion is, I think we had best take our leave. I wish to speak with Lord Milton first."

Whether Lord Tewksbury feared she might cause a scene or say something she'd regret, Phoebe didn't care. She was suddenly eager to escape Stephen's probing eyes, his inflexible point of view.

Stephen watched Phoebe's retreating back, unaccustomed to the long-dormant emotions swirling throughout his body. What right did she have to spin into his life like a damned whirlwind and make him feel the things he did, inspire him to dream impossible dreams? He had been content.

Someone behind him cleared his throat. Whipping about on his heels, Stephen turned a searing gaze on his friends. "Do not ask."

"Ask what?" Winston said, his hands held up in submission.

"I already gave up trying to understand, my friend," Rhys added.

"I haven't," snorted Elizabeth. "What if Tewksbury gives serious suit, which, if you ask my opinion, he is doing at this very moment?"

"Phoebe is a grown woman, capable of making her own decisions. She knows what I offer."

"And pray tell what is that?" asked Elizabeth. When Stephen offered no explanation, Elizabeth turned her attention to Winston.

Winston vigorously rubbed the back of his neck. "I have no intention of telling you his proposal. Let the man hang by himself if he wishes, but trust me, my dear, you're better off not knowing."

"According to whom?" Crossing her arms beneath her breasts, she scowled at all three men.

In self-defense, Rhys held his hands in the air, mimicking Winston's earlier surrender. "Remember I just arrived. I know nothing."

She snorted. "Stephen Roland Lambert, if you value your sanity or your privacy, you will tell me what I ask. Otherwise, I vow to make your life miserable."

This was not the first time he'd gone toe to toe with Elizabeth, and Stephen doubted it would be the last. Leaning his nose within inches of hers, he enunciated each word quite clearly so there'd be no misunderstanding. "I offered Phoebe a logical solution to her problem: become my mistress. Her alternative is to marry some insufferable coxcomb whose company she'll barely tolerate."

Heedless of the nearby couples, Elizabeth let loose a stream of incredulous remarks. Then, she sighed, her shoulders heaving. Clasping Stephen's cheeks between her hands, she said, "My dear friend, you have more hair than wit. You gave Phoebe no choice at all. And if you choose to let her go with Tewksbury, you might as well turn down the covers of his marital bed." She offered no chance for rebuttal, simply let him standing beside Winston and Rhys.

"She never was one to hold back her opinion," Winston said. "I spoke my mind the other day. The decision is yours."

Winston followed in Elizabeth's wake, leaving Stephen with their words and his private demons.

"Will you listen to what *I* say?" Rhys asked quietly.

"Why is it everyone finds such pleasure in offering their opinion?"

Rhys grinned. "My friend, we seem far wiser that way. Why would we examine our own problems? Others' are more easily solved. Or so we think."

"Say your piece."

"Do you remember when you came to the gypsy camp for the first time, searching for answers? As a child?"

"Yes, I beat you to a bloody pulp."

"Hah," he chortled. "I remember it the 'other way. But who am I to quibble over minor details? You came to find a devil in gypsy clothing, the one responsible for all your misery. Finding no real answers, you swore your great-grandfather's indiscretion would not stop you from living your life as you saw fit. You claimed each man was responsible for his own actions. What has happened to that man? You seem to have forgotten your vow."

"Yes. I paraded 'round London like a neck-or-nothing young blood, intent on only my desires. I was going to prove to the world that the Badrick curse was nothing more than a silly superstition. I set my sights on the sweetest, most innocent female I could, a rose amongst the snapdragons of our society. My actions produced disastrous results."

"It is not uncommon for men to lose their wives."

"*Other men* have no legacy of death preceding them." Stephen shoved his hands into his trouser pockets and stared at the distant corner of the room, seeing nothing but a gravestone bearing Phoebe's name. "Rhys, I don't think I'd survive if anything happened to Phoebe."

"Do you love her?"

Stephen clamped his mouth shut.

"Refusing to acknowledge your heart does not eliminate the emotion or its truth. Ask yourself these questions before you decide your future. Would you be better off without Phoebe? Can you return to a life alone and be content? Could you bear to see her on the arm of another man, heavy with his child? Or would you rather grasp whatever time you have, long or short, and love her, to be together and be happy? Put your past behind you. Believe in the man you've become. Once you do, anything is possible. Now, if you will excuse me, there is a lovely brunette widow I have wanted to meet all evening. Send me a note if you need my assistance."

Rhys's questions were identical to those that Stephen had asked himself. As he stood alone, he reflected that he had spent most of his life in solitude. He'd seen to that. He'd purposely alienated himself from people and society. He'd shielded himself from the constant temptation to take what he wanted, what he couldn't have.

Since Phoebe waltzed into Wyman's study, he'd begun to live again. To feel. And he liked the change. The implication of that thought was frightening. Suddenly the room seemed unbearably crowded. Circling the perimeter of the gallery, he veered into a small antechamber with three solitary statues. Ironically, seeking escape, he'd come face-to-face with her.

Phoebe leaned against a wall, her head drooped. He spoke before he realized he'd said a word.

Her head jerked up. Pressing herself from the wall, she squared her shoulders like a sentry caught lagging at his post. "What do you want?"

She seemed reticent to talk, to remain with him alone, which bothered him more than he cared to admit. The anguish in her voice, the acceptance of defeat, chilled his blood. He scanned the room to ensure their privacy. Satisfied, he said, "We need to talk."

"I thought you made your feelings perfectly clear."

"Are you going to marry Tewksbury?"

"He hasn't asked me yet. I have four days left."

Damn, but he wanted to hold her. He inched closer. When she distanced herself from him, he raised his arm midway in the air in a helpless gesture. "You told me you loved me."

"I'm beginning to think love's an illusion after all."

"The hell it is."

"As you've said many times, we've shared passion and

certainly lust. I've discovered those emotions burn fast and furiously, leaving only ashes."

"Damn it, you know I care."

"But not enough to chance what we might find together," she blurted out. Suddenly overwhelmed by the torment of the last few weeks, she wrapped her arms protectively about her stomach as if the action might ease her sorrow. "Unless you have something else to say, please leave me alone."

"I never meant to hurt you."

Yet he had. He'd been brutally honest from the very beginning. In all fairness, she couldn't blame him for her current situation. That fact did nothing to ease her heartbreak. Stephen was a mere two feet from her, yet he might as well have stood on the moon. No longer content to remain still, she circled one of the three statues. "I don't blame you for any of this. I understand your fear. I think I even accept it now. It's not your fault. It's mine. You are who you are. I tried to make you different." Once she accepted the truth, that her future lay elsewhere than with this man, the words came more easily.

"From the very beginning I refused to listen to you. In my naïveté, I believed that if I wanted it badly enough, I could charm you into marriage. The truth is that no one can force another to do his bidding. I would live every day trying to make you love me. Day after day you would withhold yourself from me for fear I might die. If you married me with any reservation, you would hate your life and eventually me. I couldn't live like that."

"You could be happy with another man?"

After a long pause, during which she struggled to maintain control of her emotions, she answered. "I hope to be content." He looked as though she'd struck him. How could he be shocked? She'd been honest with him as well. Tears threatened to spill. She refused to give him the satisfaction of witnessing her pain, and she escaped to the doorway. "I wish you well, Stephen Lambert. Thank you for the time we shared. I shall it cherish forever."

Tears glistened on her pale cheeks. He felt the pang of guilt and his greatest fear yet. For the first time, he truly considered that he might be wrong. That Phoebe might, just possibly, marry someone else. Could he change a lifetime of thinking, of believing? That vexing question was not quickly answered. And time was running out.

Chapter Twenty-one

Together, Phoebe and Lord Tewksbury wandered the pebbled path of Hildegard's garden, the air heavy with the scent of freshly tilled dirt and the promise of rain. Although the weather had blessed them with a lovely spring day, like Phoebe's recent moods, it could change from moment to moment.

Birds chirped in the trees and bees busied themselves collecting nectar from the budding flowers. A slight breeze teased Phoebe's curls, reminding her of Stephen's feather-like caresses.

She quickly scolded herself for her foolishness. Now was not the time to be thinking about that man. Lord Tewksbury was here with a matter of great importance. She feared the decision she might have to make. She circled toward a large trellis covered with wisteria and lowered herself to the small bench beneath.

"Woolgathering?" Lord Tewksbury asked as his shadow fell across the bench.

Her heart devoid of any real joy, Phoebe smiled. "You caught me. Please sit?"

Lord Tewksbury did so, angling his body to face hers. "I believe you know why I came today. The past week has been delightful and unless my powers of deduction are greatly impaired, I think you enjoyed my company as well." He plucked a purple flower from the nearby bush and extended the gift to Phoebe. As their fingers brushed, he entwined her hand with his. "Phoebe, I would be honored if you would be my wife."

She fought the impulse to free her hand and conceal it in her skirts. The tremble that shook her body was something else altogether. It was as plain as the concern on Lord Tewksbury's face.

He said, "I thought I made my intentions perfectly clear. Was I wrong? Did I misinterpret your need to marry?"

"No, sir, you did not."

"Splendid." He gave her hand a gentle squeeze. "By my calculation, you must wed in three days. I see no reason to wait. I took the liberty of procuring a special license. I would like to marry tomorrow with my daughter in attendance."

"You've been quite thorough, haven't you?"

"I apologize that I cannot offer more than this."

"You offer more than I expected."

"Best to understand now, Phoebe. I leave very little to chance. I want a wife and a mother and someone to bear an heir. My proposal likely seems cold-hearted, but I would not make it if I didn't think we could be happy. Are you willing to take the risk?"

"I appreciate your honesty and you deserve mine before this discussion goes any further. I still care a great deal for Lord Badrick."

"I gathered as much from the other night at the museum. Will you be faithful to me?"

She wanted to be insulted, but he had every right to ask such a question. "Be assured that if I accept your proposal, I would never do anything to embarrass or shame you."

"You're an honorable young woman. If I truly considered your infidelity a possibility, we would not be having this discussion. I think you needed to hear yourself say the words." He grinned, a warm boyish smile. "Perhaps *I* needed to hear the words as well."

Her mood had improved with the conversation. His quiet acceptance made her next request easier to ask. "In all fairness to both you and myself, there is something I must do."

His expression filled with understanding. "You wish to contact Lord Badrick."

"I must."

"Is that wise?"

"I owe him the truth. He will come to see me or not. Either way, I shall have my answer. I will send you a note tomorrow morning. If need be, I can be ready to travel by the afternoon."

He clasped her chin in his fingertips. Knowing he intended to kiss her, she allowed her eyes to drift shut. His lips met hers in a sweet, soothing kiss. She felt no fire, but neither did she experience any disgust. He collected his hat and stood. "I shan't wish you luck, for his good fortune would be my loss. Whatever you choose, I will understand."

She watched his retreating back. Theirs would never be a passionate marriage, rather one forged of friendship and respect. She could be content.

Stephen's dart sailed through the smoky haze of the Lusty Dog and landed in the cutout bottom of a whiskey barrel that served as a target. Although his opponent, a sailor with arms the size of tree limbs, grumbled and added another coin to Stephen's growing pile, the bull's-eye did nothing to ease the suffocating anxiety he felt. Ever since his conversation with Phoebe, he had tried to come to terms with losing her to Tewksbury.

This morning Stephen had escaped his house to come to terms with his recent decision. Phoebe needed him. He wanted her. And God help him, he loved her. Nothing or no one, not a curse, a vindictive Gypsy, bitter relative or even his own fears would keep him from Phoebe. It was time to bury his ghosts once and for all. Though he had made his mind up, he still needed a bit of time to accept his decision. Yanking the wooden points from the target, Stephen decided he had time for another game or two. Perhaps his mood would improve. After all, wasn't a man supposed to be happy when he proposed to his bride-to-be?

With that thought squeezing his mind, he saw Winston threading his way through the crowded tavern, oblivious to the stares and hushed whispers he attracted. Stephen's presence had been quietly accepted after a few heated glares. Evidently the presence of two lords was something to be remarked upon.

Winston stopped and swiped his hand across the nearby table to inspect the grime collected on his leather glove. He grimaced. "By Henry, this place should either be torched, or at the very least scoured with lye soap and aired for a month."

"The price one pays for anonymity, my friend. No one here prattles in my ear, nor do they cast disparaging remarks or scowls my way. How did you find me?"

"I went by your home. Your coachman implied you might be found here. He seemed unhappy, and I understand his ire. I remember this tavern from our last adventure."

"What do you want?" Stephen asked absently.

Stephen's opponent, who had been silently observing

the conversation, finally lost his patience. He shoved Winston to the side—no small feat considering Winston's powerful frame—to stand directly in front of Stephen. He grumbled, "You going to play or wag your lips? I want to win some of me blunt back."

Winston glanced superciliously the meaty hand that dared soil his linen jacket, then crossed his arms over his chest.

Stephen smoothed the whiskers of his mustache as his mood improved considerably. Perhaps a brawl was just the thing he needed to purge the last of his frustration—and in a place like this a person simply planted a facer on one man and soon the entire crowd was exchanging fisticuffs. He grinned. "Winston, meet Scoots."

"Pleased," Winston said as he gave Stephen a look of understanding. He wasn't taking the bait. "By all means, play," he said. "I'll make sure our little conversation doesn't disturb your game." Scoots's grunt was his only response. Winston started to sit down, changed his mind and leaned against the wooden beam. He nodded to Stephen's opponent. "Charming fellow. Unfortunately I don't have time today to teach him any manners. Elizabeth ordered me to find you and drag your arse—her words, mind you—back to her, at which time she intends to smash her silver tureen over your obstinate head while she enumerates the pitfalls of stupidity. Again, her words." He spread his arms wide. "So here I am."

"And you live to do to her bidding."

Winston's face blossomed into that silly, I'm-in-love expression that Stephen had grown accustomed to seeing on his friend's face. As Winston shrugged his shoulders, accepting his condition with his usual ease, he said, "What can I say? Besides, I wanted to see how you fared as well. I must say, you seem to be taking all this business in stride."

"What am I to do?" Stephen muttered more to himself than Winston, as he watched the giant score thirty-five points. He didn't really care one way or the other about the game, though he was disappointed he wasn't going to have his fight after all. " 'Tis a sorry state of affairs when a mere slip of girl lies a man low. Like a willow, he can only stand so much, then he either bends in the breeze or snaps in two. The concept of snapping is anathema to me."

Raising a brow over the remark, Winston lifted Stephen's drink and sniffed. "Waxing a bit poetic, are we? How much have you had to drink?"

"Not enough," Stephen said. He rolled the three darts in his fingers.

"Your turn," said the sailor as he swaggered between the two men.

Winston shook his head, sighed and continued to talk to Stephen. "I truly thought a woman had come along whose charms were potent enough to make you forget that ridiculous curse—someone to make you happy."

"Make me happy? Hell, since I've known Phoebe, I've been confused, agitated, frustrated and endured enough social functions to last me three lifetimes. She's willful and stubborn and she refuses to see reason unless it smacks her between her beautiful green eyes."

The giant braced his feet apart. His stance suggested they listen. "Play."

Patting the broad shoulder of his opponent, Stephen said, "No need to cob on, Scoots." He tossed a dart, pleased to score another bull's eye.

As he watched, Winston said, "Well then, everything has worked out for the best."

Stephen snorted, thinking of the life before him. He threw a dart and scored another ten points. "I shall have *no* peace. I will worry every waking moment of my day, wondering where Phoebe is and what she might be doing, whether or not she is safe. I'll go mad in short order."

"You made your choice. Put her out of your mind."

"Play," Scoots boomed. It was a demand, not a request.

Discussing Phoebe so openly revived Stephen's need to pound something or someone. Scoots was quickly becoming a likely candidate. Torn between planting the dart in the sailor's arse or the board, Stephen aimed as he said to Winston, "I think, my friend, it would be rather difficult to forget one's wife."

Winston pushed away from the beam. "Wife? Dear Heavens. Phoebe left with Lord Tewksbury this morning."

The dart flew from Stephen's hand, landing with a whack in the wooden breast of a carved seagull that sat perched on a shelf by the bar where Scoots stood. Stephen whirled about to face Winston. "Impossible. She's to marry me."

"Does she know that?" asked Winston.

"I said play," the giant boomed.

Winston planted a firm hand on the sailor's shoulder and squeezed. "The game is over, my good fellow. Go away."

"I intended to inform Phoebe this afternoon." Stephen continued as though Scoots were nonexistent. "I can't believe she would up and marry another man without so much as a by-your-leave."

"She sent you a note."

"The hell you say," snapped Stephen, his arms already in his jacket. "I received no note. What makes you think I did?"

"She said so last night at the opera."

"Well, I didn't receive a damned note. Come along. We don't have time to waste." He reached for the coins on the table.

Scoots's meaty hand landed on top of Stephen's with a resounding thud. "I want me blunt back."

There was no hope for it. Scoots refused to see the need for expediency. Stephen hung his head in resignation, balled his hand into a fist and planted it squarely on the giant's broad chin.

Chapter Twenty-two

When Winston and Stephen approached Tewksbury Manor, a lone black carriage, the sort used by a local vicar, was parked in front. Stephen cursed, then muttered a plea of mercy. They had made a brief stop at Hildegard's on the off-chance Phoebe might still be there. They'd encountered Hildegard, who'd gleefully claimed responsibility for the missing note, then in the same breath ranted and raved about the loss of Marsden Manor. Hildegard would always be a lonely, bitter woman. Stephen pitied her.

For the last hour, during the harrowing ride from London, he'd vacillated between silence and profanity. Winston had abandoned all attempts at conversation long ago. At the moment, Stephen Lambert, the Duke of Badrick, was loutish company. He leaped from the vehicle before the horses completely stopped.

Winston quickly followed, trying one last time to appeal to Stephen's common sense. "At least find out if they've married before you attack like Edward on Scotland. A

scene is the last thing you need to press your case."
Stephen charged up the stairs two at a time. "Why do I
have the feeling you're ignoring everything I say?" Winston called up.

"Because I am." Stephen rapped the brass knocker
against the giant oak door.

Knowing when to wave the flag of surrender, Winston
leaned against the brick wall and sighed. "This should be
interesting."

Stephen pounded, prepared to break the bloody door
down. When the butler finally peered out, his eyes were
round with shock. No small wonder, thought Stephen. His
jacket was torn and his eye was swollen half-shut. Winston
had fared no better in the brawl they'd just escaped. He
sported a bloody lip, a lump above his brow from a pewter
mug and more blood smattered on his lovely white cravat.
The stench of the bar from their clothing did nothing to
soothe the servant's nervousness. At the moment, Stephen
didn't give a damn. He shoved his way across the threshold. "Where the hell is Tewksbury?"

When the butler continued to gape, open-mouthed,
Stephen marched through the foyer and down the hall, his
footsteps thundering on the marble floor. He opened doors,
peeked inside, and, finding nothing, he slammed them shut
and proceeded farther. The butler practically ran to keep
up. Winston followed behind, doing his best to placate the
poor man before he dropped to the floor in a fit of
apoplexy.

A familiar tiny blonde with a mop of curls on her head
appeared at the bottom of the stairs. She tilted her head
regally and observed Stephen's approach. With all the dignity of Queen Elizabeth, the moppet wrinkled her nose and
pursed her lips. "You stink."

Stephen paused. "So good of you to notice. Where is
your father?"

She turned to the butler who was readying himself to call in reserves at the least provocation. "Go along, Simpson, I can handle this." To honor the girl's wishes, the butler skulked to a nearby room but hovered in the doorway. Bliss faced Stephen, and judging from the stern expression on her face, the chit was about to offer him the proper setdown. "What do *you* want?"

"I don't think that's any of your business."

"It is if you want my help."

Winston burst into laughter. He couldn't help it. Here stood the Duke of Badrick at his most desperate of times and he was arguing with a tot. He laughed even harder.

Stephen, who couldn't quite believe the child's insolence either, glowered at Winston. The wee tyrant before him actually expected, no, demanded, an explanation. He crossed his arms over his chest in his most authoritative manner. "If you must know, I am here to collect something that belongs to me."

She stepped closer, not the least bit fearful of him. She planted her hands on her hips, likely in the manner she had seen her father do repeatedly. "I don't believe I like you."

Good lord, Phoebe wanted one of these of her own. It was too much to comprehend. "The feeling is mutual. However, I do not have the time to discuss our feelings toward one another. Where is Miss Rafferty?"

"Why?"

"Why?" he bellowed. The butler lunged forward, as did two other servants, prepared to protect their charge. A gray-haired woman flew into the room, her feather-duster mop above her head. The cook, judging from the pot in his hand, had entered from another door down the hall. Winston raised his arm, silently requesting they wait.

Bliss trembled, but held her ground. "I won't let you hurt her."

No one deserved his anger, which stemmed from sheer

panic. Leastways not this child. Deflated, Stephen knelt before Bliss. "I hope to make Miss Rafferty very happy. I promise. I need to find her first."

Wisdom and acceptance shone in her eyes, an odd mix to be found in one so young. Bliss spun on her heels and proceeded up the steps. "All right."

The assembled group marched upstairs like a gaggle of geese with Bliss in the lead. Winston brought up the rear guard, the collected staff in between. Bliss stopped outside a pair of mahogany doors. "She's in there with my father."

"Stay calm," Winston called from stairway.

As he reached for the doorknob, Stephen said a silent prayer, a meaningful thing since he wasn't a man prone to piety. What if they were married? Dear God, what if they were making love, what if . . . ? He felt a tiny hand grasp his and squeeze. With renewed hope, he shoved the doors open.

Phoebe sat on a settee, her head nestled on Tewksbury's shoulder. White-hot rage soared through Stephen's veins; it was such a surge of jealously, he was likely going to have to kill someone after all. Then he noticed the trembling of her shoulders. Tewksbury looked up. Phoebe lifted her head. Stephen saw the tears in her eyes and lost all control. He launched himself to her side. "What have you done to her, you bastard?"

Before Stephen managed three steps, Tewksbury stood, which effectively stopped Stephen's advance.

"That's diplomacy for you," Winston muttered as he casually leaned against the doorframe. A small army of servants, whose ranks quickly expanded, surrounded him.

Stephen shot scowls at both men, finally settling his glare on Tewksbury. He spat out, "Get out of my way."

Tewksbury crossed his arms. "Do you think to force me?"

Stephen didn't dignify that comment with an answer.

"Phoebe, come out from behind him. I don't give a damn if you're married. You'll be a widow by tomorrow. He can't keep you."

Phoebe, frozen on the sofa until now, finally peeked from around Tewksbury's hip. Her eyes were puffy and red from crying—a considerable amount of crying, Stephen thought. He wanted to plant a facer on Tewksbury all over again. Clearly, *he* had put the tears in her eyes.

She said with a sniffle, "What happened to your face?"

"A minor disagreement," he answered.

"More like a minor battle," muttered Winston.

"Good evening, Winston," Phoebe said absently, as if she had just noticed his presence. She kept her eyes fixed on Stephen.

"For the love of God, we're not serving tea." In disgust, Stephen threw his hands in the air. "Could we possibly have some privacy?"

Tewksbury, Winston and Phoebe all spoke at the same time. "No."

Leaning a bit further to the side, Phoebe asked, "What do you want, Stephen?"

"Why were you crying?" he demanded.

"I felt like it."

"Damn frustrating when they do that, isn't it?" Winston said while moving to a chair where he sat and massaged his knee. "When Elizabeth cries, I want to flee the room and take her in my arms at the same time. Then she never seems to remember why she's crying."

Rising from the settee in a fluid motion, she put her hands on her hips. "I know full well why I was crying."

Stephen wanted to pull her into his arms, to kiss every vile tear from her face. "Must we do this with an audience?"

"Until I hear something to persuade me otherwise, yes," Tewksbury said.

Stephen barely restrained himself from choking the man, but killing someone was not a stellar way to begin a honeymoon—if he was going to have one. He didn't know whether he would or not. "Answer me this. Are you married?"

Deathly silence overtook the confusion of the last half-hour. The ticking of the wall clock matched the drumming in Stephen's head. He heard the rustling of Phoebe's dress, Winston's sigh, the shuffling of the servants gathered in the doorway. A dog howled somewhere outside. His future hung in the balance, dependent on one word: *yes* or *no*.

The terrifying realization that he might have arrived too late wrapped around his chest like a wide leather strap. Stephen locked stares with Tewksbury, who contented himself with making him squirm. Tewksbury's expression was as telling as a stump's. Stephen clenched his hands at his sides and waited.

Finally, Tewksbury said, "Not yet. What matter is it to you?"

The tension eased from Stephen's shoulders, but the knot in his stomach never lessened. He had yet to gain Phoebe's agreement. Glancing over his shoulder, he saw the gathered multitude watching the scene with a mix of curiosity and astonishment. There was no hope for it. No one was leaving. He spoke to Phoebe as though the room were empty. "Come home with me."

Tewksbury crossed his arms over his chest. "She stays exactly where she is."

Stephen mirrored Tewksbury's position. "Isn't that for Phoebe to decide?"

"If I remember correctly, you relinquished that right," Tewksbury answered.

"He has a point there," interjected Winston.

Phoebe moved impatiently to Tewksbury's side. "If you all don't mind, I have something to say."

She hadn't said more than a few words since he arrived. Stephen took that as a good sign. He waved his arm in a sweeping gesture. "By all means, darling."

"Don't you 'darling' me. You expect me to up and leave Lord Tewksbury on the night of our wedding? Do you realize you put me though hell? Why couldn't you have thought of this when I sent you the note?"

Taken aback by her attack, he mumbled, "I never received a note. Hildegard intercepted it."

"You never received my note?" She repeated the words more to herself than to anyone else. She looked to Winston for validation. He nodded.

Shifting his weight to one leg, Tewksbury said, "Nothing has been said to change *my* mind."

A most profound curse slipped from Stephen's lips.

The matter was settled by an unexpected source. Bliss strolled to her father's side and tugged on his jacket. "He won't hurt her anymore, Father. He promised."

The calm assurance of those words, spoken by a mere child, was simply too much to bear. Imagine, thought Stephen. Championed by a seven-year-old. His life was no longer recognizable. The beliefs he'd clung to had been whipped upside down and inside out, ripped from the past and reshaped into the present. The responsibility lay at the feet of the woman before him, the woman who had loved him and trusted him. And he *had* hurt her terribly. Softening his voice to a whisper, he said, "Phoebe, I'm truly sorry. Trust me to make this right." He wasn't above begging. Stepping forward, he added, "Please."

"I . . ." The solemn despair in Stephen's voice tugged at the wounded strings of her heart. Hope opened within her soul like the bud of a lily awakening to greet the dawn. He was a fool. But fool that he was, she loved him. She'd been sitting here, weeping all over Lord Tewksbury, apologizing because she had been unable to marry him after all. Logic and common sense dictated she stay, but her heart demanded she go. The power of her love had made only one decision possible. She had planned to return to London, to Stephen.

Now he stood before her of his own volition. Surely he hadn't come all this way to wish her well, but his reasons didn't matter. She would refuse him nothing. "I don't know what you expect from me."

"Come with me and I'll make my intentions perfectly clear." When she nodded, he gathered her into his arms. The servants blocking the doorway parted, then scattered down the hall. Winston, Tewksbury and Bliss followed Stephen and lined the balcony. Stephen called over his shoulder. "Winston, see if Tewksbury has a carriage for you. I'll be taking yours."

"I'll expect to hear from her, Badrick," called Tewksbury.

Phoebe answered with a lopsided grin. "I'll be all right. Truly." Halfway down the stairs, Phoebe said, "Wait." Stephen stopped.

Climbing from his arms, she ran up the steps and knelt beside Bliss. She whispered something in the young girl's ear. Bliss grinned and nodded. Phoebe skipped back down to Stephen. Hand in hand, they marched out the front door. Once in the carriage, Stephen settled Phoebe on his lap. "What did you say to Bliss?"

"I told her to find her father a wife who will love him to distraction, to not settle for anything less. They both deserve such a woman."

"God help him. With Bliss as his taskmistress, the poor man doesn't stand a chance."

A sense of peace swelled within her. Her questions about her future remained unanswered, but one thing was certain, she belonged at Stephen's side and in his arms. Laughing, she wrapped her body around his. "I know." She nibbled on the soft flesh of his ear, the tender bruise beside his eye.

"Phoebe."

The fire in his eyes revealed the heat within his body. Yet he made no move to kiss her or drown her in sensation. Her need to touch him shocked her. Her lips trailed down his jaw to torment the crease in his mouth as her hands drifted across shoulders. She moaned.

Capturing her wayward hands, he placed them in her lap. "If you're not careful, you'll find yourself on your back with your skirts tossed above your head."

She couldn't tear her gaze from his. Embarrassment turned to yearning. Truth be told, she rather liked his suggestion. He must have sensed her train of thought, for he whispered in her ear with that deep husky voice she adored. "Another time, my dear. First I want a bath, then I want a bed. Champagne, candles and absolute privacy."

During the entire trip, the blood pounded in her temples with the rocking of the carriage. Stephen made innocuous conversation. Had someone asked her, she doubted she'd be able to repeat a word. Her thoughts lay with the night ahead. They reached his home and were greeted by an exuberant staff who quickly rushed to meet Stephen's demands. He deposited her in a room with instructions to make herself comfortable, a feat she considered impossible. Her throat was as dry as a week-old biscuit and her limbs suddenly felt weighted like a stone.

She found a white lace nightgown draped on the bed, the fabric so sheer she briefly wondered why he wanted her to bother. A silver brush lay next to it. The man was certainly full of surprises. Once she had changed, she waited beside the window, gazing into a star-filled sky, anticipation singing through every nerve in her body.

The door opened. Wrapped in a burgundy satin robe, Stephen leaned against the frame, watching her with an intensity that set her skin to tingling. His hair, still damp, curled slightly around his ears. The robe parted at the waist to reveal the tawny muscles of his chest. Like he had so many times before, he extended his hand in invitation. She went willingly.

Lit by moonshine and candlelight, his bedroom appeared the place where dreams were made. He led her to the bed and with a slow, agonizing pace, he unlaced the bindings of the delicate gown until it pooled at her ankles. Her breath hitched as his eyes gleamed with unspoken promises and expectation.

He took her hand and guided it to the belt of his robe, and she ceased to breathe at all. With trembling hands she freed him from his clothing. She had glimpsed his masculinity before, but had never really had the opportunity to see all of him, had been far too embarrassed to stare. Even now, she couldn't believe that they had once joined body to body. Her mouth, already impossibly dry, felt like a wad of cotton had been stuck there for safekeeping and forgotten. She felt her cheeks flush.

"As bad as all that?"

Her cheeks heated more. "No . . . I . . ."

When he chuckled, she swatted him on the shoulder. "I can't believe we . . . I mean, it doesn't seem . . . I've never really seen a man's body before."

"I should hope not. And I promise we'll do just fine. Come here."

He lifted her to the center of his bed and with every delectable inch of his body, he lowered her to the periwinkle cover. The satin fabric slid sensuously against her naked body. The hair on his chest and legs teased her bare skin. She knew a single kiss would not satisfy either of them. When he pressed his lips to hers, he spoke from his heart.

She answered with her soul, claiming his tongue and drawing it into her mouth. The weeks of separation and indecision, the torturous hours of worry and despair turned to raw desire. Her gasps shifted to moans as his body slid against hers. Her kisses grew bolder while his caresses seared a path across her shoulder, over and down her breasts and beyond. With the greatest of care, as though he held a cherished treasure in his hands, he repeated the caresses over and over until she writhed in agony, her body a mass of quivering need. Using his mouth, he paid homage to every inch of her, finally settling himself between her thighs.

She nearly leapt from the bed when she felt the hot whisper of his breath at the very core of her body; then she ceased to think at all. Sensation controlled her every sigh, every whimper, every tremble as her body vibrated like the strings of a harp. Surely if the house were on fire, she'd never notice.

When neither seemed able to withstand another touch, another caress, he rolled to his back and levered Phoebe above him. She felt his manhood nudge the entrance to her. A bit embarrassed, yet more aroused, she allowed Stephen to guide her into mobility, thrilled with the novelty of making love like this.

His muscles glistened, evidence of his restraint. With every rise and fall of her hips, she climbed higher and higher, burned hotter and hotter until she shattered into a hundred fiery pieces. Stephen continued to rock her body against his until he stiffened and joined her in the magical realm of ecstasy.

In the afterglow of their lovemaking, they lay face-to-face, their legs entwined, their breath mingling as one. Trapped in a world of sensation, neither spoke a word.

Stephen traced featherlike circles across Phoebe's brow. Finally he said, "Thank God, I arrived in time."

Phoebe's fingers roamed through the dusting of hair on Stephen's chest. "I have a confession." She cast her eyes downward. "I was weeping all over Lord Tewksbury because I had decided to return to London, to you. I was afraid you wouldn't want me anymore."

He crushed her in his arms and kissed the top of her head. "Not want you? I couldn't live without you." Shifting his body, he rolled to the nearby table and reached for a small blue velvet box. He removed a gold ring, which he gently placed on her finger. Etched in the delicate band were two entwined hearts.

The ring on her finger was a close match to the one she had described when they shared stories at Chantonbury Ring. The day she'd acknowledged the love she felt. A wave of tenderness washed over her. Would she ever understand this man? She would spend a lifetime trying. "You remembered?" she said in awe.

"Silly girl. How could I forget? The day I first made love to you has been one of my fondest memories. You stole my heart that afternoon. Fool that I was, I refused to see the truth. Like that skeleton in your treasure cave, I vow to never love another woman."

"When did you—"

"I ordered the ring two days ago when I decided I had to have you or go mad. I simply needed time to reconcile my feelings with my decision. I'm truly sorry for the pain I caused you. If you'll allow it, I'll spend my life making you happy. Will you be my wife, Phoebe Rafferty? Will you do me the grave honor of sharing my life?"

One question remained unanswered. "What about the curse?"

"The thought of losing you terrifies me, but I can't exist without you. You're the one who always said love conquers all things. I'm willing to put my hands, my heart, and my future, into love's tender care. I would rather have a day, a week, or a month with you than a lifetime without. Marry me."

She'd dreamed of this moment for so long and had given up all hope of ever hearing those words from his lips. They were joyous, musical, to her ears. Happiness crescended in her like the song of a hundred violins. With all the love in her heart, she smiled. "I would be honored."

"I will go to my grave with your name on my lips, our love etched in my soul." He covered her with his body, his lips hovering an inch above hers. "And if you have any doubts, be assured I shall erase them one by one, each and every day of our lives."

Epilogue

Four years later

Phoebe passed through the picture gallery of Marsden Manor, searching for her wayward family members. The sun shone brightly, so she had a fair notion as to where they might be.

Pushing through the French doors and onto the balcony, she still marveled at the beauty of this place. She thanked the stars, the heavens, for granting her this life.

Hannah, her face so very much like Stephen's, sat on Hampson's lap. Wibolt occupied the chair across the table with Michael, now three months old, nestled in the crook of his arm, sound-asleep. Stephen leaned against the stone wall.

Hannah's face was bright with excitement. Phoebe imagined Hampson was filling her daughter's ear with some nonsensical story or feat of her infamous relative.

Phoebe grinned. To this day, she herself loved hearing those tales that Hampson told. She stepped into the sunlight and said as sternly as possible. "Have you forgotten? It seems someone is having a birthday."

Her daughter crawled from Hampson's lap, ran to her mother and jumped up and down. "Me. I'm three."

Stephen crossed to Phoebe's side as well and pulled her into his arms. He kissed her as he often did with no concern as to where they were. And, she didn't mind one bit. He said, "Hampson was telling us a delightful tale of a poor fisherman who found treasure in a sea gull's egg."

"Is it true?" Hannah asked.

Sharing a smile with her husband, Phoebe answered, "Treasure of any kind can be found in the most unexpected places. You simply need to search for it and never give up hope. Now, off to wash. Our guests will arrive shortly."

Stephen rubbed his chin. "I have no concern about Winston and Elizabeth, but Charity and Ellwood manage to lose their way every time."

Laughing, she said, "I think Charity rather likes being lost with her husband."

His brow raised a notch. "Really? Perhaps they have something after all." He guided her back toward the house. "Hampson and Wibolt, watch the children if you will. I have an inclination to lose my wife and myself below the stairs. Perhaps we'll search for our own buried treasure."

She thought of the small, but well-furnished hideaway tucked beneath the music room. "Remember our guests."

He gave her a look, and a shiver traveled down her spine. She could deny him nothing. She doubted she ever would. She'd asked for his name, expected his devotion, and received much more. He'd bestowed upon her the greatest treasure of all: his love.

315

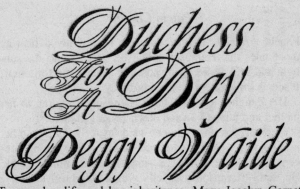

Duchess For A Day
Peggy Waide

To save her life and her inheritance, Mary Jocelyn Garnett does what she must. She marries Reynolds Blackburn—without his knowledge. And all goes well, until the Duke of Wilcott returns to find he is no longer the king of bachelors. As long as the marriage is never consummated, Jocelyn knows, it can be annulled—just as soon as she has avenged her family and reacquired her birthright. Unfortunately, her blasted husband appears to be attracted to her! Worse, Reyn is handsome and clever, and she fears her husband might assume that she is one of many women who are simply after his title. After one breathless kiss, however, Jocelyn swears that she will not be duchess for a day, but Reyn's for a lifetime.

___4554-0 $4.99 US/$5.99 CAN

Dorchester Publishing Co., Inc.
P.O. Box 6640
Wayne, PA 19087-8640

Upon A Moon-Dark Moor

Rebecca Brandewyne

From the day Draco sweeps into Highclyffe Hall, Maggie knows he is her soulmate; the two are kindred spirits, both as mysterious and untamable as the wild moors of the rocky Cornish coast. Inexplicably drawn to this son of a Gypsy girl and an English ne'er-do-well, Maggie surrenders herself to his embrace. Hand in hand, they explore the unfathomable depths of their passion. But as the seeds of their desire grow into an irrefutable love, its consequences threaten to destroy their union. Only together can Maggie and Draco overcome the whispered scandals that haunt them and carve a future for their love.

___52336-1 $5.50 US/$6.50 CAN

Prince Of Thieves

Saranne Dawson

Lord Roderic Hode, the former Earl of Varley, is Maryana's king's sworn enemy and now leads a rogue band of thieves who steals from the rich and gives to the poor. But when she looks into Roderic's blazing eyes, she sees his passion for life, for his people, for her. Deep in the forest, he takes her to the peak of ecstasy and joins their souls with a desire sanctioned only by love. Torn between her heritage and a love that knows no bounds, Maryana will gladly renounce her people if only she can forever remain in the strong arms of her prince of thieves.

___52288-8 $5.50 US/$6.50 CAN

Exquisitely beautiful, fiery Katherine McGregor has no
qualms about posing as a doxy, if the charade will strike a
blow against the hated English, until she is captured by the
infuriating Major James Burke. Now her very life depends
on her ability to convince the arrogant English officer that
she is a common strumpet, not a Scottish spy. Skillfully,
Burke uncovers her secrets, even as he arouses her senses,
claiming there is just one way she can prove herself a
tart . . . But how can she give him her yearning body, when
she fears he will take her tender heart as well?

___4419-6 $5.99 US/$6.99 CAN

Dorchester Publishing Co., Inc.
P.O. Box 6640
Wayne, PA 19087-8640

Please add $1.75 for shipping and handling for the first book and
$.50 for each book thereafter. NY, NYC, and PA residents,
please add appropriate sales tax. No cash, stamps, or C.O.D.s. All
orders shipped within 6 weeks via postal service book rate.
Canadian orders require $2.00 extra postage and must be paid in
U.S. dollars through a U.S. banking facility.

Name_____
Address_____
City_____State_____Zip_____
I have enclosed $_____ in payment for the checked book(s).
Payment <u>must</u> accompany all orders. ❏ Please send a free catalog.
    CHECK OUT OUR WEBSITE! www.dorchesterpub.com